For my short-fuse girlies who fear their passion
burns too hot for anyone to hold on.
Every part of you is lovable, especially your fire.

And for Brandon, who embraces my flames instead
of dousing them. Thank you for loving every part of me,
even the parts that make me neurotic while writing.

Chapter 1

THEA

Whoever came up with the phrase "diamonds are a girl's best friend" is a dirty liar.

The gigantic rock catches the light, sending a swirl of colors around it, like living inside a kaleidoscope. But the brightness is nothing compared to the smile on my little sister's face as she wiggles her fingers.

There were a lot of things I expected when I came in for my shift at Cibare, an intimate Italian restaurant in our small town halfway between Orlando and Daytona Beach. Having to tolerate creepy men so I can get enough tips to pay my rent. Knowing I'll have twice the number of tables as usual because our asshole manager cut down on the staff to *trim the fat*. Avoiding said asshole boss at all costs.

What I *didn't* have on my bingo card was my twenty-three-year-old sister showing up in my section, waving around an engagement ring the size of the Hope Diamond while yelling, "Surprise!"

"It's beautiful, isn't it?" Addy asks with a sigh, straightening the ring when it slides sideways on her finger. "Harrison said we can get it sized so it stops twisting like that, but I can't bear the idea of taking it off."

Harrison. The man my baby sister is apparently marrying. This is the first time I've heard the name. I didn't even know he existed before today, a fact I don't have time to unpack when there's someone at one of my tables yelling about the amount of ice in her iced tea, another patron calling out, "When you have a second," and a third frantically waving his hand through the air like an inflatable tube man to signal for the check. The terrifying stack of bills at home is the only thing keeping me from blowing them all off and demanding an—inevitably long—explanation. Why would Addy hide a guy she's dating, much less serious enough about to marry?

A voice in the back of my mind whispers *he* isn't the one she's hiding.

I shake off the intrusive thought. She loves me. We've been there for each other through everything. Thea and Adelaide. Tia and Addy. The Pappas girls. Just the two of us.

Until now.

I keep my eyes glued to Addy, pretending like I don't see Tube Man waving even more aggressively in my periphery. "So, Harrison?"

A dreamy look takes over her face, blissed out like our mom after one hit too far. Not that she'd remember those days.

"He's the best, Tia," she says, the lifelong nickname that belongs solely to her slipping easily from her tongue. "If I could make a perfect man, he'd be it. I laugh with him, like, all the time. And he's gorgeous. The most beautiful eyes I've ever seen."

Another pair of eyes—the one I guarantee would actually win the mantle of Most Beautiful Eyes—flash in my mind, and I push the memory away.

"He sounds great, Addy," I say. "But . . . isn't it fast?"

Her body stiffens and her smile slips before she plasters it back in place, like a construction worker half-heartedly spackling the side of a building for repair.

"We knew each other for over a year before we started dating."

"Because he's your boss," I say slowly, still working through the sixty-second info dump she gave me when I walked up.

She breathes deeply through her nose, then slips on a patient, if slightly exasperated, smile. "Harrison is *not* my boss. He *was* my supervisor, but he moved to another department almost a year before he asked me out."

"Another department of the company his family owns that you work for. I know I'm not a *professional*"—I put the word in air quotes—"but isn't that, like, a big no-no?"

"There's no conflict if I'm not reporting to him," she says, her voice going higher with each word, and I imagine a timer counting down on her forehead, a bomb about to explode. But before it can, she sucks in another breath, calming the rage in a way I never mastered. "I know him. I *love* him. And I'm not giving up my soulmate because the way we met isn't perfect. I've never felt connected to someone like this before."

I tense my muscles to stop my flinch in its tracks. It's not that I don't want her to find someone to spend her life with. It's just that she's slowly slipped away from me over the years since I aged out of the foster system and we were separated. But this moment, her creating a family of her own, feels like the final step in our relationship's inevitable doom.

"Why the rush? You're so young."

She's barely out of college with a little over a year in the real world. I'm five years older and have no idea what I want in life. How can she?

"Why should I wait?" she asks, her pleasant demeanor holding up, but the tightness in her words—something only I'd notice—gives away her frustration. "I want to marry him. He wants to marry me."

"Yeah, but—"

"Stop, Thea," she says. Her use of my real name is like a slap to the face. "Have *I* ever done something irresponsible?"

The implication is clear. She's the levelheaded one. The one who always makes the right decision, who thinks things through and weighs all options before jumping in.

Meanwhile, I'm the screwup. The one who lets my emotions get the best of me. My temper and inflexibility have cost us plenty over the years.

"I'll give you a minute to look over the menu," I say around the knot in my throat, rushing to check on my tables before Addy can say anything else.

I should go straight to the man whose frustration over the wait has gotten progressively louder, but I need a friendly face, so I stop by the young couple's table near the front. The boyfriend has a gleam of sweat on his forehead, and I give him an encouraging smile, a nonverbal reminder that I have his back. The ring will come out with dessert, just as we planned earlier today.

Moments like these are what keep me here. Cibare is one of the nicer restaurants in town, a place families and friends come to celebrate big events. I get to watch and play a small part in these happy moments that build a life. Pour the wine that the couple will use to toast to twenty years. Help put the young girl at ease when her parents bring her out to a fancy birthday dinner. Take the picture that will go on the fridge of the family celebrating their son's college graduation. Things I never got to experience.

I swing by Tube Man's table to put him out of his misery before heading back to Addy.

She takes my hand as soon as I come into reach. "I know this is all . . . unexpected, but I need your support. He loves me, and I love him just as much. It's my chance to build a family. Please."

The family I've always kept her from. She doesn't say it, I don't know if she even thinks it, but I feel the words in my bones.

"Please, Thea. Can you support me?"

I swallow thickly. "Of course."

The serious expression melts from her face, transforming

into a wild glee as she stands so quickly her chair teeters on its back legs.

"Thank you, Tia!" she squeals, throwing her arms around me.

And just like that, we're back to solid ground. She always did forgive me too easily.

"You're working, so I won't go through it all now, but I'm going to need your help as my maid of honor. It'll be nuts trying to get this all sorted out in the next month."

My knees buckle, and I drop into the seat across from her. "A month?"

She glances down at me, her head tilting to the side. "Didn't I mention that?"

"No, Adelaide," I say, and she scowls at the use of her full name. "You did *not* mention that you were marrying the guy you've been dating for three months a month from now."

She shrugs.

I barely hold back my scream. If I'm going to help her realize her plan is fucking bonkers, I need to find another approach.

"Why?" I ask, forcing a level of nonchalance into my voice to keep her defenses from going up again. "Your wedding should be perfect, and we'll have so much fun taking our time to make it exactly what you want."

"His family has a vineyard in the Blue Ridge Mountains. The mountains, Tia! Our whole lives we've talked about running away to the mountains. It's a sign from the universe, right?"

The first time in her life Addy has played into anything even approaching New Age thinking, and it's making her run off and marry a guy she's just started dating. Great. Of course she couldn't start with something small, like an interest in crystals.

"They host weddings, and they had a last-minute cancellation. Pretty much everyone except his immediate family lives up there, and I only have you and the Fischers"—I can't hold back my flinch this time, though I don't think she notices—"so it makes sense to go there. Plus, it's special. He spent his summers there with his cousins and brother. You're going to be shocked by how beautiful it is."

I've been to the Blue Ridge Mountains, but she doesn't know that.

Addy was a sophomore in college when I got hit with the world's worst string of luck. I kept it quiet because I didn't need her swooping in when she should have been focusing on school.

But a girl's gotta eat. So when my best friend came to me with the opportunity to make a little money by pretending to be his other friend's girlfriend, it was an easy call. I knew his friend—Owen—had to be a good guy because Vaughn wouldn't put me in a dangerous position. So up Owen and I flew to North Carolina and spent the weekend pretending we were wildly in love to keep his family off his back. I walked away with several months' rent and the relief that I wouldn't have to ask my baby sister, who had been saving for school since she was old enough to realize it was a thing, to give me some of her college fund.

And then, I have a horrifying thought. A family in our small town with a vineyard in the Blue Ridge Mountains. Owen had a little brother. Shit, I can't remember his name. It's a big mountain range, but the similarities are too many to ignore.

"Addy," I start as the acid in my stomach churns and I fight the urge to throw up. "What's Harrison's last name?"

"Hayes. Why?"

I hold in the breath of relief as the nausea fades. That isn't Owen's last name. It's a bizarre coincidence, but at least I won't have to come clean about what we did or make a scene at her wedding.

I shake my head dismissively, and she watches me, her face pinching. She has the same strong, dark brows and thick brown hair as our mother. With her lightly tanned skin, she'd fit right in with the Greek family that gave us our last name, even if we have no real connection to any of them. I, on the other hand, inherited my father's bright blond hair, or so my mother said when I was little. I remember resenting that Addy looks so much like Mom when I only got her dark brown eyes. I spent hours staring in the mirror after she died, like it was a portal to the next life, and if my gaze didn't stray it would actually be her looking back.

Addy's lips purse, and I know she's chewing on the inside of her mouth, a tell she's had since childhood.

"What's wrong?" I ask.

She immediately stops, then sighs. "I just want it all to be perfect. He has this giant extended family, and I haven't met them yet. What if they don't like me?" Her voice lowers to a whisper. "What if I lose him?"

I know where the fear stems from. It was all those families over the years who told us they couldn't afford to keep us, or handle the work of keeping us, or just straight up didn't want to keep us.

But what she doesn't realize—or never admits out loud—is that *she* was never the problem. Addy was smart, well-behaved, rational to the point of unemotional. *I* drove away every family stable enough to keep us long-term, and since the Florida foster system doesn't separate siblings except in extreme cases, I dragged her right along with me.

I won't cost her another family.

"How could anyone not love you?" I ask.

Her lips pinch again. "His mom doesn't."

"I can't believe that."

"She . . . I don't know how to explain it. She just kind of ignores me. I can't break through. This is my chance to change all that. We'll have a week in North Carolina to prepare wedding stuff and you can help me win her over. You'll be there? Right?"

My stomach churns over the idea of being away for a week. This isn't like Addy's cushy salaried job with paid time off, but she's looking at me with so much desperation that I already know I'll take extra shifts over the next few weeks to make it work.

"I'll be with you the whole time. It'll be perfect. I won't let it be any other way."

Tears fill her eyes. "Promise?"

"Yes. No one can stop the Pappas sisters, right?"

Addy kindly doesn't correct me, even though we both know the invitation will say Adelaide Fischer, not Adelaide Pappas.

She hooks her pinky through mine and lets out a relieved breath.

"Pappas," a loud voice echoes through the restaurant, making patrons jump. I jump, too, flying out of my seat. This time, the chair *does* tip over, smacking into the back of another patron's chair and earning me a scowl over her shoulder.

My boss, Gordon, barrels over. "My office. Now."

I glance around at my colleagues, who quickly avert their gazes. Addy grabs my hand but I pull away, giving her a shaky smile before following Gordon.

The door has barely closed when Gordon says, "You're fired."

I expected to be scolded for sitting down at one of my tables. Not *fired*.

"But . . . but I've worked here for over a decade."

"We both know you've been trouble for over a decade, too."

I refuse to let him see me react, even if his words cut. He's the worst, but Cibare has been the closest thing to a home, the only constant in my life besides Addy and Vaughn.

I *was* difficult when I started here at sixteen, an angry kid just looking to save some money for when I aged out of the system. And, I guess, at seventeen, too. Fine, eighteen, nineteen, and twenty weren't pretty either. I've always been quick to anger, and spending the last ten years of my childhood moving from home to home only heightened my fight reflex. I'd have been fired years ago if the owner—Stella—hadn't taken a liking

Praise for *The Best I Never Had*

"*The Best I Never Had* is a wonderfully tender, swoony, and steamy second-chance love affair. Thea and Owen sizzle with unresolved chemistry (and, boy, do they fix it!) set against a stunning setting, all the delightfully fun high jinks of wedding planning, and a vibrant cast of characters. This book is also a love letter to eldest daughters and women who feel like they're always a little bit too much, and promises that they are so deserving of their beautiful happily ever afters!"

—Mallory Marlowe, *USA Today* bestselling author of *Love and Other Conspiracies*

"A complicated, layered heroine, deliciously sultry spice, and a heartwarming ending that feels completely earned? Must be an Amy Buchanan novel! *The Best I Never Had* had me engrossed from beginning to end, with one of the freshest takes on fake dating I've ever read."

—Katie Naymon, author of *You Between the Lines*

"Deliciously hot, poignant, and brimming with tenderness . . . Amy Buchanan is at her best in this smart, sexy romp that paints a deeply romantic portrait of love, identity, and the family we choose for ourselves."

—Heather McBreen, author of *Wedding Dashers*

"A truly beautiful, funny, steamy story that turns the fake-dating trope on its head in all the best ways."

—Sarah T. Dubb, author of *Birding with Benefits*

"Amy Buchanan has written another hit! With a sister's wedding, a secret, and a fresh twist on fake dating, *The Best I Never Had* had all the vibes of my favorite '90s rom-coms! A pure delight from start to finish, filled with so much tenderness, swoon, and heat!"

—Naina Kumar, *USA Today* bestselling author of *Flirting with Disaster*

"*The Best I Never Had* is a fun twist on two of my favorite tropes, fake dating and second-chance romance. With a hilarious cast of secondary characters, a dreamy forced-proximity setting, and some serious steam, this is a must-read for any rom-com fan."

—Falon Ballard, *USA Today* bestselling author of *Change of Heart*

"Amy Buchanan shines incandescently bright in her sophomore novel *The Best I Never Had*. Perfect for fans of Tessa Bailey. Thea and Owen's chemistry is sizzling off the page. I wanted to give them each a hug, as the burden of being the stronger older siblings was often too great to bear. Buchanan writes delicious sexual tension, hilarious rom-com high jinks, and such an endearing and emotional tribute to sisterhood. This book is one I'll find myself returning to when I need a good laugh and cry."

—Danica Nava, *USA Today* bestselling author of *Love Is a War Song*

Praise for *Let's Call a Truce*

"Buchanan's debut hits all of the right notes . . . This twist on the enemies-to-lovers trope that also sensitively explores dating while grieving is perfect for fans of workplace romances."

—*Library Journal*

"Amy Buchanan's *Let's Call a Truce* starts as a tension-filled conflict between workplace nemeses but ends as a touching story of love and family. The struggles Juliana faces as a widowed mother trying to make her way back into the workplace felt so real, and it's so satisfying to watch her realize that instead of her greatest enemy, Ben might just be her biggest supporter. As a Florida native myself, I also couldn't help but love the way Buchanan brought that setting to life! *Let's Call a Truce* felt like a real, lived-in romance between two people who deserve a new beginning, and who found it with each other."

—Alicia Thompson, *USA Today* bestselling author of *With Love, from Cold World*

"Amy Buchanan's debut had me chuckling one minute and choked up with emotion the next. With a perfect balance of LOL moments, punchy banter laced with sexual tension, and heartwarming moments of found family, grief, and second chances in love, *Let's Call a Truce* is an outstanding debut by a fresh voice in contemporary romance."

—Meredith Schorr, author of *As Seen on TV*

"Featuring one of the most swoon-worthy lines I've ever read from a hero, *Let's Call a Truce* delivers a heartwarming and engrossing story that beautifully explores love after loss."

—Livy Hart, author of *Planes, Trains, and All the Feels*

"Touching and swoon-worthy, *Let's Call a Truce* is a truly enjoyable debut that wrings laughter and tears from realistic life situations. A real treat!"

—Jayne Denker, author of *The Rom-Com Agenda*

"Filled to the brim with courage and compassion, *Let's Call a Truce* is by turns hilarious, heart-wrenching, and scorchingly hot. Amy Buchanan deftly navigates the demands of parenthood and the trepidation of love after loss in this superb debut. From sizzling banter and forbidden office trysts to aching scenes of two parents trying their best, this novel delivered a romance I'll never forget."

—Alexandra Vasti, author of *Ne'er Duke Well*

"Amy Buchanan's debut novel is both meltingly sweet and scorchingly hot. Juliana is a complicated, relatable heroine, and I was rooting for her at every step of her heartfelt and hard-fought journey to happily ever after."

—Diana Biller, author of *Hotel of Secrets*

"A fresh single-parent spin on workplace-enemies-to-lovers that will delight fans of *The Hating Game*."

—Kate Canterbary, author of *In a Jam*

"Office rivals to lovers is my kryptonite and this book delivers in every way. I laughed, I swooned, I read the steamy scenes twice! Forever a fan of Amy Buchanan!"

—Kate Robb, author of *This Spells Love*

"Amy's book left me feeling invigorated and hopeful. *Let's Call a Truce* is a richly crafted love story, with characters who leapt off the page and directly into my heart. A joy to read!"

—Tarah DeWitt, *USA Today* bestselling author

Also by Amy Buchanan

Let's Call a Truce

The Best I Never Had

A Novel

Amy Buchanan

ST. MARTIN'S GRIFFIN
NEW YORK

This is a work of fiction. All of the names, characters, organizations, places, and events portrayed in this work are either products of the author's imagination or used fictitiously.

First published in the United States by St. Martin's Griffin, an imprint of St. Martin's Publishing Group

EU Representative: Macmillan Publishers Ireland Ltd, 1st Floor, The Liffey Trust Centre, 117–126 Sheriff Street Upper, Dublin 1, D01 YC43

www.stmartins.com

Designed by Meryl Sussman Levavi

The Library of Congress Cataloging-in-Publication Data is available upon request.

ISBN 978-1-250-34158-7 (trade paperback)
ISBN 978-1-250-34159-4 (ebook)

First Edition: 2026

10 9 8 7 6 5 4 3 2 1

to me. But I'd fought like hell to get under control and became the perfect employee.

But in Gordon's eyes, I'll always be the sixteen-year-old girl who screamed at a set of parents that if they didn't want to take care of their kid—who they let wander into the dangerous kitchen—they shouldn't have had her in the first place.

I lay my hand over my stomach and force in a calming breath from my diaphragm—a coping mechanism from therapist number two set up by foster mom number five.

"What we *both know* is that I've been a great employee. I've given my entire adult life to this restaurant, and I think I deserve an explanation."

"A great employee?" he scoffs, and I bite my tongue to hold back my response. "You think a *great employee* would sit at a table during their shift?"

I swallow my pride—at great personal cost. "Please, Gordon. I shouldn't have done that. I'm sorry, but is that worth firing me over?"

Gordon's lips twist in a deranged smile. He's getting off on the power, wants to see me beg, and it sets my blood on fire.

"I've been telling Stella for years that you don't pull your weight," he says, clucking his tongue. A lie, and we both know it. "Sitting down while poor Lindsey's managing eight tables."

"Lindsey's managing eight tables tonight—just like me—because you fired everyone," I say through gritted teeth.

He shrugs. "The restaurant industry's tough."

The fucking audacity. A couple of days after he let go over half the staff, he was bragging to Lindsey about his raise and promising if she said yes, their date would be epic. Gordon's two specialties—selfishness and sexual harassment.

"If by 'tough' you mean full of dicks who fire hardworking staff to give themselves raises, you're right," I spit out. "Pathetic."

He stands abruptly, knocking over the Coke Zero on the

edge of his desk. I get a perverse sort of pleasure watching him scramble to right it while the dark brown liquid soaks through his papers.

But the frantic moment fades, leaving him towering over me with a sinister glee in his eyes. "I can tell you I'm of greater value than a bitchy waitress who thinks too highly of herself."

My eyebrows shoot up my forehead. He wants bitchy? I can give him bitchy. "Not sure why I'm surprised. Useless assholes always put others down to make themselves feel better."

Gordon's face turns a satisfying shade of puce. "Get out! If I see you on this property again, I'm going to send your ass to jail where you belong."

"Don't worry about that, Gordo," I say. "I doubt any woman comes back for seconds after an interaction with you."

His growl of irritation is like a balm to the open wound of losing Cibare. I turn my back and force my head high, letting the back door close behind me with a dramatic final thud.

I'm left in the alley behind the building with nothing but the hole in my heart where Cibare had been. Another home lost because of my temper. Like all those times I picked fights that led to Addy and I being moved again.

The thought of Addy brings me crashing back down to reality. Addy, still sitting in the restaurant daydreaming about her too-soon wedding. How am I supposed to help her connect with her new family when I'm a mess who can't control her temper? No matter how hard I try, I always end up blowing up my happiness, and nine times out of ten, the blast goes wide enough to hit Addy, too. I refuse to let it happen again.

I can do this. I'll be the perfect, drama-free maid of honor at the perfect, drama-free wedding.

I'll get her the family she's always deserved.

Chapter 2

OWEN

***"What would you** do if this was real, Owen?"*

I stare down at a vision of perfection in a flowing red dress. My hand on her hip flexes involuntarily, bunching the fabric and pulling her another centimeter closer.

"If this was real?" I ask.

Her eyes flick down to my lips. "Yeah. If we weren't putting on a show."

I tense and glance around the dance floor to make sure no one's close enough to hear. I shift closer still, suppressing a groan when her chest brushes mine. She lets out a little gasp at the contact, sending signals my body is desperate to answer.

I hold her eyes, the dark brown like a cavern, tempting me to jump just to see how far I can fall. "I'd drag you off this dance floor and around the back of the building so I didn't have to share you in that incredible dress."

She bites her plush bottom lip, her eyes never straying from mine. "Then do it."

I turn, my grip slipping from her waist to her hand, and tug her along behind me, her laughter echoing off the wall of windows overlooking the vineyard. A few of my family members watch us with knowing smiles, but I'm not letting anyone distract me.

I pull her behind the stand-alone ballroom. She stops, walking back a few steps with her eyes pinned to mine. Her back hits the siding, and she smiles, wide and tempting.

"Then what?" she asks, a breathiness to her low, sensual voice.

"Then I'd pin you to that wall and kiss you until you knew you were mine."

Her eyes flare. "Then do it."

I'm on her in a second, her body braced between mine and the wall behind her. I moan at her taste as our tongues tangle together. My hands grip her from behind, lifting until her legs wrap around me, the slits on each side of her dress dropping away from her thighs. She grinds against me, making me harder with each movement until I'm sure I'll die if I'm not inside her.

"Owen, take me to our room. Now," she says with such vehemence, such passion, that I almost come there.

"No," I choke out. "Here. Right now."

"Yes," she sighs, her hands diving for the button of my—

A loud banging on my door makes me shoot up straight. A quick glance at my lap tells me I'm not the only thing that's up.

This happens way too often. The memory of that weekend, of Thea in that insane dress, forces its way into my subconscious. Every few months, there she is, like she can feel me forgetting her and needs to reinforce her place in my mind.

It's frustrating. She made it clear she doesn't want to date me, and I don't want to date her either. A woman like that would destroy me, run me into the ground trying to keep up with her. She's excitement personified, while I'm . . . good ol' Owen. Reliable, but boring. There's no way a woman like her would go for me if money weren't involved.

So why won't she go away?

The taste of Dream Thea is still on my tongue, mint and a bite of the whiskey she favors. A fabricated flavor, since I never actually got a taste. In the real world, I didn't drag her off the dance floor. I brushed off her question and focused my attention on my Uncle Dennis trying to twerk on the edge of the dance floor to fend off the same problem I'm fighting now.

But my mind is creative. It fills in all the gaps I left in our relationship. *Fake relationship*, I remind myself.

The door rattles again. "Wake up, Owen."

I groan into my pillow, willing away my condition while simultaneously wishing I could sink back into the dream. I grab my phone and groan again: 6:57 AM. My alarm would have gone off at seven anyway, but I feel cheated out of those three minutes. Maybe my brain would have finally sealed the deal with Thea. No matter how many fantasies it creates—and there have been a lot of fantasies—sex seems off the table, like it knows no matter how hard it tries, it won't do Thea justice.

Another knock. "Wakey, wakey, big brother."

I never should have given my brother a spare key.

"Give me a minute, Harrison. Jeez."

The knocking continues, picking up a rhythm that tells me he's singing something under his breath while I pull on a pair of sweatpants and a T-shirt. His fist punches my shoulder instead of the door when I swing it open, his blue-green eyes that match mine cast to the ceiling like he's watching an invisible music performance.

He smiles at my scowl. "About time, butthead."

"You are a literal child, Harrison," I say.

"See, if I was a literal child I wouldn't be able to tell you that's literally the wrong use of 'literal.'"

I manage to hold on to my scowl for three seconds before breaking out in a smile. "Touché."

I follow my brother through the open living space, and he plops himself down at the kitchen bar. I ruffle his hair as I pass, and the solid punch to my bicep is another reminder that Harrison isn't my baby brother anymore.

I grab a pan from the hanging rack as I round the counter, pulling out ingredients from the refrigerator in a set of moves so practiced over the years of cooking for Harrison that I can do it mindlessly. I set about whisking the eggs and cheese together while the pan heats.

"No muffins?" Harrison asks, eyeing the counter of my long, narrow kitchen.

"Been too busy at work to bake," I remind my brother, even though the work at our company has always run me more ragged than him.

I brew our coffee while the eggs cook, Harrison sitting in comfortable silence while I work. I fix his mug—three horrendously large scoops of sugar with a bit of the powdered creamer I keep for him—then pour my black coffee, gulping down the liquid and definitively *not* thinking about the fact that it's the same color of Thea's dilated eyes in my dream, most of the chocolate brown taken over by her blown pupils.

I don't regret not kissing her when I had the chance.

Okay, 90 percent of the time I don't regret it, and that 10 percent likes to run wild with what-ifs in my dreams.

With Harrison's breakfast ready, I snag myself a banana from the counter and settle across from him. "I know you love me, but you're not here for a pre-work get-together. What's up?"

"Can't a man visit his brother?"

I lift an eyebrow. "He can. But not before seven in the morning, and especially not when he's going to see said brother in less than an hour at the office."

Two years ago, when Harrison graduated from the small liberal arts college he went to in New England, he moved back home to join me at Hayes Electric, our family's electrical contracting company. It was our dad's dream, and he had worked tirelessly to make it successful. And to keep it successful, even after he got sick. He and I spent long hours sitting on his hospital bed, sheets of paper spread across it while he explained the ins and outs of the company. He was so proud that I'd take it over one day, even though he wouldn't be there to see it.

And then he was gone, with nothing but his expectations left behind. And a grieving widow who fluctuated between debilitating despair and extreme bursts of productivity so she could *maintain her husband's legacy for his sons*, forcing all of her five-year-old's care onto her thirteen-year-old.

Harrison takes a bite of his eggs, his hum of appreciation bringing me back to the present. "These are great, Owen."

"I'm sure. Now spill."

He smiles down at his plate. "You know Addy said yes?"

I nod, clapping him on the shoulder. "I'm happy for you, man."

My loud, self-assured little brother blushes. "I can't believe she's marrying me. I don't know how I tricked a woman like her into loving me."

"I agree. She's far too smart and beautiful for the likes of you," I tease.

In truth, I don't get it. I've only met Harrison's girlfriend—fiancée, I guess—a handful of times. She works at Hayes with us, but there's no overlap in our roles. Addy's sweet, if a little bland. Like a doll with eyes that blink and a voice box to speak, but whose expression never changes. But Harrison loves her, and that's all that matters.

"We called Nana to tell her about the engagement, and she mentioned there was an unexpected cancellation at the vineyard."

"That's great." Every Ellis—our mom's side of the family—in the past three generations has been married at Black Bear Winery, and Harrison's always wanted to follow in their footsteps.

Our family here in Florida is small, just us and our mom. But for two months every summer, before real life and jobs took over, we got to run wild with our extended family in the Blue Ridge Mountains. Four aunts and uncles, too many cousins to count, and our grandmother. The untamable, unconquerable Cecily Ellis. It's home, in every way that matters.

But my family, my company, needs me here.

"When's the big day?" I ask.

"The twelfth of August," he says with a guilty smile.

I flip through the calendar on my phone, landing on the date. "You're getting married on a Sunday?"

"No." He clears his throat. "You're in the wrong year."

I look up at him so quickly my head spins. "Please tell me you're waiting a couple years to get married and not getting married next month."

He smiles wide, almost manically. "I'm getting married next month!"

I run my hands down my face. "Mom's going to have a conniption."

"She's just happy one of us is getting married," he says with a laugh.

"I'm thirty-two, not fifty! She acts like she has to save me from becoming a decrepit bachelor."

Harrison laughs at my misery. "So, who are you going to bring to the wedding?"

"I thought we agreed you wouldn't come over before I had my coffee, *Mom*."

Harrison lets out a whine. "Was that an attempt at a joke? Haven't we established you should leave the jokes to the funny people?"

He chuckles, and if he notices the forced nature of my laugh, he says nothing.

I know who I am. I'm not the fun brother. Definitely not the *funny* brother. But every reminder feels like a jab between the ribs.

"Then stop grilling me about my love life," I say.

He chews his eggs, tapping the fork against his lips. "Is this where you tell me you're still hung up on Thea?"

No one in my family—not even my brother who I love more than anyone in the world—knows the real story there, how I was so desperate to get my mom off my back I let a friend set me up with a fake girlfriend for my cousin's wedding. How she won my family over within the first day, and how I've used my "heartbreak" over the split to avoid setups for the past few years. You'd think they'd question me still being obsessed with this woman, but she wormed her way into their hearts so thoroughly over the course of three days that they're still mourning her loss, too.

I narrow my eyes at him. "It was a tough breakup, okay?"

"Are we talking about Thea?" my mother's voice calls, and I look over Harrison's shoulder to see her kicking the front door closed behind her.

I really need to get those spare keys back.

"I was just saying that I'm not ready to take some random woman to an out-of-town family wedding," I say. "Plus, I'm sure there'll be plenty of things you need help with."

"It's time for you to move on, Owen," Harrison says around a mouthful of eggs, like I didn't teach him better manners than that. "Addy's got a sister, you know? Tia. I haven't met her yet, but if she's anything like Addy, you'd be a lucky man."

There is no way I'm hooking up with my brother's soon-to-be sister-in-law.

Harrison claps his hands together as he stands, leaving his dish on the bar. "I'll let Addy know we're going to set you two up."

"Don't you dare," I yell at his back.

"You could always call Thea. Patch things up with her." He laughs and lets the apartment door swing shut behind him.

I'd be lying if I said the thought didn't cross my mind. Camila's wedding was so much better with her there, but I can't call Thea. First, it would probably be a horrible decision based on the explicit dreams. Second, she conveniently deleted her number from my phone while I was filling the gas tank on our way home from the airport. I could get her contact information from Vaughn, but I got the message loud and clear.

Mom nods to the door where my baby brother just disappeared, abandoning me. "He's right about moving on. You know I loved Thea, too, but you can't just stop living."

She's one to talk.

I rub a hand down my face. It's too early to deal with this. "Can't we just leave it alone until after the wedding? I want to enjoy my time in Elk Ridge."

Her jaw tightens. "Your grandmother is going to try to steal you again."

"Come on, Mom. You know I won't say yes to moving up there until she asks at least five more times," I say, giving her a little nudge. I realize my mistake the moment she gasps, clutching her chest. "Mom, it's a joke."

Tears flood her eyes, and she stares blankly at the bland tan wall that I never got around to decorating. "I know. You'd never abandon us like that. But even the idea makes me . . ."

I hedge, trying to head off what's coming next, but it's like trying to stop a moving train with my bare hands. "Mom, come on."

She places her middle finger between her eyes, rubbing at the spot. Step one in her breakdown process.

Before Dad died, she'd been so focused on his treatment that she left most of Harrison's care to me. But even if she wasn't around much, she was reliable when she was. Present.

When the doctors gave that final diagnosis—told them it was a question of when, not if—it all started falling apart. I'd ask if I could sleep over at a friend's house instead of watching Harrison, and she'd scream that if I cared so much about that friend, I should join their family instead. Or I'd mention I was tired of working on job sites after school, and she'd spend the week in bed, crying about how Dad was going to be forgotten.

I'd assumed those reactions would fade, but if anything, they've gotten worse. She and Dad were childhood sweethearts, and her identity was wrapped around him. My life became her new focus, making sure I hit the milestones my father imagined for me. The degree he said would be most helpful for the job. A role as president of the company before I was qualified to take it. And, once those goals were achieved, making sure I found the right type of woman to settle down with and have kids to carry on the family legacy, regardless of whether that was what I wanted. Every time I push back—or seem like I'm even *thinking* of pushing back—she loses it, and I'm left to pick up the pieces.

She's going to be even more emotional once we get to North Carolina. I need to be careful, or she's going to spend the entire wedding week in bed and miss all of Harrison's big moments. I won't let my—clearly poor—attempt at humor derail one of the most important moments of his life.

"Please, Mom, I was just kidding. How could I consider leaving Hayes? And you and Harrison? It's unthinkable."

It's true. How could I leave them when they need me so much? Someone has to manage Mom and keep the company afloat while Harrison bounces from role to role.

She sniffs, wiping at the tears that have started to dry on her face. "So you aren't saying you hate your job?"

"Of course I don't," I say, only half lying. I love that I'm keeping Dad's dream alive. And the work's fine. I get to see Harrison every day. The pay's good. Do I really have the right to complain?

Mom's face relaxes as she links her arm through mine, laying her head on my shoulder.

"I wish he was going to be there," she whispers, and an invisible hand wraps around my heart.

"Me too."

There's so much I wish my dad had been here for. To scream in the stands of my last baseball game. To talk me through what ended up being an epic fail the first time I asked out a girl. For our graduations.

But he's not here. It's all on me, so I'll make sure that whatever else happens, Mom's kept happy. And in one month, that woman will be planted in the front row where she belongs, watching her youngest son pledge his life to the woman he loves.

Chapter 3

THEA

I stare at the small, unimposing restaurant, just another spot in this small, unimposing town. The drive through looked familiar, in the way all these mountain towns look alike. When I came to the area with Owen, we made a game out of finding something unique in each of the tiny, near identical towns on the drive from the Asheville airport to his family's property. A store that sold both fishing bait and fine women's clothing; a restaurant called Hawk's Landing that had a massive moose statue in front of it; a taxidermist that had three dozen stuffed animals on the front porch.

It had been a surprisingly fun way to pass the two-hour drive with a stranger.

This trip up has been a less pleasant experience. Instead of a quick flight, I had an eight-hour drive, and instead of the promise of financial security at the end, I have a mountain of bills and no income waiting for me. I've spent the past few weeks trying to find a new server job, but no one's hiring. One of my old coworkers connected me with a catering company, but those gigs are unreliable and exhausting. I can't do that forever.

But that's a problem for future Thea. Present Thea has enough to worry about, like getting my ass to this party.

I shoot off a quick text to my best friend.

Thea: Made it alive and partially sane

Vaughn: Change your mind about me coming yet?

I fight off the urge to beg him to jump on the next plane. He'd come and run interference for the awkwardness I'll create, but I don't want him saving me. I don't want Addy to see me rolling up with my best friend—who wasn't invited—like a child who needs a babysitter. This is my chance to show up for her, to prove that all those mistakes of the past don't define our relationship.

Thea: It's just my sister's wedding! It'll be great!

Vaughn: Two exclamation points in one text? You're clearly having a breakdown. Booking my flight now

Thea: Fuck off. Love you.

Vaughn: Same

I flip down the visor to check my makeup one last time. I'd done it in pieces at red lights, frantically spreading on my concealer or making it through one eyebrow before it switched back to green, and I'm sure I'll find a giant mascara smudge.

I'd planned on arriving hours ago, giving myself time to settle into the hotel before the welcome party, but the universe was against me. First, there was a massive accident on I-75. Then, in an attempt to make up the time lost, I got pulled over for speeding. I don't speed. I can't afford to speed—either the ticket itself or the increase in insurance costs—but I was so anxious to get up here, to make sure Addy had someone in her corner, that I broke my own rule. And am paying for it. Literally.

When I enter the restaurant, the hostess greets me with a cheery "Welcome! You here for the Hayes party?"

"Yeah," I answer, fiddling with my dress. It's a little much for this dinner, but they have too many wedding events planned, and I have limited options.

"This way, then." She talks as we walk, even though I don't register half her words, before she pulls back the curtain to the private room. "Have a great time."

I push into the party. Addy's across the room, outfitted in a perfect white dress. It's stunning, but still demure, like she's been reincarnated as an article of clothing.

For the first time in person, I see the man who's marrying my sister. He's tall, with thick blond hair and a confident smile. He maintains contact with Addy the whole time I watch them—a hand moving up and down her back, an arm slung around her shoulder, fingers twined together—like he can't keep his hands still when she's near. Loving. Reassuring. And when Addy smiles up at him, it knocks the breath out of me.

Addy's always smiling, the result of a desire to be what everyone wants at all times. She's never angry, never disappointed. But it's all an act—a desperate attempt to hold on to love where she can find it—and I see through it every time. That isn't the smile *I* receive from her, genuine and joyful, with a touch of mischief. That smile has always been reserved for me, and me alone.

But Harrison doesn't get my smile, either. This smile is so wide it splits her face, enormous, perfect, and tinged with the slightest bit of awe, like she can't believe the person she's looking at is real. I love it for her and am terrified of it in equal measure.

I study Harrison more closely. There's something familiar about him. When I saw his picture last month, I thought I must have served him at Cibare. But now? It feels like more, and I can't put my finger on it. The woman they're talking to is familiar, too. Like my attention summons hers, she looks up at me and gasps.

Addy turns to me, *my* smile lighting her face before she calls out "Tia!" right as her husband-to-be hollers, "What?"

I reach around me, double-checking my dress isn't tucked into my underwear from my backseat dressing room session, the cool of the red silk caressing my fingers.

My butt isn't on display, regardless of how the group is looking at me.

I scan the room, trying to figure out what I've done in less than two minutes that has everyone looking at me like I ate the cake while they were in the bathroom.

I spot a woman who will stick in my mind forever, and my stomach drops to the floor. Beautiful in an unattainable way, but those soft features from three years ago are now twisted in shock.

And then I'm spinning again, looking for the person I know has to be here. The sea of faces blurs together, my rising panic making everything merge.

"Thea?" The deep rumble of his voice sends goosebumps along my arms.

I turn toward the sound, finding the most beautiful eyes I've ever seen boring into me from a few feet away. Dark navy circles the iris, fading into a blue so clear it's nearly silver. If I were closer, I'd see the crystal green ringing his pupils, like his creator couldn't decide on an eye color and chose to give him all the best ones.

He's still perfect. The type of perfect that makes me want to reach out and ruffle him, just to see how he'll react. No one should be that perfect.

The suit clings to his broad shoulders, tapering down at his waist. His light brown hair is a bit tousled, like he ran out of time to do it. On anyone else, it would seem like an attempt at the too-cool-to-primp look, but on him I'd bet anything it's genuine. He was probably helping the staff set up or clearing up some last-minute plans for the wedding, even though it isn't his job.

My panic is reflected at me, and I back away on pure instinct. My legs hit a piece of furniture and the momentum has me tipping backward, landing in something that makes a wet, squishing sound.

The entire room gasps.

I close my eyes for a count of three before confirming what I already know. My ass is planted comfortably on the huge cake they made for the party.

I scramble off the table, the sound of cake chunks plopping to the floor punctuating each movement.

The room is silent, so much worse than if everyone started piling on questions, and my anxious brain decides it has to fill the silence, no matter what comes out.

"I guess dessert is out, unless some of you like eating ass." My eyes fly wide at my words, a new form of panic gripping my throat as people across the room gasp again. Owen runs his hand back and forth over his mouth. "Oh my god. I can't believe I just said that. And that. Why isn't my brain working? Stop talking, Thea."

A cackling sounds from the side of the room, and I turn to find Owen's grandmother bent over in laughter. Some of the other partygoers join her, but I can't laugh along when the walls feel like they're falling in on me.

I should go to Addy, apologize for making a scene right after I got here, but I can't look at her face right now. Can't see the disappointment or frustration she's bound to have, so I run. I don't stop, rushing past the diners at their romantically set tables until I push out of the restaurant, gulping in air.

The bell on the door chimes a second later. I turn, expecting to find Addy, but am greeted by those eyes again.

"Hey, Thea," Owen says, as calm and collected as ever, his eyes traveling down the line of my dress. A dress he bought me three years ago after I told him I didn't have anything nice enough to wear to his cousin's wedding. When I'd come out of the bathroom back then, his eyes had bugged out and warmth had bloomed through my limbs.

His gaze now is less admiring and more assessing, probably determining how thoroughly I've ruined a very expensive dress. I'd looked up the brand after I got home and choked on my spit when I saw what these dresses were going for. And I just planted it right in the welcome cake.

So much for not making a scene.

"How the fuck is this happening?" I ask, running both hands up into my hair, only to belatedly remember they're covered in icing. I wince, pulling one blond curl in front of my face to see just how badly I'd destroyed my hair. It looks like I'm a high schooler who thought putting in blue streaks would make me *cool* and *unique*.

"What are you doing here?" Owen asks.

"What am *I* doing here? I'm here for my sister's wedding! What are *you* doing here?"

"Brother's," he says with a laugh lacking in all humor. "What are the chances?"

Slim to none. But the universe has never given me good chances. Why would it start now?

"But your last name isn't Hayes," I say with a petulant stomp of my foot.

His brows pull together. "Yes, it is."

"No, it isn't!" I yell.

He crosses his thick arms over his chest. "I think I'd know my own last name, Thea."

"Your last name is Ellis."

He keeps his arms folded but rubs a hand over his brow. "The Ellises are my mom's side of the family. They're the ones who own the vineyard where Camila got married. I promise you my last name is, and always has been, Hayes."

"I've never heard the name Hayes in my life."

That's probably a lie, but if I have, it never stuck, where the last name Ellis is burned in my mind. I pace the sidewalk, new patrons shooting me concerned glances. But of course they would. I'm covered in food and walking back and forth muttering "fuck" to myself on repeat.

"What do we do? I promised myself I wouldn't mess up Addy's wedding, and now every person in that room except for the most important one thinks we dated."

"Yes," Owen says with perfect composure. "You should also know that I've used our breakup as an excuse to get out of matchmaking schemes ever since."

My pacing stops so abruptly I teeter in my heels as my eyes go wide. "I'm sorry, what? It's been *three years*!"

Nothing changes in his expression but there's a slight gleam to his eye. "You leave an impression."

I finally crack a smile at that. "You're so full of shit."

Owen smiles back, the first I've seen since we arrived, and something deep in my stomach tightens in response. He's way too buttoned up, not my type, but when his already handsome face is transformed by a slight curve of his lips, it feels like my world is tilting on its axis.

I shake off the distraction. "So, we go in there and come clean? Tell them it was all fake? It'll be awkward for a few minutes, but then we can all move on and focus on the wedding."

Owen nods thoughtfully, running his tongue over his teeth. "Or, and just hear me out, we don't come clean."

A scoff rips from my throat. "Hilarious."

He rolls his lips together like he's trying to hide a smile, and I can't help but home in on the action. "I just don't see why we need to jump straight to telling the truth without at least talking through our options."

I hum. "What about Addy? She knows my dating history, or lack of dating history. If we go in there pretending like we were in this serious relationship, she'll know it's bullshit."

"Will she, though?" Owen asks, his face pinching together in skepticism. "She's twenty-three. She would have been, what? A sophomore or junior in college when this all happened. We can just tell her she was distracted with school."

"You can't be serious."

He lifts his hands with a little shrug that says, *But can't I?* My teeth clamp around my nail, chewing nervously before remembering how long I spent on them to make it look like I'd been able to afford a nice manicure for the wedding.

"Look, you don't want this week ruined for Addy, right? And I don't want this week ruined for Harrison. Keeping up the lie is the best way to ensure they make it down the aisle without drama."

I anchor my hands on my hips to keep my poor nails away from my teeth. "What are we looking at here?"

Owen crosses his arms. "If we tell them the truth?" I raise my eyebrow at the "if," but I nod. "I can't tell you exactly how it'll pan out, but it wouldn't be good. My mom's moods are unpredictable, and this *will* set her off. She's already emotional because Harrison's getting married without our dad here, and it wouldn't take much to push her over the edge. I'm guessing it'll be the main—if not only—topic of conversation all week, assuming she shows up to the wedding at all."

And it will reflect poorly on Addy. I think about the desperate gleam in her eye when she told me about the engagement, how she said she needed my help to win over her soon-to-be mother-in-law. I can't help if Diana decides she can't trust me.

I run my hands back up into my hair again—it's already streaked with icing, so I might as well lean into the stress relief and consider my options. I promised no drama, and this seems like the easiest option.

"If we do this—and I'm not saying I agree—how does this work?" I ask.

"Well, we broke up, and I'm still devastated," Owen says. When I snort my response, a conspiratorial smile takes over his face, more devious than I thought him capable of. It's kind of hot. "We go back in there and let them believe what they already believe."

"And you think people will buy that?" I ask. The idea of *him* pining over *me* is just absurd.

Owen's brow furrows. "Of course they will. My cousins may have a bit of fun at our expense, but if you want to avoid drama, I promise, this is the best way to do it."

I think of the way Addy smiled at her fiancé. Open and joyful and so fucking optimistic it made my insides feel like they were going through a spin cycle. She's always wanted a family like this, and my people-pleasing little sister will be crushed if she can't get her mother-in-law's approval.

What's one week of maintaining this bizarre lie in the grand scheme of her life? After the wedding, I won't see them. It'll be just like with the Fischers. Addy will go do all the family things that I'm not invited to. Owen will find someone and fall head over heels. I'll stop being "Owen's ex" and just be the sister they know exists on the other side of the family, but who they never think about. It'll be easy.

"Fine, but *no one* can know. Just the two of us." I wait for Owen to nod his agreement, then mutter, "This is going to be such a shit show."

"It'll be fine," Owen says as he starts back toward the restaurant.

He stops next to me, looking straight into my eyes. With my heels, he's only an inch taller than me, putting our faces too close together. He places a hand on my hip, his touch burning through the fabric.

"It's great to see you, Thea. You still look beautiful in that dress," he says quietly, and the words rush through my veins like a shot of adrenaline. He pulls his hand back, realizing he got some icing on his pointer and middle fingers when he touched me. He slips the digits into his mouth, sucking it off.

"Shame about the cake. It was delicious," he says, face deadpan.

I bark out a laugh. His eyebrows pull together in surprise for a half second, then he looks away, a small, almost shy smile curving his lips.

Without another word, he walks back into the restaurant, and my eyes trail him of their own accord.

"He's right," I mutter to myself. "This is fine. Everything will be fine."

I take one last breath before forcing myself to march back into the restaurant, wholly unprepared for what's to come.

Chapter 4

THEA

I've had plenty of rock-bottom moments in my life. Like the time I got back together with an asshole ex-boyfriend because I needed a place to stay. Or when the top three buttons of my uniform blouse popped open at work and no one had the balls to tell me my boobs were out for half my shift. I thought accidentally flashing a bunch of families would be my lowest point. Face in the dirt. Nowhere else to go.

But the universe had apparently decided rock bottom wasn't enough for little old me, and chose instead to push me through the Earth's crust and boil me in hot magma made of my own embarrassment and shitty decisions.

The Earth's core is a bathroom in the Blue Ridge Mountains, where I stand, stripped down to my bra and hole-filled shapewear, with streaks of blue icing in my hair.

My once beautiful dress is half soaked under the stream of warm water. I stare at the red fabric, realizing I should have googled "how to clean stains on silk" before sticking it in the sink. Now my dress is 50 percent covered in cake, 50 percent drowned in water, and 100 percent ruined.

I also now realize I should have gone to the car for a change of clothes *before* stripping. I wonder how people will react if I walk through the front of the restaurant like this. And will Addy bail me out of jail after I'm arrested for public indecency?

Behind me, a sliver of the bathroom door opens, and Addy's head peeks around just as she says, "You in here, Tia?"

I hate that I just arrived, and I've already brought out Addy's worried voice. It's the same one she used at seven when she brought me frozen peas to ice my first black eye from a fight with our much bigger foster sister. Or at nine, while she petted my hair as I cried over losing my first job as a cashier because while shopping there may have been a pleasure, I apparently was not. Or at ten, when she listened to me rage about the boy I thought loved me, who promptly followed up taking my virginity with *Come on, babe, you know this is just fun*. In retrospect, my baby sister didn't need the details on that one.

I watch her expression closely as she comes inside, letting the door swing closed. Her strong brows are wrinkled, and she slips a hand over her mouth as her eyes track the dress in the sink, then my mostly exposed body, and up to the blue streaks in my hair.

She removes her hand, opening her mouth to say something, but instead a wild laugh bursts out of her, so forceful she drops back against the door. Relief courses through me. This situation is a disaster, but at least she's not upset with me. And I love this laugh, the free, genuine sound that's pure joy and amusement. None of the forced levity she puts on for others.

She wipes at her eyes. "I'm"—another laugh—"Oh my god"—the chuckles swirl around us—"I'm so sorry. I can't stop."

I twirl away from her, showing off the pièce de résistance, matching holes on the middle of each butt cheek. "You think that's funny, look at my ass nipples."

She devolves into laughter again, and I brace myself. Wait for it . . . wait for it . . .

Her blasting snort echoes off the bathroom tile, and a satisfied smile splits my face. That snort has been my guiding light for years, the ultimate sign that Addy is happy, amused, and, most important, comfortable. I hope Harrison pulls out her snort, even as a selfish part of me hopes it's something that will remain mine alone.

Addy walks over, wiping the last of the tears from the corners of her eyes, then wraps her arms around my waist from behind. She's so much shorter than me that I can't see her face in the mirror, but I feel her cheek against my shoulder blade, the way her love twines around my heart the same way her arms twine around my body.

"You okay?" she whispers.

"I'm fine," I say, having to clear my throat to get the words out as I shimmy out of her embrace to face her. "And you've been patient, so hit me with your questions."

She looks a bit sheepish, but then dives in. "What the heck is going on?"

I lean back against the counter and take a steadying breath, preparing to lie to my baby sister for the first time in my life. We agreed when we were young that if we could only count on each other, we had to *really* count on each other. No lies.

But if I tell her the truth, it'll go one of two ways. Either she'll demand we come clean, and the rest of the week will be spent with people gossiping and making Addy feel like she's not welcome. Or she'll agree that keeping up the ruse is best, and she'll spend her wedding stressed about the truth coming out. I've taken so much from her over the years, and I won't take this moment, too.

"Owen and I dated," I say.

She blinks like I just told her the Earth is a tiny ball sitting in a giant's hand. "You and Owen? Clean-cut, serious Owen?"

Indignation shoots through me. I know who I am, but her utter shock feels like an insult. "Is that really so unbelievable?"

She lets out a little chuckle. "I mean, you aren't the first people I'd put together."

I huff. "Yeah, well, we did."

"Oh, come on. I didn't mean it like that!" Addy says. "How don't I know about this?"

"It was your junior year. We didn't talk as much because I wanted you to focus on school."

She looks hurt, and I hate myself a little more. "It was serious enough for you to meet his family, but not for him to meet me?"

I pinch my lips to avoid saying she'd be the first person I'd introduce to a real boyfriend. "There was a family wedding."

"Why have you never mentioned him? Did he . . ." she trails off, her shoulders steeling as her eyes go hard. "Did he hurt you?"

A guffaw explodes out of me. "God, no. You've met Owen. Do you think that man would ever hurt anyone?"

Her lip twitches, but she doesn't let it go. "I didn't mean physically. Did he break your heart?"

My smile falls. We didn't break each other's hearts, but his family thinks we did, and I need to give her an answer that doesn't contradict what Harrison is going to tell her tonight.

I hate lying so much.

"I think we both changed each other in a lot of ways," I say hesitantly, "but we're okay. We just talked, and we both agree there's no need for drama."

Technically, that part isn't even a lie. Neither of us wants the drama of our deception coming out and ruining the wedding. If she thinks I mean drama between us, that's on her.

She releases a sigh, all the tension flowing from her body as she plants her hands on the countertop. "What's your plan?"

"Plan?" I squeak out. I've never been much of a planner.

"You two probably don't want to see each other much, right? It has to be hard, even if you're fine now."

"I don't know if we need a *plan*—"

"I'll move things around," she says, nodding her head once

like she's leading a board meeting and just got everyone's approval.

"I mean, we're the maid of honor and best man. I don't know how—"

She takes my hand, squeezing tight as fierce determination takes over her face. "There's plenty to do where you won't have to overlap. You're my sister. I'm not making you do something you aren't comfortable with."

There's a small, concerning pinch behind my breastbone, and I recognize it for the disappointment it is. I had fun with Owen that weekend, and part of me was excited for another chance to be around him.

Plus, I've seen Addy's schedule. There are a dozen events, and at least some of those will include both me and Owen. I don't want her spending the week stressed about keeping us apart.

"Please don't worry about this. We broke up years ago. Both of us are fine. I just want to focus on the wedding and all the amazing things you've put together."

Addy opens her mouth like she's about to argue, but the bathroom door creaks open again. Owen's mother, Diana, slips in with a dress in one hand and a toiletries bag in the other. I fumble for the silk dress, pulling the wet, uncomfortable fabric over my hips, more to hide my embarrassingly ratty Spanx than to cover myself.

"Quite an eventful evening," Diana says with a soft smile, holding the dress out to me.

"Oh, thank you, but I'm fine," I say.

Diana clucks. "I hate to tell you this, but that dress is ruined."

I glance over my shoulder at my ass, which is a darker blue now, almost purple, with the combination of the light blue icing, red fabric, and terrible attempts to rinse the icing away. "It's not my best look, but I'll be fine."

"Is she always this stubborn?" she asks Addy, the lightest Southern drawl snaking through her voice.

Addy snorts, then clears her throat. "Yes."

When I don't respond, Diana grabs my hand, placing the dress directly into it. It is a lovely light blue, ironically almost the exact color of the cake I sank my ass into.

"Do you have dresses lying around?" I ask.

She smiles and gestures for me to dress while she spins to face the wall, giving me the illusion of privacy even though she's already seen everything I have going on.

"It's my niece's," she says. "She lives a couple blocks away, and you're about the same size. I'm sorry it's wrinkled."

Wrinkled, but otherwise flawless, if a bit short on my tall frame. It hugs my hips beautifully, and the light material swirls a few inches above my knees, soft and flirtatious. Addy runs her hand down the back, letting out a soft sigh.

"It's beautiful," I say, and Diana turns around to look at me. "Thank you."

"I knew it would fit perfectly," she says, towing me to the little primping area, complete with vanity and padded benches.

Diana's a tall woman, but even she can't comfortably reach my hair with my three-inch heels that put me at six feet. She encourages me to sit, then plants the toiletries bag on the counter, fishing out a comb. She wets the teeth and works it through my icing-covered hair without a word.

I let my eyes drift shut at the soft way she's working it through my curls. Addy and Diana start chatting, but I let their words fade into an incoherent jumble as I enjoy the tenderness. It's a beautiful feeling, being pampered by someone else, and something I haven't experienced since before my mom lost herself to her addiction again. Diana gathers my mass of hair, making quick work of pulling it back into an elaborate fishtail braid and draping it over my shoulder.

I twist my head to see the side angle. "That's incredible!"

"I always wanted a daughter," she says with a conspiratorial look in her eyes that racks me with guilt. I hate lying when she's been good to me.

I catch Addy's reflection in the mirror. She's looking at Diana with such open longing that it feels like a knife to the gut. She glances away a second later, blinking down at the toiletries as she packs them away for Diana.

"Thank god for Addy," I say, and Addy's head whips up, catching my eyes in the mirror but leaving too quickly for me to catch the emotion in them.

"Yes," she says, wrapping one of her arms around Addy's shoulders. "And you've brought Thea back into my son's life."

"Diana," I start, my tone placating, as I shoot a nervous glance at Addy.

"You two were just . . ." she trails off, waving a hand in front of her eyes before turning her attention back to my braid.

"Whoever ends up with him will be very, very lucky," I say, meaning every word. "Should we get back out there?"

Diana's lips twist in an indulgent smile that tells me there's plenty more to come, but she nods and lets me lead the way out. When we enter the room, we split off. She heads over to her mother holding court in her gorgeous gown, and Addy drags me straight for Harrison, who's talking in a group with Owen and a handful of people around our age.

Owen catches my eye and mouths, *You okay?*

I nod, and another tug on my hand from Addy has me stumbling the last foot into the group.

"Baby," she says to Harrison, bouncing on her toes. "This is Tia! I mean, I guess you already know her, but still!"

Harrison throws his arm around Addy's shoulder, giving her a light kiss on the forehead as he chuckles onto her skin. "When you said Tia all those times, I assumed that was her actual name."

"It might as well be to me!" She giggles and smiles up at him like he hung the moon, before turning to the rest of the group. "This is my sister, Thea. Thea, these are Harrison's cousins."

She lists off names like she's known them for decades, and I can imagine the flashcards she probably forced Harrison to make so she didn't mess anything up.

One of the younger cousins I recognize but can't name steps forward. He lifts my hand to his mouth, brushing a kiss over my knuckles. "The lovely Thea. We're so excited to have you back with us."

I'm not conceited enough to believe this kid's actually excited about me being here. This is the Ellis dynamic, each cousin teasing and poking to see who can get the biggest reaction. I'm just their latest prop.

Owen snatches my hand away from him, and the graze of his fingers sets off a tingle through my arm in a way his cousin's lips can't touch. "Nice try, Gabriel."

He raises his hands. "What? A man can't shoot his shot?"

"No," he practically growls, and even though it's an act for his family's sake, the single, low syllable affects me more than it should.

"Come on, Owen," another cousin says. "Just because you couldn't lock it down doesn't mean the rest of us shouldn't try."

Addy chuckles nervously and leaves Harrison's side to squeeze between me and Owen, wrapping her arm around my waist. She opens her mouth but can't get out whatever she wanted to say before the cousins jump back in.

"Pretty sure Thea isn't interested in dating children," Owen says with a half smile that shows just how much he loves this, the give and take with his big family.

"I'm not a child!" Gabriel says with the petulance of the child Owen accused him of being. "I'm twenty-two."

Another cousin steps forward, this one with slight graying around the temples that works well for him. "No, Owen's right, Thea deserves someone more dignified."

"If by dignified, you mean half in the grave," Owen says, and he lets out a little *oof* when the new cousin punches him in the stomach.

Camila, the bride at the last wedding and the only cousin in the circle I could have named, lays a hand on her small bump. "You can be my mistress if you want to avoid the pestering from these bozos."

I laugh and point at Camila, running my eyes over the group. "That's the first tempting offer I've received."

Gabriel comes to my other side and throws his arm around my shoulder, sandwiching me between him and Addy.

"Don't be like that," he says. "People tell me all the time I look like a young Owen." I can see it. Besides the deep tan skin he inherited from his Mexican mother, he could be Owen's clone. He has the same sharp jawline and kaleidoscope eyes, but there's a playfulness to him that's missing from Owen's strong, stoic features. "Imagine it. The same good looks, but with the stamina of a young man and an actual sense of humor."

The group laughs, but I catch Owen's flinch. Teasing may be the Ellises' love language, but something about that particular insult hurt Owen, and it sparks an unexpected protective fury in me.

"Maybe you assholes just aren't smart enough to get his sense of humor." The words, tipped with venom, explode out of me before they've fully formed in my mind, and the entire group goes silent.

I shift uncomfortably on my feet as they blink at me. My eyes land on Addy, who is looking between each of the cousins in panic. I can practically see the thoughts behind her deep brown eyes. *Thea once again can't control her temper.*

Why am I like this? Why do I always get angry and say the wrong thing? I have to get this back on track for Addy's sake.

I force a shit-eating grin, nudging Gabriel with my elbow. "At least he can make me laugh at all, unlike you that weekend."

The cousins all bust out in mock outrage, except for Gabriel, who plants a smacking kiss on my cheek. "I knew you remembered me."

The cousins start in on each other again and the conversation moves on. But I catch Owen's eye over Addy's shoulder, and he's looking at me with such soft gratitude that I almost melt on the spot.

And in that moment, I think that pretending to have once been in love with Owen Hayes doesn't seem all that difficult.

Chapter 5

OWEN

I never thought I'd see Thea Pappas again.

At least, not outside my dreams. She looks just like she did three years ago. Her blond hair is the same, bouncing a few inches past her shoulders in tight ringlets that would probably reach down to the tantalizing curve at the bottom of her back if straightened. Her dark eyes still dart around any room she's in, and I could never tell if it was nervousness or if she was just too curious not to know everything at once. Hell, she was even wearing the same dress she wore to the wedding. I expected her to behave like she would in one of my dreams, to drag me out of the room to make out against a wall or walk up to me and say something inappropriate.

To be fair, she did say something inappropriate, but that's not the type of inappropriate my mind creates for her.

My family has once again flocked to her. They're having fun messing with me, but she also just fits with them, giving back whatever they throw out.

I spot my mom and Aunt Dawn slinking over, and I try to catch Thea's eye so she can escape. She's too engrossed in a story Camila's telling about her and her wife's honeymoon to notice.

"Thea, I wanted to introduce you to my twin sister, Dawn. She's coordinating the wedding, and I'm sure you'll spend lots of time together this week. Plus, it's good to get to know family."

Thea's eyes flick to mine and then back. "I'm excited to get to know *Addy's* new family this week."

The emphasis on Addy leaves no question for anyone in the group where Thea stands on our relationship, but either Mom is the exception or she just doesn't care.

"Addy's family," she says, puffing out air. "Like you weren't part of the family long before she came into the picture."

Addy tenses beside Thea, her eyes dropping to the floor. Thea's face goes dark. I don't know what's going to come out of those beautiful lips when she opens them, but it won't work out well for anyone involved, including Addy.

"Who the hell says that?" Thea asks, her fingers twisting into fists so tight her knuckles turn white.

My mom sputters, "I . . . I was just being welcoming."

Thea's lips twist into a menacing grin. "You call that welcoming? I'd hate to see what you're like when you don't want someone around."

She's incredible like this. Vicious and pissed and ready to jump into any fight necessary to protect her sister. The anger brings a flush to her cheeks and brightness to her eyes. I could watch her all night.

A squeak from next to Thea pulls my attention away. Addy's there with red splotches on her cheeks. She turns on her heel, speedwalking out of the room. Thea's entire demeanor shifts in an instant, her skin blanching and her shoulders caving in. She follows immediately, Harrison right on her heels.

"Mom, can I talk to you?" I drag her away by the arm before she can answer.

Mom huffs as I bring her to a stop just beyond the curtain separating off the party from the rest of the restaurant. "Can you believe that girl? How could she talk to me like that?"

For a second, I consider letting her stay mad at Thea. It'd be easier for me if she didn't want us to reconcile, if she spent the week trying to keep us apart instead of pushing us together.

But Thea was right to say what she said, and I can't bring myself to let her reaction be treated like a bad thing.

"She was right, Mom," I say, and Mom's eyes go wide, her hand coming to her chest like I struck her.

"How can you say that?"

"You hurt Addy. She was protecting her sister. That's a *good* thing. Do you not see it, or do you just not care?"

Mom blinks like she's fighting back tears, but there's no moisture in her eyes. "Of course I don't want to hurt Addy."

"I know you'd never hurt someone on purpose," I say. A bit of flattery will go a long way in easing this situation. "You're too kind for that, so you have to stop."

She shrugs innocently, but her eyes darting around the room tell a different story. "Stop what?"

"Stop trying to force something with Thea. We broke up. It sucked. We've moved on."

She lifts a brow. "Moved on? Did I imagine you saying you couldn't meet my friend's daughter for a coffee a few weeks ago because you *aren't ready for a new relationship*?"

Okay, well, that plan has officially shot me in the foot.

I sigh and decide to try another route. "I may not be over her, but you taught me to respect my partner's wishes. If Thea doesn't think we're the right fit, I won't force her into a relationship against her will."

She scoffs. "Reminding her of all the reasons you're so lovable is not *forcing her into a relationship*."

"You were just mad at the way she spoke to you. Why would you want me to get back together with her?"

"You were right. She was protecting her sister. Those protective instincts will be great when you have kids." God, the kid conversation again. She won't stop until I carry on the Hayes legacy. "This is your chance to reconnect with the love of your life."

"I never said she was the lo—"

"Some of us don't get second chances."

Her voice breaks on the last few words, and she presses her middle finger to the space between her eyebrows.

Step one.

Part of me wants to cave, to tell her I'll try, but Thea's not here as my fake girlfriend this time. She's here for the wedding and doesn't need me trying to "win her back" while she's supporting her sister.

"I'm not going to do that to Thea. She knows how I felt about her, and if she still has feelings for me, she'll make sure I know."

Mom brings her other middle finger to join the first. Step two completed.

"I just don't understand why you're not willing to try."

"And I don't understand why you're so fixated on getting me back together with someone who doesn't want me."

The words come out harsher than expected, and I don't know if it's my frustration at Mom or the tightness in my chest when I think about how Thea really doesn't want me. She made it clear when she deleted her number. I don't even know why it bothers me when I may not have called her to begin with.

But even as I tell myself that, I know it for the lie it is. I would have called her. That weekend had been amazing, and I felt so sure it wasn't forced on her part until I tried to pull up her contact in my phone and realized she wanted nothing to do with me now that money wasn't changing hands.

Mom gasps, tears flooding her eyes, and I immediately regret speaking so forcefully. She's too fragile for that. Her hands drop from her head to her sternum, where she rubs like she's buffing out the emotions like a scratch on a car.

"I'm not feeling well," she says weakly. "I think I'll head back to the inn."

"Mom," I say gently. "Come on. Don't leave. I'm sorry."

She waves, already walking toward the exit. If I don't stop

her, she'll end up missing everything tomorrow. And I will, too. I'll spend the day trying to coax her out of bed so she doesn't miss something big, like the time we both missed Harrison's elementary school graduation because I told her I wanted to do an internship with a company besides Hayes and she decided it meant I was abandoning the family.

"I'll try," I call out to her back, and she pauses, waiting for me to go on. "I'll talk to Thea."

She spins to face me, a few of the clouds gone from her face. "I'm happy to hear that. I'll see you tomorrow for the game."

I breathe out a sigh of relief. She's still leaving, but if she's saying she'll be there tomorrow, she's in a much better place than she would have been otherwise.

Now I just have to break it to Thea that things got a bit more complicated.

* * *

I pace in front of the hotel room door, wondering if going to my cousin for Thea's room number is the creepiest thing I've ever done.

I'm not here for a creepy reason. Not because she still knocks the wind out of my lungs in that red dress or because her ridiculous antics made me feel lighter than I have in years or because she called out my family while they were ragging on me. All that's true, but it's not why I'm here now.

There are things we need to discuss, like what went down when we "broke up" and how I'm "trying to win her back" this week. An anxiety-driven vision of her saying *I* broke up with *her* and my mom declaring us still in love and, therefore, back together is enough to get me to knock.

The door swings open a few seconds later and I'm greeted by what might be the most glorious sight in the world. Thea's fresh from the shower, droplets from the messy bun she has piled on top of her head running down the sides of her neck.

A few curls have escaped, framing the soft curve of her cheeks. Her oversized sweatshirt hides the tiny sleep shorts that peek out as she shifts her weight onto one foot, and my fingers twitch with the desire to play with the hemline.

God, she's beautiful.

She clears her throat, and I realize I've been staring, openly and unabashedly. I have to get this under control.

"I thought we should check in," I say.

She glances down the hallway for prying eyes, and then steps back to let me in. The room is set up like mine. A comfortable king bed. An antique desk from one of my uncle Doug and aunt Ximena's thrifting trips. No charging station or any of the other modern amenities I know Camila's been on them to add.

I grab the back of the old wood chair at the desk and gesture for her to sit on the bed across from me to put some distance between us.

Thea sighs as she drops onto the bed. "Scale of one to ten, how much does your mom hate me now?"

"The good news: she doesn't hate you. The bad: she desperately wants us to get back together. How's Addy doing?"

Thea throws herself back, bouncing slightly on the bed as she groans. "I think she's okay. I just need to keep that sort of reaction under control. No more awkwardness, no more fuckups."

"Speaking of that," I say, and she pushes herself back to sitting. "We should make sure we're on the same page."

"Okay, so let's walk through everything. You said we were together for a year?" she asks.

"Yeah. You ended it and I was—am—heartbroken," I say.

Thea lets out an unflattering noise somewhere between a scoff and a snort. It's tragic how adorable I find it. "I don't see how people will believe that."

Her statement seems genuine, but it doesn't compute for me. She's stunningly beautiful, funny, and interesting. Why wouldn't my family believe she broke my heart? Did she not see the way my cousins fell all over themselves to get close to her? And it was only half to screw with me.

"Why wouldn't they?" I ask, and she lets her head fall to the side, widening her eyes in a way that says, *Come on, Owen*. "No, if you think it won't work, I need to get why."

"You're really going to make me say it?" She meets my eyes again, but I stubbornly cross my arms. "You're out of my league."

I laugh, because what else can you do when the most perfect person in the world thinks *anyone* is out of their league? "You're messing with me."

"No, I'm not," she says, her voice going to the highest octave I've heard from her, and I pull back on my laughter. "This whole family is smart and put together, and I don't fit in here."

"You held your own that weekend and tonight at the welcome party."

"When I called your cousins assholes?" she asks wryly.

"They *are* assholes," I say, and Thea covers her face with both hands to hide her laughter. It takes everything in me not to move to her bed and peel her hands away, to soak in the sound and the way her wide eyes crinkle when she laughs.

I cough into my fist, refocusing on the problem at hand. "There is one concern. My mom's determined to get me back together with the *love of my life*."

I put a sarcastic twist on those last four words, but something deep inside jumps in response.

"She . . . um . . . she wants me to try to win you back."

Thea's eyes go wide. "And you told her no."

I rub a hand over my brow. "Mom gets these moods. Sometimes she ends up in bed for weeks, and I figured we can't afford that."

Thea starts chewing on her lip, and I lean toward her. There are still a couple of feet between us, but it's enough to get a whiff of her scent. Nothing flowery for Thea. It's deeper, a spicy, addictive fragrance I didn't realize until now I've been trying—and failing—to recreate with my baked goods. Harrison had asked why I suddenly put cinnamon in everything. I didn't have an answer then. Guess I do now.

"I won't do anything to make you uncomfortable," I say. "Just me seeking you out a few times here and there. Is that okay?"

"Why can't anything be easy?" Thea's head drops back as she groans toward the ceiling. "Fine. Addy wants your mom at the wedding, and I want to give Addy whatever she wants. She deserves that after everything else."

I almost ask what "everything else" is. She was so closed off that weekend, keeping everything fun and light. Every question I asked slid off her like water, and I was left with nothing but an enigmatic memory. Now I have her here again, and I want to know more.

But it's been a long day, and I can't handle the inevitable rejection. "Fair warning, my mom and her sisters will be obnoxious."

"I can take it," Thea says, and it shouldn't make my mind go to places it has no right to be. Thea, on her back, begging me for it. Promising she can take it all.

I stand abruptly, needing to get the hell out of this room. "Great. Then we're all set."

Thea walks me out, leaning in the doorway when I turn to say goodbye. For a second, all I can do is stare. There's something more delicate about her now, face free of makeup, the escaped curls having dried into ringlets. My hand desperately wants to see if they're as soft as they look.

"Are you tempted, Owen?" she asks quietly.

I can't stop my eyes from flicking to her lips. Yes, I'm tempted. So tempted that my body sways forward on instinct.

"Tempted?" I ask, my voice scratchy, like it's been hours instead of seconds since I used it.

"To come clean," she says, and my body jolts backward. "You don't strike me as the type who does well with lying, and it's going to be a week this time instead of a few days. I need to know you're in this with me."

She's not asking if I'm tempted by her. Just because I'm drawn to Thea doesn't mean she feels the same. When she says I'm out of her league, she means on paper, not in reality. If she was interested—if she'd felt even an ounce of the connection I felt then—she wouldn't have deleted her number from my phone. She would have left the door open for something more.

"No," I answer, knowing that whatever confusing feelings are swirling inside me, telling my mother the truth is the last thing I want. "I don't want to deal with the drama any more than you do."

I knock on the frame of her door, giving her a tight smile I hope looks less awkward than it feels, then turn to leave. I make it only a few steps down the hall when her voice stops me.

"A dentist's office that doubles as an art supply store," she says.

It takes a few seconds for her words to sink in, for me to realize she's referencing our drive from the airport to Elk Ridge for Camila's wedding. I'd been so nervous that I barely spoke on the flight up. Every time I opened my mouth—to ask what she thought about the mountains or to tell her something about myself—I was struck by a wave of self-consciousness that made me clam up.

I was mortified when the first thing I could force out was an abrupt "Fresh meat."

She stared at me like I was Jack the Ripper. My body went so hot I thought I was going to burn a hole right through the car and drop onto the pavement below.

I gestured toward the building I was trying to point out. It was a run-down, wooden house straight out of *The Texas Chain Saw Massacre* with nothing but a giant hand-painted sign that read FRESH MEAT. I'd seen a lot of weird places in my years up here, but that one took the cake.

Thea's body relaxed as she took in the structure. "Do you think anyone actually stops there?"

"Do you think everyone who *does* stop there is a cannibal?" I asked, shuddering.

Thea laughed, and I glanced away from the road just long enough to see the crinkle of her eyes. "That's not even the strangest place I've spotted on this drive."

We spent the next hour scanning every storefront, both trying to one-up the other. By the time we reached Elk Ridge, I'd shaken off the last of my nerves around her.

I'm shocked she remembers. That something that small made it into her long-term memory storage.

When I don't speak, Thea shifts on her feet. "Never mind, sorry. It was silly."

I take a step toward her before she can disappear into her room. "There's no way you found a dentist's office slash art supply store."

She narrows her eyes at me, a smirk playing on the corner of her lips. "Are you calling me a liar?"

"Might be," I say, running a hand over my mouth to hide my smile. "Gotta back up a statement like that with proof."

She tugs her bottom lip between her teeth, and it's a battle to keep my eyes on hers instead of tracking the movement. "Fine. We've got a week up here. I'll find it again and get you a damn picture."

I chuckle, ducking my head for a moment to hide how much she affects me. "Can't wait. I'll see you tomorrow?"

Thea nods as I back away. And that image—wild curls and soft curves, long legs and deep brown eyes—is the only thing I see in my dreams that night.

Chapter 6

OWEN

The air is different here. Fresh and clean, with a bite that only exists in the mountains. The rolling hills of my grandmother's property reach out before me. If I turn slightly to the right, vines dominate my vision, crisscrossing over the slopes. French American hybrids my grandmother and Uncle Dennis have spent five decades cultivating instead of the traditional European species.

A quick swivel to the left, and the slopes are covered instead with young Christmas trees, still a few years out from harvesting. The brainchild of Aunt Debra.

I'm on the back porch of the main house, Uncle Doug's passion project, which acts as an inn, restaurant, and consignment shop of locally sourced keepsakes.

On one of the slopes in the distance, a ten-minute scenic walk from the main house, are the event spaces, perfect for the dozens of weddings hosted each year by Aunt Dawn, including the ballroom from my latest dream. My mind conjures a flash of red, the broad smile on Thea's face as she backs up against the building, and I force my gaze to the wood planks of the porch floor to get rid of the image.

I love the summer mornings here, when the chill has everyone reaching for a blanket and a warm cup of coffee. The sun has just crested the mountains, casting a glow over the vines. Within a few hours, it'll force everyone to shed their layers and bask in the heat, but for now, it's just me and the sunrise.

A lone deer wanders through the vines, nibbling on a grape. I wonder how it made it past the fence, knowing Uncle Dennis will have a conniption when he spots it, but it's nice to share the quiet of the morning with another creature.

"You're looking damned pensive for a man on vacation," Nana says.

She places a coffee mug on the thick railing in front of me, and I lift it to my lips as I turn to face her.

"Can we call a wedding with my extended family a vacation? Because y'all are exhausting. I think I'm going to need a vacation from this *vacation*."

"You're looking for a slap upside your head, aren't you, boy?" she asks, hands anchored to her hips as she glares. It holds up for a solid five seconds before she chuckles and wraps her arms around me. "I've missed you, peanut."

She's small, only coming up to my shoulder, but her hug still surrounds me, letting me sink into her affection like a warm bath. "Missed you, too, Nana."

"Thinking through the logistics of your move up here?" she asks, gazing out over her kingdom, and I fight back my scoff.

My grandmother, a natural powerhouse of a woman, has never been denied anything a day in her life. She came from money. Serious money. The type of money that makes life completely accessible.

But when Nana's father died unexpectedly, he left the entire family fortune to his only child, who used it to run off from the pressures of "high society," as she calls it, and buy this land. She built a beautiful life here and has been trying to bring me into the fold as long as I can remember.

In my head, I let myself indulge. Just for a minute. What would it be like to stay here? My eyes flit over the peaks, soaking in the beauty before me. The only place I've ever felt at peace.

Childhood summers spent here, running through the vines with no responsibilities. Staying out until sunset, knowing that one of the adults would deal with dinner instead of me having to sort it out. The fresh mountain air filling my lungs instead of the stale hospital scent or construction dust that dominated the rest of the year. The only time in my life where I experienced freedom, when I wasn't being pulled in a million directions at once.

But it's a dream. Home is my reality. Hayes Electric is my responsibility. No, my gift. It's an honor to maintain the legacy.

"Next year, Nana," I say, throwing my arm over her shoulder, and she doesn't fight off her own scoff at the response I've given her since she started asking me at eighteen.

We turn back to the mountains, leaning against the railing and drinking our coffees. There's comfort in the silence. I don't know how much time passes, but eventually our drinks are gone and the sun is high in the sky.

Our peace is interrupted when Harrison flies out onto the porch. "There you are. I've been looking everywhere for you."

Nana jumps in. "Is that how you greet your grandmother? Without so much as a 'how are you'?"

Harrison puts on his most charming smile—the one that's gotten him out of plenty of trouble over the years—and wraps her up in a bear hug. "Good morning, Nana! You're looking particularly beautiful this morning. How are you?"

She laughs as she pushes her way out of his arms. "You're full of shit, and I love you for it. I'll leave you to it. I should deal with that damn deer."

The moment she's gone, Harrison spins to me. "Where were you last night?"

Crap. He must have come by my room while I was talking with Thea. "Just wandering around the property."

Harrison's eyes narrow. "So you weren't avoiding talking to me about the Thea situation and how perfect it is?"

I groan, dropping my head into my hands. "Not you, too."

"Yes, me, too! A month ago, I told you I wanted to set you

up with Addy's sister, and now we find out she's the woman you've never gotten over. It's fate, man."

"It's not fate, and I'm not going to win her back."

"Not with that attitude, you aren't," he says, shaking his head in mock judgment.

Harrison's default setting is positivity, so certain that things will work out in his favor, which makes sense when I've always been there to cover for him. It was okay when he got caught drinking in high school because I talked the cop into letting him off. Everything was fine when he left his internship in the middle of the semester because he had a job lined up with me after college. It's worked out each time he moved to a different department of the company because I was there shifting responsibilities around to cover him.

I scrub my hands down my face. "How could you not have known it was Thea? This is your soon-to-be sister-in-law."

He shrugs, unbothered by my despair. "She calls her Tia."

"You never saw a picture?" He shrugs. "You're telling me that Addy doesn't have a single picture of her sister in her apartment?"

Harrison's usually cheerful face hardens. "Addy doesn't have photos up in her apartment. She's got a thing about settling into a place, which I think is fair after everything they went through in their childhood. We're working on it."

It feels like I should apologize, but I don't understand what I'm apologizing for, and I can't ask for more information about their past without revealing that I never actually dated Thea. I should know it all.

I *want* to know it all.

Harrison shakes off the cloud, smiling that broad, dimpled smile. "Which is why I plan on spending the rest of my life filling that woman's walls with more good memories than she knows what to do with."

A part of me is still on the fence about this marriage, but

when Harrison talks about Addy with complete devotion woven into every word, I can't help but get pulled into the magic.

I clap him on the shoulder. "What happened to my wild little brother who loved keg stands and late-night parties?"

"He's been thoroughly and completely tamed, and he's grateful for it."

"I'm happy for you," I say, and find I mean it. No hesitations. "But about Thea, don't pull anything. I'll talk to her if I think she's open to it."

Harrison lifts his hands in submission as the doors swing open behind him. He spins with an eagerness that would have embarrassed him pre-Addy, and his face lights up. Two long steps, and he's sweeping her up in his arms.

"Missed you," he murmurs, kissing her neck in a move that feels way too intimate for it to happen in front of their siblings.

Addy's laughter echoes around us. "It's been an hour!"

"You're right. Let's never do it again."

Thea's a step behind, having to dodge Addy's flying feet. She looks beautiful, with her curls piled on top of her head in a messy bun. We share a quick smile before I look away, afraid of what Addy and Harrison will read between us.

Harrison looks at me over Addy's head. "You ready to go?"

I swallow the groan climbing my throat. I forgot Harrison said he was planning something for just the four of us so we could all get to know each other. I'd been worried it was all a big matchmaking scheme. Now, I'm even more worried.

"Just need to pop upstairs and grab my wallet," I say.

"Don't forget a bathing suit," Harrison calls at my back.

I pause with my hand on the door, looking at the group over my shoulder. "Harrison. No."

A sense of dread floods my body when Harrison wiggles his eyebrows. "Yes."

* * *

Is there anything more uncomfortable than being stuck in a car with a group of people and not knowing how to behave? Are Thea and I friends? Keeping a respectful, cautious distance? Should I pretend like we never dated? That certainly would be the easiest option.

At least I have a bit of distance from her. Harrison's up front in the passenger seat while the girls hang in the back. The ride so far has been full of Harrison's chatter, telling Thea all about his history with Addy. The first time they met ("She was the most beautiful person I'd ever seen"). When he knew he loved her ("Ages before she loved me"). His proposal story ("I was so nervous").

Addy's usual forced smile has relaxed into something more natural. She still lets Harrison take the lead like she did at the welcome party, but she jumps in now and then with a comment or correction instead of standing to the side like a garden statue, pretty, but with none of the engaging energy of the plants around her. For the first time, I wonder if she's more. Maybe a flower herself that can't bloom in the shade of others.

I've always loved basking in the glow of Harrison's enthusiasm, and from the glimpses I've gotten of Thea, she feels the same. Her shoulders are relaxed, her eyes bright, and every time he makes a joke, she throws her head back, her laughter bouncing around the car like it's coming through the very best sound system.

"Tell me about yourself," Harrison says to her, turning all the way around in his seat to face them.

"Um, well . . . I was a server at Cibare. This small Italian restaurant near downtown," she says, stumbling over her words in a self-conscious way that doesn't feel like Thea at all.

My mind snags on the past tense, a knot filling my throat. "Was?"

She loved her job. At Camila's wedding, she told my family about helping one of her favorite regulars plan a massive surprise fiftieth anniversary party for his wife, complete with all their out-of-town grandkids. She practically glowed. I could have listened to her tell stories about Cibare all night.

Thea meets my eyes in the rearview, shrugging. She doesn't want to talk about it in front of Harrison, but the idea of saying nothing feels wrong. I mouth *I'm sorry*, and she nods, blinking rapidly.

"I love that place!" Harrison's face lights up, oblivious to the tension in Thea's shoulders. "We went there all the time. It was our family's special occasion restaurant. We haven't been there since my senior year of college. Owen, why haven't we . . ."

He puts two and two together. His senior year was three years ago, when Thea and I "broke up."

A heavy awkwardness settles in the car. I want to turn this around, but my mind starts spiraling. This is going to be the most agonizing day, the most agonizing week. Everyone's going to find out we faked our relationship, and Harrison's wedding will be ruined. I'll spend the rest of my life dealing with the fallout with Mom.

Like Thea can sense my panic, she leans forward, squeezing my shoulder and grounding me. "Pickup truck selling produce out of the bed."

I swivel my head to spot what she's talking about, and sure enough, there's a truck on the side of the road with a small sign advertising their produce.

I click my tongue. "Not weird enough. You can find that all over Florida, too."

"True," she says. "But are those pickups also selling animal feed?"

We're past it now, but I look over my shoulder as if I can see through the sign like Superman. "I didn't see that."

"Not my fault if you don't look close enough."

I catch her eye in the rearview mirror; she has a teasing

smile on her lips and a challenging glint in her eye. "Fine, I'll accept it, but barely."

She rolls her lips together. "You know, this has turned into a very one-sided game. Why don't you contribute if you're going to be so judgy?"

My lips tilt up of their own accord. Even when she's being bratty, she's captivating. "I apologize for focusing on the road. I'll prioritize the game over our safety in the future."

She scrunches her nose, and a laugh bursts out of me. As the sound fades, the silence sets in. I glance to the side to see Harrison staring at me with glee, and I realize in our attempt to stop one type of awkwardness, we've just created another.

I flick on my blinker, breaking the moment. "We're here."

"Where exactly is here?" Addy asks, eyeing the woods around us.

Harrison's face twists in a devious smile. "Sliding Rock."

Chapter 7

THEA

"Nope," Addy says, her fists anchored on her hips as she faces off with Harrison. "No fucking way."

My sister rarely curses, but this time it's well earned. We're standing on a wooden platform looking out at a waterfall, gently sloping rocks with a constant stream of water flowing over them. Visitor after visitor takes their place at the top, scooching as the stream builds up enough strength to carry them along the sixty-foot slope until they land in a pool of water at the bottom. I shiver just looking at it.

The angle of the rocks isn't too steep. So why is everyone speeding down the incline like Mario Andretti trying to win the Daytona 500?

This is no human-engineered slide where you know what you're getting. Each slider moves down the rocks differently, completely at the whims of nature, the slightest shift of their weight getting them caught up in a different current and sending them along a new path.

"When you said Sliding Rock, you literally meant a rock you slide on," I say, tilting my head as a family of five stretches across the wide top of the rock, counting down before pushing off.

Owen chuckles next to me. "Not the most creative name."

"This can't be safe," I say as two friends going down collide, their shoulders slamming together.

"Which is why we won't be going on it," Addy says.

"It isn't dangerous," Owen says, his brow furrowed like he's working through every scenario. "People have been doing it for hundreds of years."

Harrison slides his arms around Addy's waist, tugging her close to him. "Come on, babe. You know you want to go."

He's right. Life has forced Addy into the perfect, responsible box, but she's got an adrenaline streak. Like last year, when she took me to Universal for my birthday and I convinced her to go on the VelociCoaster. I spent the next two hours with my head in a toilet while she rode it three more times. I always wonder who she'd be if we'd been raised differently, in a home that provided the security for her to explore her wild side instead of dozens that required to her to always be levelheaded.

When Addy huffs, Harrison pulls her closer. "If you try it and you don't want to go again, I'll grow out that beard you've been begging me for."

Addy turns her head so she can see him. "And no backing out when it gets all patchy to start?"

"I swear. That's how confident I am that you'll love this."

Addy shakes out her arms. "Fine. I'll do it. Once."

Harrison plants a smacking kiss on her cheek. "That's my girl."

I step closer to Owen, dropping my voice to a whisper. "Are they always this nauseatingly adorable?"

"Worse," he whispers back, the corner of his mouth tugging up. "You up for it?"

I'm about to open my mouth to say *hell no*. My visit to Universal was enough to show me that I do not, in fact, enjoy the feeling of my stomach swooping. As for the drop into freezing cold water at the end, who *does* like that? You don't grow up in Florida and willingly put yourself in water below seventy degrees.

But before I can speak, Addy says, "If I'm doing it, Thea's doing it."

I can't help but laugh at the way she shimmies her shoulders.

She'd let me back out if I thought I couldn't handle it, but she gets so few moments like this, carefree and joyful, and I want to be a part of this memory for her.

Owen catches my eye, and I see the challenge there, like he's sure I'm going to bail at any second.

"You think I'm too scared?"

His small smile grows. "It's cold. I mean, *really* cold. Like, *can't feel your limbs after* cold."

"Trying to scare me off, Hayes?"

Owen smirks. "Just giving you fair warning, Pappas."

I start to respond, but all brain function is wiped out when Owen grabs the back of his shirt, pulling it off in one smooth motion. My mouth goes dry as the Sahara at the expanse of tan skin before me. He's all lean muscle, not jacked like men who spend hours at the gym so they can brag about how much they can lift, and I'm struck with the overwhelming desire to see if those pecs are as solid as they look.

I spin away from him, hoping it was quick enough that none of our group—most especially him—caught my ogling. I lift my tank top over my head, unsnapping my jean shorts and letting them drop to the wood deck, unable to resist looking over my shoulder to see if Owen's watching me like I watched him.

He's not.

He's at the side of the deck, hands gripping the wooden railing as he watches the swimmers glide through the pool to the steps. I shouldn't be disappointed by that.

"Carry me over," Addy says to Harrison when she realizes we'll have to walk through ankle-deep water to reach the hill leading to the top. "If I feel the temperature of the water, I'll chicken out."

"My pleasure," Harrison says, grabbing Addy and throwing her over his shoulder like a sack of potatoes. She screams and beats at his back, but he just laughs louder, intentionally splashing through the water to mess with her.

I get what Addy sees in him. He's genuine, all his thoughts and opinions written across his face. Addy will always know where she stands with him.

"Need a ride, too?" Owen asks, his low voice tugging at something deep in my stomach.

"Nah," I say. "I like to know what pain I'm getting into before it hits."

I spend the fifteen-second walk through the water to the—blessedly dry—line muttering every curse I know. The deep pool at the bottom of the waterfall taunts me while we wait for our turn, and my stomach churns with each step up the hill.

When we get to the top, Harrison pulls Addy between his legs. She squeals as the cold water slides around her body, but Harrison's already scooching them forward. Addy's screeched "Oh my god" reaches all the way back up to us until they slip off the edge of the rock and into the pool.

"Our turn," Owen says, holding out a hand.

"You go ahead. I'll be right behind you."

"Liar," he says with a chuckle. "Don't back out now. You're so close."

I huff out a breath, stepping with him off the dry path and into the flow of the water.

"Holy fucking fuck, that is so fucking cold," I say, wincing at the sharp bite of the water and forgetting about the sweet family of five behind us in line. I send an apologetic glance to the parents. "I'm sorry."

"She's not wrong, Mom," the shortest of the three girls says. "It's really fucking cold."

The mom sighs and rubs a hand over her eyes while the dad stifles a laugh. "Please don't say 'fucking,' Sophie."

It's the type of family I always imagined for me and Addy, loving parents who are gentle even when we screw up. How different would life have been if we'd been raised like this?

I absently rub at the ache in my chest, but that just spreads cold water from my hands over my body. Owen watches me from about a foot away as I shiver. He holds his hand out again, and before I can question whether it's smart to exchange these small touches, I clasp it.

"Ready?" he asks, giving me the freedom to choose. Dozens of people stand in line, watching our every move, but Owen waits, holding my hand and not tugging me along.

After a few seconds during which I seriously consider hopping back up and running away, I nod. When I still don't move, he chuckles and whispers, "Need some help?"

"Yes, please," I whimper back.

He pulls me along with him, the current strengthening until we lose all control. I squeeze his hand so tight that his bones may snap, but he never tries to escape, keeping my hand in his as we fly down the mountain. It's a bumpy ride, nothing like the man-made slides at the cheap water parks around Central Florida. The current takes us away from each other, but Owen gives my hand a tug to bring us back together. He only lets go when we land in the icy pool. It's like a million tiny pinpricks, but it's also a shot of adrenaline.

We're both laughing when we break the surface of the little pool. His eyes are shining, the silver droplets of water scattered across his lashes making his eyes even brighter.

"Holy shit," I say. "That was incredible."

"Going again?" he asks.

"Oh, hell no," I say, and he throws his head back with a big, booming laugh that sinks into my bones.

We swim over to the steps, slipping on the rocks. Owen places a hand on my waist after one particularly slippery rock, and that one little touch wakes up my senses more than the dip in the freezing water.

"Let's go again," Harrison says when we meet them at the top of the steps. Addy bounces on her toes, and I know I'm going to cave.

"Once is enough for me," Owen says. "Thea, want to hang in the sun while they go?"

Warmth spreads through my limbs at the soft smile on his face. He wants to go again. He said so in the pool thirty seconds ago, but he's willing to sit it out so I'm not the bad guy.

"Yeah," I say, trying to pull back on my smile. "That sounds great."

Harrison and Addy shoot off to the line. A few seconds later, a towel covers my shoulders. I turn to find Owen, still gloriously shirtless with water droplets dusting his broad shoulders.

"You don't have to give me your towel," I say, shrugging it off. "I should have thought about needing one when Addy told me to wear a bathing suit."

He grabs the side sliding off my shoulder and tugs it back into place. "It's fine."

"No, it's not, you have to be cold, too, and I—"

"Keep the towel, Thea." His voice is low. Commanding. A shiver moves through me for a whole different reason than the cold water.

We find a spot at the edge of the deck with the most direct sunlight. The weather's warmed up since this morning, but it's still chilly in the shade, and I need every bit of warmth possible.

"I'm guessing you came out here every summer growing up?" I ask, shifting my body so I can look at him.

He mirrors my position, running a hand across the back of his neck as he smiles. "Yeah, a few times. Aunt Dawn has this giant bus to shuttle people back and forth to town for wedding events, but during the week, she'd let us take it out. The cousins would pile in and head out here to cool off."

I shudder. "Cool off."

He reaches out and nudges my hip. "Come on, it wasn't so bad, was it?"

"No, but once is enough. I can't imagine choosing to do this every single year."

He tilts his head. "How did *you* spend your summers?"

I pause at the question. My summers were nothing like his. There was no giant family waiting to welcome me back with open arms. I never went on fancy trips or had a change of scene. Our foster parents didn't have the money, and if they did, I doubt they'd have spent it on us. My summers were spent walking around town for an excuse to get away from the house.

There was one time when our eighth foster mother took us all to the beach for the day. Of all our parents, she was my favorite. Kind, but she also didn't push me. Most of my foster parents were either so authoritarian that I felt like I had to rebel, or they desperately tried to connect with me and ended up mad when their techniques didn't work, like I must be broken. Soledad gave me space, let me come to her like the wild animal I was.

One day, she loaded all five of her foster kids in her Suburban and took us out to New Smyrna Beach for the day. It wasn't fancy—we didn't have any boogie boards or toys to make sandcastles—but we spent the day splashing in the waves, and before we left, she bought us all one-dollar soft serve ice cream from the stand down the beach. It was one of my happiest memories.

But Soledad wasn't looking to adopt, and by the end of summer, Addy and I had been moved to another home.

I haven't thought about her, or that magical day, in years. I never talk about my past, but with Owen's earnest eyes on me, I want to share it. To tell him about the bad days so he can understand how special those good days were.

"My summers were—"

I'm cut off when Harrison, soaking wet and beaming, jumps on Owen, shaking his hair like a dog and sprinkling us both with water. "How're we doing on time?"

"We need to head out in ten if we're going to make it back."

"Perfect," Harrison says, grabbing Addy's hand and tugging her away. "Time for one more."

"Only one more, Harrison," Owen calls at his back. His tone is stern, but the half smile on his face is indulgent.

"You've got that dad voice down," I say.

His smile drops a bit, and I wonder what I said wrong. "Yeah, but you were telling me about your summers."

I was, but the moment's passed. Laying out all my trauma while surrounded by joy and happy families feels like too much.

"Oh, you know. Typical Florida kid. Summers at New Smyrna Beach. Not as exciting as all this."

Owen's lips tip up. "Oh, I don't know. Shark bite capital of the world sounds pretty exciting to me."

"Excellent point. You should never underestimate the excitement of having to fight for your life."

He eyes my arms, pursing his lips. "I don't know if you could take on a shark."

I jab him in the chest, ignoring the fact that it *is* as hard as I imagined. "Hey! I'm scrappy."

He chuckles, looking out over the waterfall. "Now, that I *do* believe."

I'm not sure if he means it as a compliment, but I take it as one, preening under the praise. "Thank you."

A few minutes later, Harrison and Addy finish up their final run so we can head back to the car. Addy slips her arm through mine, pulling us a few feet behind the boys.

"You doing okay?" she asks in a hushed voice. "You know, with all the Owen stuff? It's been a lot of time with him today."

A true smile splits my face, because I'm doing better than okay. This morning was fun. Unexpected. "Yeah, I'm fine. I told you not to worry about it. We're good."

She smiles, but it's strained around the edges, more like the one she gives the rest of the world. "Good. Great. So happy to hear that."

We make it another ten steps in silence before she speaks again.

"I need to ask you something. For something, really. A favor." She sucks in a fortifying breath. "Please don't get involved with Owen again."

I'm stunned into silence. When she said a favor, my mind went to the wedding. Steaming her dress or helping with the seating chart. Not this.

Before I can speak, she jumps in. "I didn't get it before, but I see it now. The chemistry between you. But things are different than they were three years ago. My life is so wrapped up with his. Not only am I marrying his brother, but he's my boss."

I laugh to disguise the discomfort I feel at her request. "He's not really your boss. It would have been better if he *was*. You talk so much about work and your team, I'd have been able to put two and two together before we got blindsided at the welcome party."

"He's the president of the company, Tia. He's *everyone's* boss. It doesn't matter that I don't report to him. He could have me fired with a single word." It's on the tip of my tongue to point out that Owen would *never* fire an employee out of spite, but I know where the fear comes from. The insecurity of our childhood makes it hard to trust a good thing. "All my happiness is connected to this one family, and that's terrifying. You know, the whole eggs-and-basket thing."

"And me and Owen would tip over your basket?" I don't know why I'm arguing when I have no intention of dating Owen, but something about it feels like sandpaper to skin.

"Well, you tried once, and it didn't work, right? I know how easy it is to fall back into old feelings when you're forced close together."

She's thinking about her toxic college boyfriend, the one who broke up with her before each break, only to pull her back in when it was easy for him. I'd get the same call every semester. *It's different now* and *We'll work this time*, until her senior year when she started recognizing she's worth more than a man who treats her like a convenience. She told me she'd never have gotten back together with him the first time if they hadn't been forced to spend time together for class.

I hate that she's equating Owen to that human equivalent of a trash can.

She worries her lip with her teeth. "If you guys wanted to get back together, wouldn't you have called each other before this? When we get back home, all those issues that broke you up will still be there, but now I'll be in the middle."

I want to push back, but she's right. We may not have had the first time she thinks we did, but I've ruined every real relationship. She's seen my pattern of behavior. I get excited about a new guy. We go out for a little. I struggle to open myself up and trust them. We blow up in spectacular fashion. I'm not surprised she doesn't want me anywhere near her future brother-in-law.

I force out a smile. "Owen and I are on the same page. You have nothing to worry about."

I mean the words as I say them, but when Owen smiles at me over his shoulder, I think I may have just lied to my baby sister for a second time.

Chapter 8

OWEN

We make it back with just enough time to change and meet up with everyone. Thea was quieter than usual on the drive back. I got nothing more than a small chuckle when I pointed out the Textbooks and Mystical Crystals storefront. I wanted to ask if something was wrong but worried about doing it in front of Harrison and Addy.

I jog up to the ballroom where the event planning offices are to snag the key to the bus. My aunt put a giant yellow key chain on them years ago to keep us from losing them, and I swing them around my finger as I head to bring the bus around front.

It's an Ellis family tradition to have at least one sporting event when we're all together. Everyone's so competitive—probably unhealthily so—and it's nice to be our most obnoxious selves for an afternoon, knowing that our competitors will trash-talk us all day but still love us that night. When we're together for a special occasion, the family member of honor gets to pick the event.

For Camila's wedding, she set up a massive croquet tournament on the events lawn. Thea took one look at it and said, "What sort of fancy-ass *Bridgerton* hell is this?"

Her eyes had gone so wide I could see the whites around her irises, but the whole family was with her. We'd all been giving Camila—the least athletic cousin—crap about her choice for weeks, and a dozen cousins sought me out during the game to comment on how perfect Thea was for our family.

When it became abundantly clear that neither Thea nor I

were going to win, I asked if she'd be open to some light sabotage. Thea took to it beautifully, strategizing on the best ways to screw over my more successful cousins. At one point, she sent Camila's ball flying so far that it went off the lawn and all the way down the sloped path to the inn. She'd been two swings away from winning, and she'd dropped to her knees, screaming to the sky, while I scooped Thea up in my arms, swinging her around as we cheered like we'd won the World Series.

There'll be no need for sabotage this time. Harrison picked baseball, and I've never loved him more. It's been years since I swung a bat, but some things your body doesn't forget.

Most of my family is waiting when I pull the bus to the front of the inn. I hop off as they start loading up, lugging coolers of beer I'm sure they'll pop open as soon as they sit. Let them drink. The drunker they get, the worse they'll play. Then again, I should keep *my* team sober.

Thea's in the middle of the pack and stops next to where I'm leaning against the side. Her gaze slides up my joggers and T-shirt, pausing for a moment on the baseball cap I tugged on as I ran out the door. I wish I could see myself through her eyes, to know for sure if that's heat flaring in them or just my hopeful thinking.

"So this is the famed family bus," she says.

"The very one." I pat the side. "She gets us where we need to go safely, and we reward her by only vomiting in her once every fifth trip."

Thea's head tilts back as she laughs, and it's like I've been filled with helium and am at risk of floating away. When her laughter cuts off abruptly, I follow her gaze over my shoulder and spot Addy watching us. Thea pastes on a fake smile, and it feels like I've been poked with a needle, that buoyant feeling seeping out of my body. She mounts the stairs without another word, and I'm left staring after her, wondering what just happened.

Harrison pops up next to me before I can bring myself to look away. "You ready for this?"

"Depends. Did you stack the teams in your favor?"

"Like I need to cheat to take you down."

I smack the back of his head and he laughs, jumping a couple of feet away from me.

His cocky smile slips and he shuffles his feet in an uncharacteristic show of nervousness. "Hey, when you have a minute, I was hoping we could talk. About the business."

I've heard this speech before, and I know where it leads. He's gotten what he needs from the estimating department—just like accounts payable and operations before this—and he thinks he should move. Which means I'll need to find a new estimator and figure out where I can fit Harrison without upending everyone's work. The added responsibility lands like an anvil on my shoulders, and I worry my knees will buckle under the pressure.

"I mean," Harrison continues, "right now isn't the best time, but I just thought, you know, we're both here and we might as well talk. Not, like, right now, just in general."

I force a smile. "Yeah, we can talk about it."

A breath whooshes out of him, and he smiles that brilliant Harrison smile that's charmed every person he's ever met. "Awesome. Great. Thanks, Owen. Now let's get on the bus so I can hand you your old ass."

He bounds up the steps, and I call after him, "Have you seen Mom?"

There are only a few stragglers loading up, and I haven't spotted her yet.

"No, I haven't seen her since last night," Harrison says.

My stomach drops. I've been so caught up I didn't think to check on her. This wouldn't be the first time she said she was fine, then disappeared for a couple of days. I pull out my phone and dial her.

She answers on the first ring. "I know, I know. I'm late. I'm on my way, but if it's too much of an inconvenience, you can leave me."

I hold in my sigh of relief. "Not an inconvenience. Just making sure you're okay."

"Why wouldn't I be?" she says, hanging up as she walks through the front door, "I'm here with my family. My youngest son is getting married, and my older son has another shot at love."

She skips up the stairs of the bus, patting me on the cheek as she passes, and all my excitement for the day curdles into anxiety.

* * *

I stare Harrison down from the pitcher's mound, clocking his cocky smile and the way he casually swings the bat to warm up. He points it at Addy in the dugout, blowing her a kiss as he steps up to the plate.

"Better get your head in the game, baby brother," I call out.

His grin grows at my goading. "Doesn't take much concentration to hit one of your pitches."

I toss the ball up and down a few times. "Don't forget who taught you how to swing that bat."

"Yeah, then you quit, while I just got better."

You quit.

He thinks I got tired of the game, too young to realize my practices were replaced with caring for him. While my old teammates were fielding ground balls, I was sitting in the pick-up line at the elementary school. Then I was in college and working, and the closest I got to a baseball diamond was sitting in the stands at Harrison's games.

Regardless of what Harrison thinks, I haven't lost my love of the game. Or my skill, which I prove with a fastball that flies right past Harrison's bat, sinking into my cousin Johnny's glove with a satisfying thud.

"Strike one," Johnny bellows, even though it's not his job.

This is why I wanted Johnny as catcher. He can catch my pitches, but more important, he's the best at screwing with the rest of our cousins, muttering trash talk I can't hear but can see the impact of as each batter glares at him.

I lift my hand to my ear with a smug grin. "What was that about my pitches?"

"I wasn't ready," Harrison says, knocking his bat on the plate in frustration. "Won't happen again."

Johnny tosses me the ball. "Ready now? Just want to make sure."

Harrison glowers, and I let the ball fly again, savoring the shifting of my muscles, the way the ball rolls from my fingers. This time, the bat connects. The line drive threads between second and third base, and Harrison easily makes it onto first before my team snatches it up.

I'm scowling when I turn back to home plate and find Thea waiting. She looks adorable with her blond curls flaring out from beneath the helmet. Thea lifts the bat, positioning it awkwardly in her hands. Her body's hugging the plate, and she's taken such an open stance that she's nearly facing me.

"Over a year with this girl, and you never taught her how to hold a bat?" Johnny calls out.

Thea narrows her eyes. "Owen never complained about how I held a bat before."

Johnny howls, throwing his mitt on the ground so he can clap. I laugh, too, rubbing my hand over my eyes. This woman just can't help herself.

I should throw the ball, let her learn the hard way. She's not on my team, and it's every man for himself in the Ellises—even between couples—but I want her to have fun more than I want to win.

As I jog over from the mound, Gabriel calls out from his spot as shortstop, "You can't help her! She's the enemy. Where's the loyalty to your team?"

I don't look away from Thea as I call out, "How would that be an earned victory? It's like playing a baby."

"I can think of a few other ways to use this bat," Thea grumbles, twisting it in her hands. There's a fire behind her dark smile that tells me she's thinking about going full enforcer and using the bat on me instead.

"You want to beat me with that bat, or do you want to learn how to use it so you have a chance of actually beating me?" I ask, and she mumbles a reluctant "fine."

I come to stand behind her, grabbing her by the waist and shifting her farther from the plate, helping her line her feet up a bit more than shoulder-width apart. Thea lifts the bat, and I place my left hand over hers, using my right to adjust her grip until her hands are stacked. My arms encircle her, and I can't resist breathing in her spicy scent.

"When you swing," I whisper, and a shiver goes through Thea's body, "make sure to follow through. Then run like hell to the base."

"Assuming I hit the ball," Thea says, twisting her body to look at me. I shift back to keep her from brushing against me.

"Have a little faith in yourself, Thea," I say, and run back to the mound.

"Can we play baseball now?" Gabriel whines.

I mouth to Thea, *You ready?* She nods back, and I give her a soft toss. The bat connects, sending a fly ball far into the outfield.

"Holy shit!" Thea screams.

I holler back, "Run!"

My outfielder fumbles the catch, and Thea makes it to second base. As soon as she stops running, she turns to me, holding her arms out wide as if to say, *Did you see that?* It feels like a sparkler's been lit behind my sternum, and I can't hold back my answering smile.

"Impressive," I call out.

"Beginner's luck, I'm sure," she says with a little shrug.

I turn back to home plate, where Harrison is celebrating his run with Tommy, Johnny's identical twin brother, who's up to bat. Johnny's ribbing goes to a new level with Tommy, distracting him enough for me to get the first two pitches past him. He successfully hits the third, the ball flying straight from his bat into Gabriel's glove.

Thea starts toward third base the second Tommy's bat connects, and Gabriel runs after her. She's a couple of feet from the base when his glove connects with her back, sending her forward and sliding against the clay. She shouts loud enough for me to hear her a half field away, and I go sprinting to her.

"What was that, Gabriel?" I yell as I help Thea roll over. There's blood running from her elbow.

"I'm so sorry, Thea," Gabriel says. "I didn't mean to hit you so hard."

She gives him a weak smile, wincing when I shift her arm to get a better look. "It's fine. All's fair in love and baseball, right?"

Addy and my mother come running out of the dugout, dropping next to Thea. "Oh my god, Tia, are you okay?"

"Yeah," she says, her eyes darting around before she says louder, "I'm fine, everyone. Get back to the game."

"I'm taking her to get fixed up," I say to Addy, sliding my arms around her and lifting her bridal style. There's a small office in the center of the park near the restrooms. I'm sure they have a first aid kit.

"I really am fine," Thea says, wiggling in my arms.

I pin her with a hard stare. "You have blood running down your arm."

Addy dusts off her hands as she stands. "I'll help."

"Stop. It's a scrape. Please don't miss out on this with Harrison's family. Getting time with them is important to you," Thea says, and Addy glances out at the field. "It'll take a couple minutes to clean it up. Stay. Please."

My mom wraps her arm through Addy's. "Let Owen handle it. He'll take excellent care of her."

Mom winks at me, and I stifle my eye roll. Addy's lips pinch, but she nods, and I walk off with Thea still in my arms.

"You know I can walk, right?" Thea asks, lifting a brow at me. "It's my elbow, not my leg."

I shrug, tugging her closer to my body. "No need to exert yourself. You're injured."

She laughs but doesn't push for me to put her down. I love the way she feels in my arms, so I'll keep her there if I can get away with it.

Once we reach the office, I set her down on a low wall next to a pillar. She leans back against it while I run inside to grab the first aid kit and then into the bathroom to wash the clay off my hands. I sit down on the wall, sliding close and twisting my baseball cap backward so I can get a better look. She whimpers, and I glance up to find her bottom lip trapped between her teeth.

"Does it hurt?" I ask.

Her throat bobs. "No, it's okay."

"You don't have to be tough for me," I say, and she grits her teeth as I run a saline wipe over the scrape to clean it.

"Thank you," she whispers as I finish bandaging her arm.

Curls have escaped from her low ponytail and there's a smudge of clay on her cheek. She's never looked more beautiful. "Of course."

She leans back on the pillar again. "I should have known you were a baseball guy."

I laugh, bracing my elbows on my knees. "What's that supposed to mean?"

She waves her hand in my direction. "Just all of this. The

good ol' boy, Captain America thing you have going on. You're like baseball in human form."

I laugh again, and I realize I've laughed more in the past day with Thea than I have in years. "If I'm baseball, what are you?"

She tilts her head in thought. "I don't know. Street fighting? Oh! WWE!"

"Oh really?" I say, my eyebrows flying up, and she nods. "I can see it now. Thea Shark, going for WWE SmackDown champion."

Her grin grows into a full-blown smile. "Thea Shark?"

"Since you learned all your skills from fighting off the sharks at New Smyrna Beach, obviously."

Thea tilts her head back against the pillar, letting out a throaty laugh that draws attention from every man in a twenty-foot radius. I want to lock her away from their view. To hoard that laugh for myself. To find out what it feels like against my lips.

I take her arm in my hand again, turning it so I can check on the bandage. There's nothing more to do, but I need something to distract myself from the tempting woman in front of me.

"Addy asked me to keep my distance from you," she says, and my head snaps up.

"Why? What did I do?"

Why wouldn't she like me? We haven't interacted much, but I don't think I've done anything that would make her warn her sister off me.

Thea grimaces. "It's not you. She's worried about drama. Look at it from her perspective. We dated and had a big, dramatic breakup that left you heartbroken. She just thinks it'll be better if we, you know, don't fall back into 'old feelings.'"

I know it was all fake, but the sarcasm that laces her tone when she puts air quotes around "old feelings" pinches behind my breastbone. It's not fair to her. She agreed to be my fake girlfriend for a weekend, then my fake ex for the week. I can't push my confusing feelings on her.

So instead, I say, "That may work. Me seeking you out and you trying to avoid me. Kind of plays into the narrative."

She tilts her head to the side, one curl falling across her eyes. "True."

I can't tell if there's hesitation in her voice or if I'm just hearing what I want to hear, but it doesn't matter. At the end of the day, she's going to make the best choice for Addy.

"Starting tomorrow, we avoid each other?" she asks.

I nod. "Simple enough. I'll come over to you a couple more times to sell it to my mom but then leave you alone from there."

"Yeah, right. That's good. The easiest way to avoid drama."

"The best thing for Harrison and Addy."

"And it's their special week," she adds, like she's convincing herself of our plan's merits, and it soothes some of the sting.

"Exactly."

Our gazes collide, and there's so much that I want to say. That I loved spending the day with her. That I hate that she'll be near, and I won't be able to talk to her. That even though everything with us has been fake, I hope she knows how special she is.

But all that will do is make this thing more uncomfortable.

"I guess this is goodbye, then," I say instead.

She looks away, a smirk gracing those full lips. "Thanks for the memories."

"Even though they weren't so great?"

She laughs again, and I've never felt more accomplished.

"We should get back to the game," she says, standing and dusting her hands off on her shorts.

We walk back in silence. And later that night, as I lay in bed trying not to think about Thea, I kick myself for not stealing those last few minutes with her.

Chapter 9

THEA

The chilly mountain air brushes over my skin as we walk through the vines the next morning. This is the only place I've been besides Florida, but I can't imagine anywhere more beautiful. The surrounding mountains stretch out before us, smooth rolling peaks that remind me of the Atlantic Ocean on a clear day.

We're a small group compared to yesterday's family-wide game, and it's like I'm under a microscope. Diana's eyes have been boring into me for an hour.

Owen's uncle talks us through the history of the grapes, encouraging us to grab one off the vine and pop it into our mouths. I snatch it greedily, raising it to my nose to inhale the gorgeous, fruity smell before slipping it between my lips . . . and immediately regret it. The skin is thick, and when it bursts in my mouth, the bitter taste takes root in a way I don't think I'll ever get rid of. I share a look with Addy, whose face reflects what I'm feeling.

I spit it out on the ground before I can stop myself. If this is what the grapes taste like, what sort of wine will we be subjected to this week? When I look back at Addy, her face is horrified.

"What are you doing?" she cries out, looking around at the group before her eyes land on Dennis and she forces a smile, folding her hands in front of her. "The grape was delicious."

The group watches us for a handful of seconds before bursting into laughter.

"Wine grapes are notoriously bitter," Dennis says when he gets control of himself. "We wouldn't eat them. And if we need to taste them, we do what Thea did—take a sample to test and then spit it out. Sure you're not an Ellis?"

Dennis gives me a wink, and I feel an overwhelming sense of relief that yet another screwup on my part is working out in my favor. Addy has her fakest smile on, and I know she's not ready to forgive me for doing something so rude, even with the family laughing about it.

"I'm sorry," I whisper to her.

"It's fine, Thea," she says, but the use of my full name lands like a bee sting—sharp, quick, and way more painful than it has any right to be.

Dennis is still laughing as he plucks a grape himself and tosses it up like he's going to catch it in his mouth, only to nab it from the air before it can land. "Just a bit of hazing for the new family members."

I know he means Addy and that my qualification as a family member is about my connection to her, but I can't stop the small pang of longing. This *will* be her family soon, and I'll be on the outside. Harrison wraps his arms around Addy from behind, nuzzling into her neck and whispering words for her ears only. She relaxes in his arms, her fake smile fading into something genuine and soft, and I turn away from the intimate moment. My eyes flick over to Owen, who's watching me with a small smile of his own. He walks over and hands me his water bottle.

"Sorry," he whispers as I tilt the bottle against my lips, steadily ignoring the fact that they're touching the same place his did a few minutes ago.

I shake my head in mock outrage as I hand it back. "Is there no loyalty?"

"Did the baseball game teach you nothing? Every man for himself in the Ellises."

His smile grows, and I notice a subtle indent in his cheek. Not a full dimple. A tease. I ignore the tug inside me that wants to poke and prod to see just how big he'd have to smile to give me the whole thing. He shifts another inch closer, and his scent wraps around me, something deep and earthy, but with a sweetness underlying it all. I can't stop myself from taking in a lungful.

I step away to put some distance between us, a ball of guilt lodging in my throat. My heel catches on something, and I tip backward, my ass and my scraped elbow coming down hard on the path.

Addy rushes over. "Are you okay, Tia?"

I wince, brushing the dirt from the bandage on my elbow. "Can't seem to keep my feet under me since I got here."

A hand appears in my periphery, and I glance up to see Owen offering his help with a teasing tilt of his lips. I resist the urge to take it, pushing myself to stand. If this bothers him, I don't look at him long enough to find out. I'm here to support Addy, not get caught up in Owen.

"I'm fine," I say to Addy. "It won't happen again."

I mean it. No more. No shared smiles. No leaning to catch a whiff of Owen's signature scent. It's none of my business if Owen has a dimple when he smiles big enough. I won't risk my relationship with Addy for anything.

Addy runs up to join Harrison near the front, and I watch as she turns to Diana and Dennis, the forced smile sliding into place. I want to pop into the group, tell ridiculous jokes until Addy's facade breaks, revealing her true self below. I'm so focused on Addy that I don't realize I'm by myself, a lone gazelle ready to be picked off by the lions.

"Hello, dear," Owen's grandmother says as she joins me at the back of the group.

"Hi, Cece," I say with what I hope isn't an awkward smile. The two of us haven't spoken yet on this trip, but she was welcoming the first time I came up. "It's good to see you again."

"The feeling's mutual. Do you mind taking a rest with me? There's a lovely clearing around the corner of these vines, and my old bones struggle with these hikes."

I watch in terror as the rest of the group heads up the mountain, leaving us behind. "Shouldn't we keep up with them? Or at least let them know?"

"I already told them," she says, tucking my arm through hers and towing me in the other direction. "Plus, I'd like some time to get to know my future granddaughter-in-law."

"You're thinking of my sister, not me," I say, craning my head to see if I can call Addy over.

She waves a hand. "Oh, this old mind of mine. But you'll do for now."

Something tells me there's nothing old about Cece Ellis's mind, and my stomach churns. She leads me around the edge of the tall vines, and my feet falter.

There's a cleared slope ahead of us, leaving nothing to interrupt the stunning view. It's breathtaking, rolling green mountains with a few houses dotting them, a hint of life amid the wild. I want to teleport inside one, tucked away from the world. I can see myself, bundled up under a blanket in the early morning, nothing but me, a cup of coffee, and the mountains.

Cece plops down on the grass with an ease I'd expect from a teenager, not an octogenarian. *Old bones, my ass.* She pats the ground next to her, and I gingerly lower myself down. My nervous system goes on high alert, fortifying myself for a one-on-one I was so clearly manipulated into by the Ellis matriarch.

When she doesn't speak, I panic, stewing in the silence. Finally, I break. "Your property is gorgeous."

A smile curves half her mouth, but she keeps her eyes pinned to the horizon. "My slice of paradise."

"I read the article your son hung up in the lobby. About you starting the vineyard all by yourself."

She looks at me, and it's like she can see right through me, into me. I don't understand why, but I desperately want this woman's approval. This must be how Addy feels about Diana.

Cece's head tilts, like she's weighing the words she's going to choose next. "It was hard, leaving behind the life I'd been raised in and the person I'd been told I was. My father was a powerful man, which came with a lot of privilege but also meant I was supposed to fit a specific mold. And I was a hellion. I spent most of my life hearing that something—usually everything—was wrong with me."

I understand that feeling. Everyone I've ever met has found something wrong with me. I was too combative or too closed off. I was never just enough of anything for anyone. But there's a huge difference between someone being forced into a sexist box and someone who's just too difficult by nature.

Cece continues. "I spent a lot of time thinking I was broken, but when he was gone and there was no more guilt or pressure, I found who I really was. Found this place. I let myself be healed by the love of this town."

I can't stop my eye roll. This isn't the first time someone has talked to me about how love can fix everything, that if I had just been open to the love of my foster parents, I'd be a much easier, more pleasant person. "Oh yes, I've heard all about the healing power of love."

"You don't believe in it?"

"No, I don't. They say anyone can be healed by the magic of love, so if you experience one nice person in a lifetime of assholes and *aren't* healed, you're clearly too fucked up to be helped. It's a cop-out for society."

I'm breathing hard by the time I finish. When I look back at Cece, she's watching me with raised eyebrows.

My stomach sinks, and I scramble to fix it. "I'm sorry, I didn't—"

Her laughter cuts me off. "Take a breath, dear. I can appreciate a bit of righteous indignation. And I agree that love doesn't fix everything. But I think sometimes we get so stuck in who we believe we are—who we've been *told* we are—that coming to a new place without those expectations lets us take a step back. Giving myself that freedom allowed me to achieve my dreams."

I look back over the mountains, and we sit in a moment of silence that's only broken by the chirping of the birds.

"I've never had room for dreams," I say, so quietly I'm not sure the words even left my lips.

"There's always room for dreams, even if they aren't achievable in the moment. When we stop letting ourselves dream, we stop living."

If that's true, I don't know if I've ever lived. The only thing I've ever dreamed of is happiness for Addy, success and fulfillment and the freedom to make the choices she wants instead of the choices she feels are necessary.

Cece lifts both hands, letting them come down on her knees with a clap that echoes off the mountains. "Now, dear, are you going to tell me why you and my grandson are lying about your relationship or not?"

I sputter, and she laughs at whatever she sees on my face.

"What do you mean?" I ask, playing dumb.

"What I mean is you two have never been in a relationship. It's clear in the way he looks at you. You did not break that boy's heart."

The comment feels like a knife to the stomach. I'm not the right fit for Owen, not right for this family, but hearing that it's so laughably unbelievable that Cece clocked it from the start hurts.

"He doesn't look at me like he has—or had—feelings for me?"

"Oh, he looks at you like he has some sort of feeling about you. But he doesn't look like he's pining for something he's lost. He looks at you like he's never had a taste and is desperate for one. It's like me at Rita's now that my doctor's said I'm not allowed to eat too much fat. I may miss my favorite fried chicken, but that new item on the menu that would be delicious that I'll *never* get to eat is a whole other sort of pain."

A laugh bursts out of me, even as heat floods my cheeks. "Oh my god, Cece!"

She chuckles, leaning her elbows on her knees and turning her gaze back to the mountains. "I'm too old not to say what I mean. There's no time left for bullshit."

I bury my face in my hands. "This wedding moved so fast that neither of us knew the other was going to be here, and then we just panicked."

"Can I ask why you two lied to begin with?"

My throat closes around the words because I can't answer that question anymore. He gave me the spiel before we came up the first time. His mom was controlling and emotional and no matter how many times he told her he didn't want to be set up, she kept pushing. He needed a break. But now, really getting to know the family, I don't get it.

I peek at her from behind my hands. "I think that's a question for Owen."

I've seen more families than most, and none of them have been particularly positive. I'd stopped believing this type of family existed, big and full and loving. I don't know why the lie didn't bother me the first time. Maybe I was just so desperate for the money that I put on blinders, but now I can't unsee the love and trust here. It feels like what we're doing is corrupting that.

My jealousy over Owen's life is a living, breathing thing, slamming against my ribs and begging to be released. While Owen was busy resenting this beautiful family, Addy and I were surviving, living in a constant state of defensiveness. No mother invested in our future happiness. No cousins or aunts or grandparents to watch out for us. *This* is the family she deserves, but Owen, with his lies and manipulations, is the one who gets them?

Just then, Owen turns the corner, and my frustration boils over.

He smiles at Cece, something softer in his gaze than when he looks at the rest of his family. "Mom sent me back to check on you."

She laughs loudly. "Oh yes, I'm sure it's about checking on me and not about the charming woman keeping me company." She shoots me a wink and pops up off the ground. "I'm going to head back to the house."

"Would you like me to walk with you?" I ask, desperate to get away from Owen before I blow up on him.

"I'm much more agile than most would believe, dear. Why don't you take in the view with my grandson?"

He meets my eyes and gives a little shrug, tilting his head back toward the clearing in invitation.

I don't want to sit with him. I can barely even look at him, not in this beautiful place full of love that he doesn't appreciate. But I don't have an excuse, and Cece is already a dozen feet away from us.

As she's about to turn back between the rows, she calls out, "Oh, and Owen, do come see me when you get back. I'd love to hear why you've been lying to us all for years."

Owen's mouth drops open in shock, and I can't help but feel a surge of satisfaction. He's still gaping like a fish when Cece disappears from view.

Chapter 10

OWEN

Crap. That's not good. I'm still watching where Nana disappeared, her words echoing in my head. How does she know?

There's only one explanation, and it's standing right next to me with her hands planted on her hips and her eyes looking out at the view.

"Did you tell her?" I ask, my tone more accusatory than I intended, but I'm pissed. We agreed not to tell anyone. It's been less than forty-eight hours. Nana can be tough, but still. And without so much as a *Hey, Owen, heads-up . . .*

Her cheeks flush, and I take it as confirmation until she opens her mouth. "Did *I* tell her? No, Owen, I didn't fucking tell her."

The tension releases from my muscles, but the relief only lasts for a few seconds before I'm hit with shame. Of course she didn't tell her. Thea wouldn't do that, to me or to Addy.

"I'm sorry," I say, stepping toward her and placing my hand on her arm.

She rips it away from me. "You're not forgiven. It's a douchey thing to jump straight to me ruining this when I've done nothing wrong. She said she could tell. And of course she could, because they know you."

She paces away from me, and I follow. "Okay, I'm sorry. I didn't think they'd be paying that much attention. Is that what you're mad about?"

"I'm mad that I'm in this situation at all. I'm mad that your mom has moods that could ruin the wedding, so I'm under pressure to keep it quiet for Addy. I'm mad that everyone's watching us and wants *something* to happen, all while Addy wants me to stay far away from you, and I'm stuck in the middle lying to a group of people who have been nothing but kind and welcoming to me. And I'm really fucking mad that you made up this lie to begin with. They love you so much."

"I know they love me," I say, getting worked up, too. "You think I don't know they love me?"

"I don't fucking know. All I know is that your family is incredible. Do you know what I would have done to be a part of a family like this growing up? And you don't appreciate it at all."

"Yes, I do."

"No, you don't," she yells, "or you never would have lied to begin with."

"You don't get it," I say, unsure how to explain it.

"Oh, of course I don't. I'd never understand how hard it is to have people love me. A grandmother who knows me well enough to judge my feelings from just a look. A mother who wants me to find happiness. How difficult your life must be."

"I didn't mean it like that."

"Then how *did* you mean it? Make this make sense, Owen," she yells.

"I've given her everything!" I yell back, and Thea's pacing falters. She turns toward me, confusion written on her face, and it makes my voice drop lower. "My entire life has been chosen for me. I've had no freedom to pick for myself, and I won't let her pick my future partner, too."

I can't watch any more of the disgust on Thea's face. I plop down on the grass with the grace of a newborn horse, looking out over the view, and before I know it, I'm pouring everything out to her.

"My dad was sick my whole life. He wanted me to take over his business one day—it was his dying wish—and after he passed, that became the expectation. I think she had to keep part of him alive or her grief was going to take her with him. And so I gave her what she needed. I worked on job sites after school instead of trying out for the baseball team because he believed it was important for me to understand the labor side of the company. I went to college nearby so I could help with Harrison and keep working at Hayes, just like Mom wanted me to. I took over the mantle of president a year out of college for a company I don't love, all because *they* wanted me to."

I finally glance up at Thea, and she's looking at me like a goddess who has paused in the middle of administering her vengeful punishment to reconsider.

"I know how lucky I am," I continue, turning back to the view. If she decides I'm beyond redemption, I don't want to see it. "The business is solid and gives me the money I need to live comfortably. It's selfish to be mad. It's selfish not to accept it when I don't even know what I'd do if I had that freedom. I don't have some fantasy I've been cut off from. But I have always envied the opportunity to dream. My whole life, I've just felt . . . trapped."

Thea slowly lowers herself beside me, and even though I don't look at her, the warmth of her body's only an inch away, soothing like sunlight on a cool day. Something loosens inside me, either at saying those words or her closeness. When I look at her, she isn't looking back, instead she's studying one of the nearby trees.

"I understand feeling trapped," she says quietly, and my body shifts closer to hers. "I told you my parents passed away, but I didn't tell you all of it. I don't . . . I don't talk about it, but my dad's never been in the picture, and our mom died from an overdose when we were little. We bounced from foster home to foster home until I aged out. I mean, clearly there's a way out for some—look at Addy—but I could never see it for me."

Her words slowly sink in, and I hate myself. This is what

Harrison meant about their difficult childhood. I must look like such an asshole, complaining about my family when she never had one. My job was handed to me on a silver platter while she's fought for everything she has.

"I'm so sorry, Thea. I must sound like such a jerk."

"Only a little," she says with a teasing smile. I groan and dig my palms into my eyes, but she grabs my hand. I watch in fascination at the way she twines our fingers together. "Trauma isn't a competition. Just because things in my life have been shitty doesn't mean that you haven't struggled, too."

"Still, when you look at the facts, they've given me everything."

"Everything but a choice, and that's the most important thing," Thea says before I can spiral further. "We all deserve to be in control of our own lives."

"Every time I made comments about maybe wanting something different, she sank into herself. Went back to that quiet ghost of a person she was in the months after my father passed away. After a while, it seemed unfair to keep throwing her back into that, especially since it meant Harrison didn't have an engaged mom. I cared for him, but he needed her. We both did."

"That doesn't seem fair to you," she says, her thumb drifting across the back of my hand.

"It wasn't on purpose," I say, almost defensively, and Thea raises a brow in response. "I just mean, she was grieving, too. Probably always will be. I can't imagine how hard it was to watch the love of her life waste away."

"But you shouldn't be responsible for managing her grief. You were grieving, too. And a kid. How old were you?"

"Thirteen."

"Barely a teenager, with your life mapped out for you, plus the responsibility of taking care of your brother and managing your mother's emotions? Yeah, that sucks, and you have every right to say it."

I've never said this out loud, too afraid of how it would sound. I wouldn't have said it today if Thea hadn't goaded it out of me, and I feel an overwhelming gratitude for this woman. Both that she forced me to release the words out into the world, and that she met the confession with so much patience and acceptance. I feel lighter than I have in years.

Her hand is still grasped in mine, grounding and supporting me. Giving me the confidence to fall into these emotions without fear, like a climber who knows they can push off the rocks because their belayer won't let them hit the ground.

We both turn back to the view, sitting in silence for a few minutes.

"It's hard to feel trapped here," I say, "with nothing but open sky and rolling hills."

"Yeah," Thea whispers. "There's something magical about this place."

I've felt that, too. This little sliver of the mountains has been a hideaway from the pressures of my life. But being here with Thea feels even more special.

The two of us sit for a few more minutes, not speaking and just soaking in the mountains. It's safe and comfortable, even though it can't last. Soon enough, we'll go back to the main house and once again be "exes" with a complicated history. She'll keep her distance, and I'll pretend I'm not watching her.

Even knowing I should move away, to give each other space just like we're supposed to, I can't bring myself to let go of her hand. And she doesn't let go either.

Chapter 11

THEA

The service in my room is so bad that it takes three attempts before the video call to my best friend goes through.

"Make it fast, ma'am," he says, propping his phone up on the mirror of his bathroom vanity, running each hand along the line where his fade gives way to his tight black curls. "You're eating into my getting ready time. I've got a date tonight."

"Your date can wait," I say. "I'm having an emergency."

Vaughn swipes his phone off the counter, walking out into his living room and plopping on the couch. "Oh shit, sorry. What's up?"

"Remember that time you convinced me to come up to North Carolina to be your friend's fake girlfriend?"

He gives me a flat stare. "You mean that time I helped you make rent by setting you up with my hot cowork . . ." His sentence trails off as he registers where this conversation is going. "No fucking way."

"Yes fucking way. It's a disaster!"

He has the audacity to laugh, the light brown skin around his eyes crinkling. "How'd they react when you came clean?"

I pull my lip between my teeth. "We didn't exactly . . . come clean."

He groans. "Seriously?"

"His family would be pissed. And his mom's emotional because her dead husband isn't here for her son's wedding and Addy's already scared she won't be accepted by them and Owen doesn't want to deal with the fallout. And, I don't know, I want to help him, too."

I want to give him this little sliver of freedom, even if it's not as much as he deserves.

Vaughn studies me for a minute. "Fuuuuuuuuck, you're going to fall in love with him."

My stomach flips like I've been thrown out of a plane with no parachute, but I force an eye roll. "No, I'm not."

"Yes, you are." He laughs, but there's a hard edge to it. He leans forward, bringing his face closer to the camera. "Thee, be careful."

"There's nothing to be careful about," I say, breaking eye contact so he can't see the lie. "And if there was, aren't you the person who's spent years telling me he's a great guy?"

I don't even know why I include that last bit. Obviously, Owen's a good guy, but that doesn't matter.

"Yes, he *is* a great guy. And I meant it all those times I said it. But he's about to be Addy's brother-in-law. The two of you have concocted this massive deception, and getting emotionally involved will just make things messier."

"He says like she's unaware of her own predicament," I mumble.

"You know how Addy's going to react if this comes out. She'll get pissed and take it—"

"Don't insult my sister," I say with so much venom that it slithers through the phone to poison my friend.

He sighs. "I'm sorry, I shouldn't have said anything. But I've watched you beat yourself up over things with Addy for years."

"I don't do that."

He levels me with a stare. "What about that time we got drunk at De Leon Springs and had to call her to pick us up? A totally normal thing for a Saturday, but you cried after she dropped us off because you were, and I quote, 'so irresponsible.'"

"She had to leave a work picnic to get me!" I yell.

"That you didn't know she was at. She could have told you to call a rideshare, but she didn't. And you beat yourself up for weeks."

What Vaughn doesn't realize is that the day at the springs wasn't an isolated incident. Yes, it sounds normal and reasonable, but it's mixed in with the years of me screwing up and dragging Addy down with me.

"You're going to do the same thing if something happens at the wedding, and I don't want that for you. So stay away from Owen." I don't answer, and he stares at me long enough that I think the connection has dropped until he sighs. "Just think about it, okay?"

I nod, saying a quick goodbye so he can get to his date and I can hype myself up before meeting up with Owen's family. Because even though my knee-jerk reaction is to fight Vaughn's comments, he is right. My best bet to keep Addy happy is to stay away from Owen Hayes.

* * *

Thirty minutes later, everyone's gathered in the lobby, ready to head out for the joint bachelor/bachelorette party.

I spot the person I'm absolutely not going to talk to under any circumstances. His back is to me, his jeans hugging his ass and thick thighs. But I'm not noticing that. I'm being responsible, because I'm not here for my own fun. I'm here to give Addy the future she's always wanted.

Gabriel bounds over like the puppy dog he is, throwing his arm around my shoulders again. "How can I earn your forgiveness, oh perfect one?"

"What?" I ask, the word broken by a laugh.

He gestures to my elbow. "For injuring you. I'll spend the rest of my life paying my penance."

I chuckle at his enthusiasm. "It'll heal up in a day or so. No need for self-flagellation."

"Thank god for that. In that case, are you ready to fall in love with me?" he asks with a cheeky smile, and I poke him in the side. He jumps a few steps away. "Wait until you hear me play, and then we'll talk."

We're heading into town tonight to a dive bar that's apparently the *greatest place ever to party*, which sounds like a pretty big declaration for a town with about four stores. But I was promised live music, and that's all I need to get on board.

"You're in the band?"

Gabriel gives me a cocky smile. "I am. Does knowing I'm a musician change anything for you?"

I laugh loudly, and the noise catches Owen's attention. He looks over his shoulder, catching my eye and giving me a small smile that has everything in me tightening up.

Shit.

I turn my focus away, to anything besides the way the slight tilt of his lips makes me feel. Gabriel slips a flask out of his back pocket, handing it in my direction with a playful glance at Owen.

"Need a nip of courage?"

I sigh, swiping the container and letting the cool metal ground me. The cheap whiskey burns, but it gives me something tangible to focus on.

Camila slides up to our group, hip-checking Gabriel. "Is my little brother giving you trouble again?"

Gabriel sighs wistfully. "Thea Ellis-Gutiérrez has a nice ring to it, doesn't it?"

I shake my head. "He's a very charming fetus."

Gabriel clutches his chest like I've stabbed him while Camila's wife, Mira, comes up behind her, wrapping her arms around her waist and laying her hands gently on the swell there.

Camila pops a kiss on her cheek. "Babe, fair warning, I offered Thea the role of my mistress to get the boys off her back."

Mira pins me with a hard stare, like I actually intend to steal Camila away in the night, and a shiver runs down my spine. The sheet of her gorgeous black hair slides over both their shoulders as she shakes her head. "Not okay with that."

Camila hums. "What if she was a weird live-in mistress who handles nighttime feedings?"

"Yeah, I'm going to pass on that one." I take one last swig before passing the flask back to Gabriel. "No one wants me in charge of keeping a child alive. Who's on bus-driving duty tonight?"

"That's Owen's job," Camila says.

"He drove to the baseball game," I say.

"Owen always drives," Gabriel says. "Didn't he do it the last time y'all were here?"

"No, we didn't go off property during my wedding," Camila says.

"Our wedding," Mira answers with a little nudge, her light Indian accent slipping through the syllables, and Camila smiles up at her guiltily.

"Wait," I say, even though they're already moving on to something else. "Owen always drives?"

They blink at me.

"Yes," Camila says, drawing out the word like doing so will help her see the logic behind the question.

"Why is it always Owen?"

Camila and Gabriel look at each other, confusion etched on their faces, like the question has never occurred to them.

"It just . . . is," Gabriel says, the last word turning up like a question.

Camila laughs. "Owen's always been the dad of the group. He likes making sure everyone's safe."

I don't point out that she's pregnant and can't drink, but

from the way everyone's eyes flick to her bump, we're all thinking it. I'm this close to calling it out, but inserting myself into the family dynamics is the opposite of what I said I would do. Owen's role in the family is not my problem.

Owen hops up on the coffee table in one of the sitting areas and cups his hands around his mouth. "Anyone planning on using my services—"

"What sort of services, Owen?" one of the cousins calls from the back in a fake feminine voice that has the group cracking up.

Owen levels a stare across the group, and everyone quiets down, giggling behind their hands like scolded schoolchildren. "This bus is leaving in ten minutes, so get out there."

Everyone heads for the door, but I drop back to avoid the rush.

"I'll save you a seat," Gabriel says, blowing me a kiss.

"You're developing quite the fan club," Camila whispers, jerking her head in the opposite direction from Gabriel to where Owen is standing, watching us.

Owen heads my way as Camila and Mira saunter off. "You ready for this?"

"It's a night at a dive bar. You're putting me in my natural habitat," I say. If anyone wouldn't be comfortable at a dive bar, I'd guess it would be him with his pressed collared shirts and lack of tattoos.

The smile he gives me is small but no less earth-shattering. "My family can be a lot."

"I've been called a lot my whole life," I say. "I can take it."

"I know you can," he says, his voice low and quiet. It shoots through, heat rushing to every corner of my body.

I take an abrupt step back. "We should probably, you know . . . not talk like this."

Owen blinks and backs away, too. "Oh, yeah. Of course. Sorry."

Owen turns suddenly for the door and walks away from me

without another word, and I fall into step a couple of feet behind him, like a sad, reluctant baby duck. There's a tightness in his shoulders that's not normally there.

"I hear you're the permanent designated driver around here," I say. It's the opposite of what I just promised myself. I shouldn't keep encouraging conversation when I'm trying to put distance between us.

Owen flicks the keys around his finger again. "Yup."

"Don't you ever just want to let loose with your family?"

He looks over his shoulder, his feet never faltering. "Of course."

"Then why don't you?"

He lets out a heavy sigh. "Because they ask me to drive."

"Have you ever told them you don't want to?"

He stops on a dime, twirling to face me. "What's with all the questions, Thea? I thought we weren't spending time together."

It's the harshest he's ever spoken to me, and I'm a bit taken aback. But I'm also happy to see him not just saying whatever he thinks I want to hear.

"We aren't. I'm just wondering."

He runs a hand down his face. "No, I guess I've never blatantly said it before."

"Camila told me you *like* driving, that you want to take care of everyone."

Owen blinks a few times, like this is news that his brain can't process in regular time.

I shrug. "Just seems like everyone's making assumptions right now, and it may be worth a conversation."

Owen watches me for a couple of seconds, something in his gaze softening. But one of his cousins calls out from the door of the bus, and the indifferent mask slips back into place. "I can handle my family, Thea."

It feels like a slap, even though it's true. This isn't my place.

I have *no* place with this family, just a transient role to help the real new member of their family settle in.

"Yeah, of course you can. Let's go," I say, turning away from the flash of regret I spot in his eyes.

Addy and Harrison are on opposite sides of the front row, and Addy bounces as she pulls me down to sit next to her.

"I've barely seen you today," she says with a little squeeze of my arm. "Harrison can handle a bit of space."

"No, I can't," Harrison says, winking before turning his attention back to his own seat buddy.

I slip into the window seat, and Addy starts whispering about her plans to win over each of the cousins. I try to follow, but I can't focus past the buzzing in my head. Owen's the last to board the bus, and his eyes find me immediately. I break the eye contact first, refocusing on Addy and her plotting and only glancing at the back of his head a half-dozen times as the bus twists down the winding roads from the inn to downtown Elk Ridge.

I can't stop thinking about Vaughn's comments earlier. He has every right to worry, because I'm absolute shit at putting distance between me and Owen.

Chapter 12

OWEN

Frustration is still buzzing under my skin when I get to the bar. I can't even pinpoint where the anger is coming from. Whether it's at Thea for, once again, pointing out issues with my family that I've been ignoring, or at the fact that my family has so solidified my role as the reliable cousin that they believe I want to be in charge. Probably a combination of both.

And, if I'm being honest with myself, Gabriel slobbering all over Thea—and knowing I have no right to be bothered by it—hasn't helped my mood either. She's never given the slightest hint that she welcomes his attention, but I can't help but wonder.

I lost a good twenty minutes. After dropping off everyone in front of the bar, I had to go a mile away to find parking for our ridiculous bus. The air is cool again now that the sun has set, just enough of a chill to nip at my ears and nose, and the cold should extinguish the last of the embers inside me. But instead, I spend the walk turning the interaction with Thea over in my head and working myself up even more.

I was a jerk to her, and I hate myself for it.

It takes all of ten seconds after walking through the doors to realize my family has taken over. Every single one of my almost two dozen cousins have shown up, plus their spouses and partners and friends. We might as well have rented out the entire venue for the way the non-Ellis patrons get pushed to the corner.

The air in here is hot and thick; too many people are crammed into the small space. My shoes stick to the floor with each step. Gabriel's band has already started their set, mostly playing covers of top-forty songs with a country bend, and they're better than I expected. My eyes are immediately drawn to Thea, sitting with Harrison and Addy at the table closest to the stage. She clutches Addy's hands as they sing together about a sky full of stars. Harrison watches Addy with stars of his own in his eyes.

Addy's different with Thea. I noticed it at Sliding Rock—the genuine smile so different from the china doll one she uses at work—and I wonder if this is the version of Addy that Harrison fell in love with.

There's a fourth chair at the table. It would be so easy to claim the spot next to Thea. The thought has barely crossed my mind when another guy—one of maybe five people in here not connected to the Ellises—drops into the seat, sliding his thick, tattooed arm over the back of her chair and smiling down at her. It isn't surprising that people are drawn to her, but it is a solid reminder. There's no spot for me at the table, figuratively and literally.

I push my way to the bar, squeezing next to Tommy and Johnny, then ask the bartender for a whiskey ginger. Thea's drink of choice. I may not have a place next to her, but I can still get her an apology drink.

"That's not like you," Tommy says, clapping me on the shoulder and tsking. "Drinking when you're driving the family."

"Is Dad being bad?" Johnny says with a laugh.

"You're fifteen years older than me," I mumble, passing over my card to the bartender.

"You're right, and you should listen to your elders when we say don't drink and drive."

"Be nice to our boy," Misha, Johnny's wife of twenty years, says as she slaps his shoulder.

She pops a kiss on my cheek and grabs the drinks for her

and Tommy's boyfriend before sauntering back to where the two of them were gossiping in the corner. It's always like this when I'm here, a constant flow of family around me, always someone new jumping in with a joke or a tease or that little bit of love you didn't know you needed until they give it. Misha's quick show of affection is the reminder I needed of how special my time is here, how limited. I don't want to waste it brooding over Thea.

I laugh. "It's not for me, guys. You can go back to your shots without worrying how you'll get home."

"Thank god," Johnny says. "It was like I didn't even know you anymore."

I ignore the way his words bring back what Thea said, that my family thinks I'm happy to be the responsible one, that I'm doing this for me and not as a favor to them. The cold condensation of the glass grounds me in the moment, bringing my attention back to Thea. The stranger leans over and says something to her, and I watch every micro expression to see if she's interested. She laughs at whatever he said, and my jaw clenches so hard it aches.

My cousins follow my gaze, and one of them—because I'm too focused on her to even register which one is talking—says, "Good plan. Always bring gifts when you're trying to get back in a woman's good graces."

"But it looks like someone else is trying to get into her *good graces*, if you know what I mean," the other says.

I turn back to the bar, setting the glass down with so much force a bit of amber liquid splashes over the edge. This possessiveness is new to me. I don't want that man to look at her, to take her smiles and laughter. It's unfair and ridiculous when I don't have a future with her. What sort of asshole would rather see someone alone than with someone else?

Tommy throws his arms around my shoulders. "We got you, baby cousin."

"I thought I was Dad," I say.

"Family's complicated."

I elbow him, and he moves his arm around my neck, pulling my head forward and giving me a noogie like we're kids again. I try to push him off, but he spends his days moving around wine barrels and machinery, and there's no way I can overpower him. When he lets me go, I realize his twin is gone, and a stone settles in my stomach. They only split up when one of them is about to do something the other is trying to hide.

"Tommy, where is he?" I ask with narrowed eyes.

He shrugs, but his eyes widen in glee.

I spot him a half second too late. He's standing behind Thea and her new *friend*, dancing like he's consumed half the alcohol in the bar. I'm about to call out to him when the drink in his hand tilts forward, pouring directly down the tattooed guy's back. The guy jumps up, shrieking and shaking out his shirt before screaming in Johnny's face. Johnny is all faux innocence, running over to grab a towel from the bartender. Before he can get back, Tattoo Man stalks off to the bathroom.

Johnny uses the towel to wipe off the alcohol that made it onto the seat before running back to me, waving his arm with a flourish and dropping into a deep bow.

"Your throne, my liege."

"You two are fools," I say around a laugh.

Tommy yanks my head down and plants a hard kiss on the top. "We're *your* fools."

Johnny grabs the back of my shirt, pushing me in Thea's direction. "Go get your girl."

I thank them, even though she's not my girl. And she won't ever be my girl. My best case is getting back to the pseudo-friendship we had earlier today. All I want right now is to apologize for biting her head off earlier.

As I close in, Harrison stands from his seat and jumps up on the stage. Addy howls next to him, grabbing at his arm with joy radiating out of her.

"You're going to get us kicked out," she hollers over the noise of the bar, the laughter mixing with the words until she's incomprehensible. I look over at Thea, who's watching her sister with a smile tinged with sadness, and I wonder what's going on in her head.

I slide into the open seat, murmuring in her ear, "I'm pretty sure my brother's about to make a fool of himself."

She jumps at my voice, twirling to face me without realizing how close our chairs are. Her mahogany eyes are thrown wide enough to show off the flecks of gold and green hiding in their depths. Two, maybe three inches separate our mouths, and my eyes are drawn to hers like a beacon.

Thea glances behind us, and when I follow her gaze I find a half dozen of my cousins looking back with gleeful smiles, tracking every touch and glance.

She faces the stage again as she whispers, "Are they always like that?"

I chuckle, eyes still on her. "Always. There are too many of them and they're too nosy for their own good."

I turn toward them as I say the last part, raising my voice loud enough to be heard, and they scurry in different directions. Two of them run directly into each other, bouncing back and into innocent bystanders trying to enjoy their beers.

I hold up the drink before me. "A peace offering."

She watches me for a couple of seconds, leaving me hanging in suspense. "An offering?"

"An apology," I answer, needing to get this out before I chicken out and run back to the shadows. "For the way I spoke to you earlier. You were looking out for me. I'm sorry."

She swipes the drink from my hand, taking a long gulp. "No need to apologize. It wasn't my pla—"

"I want it to be your place," I say without thinking. And I do.

I want her insight and her challenges. In forty-eight hours, this woman has gotten me to admit things I never fully acknowledged before.

An emotion flashes across her face too quickly, like a shooting star you never got a chance to wish on. "You know we can't spend time together. I told Addy she didn't need to worry, and, even if I hadn't, the more we interact, the more likely we'll get caught in our lie."

I know we agreed to that, but not talking to her when she's so close feels impossible. Before I can argue, Addy comes back from the edge of the stage where Harrison's still talking to the band. Her feet falter when she sees me next to Thea, but she plasters on that fake smile as she retakes her seat. She doesn't know Thea told me that she told Thea to keep her distance from me.

God, this is already exhausting, and it's only been two days.

She leans forward to talk to me around Thea. "What in the world is your brother up to?"

"I learned long ago not to question him. Fair warning, you will be embarrassed by the end of the night," I say, lifting my cup of water in salute.

Thea tips her head as she watches him. "I never understood the urge to stand up in front of people like that."

"What are you talking about?" Addy says with a little laugh. "You wanted to be a singer."

"When I was fourteen and hadn't realized I have neither the talent nor the patience for that kind of life."

"She's a lying liar, Owen," Addy says, that fake smile twisting into something teasing and indulgent. "Don't believe her for a second. Her voice is incredible."

"Perfect segue, baby," Harrison calls from the stage, and Thea's head snaps to his so quickly I expect her to end up with whiplash.

"What does that mean?" Thea whispers, meant only for

herself, but I seem to be listening to her—and watching her—too closely.

Harrison steps up to the lead singer's microphone, dragging another stand to the front of the stage.

"Evening, y'all," he calls into the microphone, that strong Southern accent he picks up every visit slipping out. The crowd cheers in response. "The non-Ellises in the room don't know me well since my brother and I were only up here in the summers, but this place is home to us. And, because it's home and family, I was able to convince my cousin here to let me get up on stage."

He claps Gabriel on the shoulder, his guitar swinging from the force. Gabriel grimaces, mouthing an apology to the crowd, and laughter breaks out.

Harrison chuckles along with them, always quick to laugh at himself. "I know this isn't karaoke night, but we're here for a celebration. Ever since this perfect woman agreed to marry me, I've been trying to come up with an engagement present for her. She keeps saying she only wants me. Can you believe that?"

The crowd's eating him up. Some cheer and clap, some holler about how Addy's a good woman. A few of our cousins heckle Harrison, calling out that she must have been knocked over the head to want him.

He waves his hands to quiet the crowd. "But I finally found something. Addy's got the voice of an angel, and apparently so does her sister. The two of them dreamed of starting a sister singing duo, and today I'm going to make their dreams come true." He looks right at Addy now, love shining in his eyes alongside a touch of uncertainty. "I got the band to learn that song you two loved to sing."

She squeals and grabs Thea's hand. "The Pistol Annies?"

Her enthusiasm dissolves Harrison's trepidation like sugar

in water, and he preens like a rooster. "Yes, ma'am. Y'all get up here!"

Addy turns to Thea, whose face has gone white. "Let's do it!"

"Up there?" Thea asks, her hand trembling slightly.

"Yes! Please, Tia," Addy begs, clutching Thea's hand in both of hers and bringing them to her chest. "It's our song."

Thea smiles slightly. "I can't believe you told him about that."

"I've always loved singing with you, and I want him to know everything that's important to me."

Thea groans and pushes away from the table. "Let's get this over with."

Addy squeals again, bouncing on her toes before running up the stairs of the stage. Thea drags her feet but follows.

"This is going to be awesome," Harrison says as he throws himself into Thea's vacated seat.

The sisters talk to the band for a minute before setting themselves up in front of the two microphones. Thea's gaze lands on mine, and she widens her eyes in a clear *what the heck is happening* look. Heat blossoms in my chest. There are tons of people in this bar, but *I'm* the one she seeks in the crowd.

The band starts snapping their fingers before Addy joins in a cappella. The tune's familiar, a soft, seductive melody. Addy's voice is beautiful, light and clear, hitting each note with precision. Any fear that the locals would be pissed about their live music night being turned into glorified karaoke disappears.

After a few lines, Addy lets Thea take over.

And my heart stops.

Her voice is low and smoky. Less perfect than Addy's, but with so much character. And as she sings about temptation and love and sinning, I nearly crawl up on that stage to beg for a scrap of it all. I lean forward, elbows braced on my knees and my water clutched so tightly between my hands that the glass may shatter.

Addy's voice joins in with Thea's, the two of them harmonizing in practiced perfection. The sisters glance at each other, a broad smile taking over Thea's face to match Addy's. Those tempting hips swing in time with the song, and I want to stand behind her, gripping them tightly as I move with her. I want her thick curls gathered in my fist while my lips run up and down her neck, to feel the vibrations of her song moving through my body. I don't want her attention on Addy. I want her attention focused wholly and completely on me.

And then I get my wish. Thea turns back to the audience, and her eyes snag on mine. A surprised look takes over those incredible features, and I almost regret what she must see. I can imagine what I look like right now. Possessed. Starving. But there's no stopping it now. Not while she's up on that stage looking like perfection and sounding like my every dream.

She must have missed her cue, because Addy elbows her in the side, making her jump and breaking our staring contest. Thea noticeably keeps her gaze away from me after that. Or, at least, she doesn't look at me again. I hope it's an effort to keep from looking at me. Because it would take God himself appearing in this bar to get me to stop watching her.

She loosens up more as she sings, pulling the microphone out of the stand, moving toward the rapt audience closest to the stage. Each one, men and women alike, lean forward whenever she comes close like she's a magnet drawing them in.

"Goddamn," one of them says, and I'm right there with him.

The song hits an instrumental break, and Addy hollers, "Get up here and dance with us."

Harrison jumps over the front of the stage faster than I thought humanly possible. I'm halfway to standing when Gabriel spins his guitar around his back, taking Thea's hand and spinning her before pulling her back to his front. His arm wraps around her waist and he whispers something in her ear that has her laughing.

Gabriel's a good kid. A good cousin. Someone I can count on, despite his heckling. Still, I have to fight down the urge to punch him. I can see it. I'd rip him off that stage and take my rightful place behind her, slip my arms around her waist and tug her back against me while I glare at the audience, clearly communicating who she belongs to. The vision's so vivid I can feel the sliver of skin between her shirt and jeans under my fingertips.

Shit.

Someone claps me on the shoulder, and I look behind me to find the twins. I have too much family here.

"You screwed up there, cuz," Johnny says with a faux-sympathetic wince. Tommy stands next to him with a shit-eating grin.

"Yeah, I know," I say glumly. And, terrifyingly, none of it is an act.

The song winds down, thank god, ending back where it started with both sisters behind their microphones. The bar goes wild, stomping and clapping. A few people let out earsplitting whistles as others scream like they're at a Kacey Musgraves concert. Harrison grabs Addy and dips her, planting a huge kiss right there on the stage. I watch Gabriel like a hawk, waiting to see what he'll try, but he and Thea just laugh like old friends.

Harrison rushes the others off the stage and goes back up to the microphone. While Addy takes her seat, Thea eyes the two seats available. She catches my gaze, something warring behind her eyes before she lowers herself into Harrison's original seat on the other side of Addy. Right. Distance. She reminded me of that right before she went up on that stage and reorganized me at a cellular level.

"Oof, that's gotta hurt. Poor Owen," Tommy says behind me, not trying to keep his voice down, and the group of my cousins around him start whispering like old women gossiping at bingo night. At least it helps make my case that I'm still in love with her and can't be set up with other people.

I grind my teeth together and focus back on the stage where Harrison stands behind the microphone again.

"Okay, patrons of Proof Yourself. They gave y'all the performance of a lifetime, so I hope you'll be patient with me while I give my bride-to-be one more gift. It won't be anything like that, but hopefully it will be just ridiculous enough to entertain."

He takes a deep breath and steps back to the microphone, singing without backup. The notes are all wrong, so messed up that I don't recognize the song, but as the lyrics register, I realize it's "Can't Take My Eyes Off You." Which, ironically, is how I feel about Thea right now. Addy reaches for Thea, crushing her hand in a death grip as she looks at her with wide eyes.

Harrison finishes the first few lines, the entire bar shocked into silence by his complete lack of musical ability, then he pulls a whistle from beneath his shirt. Two shrill, staccato tweets later, and music starts playing out in the crowd. A trombone? A trumpet? I spin around to see a bunch of high school kids littered through the crowd playing their instruments. Not sure how Harrison convinced the owner to let in underage kids, but Addy's screaming and crying while Harrison starts singing—if we can call it that—again.

"I can't believe you set this up!" Addy calls up to him as he finishes, wiping away the tears and turning to Thea for a quick makeup check before running up the steps to throw herself at him.

"What the hell was that?" Tommy asks behind us, voicing the question I'm sure most of the bar is thinking.

"That was a recreation of a scene from Addy's favorite movie of all time," Thea answers, blinking back tears. "And while Harrison doesn't have the same singing ability as Heath Ledger, it was probably the best gift she's ever received. He really knows her, doesn't he?"

The question is directed at me. I nod, my eyes locked on her. "He does. And he loves her."

"It's just so fast," she says.

"I know. I was nervous, too."

"We can't mess this up," she whispers as she watches the happy couple on stage.

"We won't."

There's so much trust in her eyes, and I know I have to follow through with that promise. Regardless of my reaction to her, of this instinct to be closer to her, I'll see this through. For her.

Chapter 13

THEA

I keep my promise to stay away from Owen for the rest of the night. Instead of sliding into the seat next to him at the bar, I listen to Harrison tell the story—in great detail—of how he bribed the bar owner to let kids in. I let Camila tell me all about the nursery they're setting up for the baby and how she's worried about sorting out proper staffing at the inn to cover her responsibilities. Mira and I take a shot at Camila's request since she can't partake. Another cousin, whose name I can't remember now, corners me to talk about our mutual love of the Pistol Annies.

I don't speak a word to Owen, and I'd be proud of myself for that if I didn't spend the night knowing exactly where he was. If I didn't get goosebumps each time I felt him watching me.

I wish I could wash my brain clean of the way he looked at me on stage. Laser focused, so much intent in that startling gaze. I bet that's how he'd look at me from between my legs, every swipe of his tongue a study in how to make me scream his name.

Fuck.

It's the cold shower I need when Gabriel's band ends their set and he runs over, dropping to one knee before me. "Marry me."

Addy and I laugh, and Camila gives his leg a little kick.

"Get up, you maniac," she says, but Gabriel just looks at me hopefully.

When I shake my head, he pops up, unfazed by my rejection. "If you won't marry me, at least say you'll sing with us again."

I slip my arm through Addy's. "The Pappas Sisters were a one-time engagement."

Gabriel clasps his hands together. "Oh come on, *pleeeeease*?"

I look over at Addy to find her eyes shining. This is what she's always wanted, a giant family filled with love and enthusiasm.

"I wish we could," she says, "but I'll be so busy with wedding stuff."

Gabriel lifts his hand. "*You* can't, but we're asking Thea."

The muscles of Addy's arm go rigid under my hand, and for the first time since this little golden retriever came back into my life, I don't find that eager energy cute. "What the fuck, Gabriel?"

"What?" he asks, looking around the group. "What'd I do wrong?"

Camila's rubbing a hand down her face while Addy looks anywhere but me and Gabriel. I hate seeing Addy like this, the way she makes herself smaller so she doesn't cause any problems. I wish the family saw the way she was at Sliding Rock, her delighted laugh drawing stares and smiles from everyone around her. She should be admired.

Ire drips from my tone. "Walk through everything you said. If you don't see where you went wrong by the end, you're just a dick."

Gabriel's eyes go a bit hazy as he walks through the conversation in his head, then a silent *oh* shapes his lips. He takes both of Addy's hands between his.

"That wasn't how I meant it. Your voice is beautiful. Better than Thea's, even." Camila coughs, and when Gabriel glances over at her, she shakes her head. "Or, not better than Thea's"—another cough—"or *as good* as Thea's because we're not comparing?" He looks at his big sister again, who nods. "I just know you won't want to perform at your own wedding, right?"

Addy's smile is more genuine than she usually gives new people. "I get it."

"We're good?" he asks, all puppy-dog eyes and pouty lips.

"We're good," she answers.

He throws his arm around her shoulders, releasing a whooshing sound. "Good! I can't have my future sister-in-law hating me! Now, future wife, is that a yes or no?"

Addy steps out from under Gabriel's arm. "You can. If you want to. You had so much fun up there."

I nudge her. "Nah, I'm here for you."

"So? That doesn't mean you can't perform with us. We're the wedding band. It'll help with your sister's wedding stuff!"

His eagerness is sweet, but it's not going to happen. "Sorry, I'm booked."

He pouts, kicking his feet as he walks away from me. It's silly, but it feels good to be wanted. Most of the cousins' attention is driven by my past—or perceived past—with Owen, but every one of them seems genuinely interested in learning more. For someone who has always either flown under the radar or been considered a problem child, it's a strange but thrilling change.

It isn't until we're all stumbling out of the bar that I realize none of them yelled at me for snapping. Camila backed me up. Gabriel *apologized*. It lights something up in me, a warm ember of contentment.

But that warmth is nothing compared to the fire under my skin when we head back to the bus, Owen leaning against the side of the door while everyone files in. When it's my turn, Owen takes my hand, helping me step up.

I look over my shoulder at him, but his expression is composed, like touching me doesn't turn him into a human flame like it does me.

"Thank you," I say quietly.

"You're welcome."

His smile is cordial, all the fire from earlier wiped away. Maybe I imagined it. A hallucination fueled by my unfulfilled sex drive and Owen's tempting face. But then I glance back—one last look before I turn down the aisle because I can't seem to help myself—just in time to see Owen's hand flex.

And I spend the thirty-minute drive back up the mountain thinking about nothing but that hand.

* * *

An hour later, I've changed out of my tight jeans into my comfortable sleep shorts and hoodie. I almost crawl into bed and pray for a dreamless sleep, but I promised myself I'd keep an eye on job listings while I was here. The catering jobs work for now, but I don't want to do that forever.

The service is so bad in my room I can't get the employment website to load. Instead of taking that as a sign that I should go to bed and deal with it tomorrow, I go out into the hallway, sitting with my back against the door and holding my phone up until the website gets enough juice to load.

I scroll. And scroll. And scroll. There are a few server jobs, nothing as nice as Cibare—which means smaller tips—but beggars and all that. I shoot off those applications, fighting to hold on to a scrap of optimism after a month of silence on the job front.

Even though my ass is now going numb from the hard hallway carpet, it was a great night. It's been years since Addy and I sang together, and being on stage felt like magic. I close my eyes, letting my head drop back against the door while my mind drifts to that feeling, the song burrowing under my skin and the timing of my vocals hitting just right.

"Hey."

The voice breaks me out of my daydream, and I jump like a cat who's just seen aluminum foil.

"Sorry," Owen says. "I didn't mean to scare you."

I scramble to my feet. "No, I was just thinking. I didn't hear you coming down the hallway."

"What *are* you doing in the hallway?" he asks, one eyebrow quirking up in perfect time with the side of his mouth.

"The service in the room is absolute trash," I say, then suck in a sharp breath when I realize I just insulted his family's hotel. "I mean, the hotel is so nice and beautiful, and I love it here. The service just hasn't been very reliable."

He chuckles, holding out his hand for my phone, typing something in before handing it back. "You realize this is the twenty-first century, right? We have this thing called Wi-Fi."

I glance around the cozy—but old-fashioned—inn. "As much as I love this place, it isn't what I'd call high-tech."

Owen's lips twitch. "Yeah, Uncle Doug's pretty resistant to change. But cell service is a problem all over the mountains, so Wi-Fi was one change he couldn't argue his way out of."

I slip my phone into the pocket of my hoodie. "Makes sense. Thanks."

"No problem."

He smiles again, looking down the hallway like he's about to go, but a part of me isn't ready for him to leave yet.

When he takes a step away, I blurt out, "What are you doing walking the hallways so late?"

He startles a little—which, fair, I practically screamed it—but then shrugs. "Mira was too drunk to get herself to bed. She kept making jokes about how Camila's eating for two and she's drinking for two."

"Do you take care of everyone?"

He shrugs, rubbing the back of his neck. "She needed help."

"What about Camila?"

Owen laughs, loud and unencumbered, and it's such a beautiful sound, I'm temporarily stunned. "She wouldn't let Camila touch her. Said she was too drunk and would knock her down and hurt the baby. Then she waxed poetic for ten minutes about how Camila is the love of her life. It was the most I've ever heard her talk. Pretty romantic, actually."

"I'd never have taken her for the type," I say. "She's a bit terrifying."

"Nah." He shrugs one shoulder. "Tough on the outside, but worth the work of breaking through."

I'm in awe of this man and the way he's constantly giving to those around him.

"You're a really great guy," I say, more to remind myself of the type of person he is than anything else. He's not for me.

His mouth quirks up and then back down, like he's embarrassed by the compliment. "I walked a few rooms past my own. It's not like I did anything revolutionary."

He can dismiss it all he wants, but I've seen enough people to know he's special. Most people don't stick around when it's easy, but here he is sticking around when it's hard.

Owen leans against the doorframe while I take a position on the opposite side. "Did you have fun tonight?" he asks.

I bite my lip against a smile. "Yeah, surprisingly I did. I've never performed on stage."

"Thea, you were . . ." He lets out a long breath. "Incredible."

My cheeks heat, and I dip my head to hide the reaction. A lot of people tonight told me I was great, so why does this mean more?

When he realizes I'm not going to respond, he moves on. "Were my cousins okay?"

I huff out a laugh. "Well, Gabriel proposed."

Owen groans and drops his head into his hands. "That boy's a menace."

I laugh again, pulling his hands away from his face. "Stop, he's fine. Everyone was great."

"They love you."

I roll my eyes. "They're just having fun with me because

they're trying to screw with you. They'd do it to anyone you dated."

He watches me, his head slightly tilted. "No. They. Love. You."

There's an intensity in Owen's eyes, like he needs me to see and understand. But the welcome I've received makes no sense. This family is incredible. After twenty-eight years of shallow interactions and dismissals, what are the chances *they'd* be the first to want me.

"I don't understand how they even thought we were together to begin with." He opens his mouth to argue, but I refuse to be bowed, to pretend that we both don't know the vast disparity between us. Our backgrounds, our education, our bank accounts. "We've already established you're out of my league."

"We've established no such thing."

I continue like I didn't hear him, even if his words make goosebumps sprout over my arms. "I'm not the type of girl someone from your family marries."

"I don't see—"

"It just goes to show they're all desperate for you to settle down."

He takes one long stride, bringing our bodies flush as he glares down at me.

"I'm only going to say this once. They believed it because it was believable. One look at you would be enough to make anyone believe I wanted you. But then you spent three days showing everyone how wonderful you are. I'm not surprised they've spent the past three years wishing I'd get you back. You aren't good enough for my family. You're better."

I stare up at him in shock. His pupils expand, slowly overtaking the green until only the shades of blue are left. I drop my eyes to hide the riot of emotions shooting through me.

He doesn't let me take the easy way out, wrapping a large

hand around the side of my neck and using his thumb under my chin to tilt my face back to his. "Do you understand, Thea?"

The way his eyes flick to my throat tells me he feels my answering gulp against his hand, but I manage a nod.

"Good," he says just above a whisper.

His eyes slowly move back up my face. The light blue is gone now, too, leaving nothing but his blown pupils and those rings of navy. Dark and dangerous in a way I've never seen him. I expect him to walk away. He made his point. Instead, the hand on my neck tightens, a flex of his muscles that shoots straight to my core.

"I dream about you, you know?" His words coast against my lips.

My eyes widen. "You do?"

He pulls his lower lip between his teeth and a strangled whimper escapes me. His breath catches in response, and when he looks at me, there's a new hope in those depths. "I do. Every few months, like clockwork, there you are. My subconscious loves to torture me."

"Torture you how?" I ask. The breathiness of my voice should embarrass me, but I can't regret this conversation and the way he's affecting me.

"You don't want to know that." There's a hesitancy to his tone, like we're playing a game, and he doesn't know where out-of-bounds starts.

"What if I did? Want to know."

He can't stop now. If he walks away and leaves me like this, I'll never recover. I'll spend the rest of my life in a constant state of anticipation, waiting to hear the things Dream Owen and Dream Thea did in the middle of the night.

"Are you sure?" he asks, his voice still cautious, but he chuckles when I nod with too much enthusiasm. The hand around my neck moves into my hair. "It shows me these curls, wrapped around my fist." He tugs lightly, and when I tilt my head back, his other hand runs down to trace the line of my throat, then down my body to my leg. "These legs have been wrapped around me plenty of times, too." His fingers play with the hem of my sleep shorts.

"Is that all?" I ask.

He licks his lips, that smirk growing into a grin at my goading. "Not even close. You don't want me to get started on those lips. The unspeakable things they've done to me." He drops his mouth to my ear. "I wake kicking myself for not learning what you tasted like when I had my chance."

"Why didn't you?" The question rang in my head all the time. There was plenty of tension between us that weekend. I *knew* he wanted me, but he never made the move.

He pulls back, a crease forming between his brows. "I was paying you to *pretend*. I wouldn't have put you in that position."

The fact that I hadn't even considered how inappropriate that would have been is another sign of just how much better he is than me, contrary to what he believes. He's the best guy, kind and genuine. The complete package. Way too good for an emotionally unavailable, unemployed hot mess.

But that doesn't mean I can't have a small piece of him.

I look at him, my fingers curling in the fabric of his shirt. His eyes flare, the blue barely there, when I tug him another inch closer. "Are you always this good, Owen?"

He lets out a ragged breath. "Hard to remember what good even is right now."

This is the tipping point. The moment where I decide what's next. I can still walk away. We can pretend like this is nothing, another moment of the act we've been putting on for his family. But he's so close, and that scent—the sweet, earthy smell mixed with something so uniquely Owen—is short-circuiting my brain. No warnings from best friends or requests from sisters could compel me to walk away from him right now.

I push up on my toes, our lips mere centimeters apart. "Then stop trying."

He groans and wraps his hand back around my neck, hauling my mouth to his. Sparks shoot through my veins, setting every atom on fire. I slide my hands through his soft hair, tugging at the root and giving him back every ounce of passion he pours into the kiss as our mouths open in unison. He tastes fresh, the sharp minty bite of toothpaste flooding my senses, like he'd been planning to go to sleep before getting the request for help from his cousin.

His hand slides down to my leg, wrapping around my thigh and hitching it over his hip as he grinds against me, hitting the perfect place that shoots off fireworks behind my eyes. This isn't how I'd imagined Owen would kiss. I'd assumed he'd be sweet and sensuous. But this? It's a claiming, and I give myself over to him willingly.

I rip my mouth away from his, letting my head thud on the doorframe as his low moan echoes around us. Owen never stops, moving his mouth down my neck with nipping bites and the smooth run of his tongue. He bites the sensitive spot where my neck and shoulder meet and I moan again, both hands settling on his waist as I pull him against me hard.

"So much better than my dreams. God, your taste," he pants into my skin.

A shaky breath escapes me. "Pretty fun down here in the gutter, isn't it, golden boy?"

He yanks back so quickly that I would fall on my ass if it weren't for the frame behind me and the strong pressure of his hand on my thigh. Those fingers flex so tightly I wonder if he'll leave marks, and part of me relishes the thought of walking around tomorrow with the evidence of Owen's desire for me written out on my skin.

But the anguish in his face is enough to toss a bucket of cold water over my libido.

"You are not the gutter, Thea." The shock and anger in his tone make me want to disappear, to melt back into this wall until I'm a part of the hotel.

I force a laugh, pushing lightly on his stomach. The tree of a man doesn't budge. "It was a joke."

"I don't think it was," he says.

"Yeah, well, maybe that's because you have no sense of humor." The insult—my obnoxious, destructive attempt to force attention away from my insecurities—hits its mark. His beautiful face crumples and he nods, looking away from me. I remember too late his reaction when Gabriel made the same comment our first night here. "Owen, I'm sor—"

"No, you're right." He lets go of my leg, and my foot lands on the floor with a thump.

He doesn't move away, both our chests still heaving and his expression somewhere between resignation and betrayal. I stare, desperate to come up with a way to heal the wound I inflicted but unable to think of anything that wouldn't leave me bleeding out instead.

A squeak sounds down the hallway, and we both jump. When we turn, we spot Camila, eyes glued to us with delight on her face. Before we can speak, she twirls on her toes like a prima ballerina and shoots around the corner.

Owen groans. "Camila's the biggest gossip in the family."

"Shit, shit, shit, shit, shit," I mutter, pacing the hallway.

He grabs me by the arms, forcing me to stop. "I'll go after her and make sure she keeps her mouth shut."

I scoff. "Sure. How do you control the family gossip?"

"She didn't see anything. We were just standing close." *By that point* is left unsaid. "I'll make sure she knows there's nothing between us."

There really is nothing between us besides a single—scorching—kiss. So why does it hurt when he confirms it?

"Plus," he continues, "we're the closest in age. I've got plenty of blackmail on her."

His devious smile is so at odds with his normal hometown hero facade that my knees go weak all over again.

"Please don't let her ruin this, Owen," I say. "I can't do that to Addy. Promise me."

His smile fades. "I promise."

With one last glance at my lips, Owen jogs off after Camila.

Chapter 14

OWEN

I'm reeling. From the kiss—the feel of Thea under my lips and her taste on my tongue—but also from her comments. I'm angry that she sees herself that way. I'm hurt by her saying I have no sense of humor when it felt like she understood me. And I'm so turned on I don't think I'll ever feel anything else.

I let myself have one last look at her, but it doesn't make me feel better. She's tugging on her lips, still swollen from mine, while gazing off into the distance.

I sigh, jogging down the hallway and away from her without another word. Camila's only a few feet away when I turn the corner, too focused on her fingers flying across her phone screen to keep up a normal pace.

I speed up behind her, plucking the phone out of her hands before she can do any more damage. I see one of the dozens of cousin group chats—this one called Gossip Girls—with a text from Camila saying, **you'll never guess who I just caught canoodling in the hallway.**

A half-dozen replies have already come through, begging Camila for the latest gossip and throwing out their guesses. I'm relieved to see that none of them are about me. Who would guess *I* was the one acting inappropriately in public?

Camila lunges for her phone, and I place a hand on her forehead, holding her back with ease.

"Don't make me wrestle a pregnant woman, Cami," I say with a sigh.

She stands up straight, crossing her arms, her forearms resting on the small bump. "You can't keep my phone forever."

I take a step back, farther out of her reach, and toss the phone up and down a few times. "Do you think this phone should go for a little swim in the pond?"

Her eyes narrow. "You wouldn't dare."

I widen my eyes. "Of course *I* wouldn't do it. I'm responsible, sweet Owen. But accidents do happen."

She calls my bluff. "Fine, ruin my phone. I can't text everyone tonight, but I don't know how you expect to keep me from telling them tomorrow."

I slip her phone in my back pocket, holding on to it so I have time to explain, blackmail, or beg.

"Look," I say. "It wasn't what it looked like—"

"It looked like you two were having a moment." She says the last word in that singsong voice she knows drives me crazy and starts making kissing noises.

"Thea doesn't think about me like that anymore," I say, desperate to get Camila off our case. "She turned me down, okay?"

Camila's eyes narrow, and it feels like she's a telepath, poking around in my brain. "I don't buy it. What are you hiding?"

"Nothing." I cross my arms, belatedly remembering that she used to tease me about that tell whenever I was lying, but if I uncross them now, it'll look even more suspicious.

She points an accusing finger at my arms. "I know you, Owen Hayes. What aren't you telling me?"

During those summers when we were young, Camila and I had been inseparable. And even though I'd never admit it outright, she's my favorite cousin. It's natural with a family this big to find little pockets. I love all my cousins, but realistically I can't be close with every one of them, and Cami's only a month younger than me. We'd run like little heathens through the vineyard as kids. She was the person I told about my first—tragically unrequited—crush. My first sip of alcohol was from a wine bottle she stole out of her parents' tasting room. It had been wild and comfortable at the same time. But life became more complicated as we got older, and by the time I was old enough to drive, I had too many other responsibilities pulling me away from our adventures.

I want to trust her, to have someone to discuss this with, but I also can't leave Thea unprotected.

"There's nothing to tell," I say, trying for nonchalance.

Camila's face drops. "I know we haven't spent as much time together in the past few years, but I still considered you one of my closest friends."

My heart tightens. "That's some strategic use of the past tense there."

Her eyes flash. "What do you expect? You almost never come up anymore. When you do, you spend half your trip on your computer. Now you're here lying to my face, and I'm supposed to believe that our friendship is something you value?"

She's right. God, I hate it when Cami's right. As the business has grown, I've been more and more overwhelmed with work. I spend a week up here every year, but don't feel comfortable stepping away fully when there's so much pressure to maintain the success.

But my relationship with Camila is more than a few distracted visits. It's a lifetime of secrets, and she's never broken my trust when I needed her.

"Remember when we were fifteen and you told me you were gay before you were ready to tell everyone?" I ask, and her eyes narrow, knowing where this is going. "You told me that if I ever had a secret the family couldn't know, I could come to you and you'd take it to the grave."

"That's not fair! You can't use things I said against me when I was a baby."

"You can't tell any—"

"Except Mira," she says with pleading eyes.

"Fine, yes, except your wife. But no one else. Swear it on the future of this hotel." She rolls her eyes, but I push. "I'm serious, Cami. This isn't just about me. I *need* to know I can trust you with this."

Camila whines, shaking her arms a bit. "Fine, I swear on the future of the hotel."

"Thea and I . . ." I suck in a breath as I glance up and down the hallway one last time, and Cami leans forward like the pause is a black hole sucking her in. "We never dated."

Her eyes flutter so quickly that she probably just blinked more in three seconds than I do in a whole day. "I'm sorry, what?"

I shrug. "It was fake."

"But . . . why?"

I run a hand down my face. "Why do you think? Don't you remember the list my mom asked you to make of eligible women invited to your wedding? I just needed a break."

She groans, her body collapsing back against the wall. "Fuck, Owen, this is the best gossip this family's had in forever, and you want me to keep it secret?"

"I swear, Cami, if you tell anyone but Mira, I'll kill you. Thea's worried about the fallout affecting Addy. God only knows how my mom would react."

Camila's face pales a bit, and I wonder which of my mom's dramatics she's playing out in her head.

"Please," I beg, throwing myself on her mercy. "Please don't tell anyone."

"But . . ." she starts with a little whine in her voice. "Fine."

I hold her phone out, a show of trust, and she takes it back with a sigh. She types something, then holds it up. Another dozen texts have come through asking Camila where she went, but at the bottom of the chain is a new message from Camila that says, **Harrison and Addy, going at it in the hallway like they were teenagers trying to get in one last grope before curfew.**

I grimace at the image presented. "Really, Camila?"

She shrugs, a self-satisfied smile playing over her lips. "I've gotta get my fun somehow."

I shake my head, but my body sags in relief. "How are you both the worst and the best?"

The sound of my mother's voice from down the hall makes me jump. "It's been too long since I've seen you two getting up to mischief."

Camila looks at me frantically, then to my mother, then back two more times before either of us speak.

"Yeah, we're just having a grand old time," she says, rolling the *r* like a leprechaun.

Real smooth, Camila.

The upward curve of Mom's lips is paired with a confused furrow of her brows as she looks between us. "What are y'all chatting about?"

"Work," I shout.

Camila's eyes brighten, clinging to the topic. "Yes! Work! I was just telling Owen I'm taking over the inn after my maternity leave so Dad and Mom can retire."

Mom clutches Cami's hand. "Oh, darling, that's wonderful. You'll do such incredible work, and it's so rewarding carrying on the legacy."

The difference between me and Camila is that she's always wanted to take over the inn. She'd force me to play hotel with her, setting up a little table next to the inn's check-in counter so she could walk me through the process. Her parents demanded she work at other hotels before committing to the inn. They didn't want her to wake up one day and feel trapped. It may look like the same situation on the outside, but it couldn't be more different.

Tears swim in my mom's eyes, and she doesn't swipe them away when they roll down her cheeks. "I hope it's not for a long, long time, Camila, but when your parents are gone, you'll be so happy you're continuing their work. It will let you feel like they're still with you, like you're keeping them alive. Right, Owen?"

I smile, but it's tight. She and Camila are both watching me, and I can't just say nothing, so I force out a soft "Yes."

Mom doesn't need more than that and starts raving about the importance of maintaining legacy while I zone out. I'm not sure how long she talks when she finally says, "It's way past my bedtime, so I'm going to hit the hay. Don't stay up too late. We have plenty of work tomorrow."

Camila waits until she rounds the corner to nudge me. "Are you ever going to tell her you don't like your job?"

I shift on my feet. "I don't know what you're talking about?"

She lifts an eyebrow. "Sure. If you ever need someone to talk to, you know I'm here, right?"

I pull her in for a hug, popping a kiss on her head. "Says the family gossip."

She laughs and pokes me in the side. "This isn't gossip. It's your life."

"I appreciate it," I say, and I genuinely mean it, even though I won't take her up on it.

Chapter 15

THEA

I spend the night tossing and turning, wishing I hadn't deleted my number from Owen's phone all those years ago. Did he catch Camila? If he did, was he able to convince her not to say anything? If he didn't, does everyone think something happened between me and Owen?

We could always pretend we got back together for the week. A little part of me likes the idea, having an excuse to touch and enjoy him. But that's the most selfish part of me talking. Us "getting back together" would pull attention away from Addy and Harrison, and I don't want that. Plus, we'd have to fake another breakup after the wedding, which would add more drama. Right now, everyone thinks we're two people who tried to make something work and couldn't, but if they thought I broke his heart *again*, I don't think the family would look at me as favorably as they do now.

My eyes flutter open, noticing how much stronger the daylight is now. I blink at the clock on the bedside table that currently says 11:15 AM, which makes no sense since one minute ago, it was 5:38 AM. My mind wakes up enough to register that I must have—finally—fallen asleep, which is good for my body but bad for everything else. Assuming that clock's right, I'm fifteen minutes late for the crafting shower they're hosting in the ballroom. I have no idea what a crafting shower entails, but it was on the schedule of events Addy handed out when we arrived.

I dig through my suitcase, grabbing the least ratty pair of jeans I own and a T-shirt from the shitty rock band I pretended to like for a couple of months while hooking up with the lead singer. My feet aren't even fully stuffed into my sneakers before I bolt from the room.

According to the schedule—thank you, past Thea, for taking a picture—the crafting shower is in the same ballroom where the wedding reception will be on Saturday. I follow the signs as I leave the hotel, piling my curls in a bun on the top of my head as I run.

I don't know what I'm walking into. The family could be gossiping about me and Owen right now. Addy may be ready to ream me out for fucking up her wedding. I can see her imperious face, looking down her nose even from her lower height.

You hooked up with Owen last night and it's all anyone's talking about.

There was a security camera, Thea, and now everyone's watching you swallow my future brother-in-law's tongue.

Camila figured out it's all fake and she told everyone and now they think you're a terrible person and decided they hate me, too, and the wedding's off and it's all your fault.

Okay, even I can recognize that last one isn't likely, if for no other reason than Owen wants to keep our secret as much as I do. And if the wedding was canceled, they wouldn't waste their time crafting things for the reception.

I skid to a halt in front of the French doors, sucking in air from the uphill sprint. The door opens, and Diana peeks her head out. She's perfect, like always, with a pristine light pink dress that hits right above her knee. I don't know where she finds the energy to be so put together, even on a day when we're just going to sit and write out a bunch of place cards and shit.

I can't help but compare this version of Diana to the one Owen described. If you'd asked me a couple of days ago, I'd have said she's a dream parent. But I also know from experience that people give different versions of themselves to different people, and I respect Owen enough to believe what he tells me.

Her eyes slide down my outfit, one manicured eyebrow lifting slightly, but then she smiles. "We've been wondering where you were, darling. I've saved a seat for you next to Addy."

I smile, but it feels more like a wince. "My alarm didn't go off this morning."

"Nothing to worry yourself about," she says, placing an arm around my shoulder and dragging me inside.

The entire party grinds to a halt when I enter the room. And that's when I notice Diana isn't the only one put together. Out of dozens of women, I'm the only one who isn't in a dress with my hair and makeup done. Addy's sitting at the front of the room in another white outfit, this time an eyelet material with capped sleeves and a collar buttoned all the way to the top. And on her lap . . . a present.

Fuck.

One of Owen's cousins is sitting in a chair next to Addy, a little notebook dangling from her fingertips as she stares wide-eyed at me. I tug on my shirt, squirming under the scrutiny, but force myself to march over and sit in the open chair to Addy's right. The cousin jumps up, scrambling around to my seat to hand me the notebook and pen.

I glance up at her. "Thank you?"

What the hell is this for?

Addy's smile is forced as she whispers, "It's to write what gifts I receive and who they're from."

I whisper back, "I thought this was a crafting party."

"A crafting *shower*." Her tone is slightly exasperated, but she keeps that performative smile in place. "We're going to all work on the place cards and the non-floral parts of the centerpieces after I'm done opening the gifts."

I whisper, "I didn't know I was supposed to bring a gift."

The only shower I've ever attended was for one of the other servers at Cibare, but it was just a cake back by the lockers with us chipping in on a gift card. This—with the elaborately wrapped gifts and fancy dresses—is all new to me. I have something for her in my room, but I don't have time to run back to the inn. And it's too intimate of a gift to give in front of everyone.

Addy's smile shifts into something softer. "Hey, it's fine. Making it up here on such short notice is gift enough. I'm so grateful you're here."

The squeeze of her hand on mine feels like it's directly wrapped around my heart. She focuses back on the boxes around her, calling out the name on each card and thanking them profusely. The room cheers every time she breaks a ribbon while unwrapping. The lore states the bride will have one kid per ribbon she breaks, and by the eighth ribbon I start to wonder if this is Addy manifesting the big, stable family she's always wanted.

With the gifts gloriously done, we all move over to the round tables for our crafting jobs. Addy whispers that she's going to sit with new people and try to win them over, and I'm left alone to figure out where to go. I spin away when I catch Camila watching me, but she rushes over, pretty damn spritely for someone with half a basketball strapped on her stomach, and slips her arm through mine.

"Hi, Thea," she says with a little wiggle of her eyebrows.

"Camila," I say with a forced brightness. "Great to see you."

"Breathe," she whispers while towing me to a table with her mother, Cece, Diana, and Mira. "I can keep a secret."

What secret is that? I want to ask. Does she know our real secret, or does she mean finding me and Owen together in the hallway?

We set about the brainless task of filling the bottom few inches of small vases with flat glass marbles. The conversation flows around me, the comfortable exchange of people who have spent most—if not all—of their lives together, and even though I'm the outsider, I don't feel like it.

"What were you up to that kept you in bed so late?" Camila's mother, Ximena, says with a wiggle of her eyebrows.

"I wish it was something fun, but just an alarm that didn't go off," I say, and Ximena pouts. "I'm not used to waking up early since I work at night."

Camila eyes me. "What do you do?"

Oh shit, I sound like I'm a stripper, don't I?

"Server," I blurt out. "Or I was. Now I'm . . . figuring it out, I guess."

What the hell's wrong with me? I didn't plan on telling them I'm unemployed, not when Addy and I are trying to make a good impression. But luckily, before anyone can ask more questions, a woman around Diana's age heads our way. She goes for the last open seat, but Diana plops her bag down on top of it. The woman rolls her eyes, then heads to another table.

"You'll have to let it go eventually, my dear," Cece says, picking up a marble and regarding her daughter through it. "I'm all for a grudge, but you're just being obnoxious at this point."

Diana gasps like Cece has struck her. "Mama!"

Ximena wiggles her eyebrows and leans closer to me. It's abundantly clear where Camila got her love of gossip. "That's Patricia, Dennis's wife. She and Diana were best friends throughout childhood until Patricia brought their family to Orlando and didn't tell Diana. She's never forgiven her."

Diana huffed. "It's not that she didn't tell me. She blatantly lied when I asked if they were coming. If letting her boys see their family was too much of an inconvenience for her, fine"—it didn't seem fine from the way she aggressively blinks back tears—"but *lying* to me about it? That's something I can't forgive."

It seems like such a ridiculous thing to be angry about, especially years later. If a little lie like that was enough to make her give up a lifetime of friendship, how would she feel about me and Owen lying to her for years?

I meet Camila's widened gaze across the table, and my stomach plummets. She knows. Definitely knows.

And we are so fucked.

Chapter 16

THEA

Before I can fully spiral that yet another family member knows our secret, Addy and Dawn, Owen's other aunt and wedding planner extraordinaire, rush over to our table. Addy's face is contorted in horror, a look she rarely lets anyone besides me see, and my heart kicks up.

"What's going on?" I ask, jumping from my seat. I meet her halfway while Dawn continues on to the table.

Addy lets out a little hiccup-y sob. "I emailed all the vendors yesterday to confirm, and the baker wrote back that she can't make the cake anymore. She broke her arm! What are the chances?"

She throws her arms up in the air, letting them slap back down on her legs with a *thwack* that echoes through the room.

"It's okay, this is fine," I say, digging my phone out of my back pocket. "They can't be the only baker in town. We can find someone else. I'll start making a list."

"It's pointless," Addy says, swiping a hand at the tears streaming down her cheeks. "I reached out to every baker between Asheville and Tennessee, and this was the only person who was available on such short notice."

"There has to be something," I mumble as I search random key words.

Addy lets out a shuddering breath, before whispering just loud enough for me to hear, "How am I supposed to fit into this family for the rest of my life when I can't even make a wedding that meets their standards?"

I grab her face between my hands, wiping away the remaining tears with my thumbs. "Stop. This is one day, and if they judge you for it not being perfect, then fuck them."

Addy releases a shuddering breath. "But I don't want to fuck them."

The two of us stare at each other for a couple of seconds as the words fully process, then break into a fit of giggles. Addy's eyes are still watery as she drops her forehead to my shoulder.

"That didn't come out right." She hiccups, half sob, half laugh. "I just want them to like me."

Addy prides herself on being put together. On being the one all the foster families looked at as easy. She doesn't see that she's so lovable beyond the perfection, but a stressful wedding week is not the time to unpack her trauma.

I lift her head from my shoulder and kiss the top of it. "I'll sort this out. You are going to walk down the aisle in five days, marry the love of your life, and then you're going to eat the best fucking cake of your life. I promise."

Addy's eyes fill with tears again as she nods, and I let out a slow exhale. Dawn comes over, taking Addy's hand in hers and towing her over to the table. She sits her down, and we take the seats on either side of her.

"Addy, you don't need to worry about confirming things with the vendors. That's my job as your wedding planner."

Addy's face goes a bit panicked. I can tell from Dawn's expression that she's trying to take some of the pressure off, but Addy hears she overstepped.

"I'm so sorry," she says. "I just wanted to help since you're doing all of this for free."

She grasps Addy's hand. "It's my honor to help with my nephew's wedding. I want you to enjoy your time here, not be buried under your to-do list all week."

Addy releases a long breath and smiles her most agreeable smile.

"What about me?" I ask. "Is there anything I can do to help?"

Dawn eyes me speculatively. "Can you bake?"

Addy lets out her little snort, then claps her hands over her mouth in horror. "Sorry. Tia's not much of a cook."

I smack her arm. "I could with the right guidance."

She levels me with a *get real* look. "And you're going to learn how to be an expert baker in a couple days? Last time you tried to bake cookies, your entire apartment complex had to evacuate."

I stick my tongue out at her.

Dawn and Diana share a look across the table that I recognize all too well. It's the same exchange Addy and I have had a hundred times when we were conspiring. Dawn slips her phone out, typing something and sliding it onto the table, face up. It lights up a second later, and she beams.

Dawn turns back to me with a smile that I can only call devious. "If you had someone in the kitchen guiding you, could you do it?"

"I mean, I don't know," I say, but then I look at Addy's face, her once perfect makeup ruined by her tears, and I know I could figure out how to build a rocket to the moon if it would bring back her smile. "Yes, I can."

She wiggles her eyebrows at Diana. "This could be perfect."

Diana tilts her head side to side. "Maybe, but he hasn't done it as much recently. He's been keeping his focus on work, like he should, so he may not be up for it."

"But if he was? The cake would be delicious. Plus," Dawn says, glancing to me, "two birds, one stone."

"Anyone going to fill us in?" I ask. "We aren't just decoration, you know."

Addy digs her elbow into my side and whispers, "They'll tell us when they're ready."

But I don't have my sister's patience, and if I need to hound bakers to get them to squeeze in another cake, I should get a jump on that now.

Dawn chuckles. "I'm surprised you didn't guess. Owen will make it."

Addy looks at me in surprise. "He bakes?"

All three women are staring at me, waiting for a response. If we'd actually dated, I'd have tasted his baking before. Vouching for him without trying it makes me nauseous, but I can't admit I have no idea if he's good or not without blowing everything up.

"He's fantastic," I say with forced enthusiasm.

Addy lets out a sound somewhere between a sigh and a whimper. "Oh, thank god."

The door of the ballroom swings open and Owen walks through.

"You texted me?"

"Yes," Dawn answers, rushing to one of the other tables to grab an empty chair and dragging it over, placing it right next to me. "Have a seat."

Owen's eyes meet mine. I smile, a stiff, nervous thing, and he gives me a small smile back, nodding his head. I take the gesture to mean he caught up to Camila and we're okay, but my stomach still churns.

He settles into the chair next to mine, and I try to ignore the heat from his leg a few inches away from mine. There will be no giving in to the urge to shift closer.

"What's up?" Owen asks.

"How would you like to be the hero of the hour?" Dawn asks with a glint in her eye.

Owen looks around the table. At his mom and Dawn who have matching grins, at Camila and Ximena who keep looking back and forth between us like cats scoping out a delicious mouse.

"Okay," he says, drawing out the word.

"We need a cake," Diana says.

A pleased smile spreads over his face. "Oh, yeah, that's easy. You had me scared there for a minute. For what?"

Dawn looks at him like he's a sweet little imbecile. "For the wedding."

His eyes double in size. "For the wedding? I've never made a wedding cake before."

She shrugs. "A cake's a cake."

"No, a cake's not a cake. First, a wedding cake is giant and layered, not to mention all the embellishments. I have no idea how to do that."

A memory surges of us at Camila's wedding. Owen dragging me off the dance floor when they started passing out cake. Me complaining that it was my favorite song and I didn't want to miss it, but he wouldn't take no for an answer. He sat me down and demanded I close my eyes, slipping the fork between my parted lips.

"What do you taste?" he asked.

The flavors settled on my tongue, warm and familiar. "Is that booze?"

He chuckled. "Butterscotch Bourbon. Thought you might like it."

I'd opened my eyes, finding him closer than expected. The lights from the chandelier reflected in his eyes, and I was struck by the thought that this cake is what his kiss would taste like. Deep and comforting, like wrapping up in a blanket in front of a fire on a cool night.

I thought he was just hungry, but with this new information, I can see the passion for baking in the way he savored his first bite, like he was trying to identify each ingredient.

Dawn shakes her finger. "Don't BS me, boy. You know it's impossible when talking to family. I remember the cake you made for Camila's birthday a few summers ago."

Owen runs his hands up into his hair. "But this is bigger. I can't do this by myself."

A slow smile curves Dawn's lips, like she's a spider giving

directions to a fly. *Take the shortcut through this web. Trust me. You'll be fine.*

"Well," she says, "isn't it convenient, then, that Thea was *just* asking what she could do to help."

My mouth drops open. "I don't know if I'm the best person for this."

It was one thing when it was some random cousin, but being trapped in the kitchen with Owen for hours is the exact opposite of distance.

I shift in my seat. "Y'all have five thousand family members. There must be someone with more baking experience than me. Camila?"

She shakes her head, patting her belly. "I struggle around strong smells. No way I could handle it."

Dawn nods to Owen, who looks at me with a grimace. "It wouldn't just be a day. With something this big, we'd need to do a bit every day."

Dawn cuts in. "Exactly. No one else will be consistently available. Besides Addy and Harrison, but we can't have them baking their own wedding cake, now, can we?"

"There's no one else?" Addy asks, and everyone around the table shakes their heads.

I look over at Owen, who gives me a little shrug. Looks like we're baking a cake.

* * *

Why does an apron make a hot guy even hotter? Owen's mixing the dry ingredients in a bowl he's tucked under his arm, the muscles in his biceps flexing with each rotation of the spoon. He's more delicious than anything he'll whip up in this kitchen.

"Thea?"

I jump at Owen's voice, realizing he's been talking to me while my brain overlaid it with 1980s porno music.

"You can do it?" he asks in a tone that makes it clear it isn't the first time. "Mix the wet ingredients into the dry ones?"

This little experiment has two goals. First, make a test cake so Addy feels comfortable with us making the one for the actual day, and second, to figure out if I'm useless in the kitchen. With how distracted I've been by Owen, I'm afraid I'm proving the latter true.

He sets the bowl of dry ingredients in front of me and gestures to the wet ingredients that he already measured out. All I have to do is put them in and turn on the gorgeous industrial mixer.

"Yeah, no problem," I say, shifting the bowl closer. I keep my focus on the task at hand and not on the way his chuckle gusts against my neck.

Once I pour everything into the bowl, I step back, proud of myself for making it through without spilling anything. And yes, that's how low the bar is for me. I slide the mixing bowl into place and flip the mixer onto the highest setting.

"Woah, woah, woah," Owen says, rushing across the room. I spin to his voice to ask what I did wrong, but he's right there, our fronts pushed together as he reaches over my shoulder to turn the mixer to a lower setting. He grins down at me. "You weren't listening earlier, were you?"

"I was a bit distracted," I admit. He doesn't shift away, and neither do I. "I figured the faster it went, the faster we'd be done."

"Baking is all about taking your time," he says, his voice quiet. "Savoring the process. Why rush to the finish line? Getting there is half the fun."

Are we still talking about baking? Because it doesn't feel like we're talking about baking, and I'm so close to throwing myself at him, consequences be damned. Before I can make another irresponsible decision, Owen's soft gaze goes wary.

He pulls away, leaving me cold. "Anyway, you've got it now."

I can't see into his brain, don't know if he's upset or pulling away because I told him we needed distance, but my mind keeps winding back to the comment I made last night. The look of hurt on his face and the way my heart twisted in response.

"I'm sorry," I say. "For what I said last night."

He laughs, but it doesn't come anywhere close to his eyes. "No big dea—"

"It *is* a big deal," I interrupt. He doesn't speak again, and I force myself to say the words, even though they're hard. "I—I lash out. When I'm feeling vulnerable. Always have. It's easier to hurt other people than face my own shit, but I don't want to do that to you. I don't want to be someone who hurts you. So I'm sorry."

Everything in his demeanor shifts. Muscles untensing. Eyes softening. Lips twisting up. "Thank you."

I smile back, knowing this is dangerous, but also knowing it's right. Owen shouldn't carry scars from me.

"How'd you learn all of this, anyway?" I ask, gesturing to the batter.

"I, um . . ." he starts, but can't bring himself to finish whatever he was going to say. He clears his throat and tries again. "After my dad died, my mom wasn't in the place to do . . . well, anything, really. I was worried Harrison wouldn't have a birthday cake, so I started playing around with it. Then I fell in love with the process. When I'd come up here, Nana's friend who's a baker would teach me new techniques, and I'd spend the next year perfecting them before coming back to learn something new."

He moves so confidently around the kitchen, like he was born for it. I notice he smiles more easily here. His shoulders are less tense, and his movements are more fluid as he stops the mixer and pulls out the bowl. Of all the versions of Owen I've seen, I think this is my favorite.

He swipes a spoon and dips it into the batter, the smallest touch. "Here, try it."

He holds it out to me. I move closer, and I catch his Adam's apple bob before our gazes latch. I close my lips around the spoon, my eyes never leaving his, and his breath hitches. His pupils dilate at the involuntary moan that climbs my throat at the taste. It's delicious, just like I knew it would be.

The moment grows heavy between us, and he takes another step so our bodies are only a few inches apart. He brings his hand to my chin, rubbing his thumb over my bottom lip.

"Got a bit of something there," he whispers, raising his thumb to his mouth and sucking the batter off.

"Owen," I whisper.

He tosses the spoon onto the counter and brings his palms to either side of my neck, dropping his forehead to mine but not closing the distance, letting us breathe the same air. The anticipation is killing me. His lips are so close to mine, and if he doesn't close the gap, I'll lose my mind. My hands come up, landing on his stomach and scratching lightly.

With lightning speed, Owen's hands move to my waist, lifting me with ease onto the metal counter and stepping between my legs. A whimper that should embarrass me escapes my lips, and Owen runs his nose against mine.

"I can't stop thinking about that kiss," he says in a guttural voice.

"Me neither," I pant out.

He groans. "God, I need to taste you again. Please. Please, can I kiss you?"

I love the way he begs, how his hands on each of my thighs tighten while he waits for my answer. In response, I grab his shirt, pulling his lower half flush with mine. We moan in tandem, my head tilting back so our lips brush, but I don't say yes yet. Torturing him is too much fun, maybe my new favorite pastime.

I roll my hips and he lets out a hiss. "Thea," he says, a warning in his voice, almost a scolding, and I wonder how far I'd have to push him before he'd turn me over his knee and punish me.

But just as the vision flashes through my mind, I hear voices on the other side of the door. My body has never gone from turned on to panicked so quickly, like I jumped off a cliff expecting the warm Florida waters, only to realize I was doing an ice plunge.

I push him away. He stumbles a few steps, staring at me in confusion until the voices break through his lust-fogged mind, too. I flip my body back over the counter—no one can accuse us of anything if there's a literal barrier between us—but in the process I take the bowl of batter with me. It tips over, sliding across the counter space with me until it lands, upside down, on my head.

The door swings open and two middle-aged guys—carbon copies of each other—walk in. They're tall, with the same blue-green irises I'm starting to recognize as the Ellis eyes. As I wipe the cake batter from my face, I realize that one of them, not sure which, is the drunk man who spilled his drink all over that guy at the bar.

"What's happening here?" Twin One asks.

Owen looks over and sees me covered in cake. I expect him to freak out about us having to start over from the beginning, to scold me for screwing up his hard work, but instead he laughs, a booming bass. The largest smile I've ever seen spreads across his face, and I finally get to see that dimple.

"You two having a food fight in here?" Twin Two asks.

"Thea has a cake fetish," Owen says. "Sitting in them, pouring them over her head, she's not picky. It all gets her going."

The twins laugh, and Owen's smile somehow spreads even more. He looks over at me, giving me a quick wink that has my knees going weak.

"Happy to provide the entertainment," I say, walking over

to the sink. I splash away the batter from my face and wet a few paper towels, wiping away as much as possible from my hair until I can get to a shower.

"What are you two even doing?" Twin Two asks.

"We were *trying* to make a cake," Owen says, with a smaller, indulgent smile sent my way. "Harrison's baker backed out, so I'm trying to see if I can pull off a wedding cake."

"You're making the cake?" Twin One asks. "Fuck yeah! I love your cakes. Do you need help?"

Owen's eyebrow quirks up. "Nope. I've seen what you do in the kitchen."

"Can't be worse than Thea," the other twin says with a laugh.

Owen glances back, heat searing me. "Maybe not, but at least she's nice to look at."

The twins not so subtly nudge each other, looking back and forth between us. "We'll let you get to it."

When the door swings closed behind them, Owen and I stare at each other in silence for a minute, then he steps toward me with clear intent on his handsome face.

I put my hand out, stopping him before he can round the counter and mess up my control again. He blinks, but takes a few steps back.

"Owen," I say, but he cuts me off.

"No, I get it."

"It's not that I don't—"

"Come on, we don't need to do that."

"Yes, we do," I say, a bit of desperation in my voice, but he turns away with a shake of his head.

"Thea, it's fine. I'm not the kind of guy you—"

"Yes, you are," I say. He has to understand. I *need* him to understand. "If you think I don't want you, you aren't paying attention. But it's not just about me. I can't ruin this wedding."

He freezes, then slowly faces me. His expression is at war

with itself, like he thinks I'm making up an excuse to let him down easy, but he's too curious not to hear the full explanation.

"Why would you ruin the wedding?"

"Because I ruin everything, Owen! Everything I touch goes to shit. Case in point." I gesture to my batter-covered hair.

He doesn't speak, but his jaw flexes, like it's a physical battle to keep himself from speaking.

I take a deep breath, then lay it all out for him to judge. "I told you we moved a lot in foster care. But what I didn't say—what I guess I didn't want you to know—is that it was all because of me. I wasn't lying when I said I lash out. My whole life, I've been difficult. Angry and aggressive, convinced everyone had it out for me and Addy. To be fair, there were some foster parents who *did* have it out for us, but there were kind ones, too. Ones whose rules and structure I rebelled against out of principle. Each home, I pushed and pushed and pushed until I broke them, and they'd send us back."

Owen's brows pull together. "You can't blame yourself for that. You were a grieving kid, and the foster system—"

I hold up a hand, needing to get it all out. "The goal of the foster system is to reunite families. If you have a family member they hope will take you in, they move you around from home to home so you don't get too attached, which is such a fucked-up theory to begin with, but not really relevant. If you *don't* have anyone—like me and Addy—the goal is foster to adoption. They pair you with homes they think may make you a permanent part of their family. But no one could ever handle me."

I pause, my breath coming fast and shallow. Owen doesn't speak, just patiently waits like he can tell I have to get this out. Like if I don't, I'll never work up the guts to say it again.

"Addy was thirteen when I aged out. It was easier for our caseworker to place one kid than two, and she was sent back to our very first foster home. The Fischers."

Owen blinked a few times as the words registered. "The Fischers, as in—"

"As in her adoptive parents, yeah. They started the adoption process six months after Addy came back to them. If I hadn't been in the picture, they would have adopted her right away. Our mom died when she was three, so she'd never have remembered a time before them. The Fischers would have been Mom and Dad. She lived through twelve different homes, so many horrible days and nights, because I was difficult and disruptive. I won't be the reason she loses your family, too."

"I'm so sorry, Thea," he says as he moves to my side of the counter, taking my hand. We both watch as his thumb skims over mine. "But I don't understand how that stops us from exploring whatever's between us."

I slip my hand from his, backing up until I smash into the refrigerator, the cold metal dousing the heat inside me and grounding me in this choice.

"What 'us,' Owen?" He flinches, and I rush to add, "What sort of future could we have with the way this started?"

He opens his mouth, then closes it, and I can see the moment he reaches the same conclusion as me. There are only three ways this could play out.

One, we mess around in secret and risk getting caught. I can just see the way the family would gossip, throwing around speculations until the lies got too complicated to keep track of and the truth came out. Diana would either be furious or break down like Owen expects, and she wouldn't show up for the wedding. Addy would be heartbroken.

Two, we come clean and say we didn't date before but we are now, and we run into the same issue for Addy.

Three, we tell everyone we "got back together," and maintain that lie for the rest of our lives.

That's assuming we even make it the rest of our lives. It's easy for him to romanticize what could be while we're up here, surrounded by beauty and buffered from real-life stressors. He doesn't know me yet. Once he does, he'll want out, just like everyone else. I can't risk my relationship with Addy for a few weeks of fun before he breaks my heart.

"You know I'm right," I say.

He sighs. "So what do we do?"

I lift a shoulder, letting it drop back down in an overexaggerated move that rattles my body just so I can feel something besides the urge to pull Owen back between my legs. "Do what we planned to begin with? Keep our distance, get through the next five days, and move on?"

A breath shudders out of him. "Okay." He walks over to me, taking my head between his hands and placing a kiss on my forehead. I allow myself one inhale to savor his deep, sweet scent until he murmurs onto my skin, "But for the record, I'm not happy about it."

He walks back to the bowl, and I slip away to wash out my hair, focusing on getting the cake batter out instead of the fact that I'm not happy about it, either.

Chapter 17

OWEN

It's hours later, and I still can't get that moment with Thea out of my head. The way she arched into me. Her husky moan when she felt me against her. The brush of her lips against mine and her cinnamon scent wafting around me.

I also can't stop hearing her words, the insistence that she'll ruin everything for Addy. That she's broken somehow. That she wants me, too, but doesn't trust herself to have me. As much as I want to fight it, she's made her wishes clear, so I respect them.

I made the test cake alone, then avoided any overlapping tasks on Dawn's afternoon to-do list—helping Harrison with the seating chart while Thea finished up the place cards. When the family grabbed dinner, I sat on the opposite end of the table. And I determinedly kept my eyes away from her every time we passed. The limits of my control only reach so far, and my best shot at success is complete and total distance.

Now we're going to the movie in the park down in Elk Ridge, and I'm supposed to spend the night pretending like I'm not itching to speak to her.

I'm up in my room, grabbing the last few things I need before heading to the lobby when the door beeps and slides open.

"I have my hands over my eyes. Please tell me you're dressed so I can look where I'm going and not break a hip," Nana calls from the door.

I laugh. "Most people would just knock."

"Most people's grandsons haven't been avoiding them for the past twenty-four hours like a slippery little eel. Now answer the damn question."

"Yes, Nana, I'm dressed. You can drop your hand." She lowers it with a sigh, letting the door swing closed behind her. "And I haven't been avoiding you."

One of her manicured eyebrows lifts toward her gray hair. "You've turned on your heel at least three times when you've seen me. Had to make sure you didn't slither under the bed and pretend not to be here when I knocked."

I plop down on the mattress with a sigh while she takes a seat at the desk across from me. "It wasn't that—"

"Yes, yes, you weren't avoiding me. It was all coincidental and you're sorry and all the other bullshit. Can we skip that and get to the point? Why did you lie about Thea?"

She looks almost hurt—as hurt as Cece Ellis would ever let herself be—and I feel a surge of regret. I don't know how to explain this to her.

"I just . . ." I start, knowing she won't let me off the hook. "I just wanted a break."

"From?" she prompts, like she doesn't know just how pushy Mom's been.

"From the setups. From Mom, always trying to get me to the next stage of life. Having me carry on the Hayes legacy. Do you know how many times she set me up before Cami's wedding? Over a dozen. Half of them I didn't even know were setups. I got wherever she asked me to meet her and was met by some woman instead. I started developing a Pavlovian response to seeing her name on my phone."

"What did she say when you asked her to stop?"

I laugh pessimistically. "Either she got one of her headaches for a week or lectured me about how I wasn't taking my future seriously."

"Has it gotten that bad?" Nana asks, her brows pulling

together, and I realize that she doesn't know just how intense Mom has been.

"Yes," I say, deciding not to mince words. "And it's not new. It's been this bad since Dad died. I know how important it is for her that I keep his memory alive, but this isn't something I can give her. My career is one thing, but my partner in life?"

"You shouldn't have to give her anything," Nana says, then rolls her lips together like she's trying to trap in the sound. "I'll talk to her. You should have the freedom to make the choices you want in life, not the ones she wants for you."

"No," I say, the words forceful enough to make Nana jump in her seat. The last thing we need is Nana talking to Mom and setting her off before the wedding.

"Owe—"

"I'm a thirty-two-year-old man. I don't need my grandmother talking to my mother on my behalf. I'm happy with my life." *Mostly.* "Maintaining Dad's legacy is an honor. Bringing a fake girlfriend was a spur-of-the-moment, terrible idea that's come back to bite me, but there's nothing that needs to be done."

She looks like she wants to argue, but for once in her life, she lets someone else win. "We should get downstairs to meet everyone for the movie."

"Thank you, Nana."

She nods. "I'll keep my mouth shut, but I want you to think about it. You shouldn't have to live a certain way just to keep her happy."

Nana's words echo in my head as we head downstairs to meet everyone. The whole family is coming out this time, and all the aunts, uncles, and cousins have gathered into little groups to catch up while they wait. I spot Thea standing with Camila and force myself to walk the other way, joining another group of cousins. A few seconds later, my cousin Lynne—who works as Aunt Dawn's second-in-command—calls out. She tosses me the keys to the bus, the giant yellow key chain catching the light as they land in my hands.

"Anyone else want to drive tonight?" I ask the group of five around me as casually as I can. I don't know why my heart is thudding. This is my family. I love them, and they love me. So why does the idea of not doing what they want make me so jittery?

Tommy claps me on the shoulder. "We don't mind. You love driving."

I almost nod and let it drop, but then I catch sight of Thea, her head thrown back in laughter. Something about knowing she's in the room gives me a surge of confidence, even if her attention isn't directed at me.

"I'll drive," I say, "but it's not like I like it."

Everyone in the group tilts their head at the same angle—a move I've seen from Nana thousands of times—and I'm reminded of how weird it is to be around so many people who grew up with the same mannerisms.

My cousin Jourdan is the first to recover. "Since when? You always drive."

I laugh, trying to keep it light. "I always drive because y'all hand me the keys and say I'm driving."

I flick the keys around my fingers, a nervous tick I can't help whenever they end up in my hands, waiting for someone—anyone—to speak.

"Thea thought it was weird that you drive all the time when we went out to the bar," Camila speaks from behind me and I jump, not realizing they'd come over to our group. Thea's next to her with her bottom lip tucked between her teeth.

"Hi," I say, unable to stop the smile spreading over my face.

Her answering smile sends tingles to my toes. "Hi."

Camila's eyes flick between us, but she holds her tongue in front of the others. "That's why we came over here. Thea has an idea."

Thea bounces a little on her toes. "You don't want to drive tonight?"

I glance down at the keys and shrug. "I don't *mind* driving."

"That's not what I asked. Do you, Owen Hayes, *want* to drive tonight?" she asks with a raised eyebrow.

I hide my chuckle by dipping my head. "No, Thea Pappas, I don't *want* to drive."

She snatches the keys from my grasp. "Perfect."

I look over at my cousins who are eyeing her warily. Visitors always underestimate how dangerous these roads can be, and none of us is willing to die for Thea to prove a point.

"You don't want to drive, either," I say, reaching for the keys, but she pulls away, holding the keys behind her back. I'm tempted to take the excuse to wrap my arms around her, but I won't with everyone watching. "These roads are tight and winding. They're scary to drive in a regular car. It should be someone who knows them well."

Her eyebrows bounce a few times. "I agree."

Then she looks at the little clumps of the family, chatting about the latest gossip.

Her gaze lands on the closest group to us, and she calls out, "Gabriel, catch."

He turns and she lets the keys fly. His hands come up on instinct, closing around the cool metal and looking at them in confusion.

She spins in a circle as she says, "New game. Last person to touch the keys for the bus has to drive."

Everyone breaks out in cheers and laughter as Gabriel balks. "That's not fair!"

She shrugs. "Then get someone else to touch them before we leave."

He drops them down the back of Lynne's dress, who wiggles and shakes until the keys clang to the floor.

"Lynne has to drive," Gabriel calls out to the room. "She touched them last."

"Nope," Thea calls out, loud enough to reach the entire lobby. "Gotta be hands. Get creative, Gabe."

He swipes the keys up from the ground as half our cousins dig out their phones to text anyone not here so Gabriel can't trick them when they arrive.

"Owen, catch," Gabriel yells as he sends the keys back our way.

My hands lift on instinct, like my body can't stop itself from being helpful. Thea spins in front of me, and instead of catching the keys, my hands land on her hips. Her lips part on a gasp I'm desperate to swallow as the keys hit her back and fall to the floor with a satisfying thud. I look down at her, and god, we're so close. It'd take nothing for me to close the distance.

She narrows her eyes at me. "Don't you fucking dare touch those keys."

My lips twitch. "Sorry. Habit."

"Well, break it."

"Yes, ma'am," I whisper.

Her dark eyes dilate in response, and everything inside me goes taut. Her body radiates heat, and I swear the noise in the room fades, leaving nothing but the two of us. Someone coughs, and I realize the noise *did* fade because everyone's stopped talking and is now openly staring at the two of us. Thea's eyes jump straight to Addy, who's watching us with wide-eyed terror.

I yank myself away, kicking the keys back across the lobby to Gabriel. "Sorry, Gabriel. Gotta work harder than that!"

Cousins left and right start throwing out jabs at Gabriel, and Thea wanders away with Camila and Addy without so much as a glance back to me. Which is good. Distance and all that. Jourdan claps me on the back and passes over her flask while Tommy eyes me.

"Why didn't you tell us you don't like driving?" he asks.

"Why did you assume I liked driving?" I volley back, keeping my tone light.

"Because you volunteered whenever we were talking about it," he says, and I think he may be right. That while everyone else fought over who had to drive, I'd offer, take on the helpful role I'd gotten so comfortable in at home. "We're your family. You can tell us shit, you know?"

My stomach bottoms out, and I can't help but flick my eyes over to Thea. I've been so dishonest with everyone. Not just about my history with her, but about what I want and how I feel about my place in the family. I don't regret lying about Thea. I don't think I could regret *anything* that brought Thea into my life, but I do wish I'd been better with my cousins. More honest about what I want. I think I've gotten so used to what I want not mattering that I assumed they'd act the same way, and that's not fair to them.

"You're right," I say.

Tommy's brows pull together, like he was anticipating more of a fight, but then he claps his hands. "Great. Then let's get you drunk, little cousin."

"Get your own booze," Jourdan says, clutching the flask to her when Tommy reaches for it again.

Tommy dives on his baby sister, wrestling it away from her and tossing it over to me. While he holds Jourdan back, I chug the contents, then throw it back to her. She lifts it over her mouth, whining when only a couple of drops come out.

I throw an arm over her shoulder, already feeling the effects of the rum. "I'll buy you a beer when we get there."

We all spend the next fifteen minutes with our hands in our pockets, calling out a warning about Thea's game to anyone who joins the party until Gabriel admits defeat and trudges off to pull around the bus.

I feel guilty about Jourdan's flask, so I run over to the inn's restaurant to have it filled up. By the time I get back, they're all loaded up and waiting for me. The second I step on the bus, everyone stretches out in their seats. I make my way down the aisle, hearing excuse after excuse for why I can't sit with my cousins.

"No, I can't share," Jourdan says when I pass over the flask and gesture to the seat next to her. "I sprained my ankle while wrestling with Tommy and need to keep it elevated."

I didn't see her get hurt, but fine.

"Sorry," Lynne says a few seats back. "My bag's giant and I need a place to put it."

When I reach Camila near the back of the bus, she's sitting across the aisle from her wife instead of with her. She rolls her eyes. "Of course I can't share. I'm sitting for two. I need the space while I'm growing a literal human."

My brows kick up. "You sat with Mira on the way to the bar yesterday."

"This is a big developmental window. Huge changes in a short amount of time. You'll understand when your future wife is with child." The tone she uses when she says those last words is so overexaggerated, I'm surprised she doesn't stand up and take a bow like an actor in a Shakespearean play. "But I think I saw a seat in the back next to Thea."

Mira lets out a long-suffering sigh and rubs a hand across her forehead, mouthing *sorry*.

I walk past more cousins who avoid eye contact and spread themselves out like wild animals looking to defend their territory before I reach Thea.

"Do you mind?" I ask quietly.

She shrugs. "Doesn't seem like we have much choice."

I don't want her feeling like she doesn't have a choice. The idea of her feeling trapped into anything, much less spending time with me, causes a buzzing underneath my skin.

I slide into the seat, but whisper, "I won't let my cousins

pressure you into sitting with me because they came up with some harebrained scheme."

She shifts closer to hear me, and I turn my head to get a hit of her, that spicy scent that's becoming the most intoxicating smell in the world. Our gazes clash, but she doesn't move away. There's a buzzing under my skin, and I can't tell if it's from the rum or from Thea's presence.

It's dark in the bus, the two of us closed away in the back row with nothing to shine a light on what we do. It'd be so easy to slip my hand over her knee, to let my fingertips tease the seam of her jeans, higher and higher until I reach where she was aching for me earlier.

"This isn't distance," I whisper, holding on to the barest dregs of my self-control.

"Yeah," she breathes out, the word coasting over my lips.

I abruptly shift away and rub a hand over my eyes. I've never had a problem putting another person's needs before mine, so why can't I stop being so selfish with Thea? We need to talk, but we can't do it here with all my cousins' heads tilted just slightly to the side to catch the latest drama. I gesture for her phone, and when she hands it over, I save my number and send a text, sending another from my phone a few seconds later.

Owen: We should have each other's numbers again.

Thea: Yeah, that's smart.

We sit side by side. How do I follow that up? *I'm sorry my family is so invested in our potential future that they keep throwing us together? I'm sorry for so desperately wanting you that I keep forgetting we're supposed to stay away from each other? Do you want this as badly as I do?* Because it sure as hell looked like she did. I'm drafting and redrafting potential texts in my mind, but there's one thing I keep coming back to.

Owen: Why did you delete your number?

Thea's warm body tenses beside me, and her soft gasp is blaring in the silence of our little corner. My eyes stay glued to the screen as the bubbles pop up. Then disappear. Over and over and over again, her arm shifting against mine every time she types, like a tease of the words that might never come. I can't stop myself from writing again.

Owen: Did I do something? Make you feel uncomfortable?

Owen: because I thought that weekend was amazing, then when I tried to call you, realized you must not have felt the same way. But now we're here and I don't think it was all in my head, and god, Thea, I'm so confused.

From the corner of my eye, I see Thea drop her phone on her lap. I feel the jolt of our attached seats when she knocks her head back against the headrest. With every second she doesn't answer, my heart sinks further into my stomach. I'm such a jerk.

Owen: I'm sorry.

Owen: The alcohol from earlier is hitting me harder than I realized. I don't know what I was thinking.

Cornering you on a bus about why you ghosted me is not the move.

Owen: I'm so sorry.

Thea looks at me, but I can't look back. I can't see disappointment or frustration written on the lines of what has become my favorite face in the world. It's my turn to tense when her fingers start flying. It feels like ages, and when my phone buzzes in my hand, I rush to read it so quickly I fumble my phone. My lip quirks against my will at the little novel she's sent.

Thea: Don't apologize. It's a fair question. I didn't respond because I don't know how to. I didn't even fully think it through. I was sitting in your car while you were in the gas station, and your phone was there and shockingly unlocked and it just felt like the universe was telling me to do it. And I know that sounds ridiculous, but the truth is I'm a bit fucked-up. Was even more fucked-up back then. I deleted my number because I was scared you wouldn't call and I'd feel like shit. And because I was scared you WOULD call, and I'd end up ruining everything eventually and I'd feel like shit. And I didn't know how to handle the potential of having you and losing you.

She really did feel this thing between us. It's both heartbreaking and a relief. What could have been if she hadn't deleted her number? Would she have said yes to a date? Would we be three years deep into a relationship, or would we have exploded, leaving so much damage in our wake that Harrison and Addy never would have found their way to each other?

Neither of us says anything else, but her words *I didn't know how to handle the potential of having you and losing you* float in front of my eyes for the rest of the drive.

* * *

Elk Ridge's downtown looks like it stepped right out of a Hallmark film. A flat square park dominates the middle. Kids run through, jumping over each other and wrestling in the grass while their parents try to wrangle them. The park is circled by buildings on three sides, all mom-and-pop restaurants and stores. No chains in sight. People from town stop by, asking how I've been. If you boil down the time I've spent with these folks, it's only a few years, but it's been spread over my entire life, and each time I come back, they welcome me with open arms.

A group of the twins' friends come over, plying me with beer at Tommy's request. They come from all walks of life—the town doctor, a few of the mechanics who work at Jourdan's shop, the ice cream shop owner concerned about leaving the store in the hands of her teenage nephew—but they've become their own sort of family.

I haven't been drunk in ages, and I stumble off to the bathroom before the movie starts. I don't recognize the man in the mirror. My cheeks are flushed and my eyes bright, and it's not because of the booze. It's freeing, hanging out with friends and family without anyone to take care of. It's a feeling I could get used to, if not at home, at least when I visit. I think I could be happy with just that.

When I get back, my family has claimed a third of the park, spreading out on blankets and folding chairs as the sun drops below the horizon. The symphony of the mountains shifts, cicadas stopping their daytime buzzing to cede the floor to the chirps of crickets and the hoots of owls. It all mixes with the laughter of the town, the soundtrack to all my best memories. My eyes drift closed for a minute, savoring the sounds.

When I open them, Harrison waves both his arms over his head to get my attention. He's behind Addy with her pulled tight between his legs. Thea's on the blanket next to them, and in my drunken state, she seems to glow. A lighthouse shining in the distance.

"Where's the other blanket?" I ask, surprised to hear the words come out slightly slurred.

Harrison lets his body drop back with a dramatic groan that makes Addy giggle. "I'm sorry. I forgot."

Of course he did. I'm the one who takes care of him, not the other way around. I should have known better than to agree when he said he'd grab it. But now's not the time—with a mixture of rum and beer swirling around inside me and his fiancée wrapped around him—to hash it out.

"No worries, I'll sort it out."

I turn in a circle, eyeing the other blankets my cousins brought, but each of them lay out, making their bodies as big as humanly possible. When no one makes room, I decide the grass is a comfortable place to relax for a couple of hours. I plop down where I stand, laying out flat.

"What are you doing?" Thea asks as she chuckles.

I smile up at her. "Grass is soft."

She drops her head back and laughs, that deep, throaty sound, and I think it may be my favorite sound in the world. Next time, I'm gonna record it so I can play it on repeat like a new Noah Kahan album.

My favorite sound, my favorite face, my favorite scent. Is she going to take over all my favorites?

"You're pretty," I murmur.

"You're drunk," she replies, but that beautiful smile spreads even farther across her face.

"Get off the grass," Harrison says with a huff. "You know you're allergic to it."

I go up on my elbow, pointing a finger at Harrison. "Taking care is my job. Wait, taking care *of people* is my job."

Harrison rolls his eyes, but smiles, and I think how lucky I am to have him. He drives me crazy at times, and there are plenty of things I couldn't do because I was always taking care of him, but I wouldn't trade him for all the high school baseball teams and the out-of-state colleges in the world.

"I love you, little brother," I say with a gravity I didn't know I could muster with this much alcohol in my system.

"Yeah, I love you, too, drunky. Now get over here. There's plenty of room, and I don't want you with a weird rash in our wedding photos," Harrison says, shifting him and Addy a couple of inches to the left like he plans to have me sit next to Thea.

Addy grabs his arm, trying to tug him back toward me. "Let's sit in the middle. That way we can both sit next to our siblings!"

He settles Addy more firmly between his legs. "The movie's starting. Let's just sit so we don't piss off the people behind us."

Addy opens her mouth again, but I cut her off. "She doesn't want me by her sister because she's afraid I'll want to kiss her again."

Thea spreads one of her hands across her face, but I can see her smile peeking out from behind it.

Harrison laughs so loudly that people around us shush him. "You're going to be so embarrassed by all this tomorrow. Now get on the blanket."

I grumble but crawl my way off the grass as Thea shifts closer to Addy, leaving just enough room for me. My eyes meet hers, a question and request there, and she nods. This isn't what we agreed to, but the grass is starting to feel more itchy than soft, and nothing can compare to the softness of Thea's arm that brushes mine.

"This is becoming a habit," I whisper, eyes pinned to the screen.

"Have to wonder if it's intentional at this point."

"I promise, I'm not doing this on purpose," I say, suddenly worried that she thinks I'm taking advantage of the situation.

Her pinkie finger shifts an inch closer, drifting over mine. It's barely a touch, but it's a balm and a firework at the same time. "I meant your family, not you."

She moves her finger away from mine. What would she do if I grabbed it back? I know the answer to that, but my mind can't stop swirling with all the possibilities. *How to Lose a Guy in 10 Days* plays out on the screen, but there's a much more interesting movie in my mind. Thea letting out a squeak as I pull her between my legs just like Harrison has Addy positioned. The two of us whispering commentary about the movie. Getting to hear her unfiltered opinions without worrying about who's watching us.

Thea's scoff near the end of the movie breaks me out of my trance. Kate Hudson and Matthew McConaughey are reuniting on a bridge, and Thea can't stop rolling her eyes.

"Don't believe in love?" I ask, trying to keep my voice low, and when no one nearby yells at me, I assume I've succeeded.

Her mouth quirks up. "Not after less than two weeks, I don't."

"Really?" I face her fully, unable to stop my gaze from trailing down her elegant neck to the place where her pulse beats.

She doesn't look at me, but there's just enough light from the screen to see a blush come over her checks. It's adorable and new for my self-assured Thea. "Yes, really. They don't know each other. A couple weeks isn't enough time to see all the different sides of someone, and how can you love them without knowing all of them?"

"I don't know if I agree with that," I say. "You can know the core of who someone is in a few days. All the rest of it is just extra."

A terrifying thought crosses my mind—that it's only been three days with Thea back in my life and I could already see myself falling in love with her—but I'm sure it's the alcohol talking. Tomorrow, when I'm sober, I'll remember this is just attraction disguised as more.

She looks at me, raising a brow. "Are you telling me you've fallen in love in a week?"

I scoff. "I'm telling you I think it's possible. I've never fallen in love, period."

The shock on her face embarrasses me, like the fact that I've never been in love is a character flaw. And maybe she's right. I'm in my thirties and have never found anyone who stuck around long enough for us to fall in love. She must be cataloguing my red flags as we speak.

I tried to date more when I was younger. My girlfriends always found it cute how much I took care of Harrison or were amazed that I already owned my own company, but that wore off. They'd get annoyed with how much time I spent on my family, would tell me that my life was too boring, and they wanted more excitement. I may let myself indulge in the fantasy of Thea, but it would end the same way with her. She's the most exciting woman I've ever met, and I'd eventually lose her.

She meets my gaze, and I brace myself.

"I've never fallen in love, either," she says, and I feel like I've been bowled over. How could this incredible woman not have found love?

I keep my drunk tongue from saying, *I could love you*, and instead say, "That's a shame. You deserve love, Thea."

For a second, she looks as stricken as I feel, but then she turns back to the screen like the conversation never happened. And I go back to daydreaming about a future that won't exist.

Chapter 18

THEA

The next afternoon, after a morning of avoiding Owen and all my complicated feelings, Addy pulls me into her room with an excited squeal. She throws her body against the inside of the door, her back landing with a thud as she smiles at me with a bit of mania in her eyes.

"My dress was just delivered after the last round of alterations," she says, giving a little jump.

I let out an uncharacteristic squeal myself. "Can I see it? Please?"

It wrecked me when she went wedding dress shopping without me, even though I understood she was on a time crunch and couldn't wait for me to have an evening off work. That pain eased a bit when she told me how excited she was to show me. *It won't feel like* my *dress until you see me in it.*

Her body shakes like she's undergoing an exorcism. "Yes!"

Addy pulls the garment bag out of the bathroom, her body folding under the weight, but she gets it hung from the edge of the closet. A burst of tulle and lace flies out as she unzips it, but once the silhouette settles, I can see how perfect it is. An A-line ball gown with a lace overlay. The sweetheart neckline will be gorgeous on her, and the sheer lace sleeves give it a classic look. If someone had sent me into the nicest wedding dress store in the world with an unlimited budget, this is still what I'd have picked out for her.

I blink back tears as I help her into the dress, doing up the three thousand exposed buttons that run from the top of her butt to the nape of her neck. I step up behind her, my height giving me an inch on her, even with her wedding heels on.

"Addy, you're perfect," I whisper, swatting away the tear that managed to escape my blinking.

"You think so?" she asks, her voice low to match mine, like neither of us wants to share this moment, even with the silence around us.

"Yes, but wait one minute. I have something for you in my room. Don't move."

I sprint down the hall to grab the present I wasn't willing to give her in front of everyone. I dig the jewelry box out of my suitcase and sprint back. She hasn't moved an inch when I get back, staring in the mirror and running a hand over the lace like she needs to prove it's real.

I step behind her again, meeting her gaze in the mirror as I bring the box in front of her. Her brows pull together as a small smile plays on her beautiful face, but she gently takes the box from my hands.

"For your something blue," I say, my body buzzing with nervous excitement.

She pops the top of the jewelry box and gasps when she sees the dark blue teardrop gemstone. Her hand covers her mouth as she blinks back tears. "Tia, this is too much."

"It's really not," I say with a laugh. "I always thought it was a sapphire, but I took it to a jeweler a couple years ago, and it's blue topaz. Still pretty, but not worth much."

Not that I'd have ever sold it. I'd fought to keep it hidden over the years, to keep it safe for a moment like this.

"Always thought?" Addy asks, meeting my eyes in the mirror as she blinks in confusion.

Tears fill my eyes again, and I swipe them away. "It was Mom's. I saved it for us."

It wasn't easy, keeping it out of sight so none of our foster parents or siblings nabbed it, making sure it was with us on every move. It's the only thing we have left of our mother besides a few ratty pictures stuffed in a box in my closet, and I was determined not to lose it. Determined to have her be a part of this moment, even if she can't be here.

The snap of the jewelry box shakes me out of my thoughts. Addy's expression slides into that serene, fake smile I've seen pointed at so many others, and my stomach turns to lead. In the twenty-three years of Addy's life, she's never looked at *me* like that. She does a weird little curtsy bob as she hands it back to me over her shoulder.

"This is so sweet, but I already have my jewelry picked out," she says, turning her focus back to the lines of her dress.

I laugh a little, just as forced as Addy's calm expression. "Yeah, but that was before the gift. That's how surprises work."

"It's pretty, but the other jewelry goes better with my dress," she says, still not meeting my eyes.

This isn't how this was supposed to go. When I told her who it belonged to, she was supposed to tear up, too. She'd ask me to put it on her, and while I did, I'd tell her my favorite stories of Mom. Of her helping me give Addy a bottle for the first time. How she taught me every word to "Bohemian Rhapsody" so we could sing it together, her gently setting baby Addy down so we could head bang during the guitar solo. Her making up wild, elaborate stories based on a handful of random things I'd ask her to include. She wasn't a perfect person—I know that better than most—but she's a part of us. I just need to help her see that.

"This would go perfectly! It looks like it was made for this dress. Here, let's just try it on." I pop the jewelry box back open. "You need to see it with the dress."

"I really don't need to, Tia," she says, her tone sliding from the calm, fake one to something more clipped.

"Yes, you do. You can't imagine it without see—"

Addy twirls to face me, the lace and tulle swishing around

her legs like a whip primed to lash me. "I don't need to see it to know I'm not going to wear it, Thea."

My grip on the jewelry box tightens, forcing it to clap back closed. The sound echoes in the room around us while we stand off.

"But," I start before the words grind to a stop. I have no idea how to finish that sentence. "But this is for you."

"I don't want it," Addy says. There's a flash of something—almost pain—across her face, then she lifts her chin.

"Why wouldn't you want it?" I ask with a bit of desperation. "It's perfect with your dress, and you'll have a part of Mom walking down the aisle with you."

"I don't want her going down the aisle with me," she says.

I rear back. "Why not? She was our mother."

"No," Addy yells, finally breaking. "She was *your* mother. I never knew the woman. All she is to me is the junkie who got knocked up but cared more about her next hit than her daughters. Why would I want to honor a woman who didn't even care enough to stay alive for us?"

The question lands like a slap to the face, and I rear back. "She was sick, Adelaide."

I knew she didn't feel the same connection to Mom that I've always had. How could she when she doesn't even remember her? But I didn't know it was this extreme. That she'd have this visceral reaction to the idea of her being a part of her wedding day.

Addy flinches at the use of her full name. "Fine, yes. But that doesn't change the fact that she's given me nothing but a difficult life and an uncomfortable backstory."

"And a sister," I yell, and she has the audacity to rub her forehead like *I'm* the irrational one here.

Our mother is what ties us together. She's what kept us from being separated all those years, and Addy wants to pretend like she never existed?

"This doesn't need to be a fight. Please. She's nothing to me, and I'd rather spend this day focusing on my future family than the one that I could never rely on."

It doesn't escape my notice that she said "family" and not "mother." I'm fuming. I didn't make the best choices as a kid, and yes, there was a lot she lost because of me, but I've been by her side for everything. I made it clear to everyone in our homes that if they wanted a piece of Addy, they'd have to go through me first. If she wanted to leave her family—leave me—in the past, who was I to stop her.

"I'm fucking out of here," I say, stomping to the door.

"Thea," she calls behind me, and I twirl back to her with embarrassing speed, ready to hear her apology and put everything right between us. There's a flash of something that almost looks like betrayal—which makes no sense when *she's* the one betraying *me*—and then her face hardens. "I can't undo this dress myself."

Oh, fuck her.

"Why don't you call one of your reliable new family members to help you out," I say before storming out.

I stalk down the hallway, fighting the urge to slam back into Addy's room and throw out words I'd regret immediately. Staying here isn't an option. I have to get out, go anywhere, do anything to avoid the temptation to cause more damage.

I head to the hotel lobby, stopping at the coffee bar to give my hands something to do, but my first sip of caffeine sets off the jitters. The need to keep moving bites at my heels, so I head up the path to the event space where the wedding will be held in just a few days. There has to be *something* there that can occupy me. A ridiculous centerpiece to make or handwritten welcome notes Addy wants in perfect cursive. I rip the door open, slamming into a hard body right over the threshold.

"Shit," I holler as the coffee in my hands tumbles to the

ground, the contents spilling all over the floor. "Shit, fuck, dammit!"

I rip my sweater over my head as I drop to the floor, using it to soak the coffee up before it ruins the pristine hardwood. I've never had wood floors, but I know enough to know you aren't supposed to pour hot liquid all over them.

A figure squats down next to me, and a quick sideways glance tells me it's Owen. He lays his hand over mine. "Stop, Thea."

"I'm not going to ruin your family's floor, too."

He doesn't ask me what else I ruined. Why ask, when it's clear I ruin *everything*?

Owen pulls the sweater out of my hands and waves to someone, and a second later a cousin I recognize from the past few days jogs over. "Can you grab a mop for this, please?" Owen asks, such perfect politeness, easily maneuvering out of reach when I try to grab my sweater.

"Give that back," I snarl. "I need to soak up the coffee before the floor's ruined."

He moves the sweater farther out of reach. "The only thing you're ruining here is your sweater. The floor's sealed. Lynne's got it."

He stands, grabbing my hand and pulling me up before towing me behind him.

"Where are you taking me?" I ask, the impatience and anger in my tone evident.

"To rinse out this sweater before it *does* get ruined."

"Golden boy always has the answer."

He looks over his shoulder with a lifted brow, but stays quiet. He's so damn steady, his hand anchoring me even as my emotions roil, looking for an outlet.

Owen leads me into a full commercial kitchen off the ballroom. He turns on the water at one of the massive sinks, flicking his fingers under the stream until he deems it warm enough, then methodically rinses my sweater and hangs it up.

I spend the entire five-minute process prowling the kitchen like a tiger in a shitty zoo with way too much energy for the small cage I've been forced into.

He leans on the counter, drying his hands on a dishcloth. "What's wrong?"

"Pretty sure that's none of your goddamned business," I reply with a sarcastic smile, and feel a twinge of regret when the corner of his mouth pulls tighter.

This is me at my worst. Mean and angry and unable to stop my own self-destruction. He thinks he wants me, but he doesn't know me. This is the real Thea, and it's the one that will scare him away for good. At least I'll give Addy a clean break if no one in this family wants anything to do with me.

He runs his tongue over his teeth, nodding. "Does it become my business when you slam into me—still waiting on that apology, by the way—spill coffee all over the floor, and then strip in front of me?" I glance down, remembering then that I'd put nothing underneath the thin white tank top this morning, assuming my sweater would keep me covered.

"I'm so sorry for degrading your lovely family home with my near nakedness."

He flicks the dishcloth over his shoulder and crosses his arms. "Never said I was complaining."

I stop pacing, pinning him with a hard stare. "Why are you being so fucking nice to me?"

His head tilts to the side, his eyes soft. "Because you're clearly upset."

"I'm being a bitch."

His lips twitch, but he wrangles them back into a straight line. "Your words, not mine."

I run my hands up into my curls, tugging at the roots. "I had an argument with Addy."

His eyes soften. "Want to talk about it?"

"No," I say harshly, continuing to pace. "I don't want to deal with any of this. I had this wedding thrown on me and now I'm fighting with my sister, and I don't know what I'm doing and the last thing I want is to *talk* about it."

"Then what do you need?" he asks, so strong and steady it makes me want to scream. Is he always so fucking composed? I practically snarl, and he grabs my hand to make me stop in front of him. "What do you need, Thea?"

I brace for the pity I expect to find on his face, the same magnanimous look I've gotten from friends and foster parents. *Poor Thea, she can't handle her emotions.* Instead, all I see is patience, like he's willing to wait me out while I work through it all.

And suddenly, another emotion floods my veins. Need, for him to be close, to feel and experience that solidity. To know I have someone behind me, even though I've spent decades telling myself I'm fine on my own.

My fingers dive into the soft strands of his hair, yanking his body closer to me, and my lips seal over his. He lets out a surprised groan, his hands coming to my hips and squeezing, hard, before he remembers himself, lightly pushing me back.

"This isn't what you need," he says hoarsely.

"It is."

I step closer, running my lips up his throat. He's exactly what I need, what I've needed since I set eyes on him again. I've only denied myself because Addy didn't want me to pursue it, but why should I make my decisions based on her when she hardly considers me family?

"You don't want this. I understand *why* you don't want this. It would be a mistake." His words rumble against my lips, the vibrations moving through my body and making me ache in the most delicious way.

"Maybe. But I still need it. I need you."

He pulls my lips from his neck, dropping his forehead to mine. His eyes flutter closed as he lets out a shaky breath.

"I don't want to be something you regret, Thea. I *can't* be something you regret."

My heart squeezes, emotions I can't name lighting up inside me. "There isn't a moment with you I've ever regretted," I whisper across his lips.

His eyes blink open, heat and longing in the swirling colors, and then he kisses me, soft and gentle, until I escalate it with a nip to his bottom lip. He groans into my mouth, rough hands yanking me more firmly against him.

I pull back from the kiss, panting. "Take me somewhere."

"My room. Now."

He pulls me toward the exit, but I yank back. I know what will happen if we go to his room. He'll kiss me sweetly, lay me out across his king-size bed, and *make love* to me. But I'm not that girl, the one you bring breakfast in bed the next morning and who shows up at your mother's house with homemade cookies for brunch. I need to make sure he understands and accepts that. That *I* understand and accept that.

"Too far," I say.

He stares at me for a beat, then groans and drags me in the other direction, through the kitchen until we reach a large walk-in closet filled with cleaning supplies. He softly shuts the door behind us, sliding the lock into place.

"If you get us caught, we're both dead. Can you keep quiet, Thea?" he asks while stalking toward me, my back knocking into the shelves behind me.

"Won't be a problem. Unless you think you can make me scream," I taunt.

He huffs out a laugh, bringing his lips to my ear. "Don't be a brat."

Everything inside me goes tight. This side of Owen, the one I got a glimpse of when he kissed me in the hallway, is going to make me lose my mind. He runs his lips down my neck, following the line of my collarbone, not kissing me but giving enough pressure to drive me wild.

"Owen, if you don't kiss me in the next ten seconds, I'm going to walk out that door."

He pulls back, a smug smile plastered on his face as he looks deep in my eyes. Shit, cocky Owen really does it for me. "You know? I don't think you will. I think you'll let me torture you as long as I want."

I push his body back until he hits the opposite set of shelves, and the small flair of panic in his eyes that I might leave feels like a victory. But walking away right now is a physical impossibility.

He's so sturdy, always there for everyone. Who takes care of him, looks out for *his* needs? I want to play that role, even if for a short time, so I go to my knees in front of him, my hands coming to the button of his pants.

"And if I want to torture you?"

His hands come to my biceps. "This is for you. You don't need to do that."

"This *is* for me," I say.

"Thea," he says as his fingers tighten enough on my arms to pull me back to standing. "It's fine."

I groan. "Stop being so polite."

His brow furrows. "Since when is treating you with respect a bad thing?"

"It's not respect when I'm telling you what I want—when it's what you want, too—and you're denying both of us for some patriarchal sense of gallantry."

"Thea," he says cautiously.

He's so used to prioritizing everyone else, he doesn't even know how to accept putting his desires first when it's offered. But it's inside him. I could see it at the bar that night, the way he watched me. If he can stick with me through my rage, I can help him see he deserves this.

I grab either side of his face, forcing him to look at me. "Do the things you were imagining while I was on stage. It was all there in your eyes. The way you watched me?" I moan, feeling a rush of arousal at the memory. "Like you wanted to climb up there and do unspeakable things to me. I want that, too."

He lets out a shuddering breath.

I lift my chin, letting my lips drift over his with each word. "What do you want, Owen? Do you want me to walk out that door and let you keep your perfect golden-boy persona, or do you want me on my knees for you so you can fuck my mouth?"

"Fuck," he growls right before he wraps a hand around the back of my neck. The word lands like a lightning strike between my legs. He's never said it—not around me, at least—and seeing this perfect gentleman unravel at my goading is a fantasy brought to life. I want to take him apart piece by piece.

His mouth crashes against mine, everything about this kiss bigger than our first. His tongue delves between my lips, a delicious sweep. I moan into his mouth, and he spins us so I'm pinned to the shelves instead, grinding against me in a way that tells me exactly how he'll treat me in bed if he lets go. Sparks shoot behind my eyes, and I think this may be the fastest I've ever gotten this close to coming, and all without a single piece of clothing removed. He pulls back, and I chase his mouth with mine until a tightened pressure on my neck causes me to open my eyes.

Owen's gaze is dark, all colors except those rings of navy swept away by his pupils. And when he speaks again, everything in my body goes weak.

"Get on your knees, Thea."

Chapter 19

OWEN

The smile Thea gives me is the epitome of the cat who's caught the mouse, and I've never been more grateful to be caught up in anything. She lowers herself slowly, savoring the anticipation and the tension in my body. A fucking queen, even in nothing but a thin white tank top and ripped jean shorts. I should be the one on my knees, swearing my fidelity.

She undoes my pants, pulling them and my underwear down in one tug until my cock bobs up in front of her. We both pause, her staring openly while I track every expression that crosses her face—the way her deep brown eyes go wide and the delicious way she licks her lips. She leans forward to take me in her mouth, but that's not how I want this. And she told me to demand what I want. My hand wraps around her gorgeous curls, tugging her head back so she has to look at me.

"You want to know where my thoughts went when you were on that stage?" I ask as my other hand wraps around my cock, stroking myself. She nods her head. "Then put your hands behind your back."

My heart is thudding, half because she's the most perfect thing I've ever seen and half because I'm afraid she's going to turn away from me. When she was up there, I didn't just want her. I wanted complete control, to take and own every piece of her. It's a fantasy I've never felt safe enough to explore with any of my past partners, and part of me believes it'll send her running for the hills. But her lips just twist into a devilish smile as she bends her arms, laying her hands on the small of her back.

"Tongue out," I say.

She doesn't miss a beat, sticking her tongue out while keeping her eyes glued to mine.

I step closer, running the tip across her full top lip like I'm painting it, and she lets out a moan so hot, I don't know how I'll make it through more. I tap my dick on her tongue a few times, then slide between her lips. "Fuck, Thea. This mouth."

I give a short experimental thrust and—shit—nothing has ever felt so good. Thea holds my eyes the whole time, somehow smiling with her lips stretched around me.

"Is this okay?" I ask, my voice strangled, and she nods.

She tries to move her head forward, but I tighten my grip on her hair to keep her in place. This is what I want, what I have never been bold enough to ask for until Thea demanded my whole truth. My life has been about meeting the needs of others, and this freedom—the freedom to take what I want without thinking about anything but my own pleasure—sets something free inside me. She moans as I plunge into her mouth, the vibrations shooting down my cock and through every inch of my body.

I pull her mouth off me, using the controlling grip on her hair to stand her up. "Take off your shorts, then get back on your knees. I want you to make yourself come while your mouth is wrapped around me."

Thea whimpers, tugging against the hand in her hair to capture my lips as she unzips her shorts and drops them and her underwear to the floor. I almost change my mind, begging for a chance to look at her, but she drops back to her knees, her hand delving between her spread legs while she wraps her lips around me. It's the hottest sight I've ever seen, her eyes fluttering closed even as she fights to keep them on me. She sucks hard, her cheeks hollowing, and my desperate groan fills the room. And a few minutes later, when her body tenses and she moans around my cock, it takes every bit of control to keep from coming down her throat.

I pull her off me before she can push me over the edge and bring her back to her feet, pinning her to the shelves as I kiss her deeply. She pulls her tank top over her head and throws it across the room in one fluid motion and suddenly she's there, bare for me and so glorious I know I'll spend the rest of my life comparing every other woman to her.

Her breasts fit perfectly in my palms, like they were made to be there. My lips close around her nipple, increasing the suction until she writhes against me. Her hands come to the hem of my shirt, pushing it up so she can run her nails down my abs. I rip it over my head and drop it at our feet as she continues playing.

"I have to be inside you," I groan onto her lips.

"Fuck, yes," she moans in response.

I make sure she's steady on her feet before I take a few quick steps to where I kicked off my jeans, digging in the pocket for my wallet. I flip through it—cards, cash, my ID, a fucking library card for Christ's sake—but there's no condom. A frustrated sound rips from my throat and I throw my wallet across the closet. It slams against a bottle of cleaner, which teeters precariously before settling back on the shelf. I don't know which of my cousins stole the condom I keep in my wallet, but they're fucking dead when I find out.

Thea's staring at me with disappointed eyes. "No condom?"

No, but she's still right there, and I'll be damned if this ends here.

"What are you doing?" she asks in surprise as I go to my knees before her, grabbing one leg and throwing it over my shoulder. The moan she lets out when I close my lips over her clit is second only to the taste that explodes across my tongue. Fuck, I could live off only this for the rest of my life.

"If this is my only chance with you," I say, letting the breath of my words breeze over her beautiful pussy, "there's no way I'm letting it pass without tasting you."

I keep eating her like she's my last meal—honestly, I can't think of anything else I'd choose over this if I were about to die—and I'm rewarded. Her hands dive into my hair, tugging me against her while she rides my face.

"So fucking sweet, Thea," I murmur against her, and she whimpers.

My fingers tighten where my arm wraps around her thigh, keeping her open and bared to me as she squirms. My other hand closes around my cock, moving in time with my tongue over her swollen clit as she goes over the edge. Pleasure shoots up my spine seconds later, and I have just enough mental clarity to grab my shirt and come into that instead of all over the shelf supporting Thea.

I sit back on my heels as Thea's legs give out and she settles onto my lap. My arms come around her back as hers land over my shoulders, and we just hold each other.

I've always thought Thea was too bright for me, like a spark shooting off the campfires we had every summer. I'd watch them twist through the air, constantly changing directions, mesmerizing in their unpredictability. They were meant to be watched and admired, not touched. I'd assumed Thea would be the same. But instead of feeling burned, I'm warm, like the spark sunk into my soul and is heating me from the inside out.

Her face is buried in my neck, and I think, of all the incredible things that have happened in the past fifteen minutes, this is the greatest of all. She feels right in my arms, and the only negative thing in this beautiful moment is the fear of what happens next. That once she recovers, she'll walk away from me.

I'm so wrapped up in her that it takes a minute to register the moisture on my neck. I pull back to find tears streaming down her face. I wipe them away with my thumbs just for them to be replaced seconds later.

"I'm so sorry." She hiccups, her eyes glued to my chest.

"What in the world are you sorry for, Thea?" I ask, wiping at more of the tears.

She opens her mouth but cries harder, her body shaking with her sobs. I hate that she's hurting, and I'm desperate to fix it.

"I was such a bitch to you. I'm such a bitch to everybody," she says. "Why don't you hate me after all of that?"

"Hate you, because you were upset and needed to let off some steam? You're not one moment, Thea, and trust me, the good of you far outweighs the bad."

She watches me for a half second, then breaks out into sobs again. "That's not your line."

"What?" I ask, unable to stop my laughter.

"When I screw up, when I'm angry and mean and self-destructive. That's not how the script goes. You're supposed to call me out and tell me what a bitch I'm being."

My stomach drops as I realize that's what everyone else has done to her. No one's ever given her room to feel those complicated feelings without cutting her off.

I gently kiss her forehead. "Let's call this improvising, then."

"You're not supposed to be like this. It's supposed to be easy," she says.

I smile against her skin, because even if I hate that she's hurting, it feels good to know this isn't easy for her, either. Walking away from her in a few minutes will feel like my soul's being stripped from my body. But for now, I have her. And I want to do anything I can to help her feel better while she's letting me.

"Do you want to talk about what happened with Addy now?" I ask gently, tucking a curl behind her ear.

She shivers, leaning into my palm in a way that sets off a round of fireworks in my chest. "It wasn't pretty."

My mouth tugs up. "I don't mind a bit of ugly. You're too pretty as is."

There's a flash of a smile across her face—crinkled eyes and tilted lips—but it's gone too quickly.

"It was about our mom. I won't bore you with the details." It's on the tip of my tongue to say I *want* to be bored with the details, until I see the tightness around her eyes and realize she can't handle them yet. "And I just lost it."

"Why?" She tenses in my arms, and I rush to add, "Not saying you shouldn't have. I just want to understand."

She blinks at me, like the idea of someone wanting to get her is foreign. "You do?"

A breath gusts out of me. "Yes. God, Thea, I want to understand everything about you."

She looks physically pained at my words, but she leans forward, placing the softest kiss on my lips before pulling back. "Long story short, she wants to focus on her new family instead of the family who has never been there for her. So, you know, me."

Fire shoots through my veins. Anyone who interacts with the sisters can see how vehemently Thea loves Addy, how much she'd sacrifice for her sister's happiness. Before now, I'd have said it's two-sided. The only true emotion I've seen from Addy is when she talks to Thea or Harrison, flashes of something real underneath her facade.

"I'm sorry, Thea," I murmur. "You deserve a lot more raging than a couple snippy comments to me."

Thea snort-laughs into my neck, and I feel so accomplished.

"But I don't believe she meant it. It was a shitty thing for her to say, and you deserve an apology, but she loves you." She shakes her head, and I pull her face back to meet her eyes. "How could she know you as well as she does and *not* love you?"

It's too close to a confession, and I'm worried she's going to bolt. Instead, her eyes are soft, filled with gratitude and longing as a tear slides down one cheek. I kiss it away, then pull her back into my arms.

We sit, wrapped up in each other, for a few more minutes before Thea whispers, "We need to get dressed."

"I know," I say, shifting her closer in my arms. My legs have gone numb underneath me, but I'll keep her here as long as she'll let me.

"This has to stay in here," she says. "No room for improvisation in that part of the script."

I suck in a breath, my chest expanding with the motion and pushing us more tightly together. "But what if there was?"

She leans back, her strong brows pulling together. "What do you mean?"

"Did this feel like a one-time thing to you? Because it didn't for me. All of it—every time we talk and touch—feels like so much more, and I don't want to walk away."

Thea takes her plump bottom lip between her teeth, and I can see the wheels in her brain moving. She doesn't know how to make it work, but she wants to. It's clear in the way her arms tighten around my shoulders.

I push forward before she can spiral and talk herself out of it. "We can take the rest of the week to get to know each other, to make sure this is what we want. No mess or fuss before the wedding. Then, once it's done, we come clean to my mom. Tell her everything while Harrison and Addy are on their honeymoon and do whatever we need to do to placate my mom before they get home. Assuming you still want to when the week's up."

The corner of her mouth quirks up. "And assuming *you* still want to."

I bark out a laugh. "Oh, trust me, I'll still want to."

Thea watches me closely, running her fingertips along the ridge of my nose and over my cheekbone. "Are you sure? I'm . . . I'm not easy."

"Easy's overrated," I say, pairing it with a shrug that has Thea's lips twisting up for a second before they fall again.

"It could make things hard with your mom," she says, looking over my shoulder, like she can't bear to watch my face.

"You're worth making waves for."

Thea doesn't respond for what feels like eons, and my heart sinks. Maybe I misread the situation. Maybe I'm just a distraction.

"Addy may never forgive me." The words are quiet.

It's hard to resist the urge to rub at the ache in my chest. This woman—the one who has called herself "selfish" and "difficult" multiple times—has brought up how everyone except her would feel. I can't help but wonder how this lie about who she is became so ingrained in her identity, especially when she's shown nothing but selflessness to me. I want to help her see the truth. The beauty and light she brings into the world.

"You deserve happiness, too, Thea." I search her face, giving those words a moment to sink in. "Do you want this?"

I keep the question gentle, giving her the space to say no, to retreat from the feelings I can see shining out of her eyes.

"Yes."

Her whispered response barely reaches my ears, and I ask to make sure I didn't imagine it in the silence. "Yes?"

She laughs, then rolls her lips together. "Yes. I want this."

I kiss her then, slow and deep, the rumble of her laughter sliding into my body and making me feel light as air. She's it for me. My body recognized it when she looked up at me from her knees, my heart felt it when she crumpled into my arms afterward, and my soul knew it the moment I saw the tears on her cheeks. I want to be the one who lets her be angry, who holds her through it all until the anger fades enough for her to feel the real emotion underneath it.

We have four more days until the wedding. Five until Harrison and Addy say goodbye to all of us and head on their honeymoon. Which means we have to make it through six days without getting caught, to keep Thea from getting too jumpy about the risk.

Then we can start our lives together.

Chapter 20

THEA

After what feels like days, I peel myself away from Owen, already missing his warmth and the strength of his hands as they ran over my back. He puts himself back together in seconds, then leans against the shelf, his eyes trailing my movements. There's something so intimate about him watching me put myself together after so thoroughly taking each other apart.

When I look up from buttoning my shorts, he's in front of me, stern determination written on the lines of his handsome face. He brings his mouth to mine in a slow, decadent kiss.

"Owen," I scold against his lips.

"Just one more," he mumbles, like he's talking to himself more than to me. The idea that he can't walk away is intoxicating, and I sigh into the kiss.

Minutes or hours later, I push him away with a laugh. "You're dangerous."

He shrugs, that tiny smile tugging at the corner of his mouth. "It's going to be torture not being able to kiss you. You can't fault me for savoring every second."

I run my hand up the side of his neck and into his hair, watching the fascinating way his eyes drop closed at the contact. I've never had what he's given me in the last twenty minutes. When I get difficult, people walk away. Even Vaughn and Addy give me space when I get upset. No one's ever sat with me through it, like a captain ushering a ship through a storm, knowing there's beauty on the other side.

I kiss him lightly but push him away when he groans and tries to deepen it. "Thank you. For all of it."

I eye his bare chest, lean, strong muscles, and my mind swirls with images of all the potential ways he maintains this physique. Owen back in the swim trunks he wore at Sliding Rock, water sluicing down his body as he pushes out of the pool. Owen on a rowing machine, his back muscles flexing and releasing with each pull. Owen braced over me, using our activities as his own personal cardio.

"Are you planning on walking around topless?" I ask.

He scoffs, holding up the soiled shirt. "I'm not putting *this* on."

My laughter catches me off guard, deep and genuine in a way I don't think it normally sounds. His lips kick up another millimeter, and he gives me one last peck before I open the door.

Two steps out and we run into Gabriel, staring at us with wide eyes. I can just imagine what we look like—Owen in only his jeans and my hair a wild mess.

Gabriel steps forward—why is this kid everywhere?—clutching his chest. "Thea, I thought we had something special."

"It's not what it looks like," Owen says.

"Suuuuuure," he answers. "Thea, did you forget your bra in there?"

Owen thankfully steps in front of me to block Gabriel's view.

"Never had one to begin with," I say over his shoulder. "Now stop looking at my tits."

Gabriel's laugh booms through the space. "Yeah, and Owen always walks around without a shirt on."

"She spilled coffee on my shirt and we were looking for something to clean it," Owen says, coming up with a valid excuse that Gabriel doesn't buy for a second.

"Just admit you two were hooking up."

Owen denies it, but I can see from Gabriel's expression that we aren't getting away with this.

"Okay, fine," I say, hoping to at least control the narrative. "It was a bit of a backslide, but nothing else is going to happen, so can we keep this between us? We don't want to give anyone—especially Diana—the wrong impression."

Gabriel eyes us speculatively. "Fine, I won't send that very interesting message I was already writing in my head to the group chat, but on one condition."

Owen groans. "What do you want from me?"

"Not you," he says, jerking his chin in my direction. "Her."

I narrow my eyes. "If this is a weird sex thing, I'm gonna pass."

Gabriel barks out a laugh. "No, I want you to perform with us at the rehearsal dinner and wedding."

I didn't see that one coming. "You can't be serious."

"As the grave," Gabriel says, bouncing his eyebrows. "How important is my silence?"

"You're ridiculous," I say with a laugh. "I can't perform with you guys. I don't know your songs."

"I'll send you our set list. We'll do a mix of you singing the covers and one of us singing the originals."

"Even if I know the songs you're covering, I don't know how *you* perform them."

He shrugs. "I think you can make time for one measly hour-long rehearsal. You didn't practice with us before the bar performance, and look how that turned out."

"What are you even doing here?" Owen asks Gabriel, and I know it's an attempt to distract him, to give me a second to think.

He tosses something in the air and catches it, and it only takes a glimpse of bright yellow for me to recognize the bus keys. "I'm sneaking these into Lynne's desk drawer so she grabs them and has to drive the next time."

Owen lets out a bone-weary sigh as I stifle a giggle in his back. "You're going to lose them. Just wait until we get closer to the next time we're using it."

"Everyone will be on their guard by then. I already tried handing them off, and I couldn't get anyone to take them."

"Gabe—"

"Unless *you* want to take them," he says, grinning like he's about to yell *checkmate*.

Owen sighs again and reaches out, but I grab his arm and twist it behind his back. "Don't you fucking dare."

Gabriel sticks the keys back in his pocket, turning his attention to me. "What's it gonna be, Thea?"

It's a strange sensation, having someone want me involved in something enough to blackmail me into it. But singing with their band really was a rush, and if it will keep this quiet, it'll be a perfect win-win situation. Addy said it was fine, and he's right, I can find an hour.

"Fine, I'll do it."

Gabriel gives a triumphant *whoop* as Owen digs the heels of his palms into his eyes. "If you're going to sneak the keys into Lynne's desk, go now. I need to talk to Thea."

Gabriel waggles his eyebrows. "For more canoodling?"

"Cut it the fuck out, Gabriel," Owen says, and Gabriel's body jerks, jumping to attention like a soldier spotting their general approaching. "If gossip starts swirling around us, it'll distract from the wedding. Neither of us want that for Harrison and Addy. You're going to hurt people because you care more about the laugh than common decency."

Gabriel blinks a few times, then faces me. "I'm sorry."

"You're fine. But Owen's right."

"I'll keep it to myself," he says, looking fully chastised before rushing down the hall.

Owen pulls me to the side once he's turned the corner. "If you don't want to perform, I can get Gabriel to back off. Seems like he heard me."

Based on the reaction from Gabriel when Owen called him out, I'm sure he's right. But I don't want to say no. "It's okay.

Sounds kind of fun. And if you say this to Gabriel I'll deny it, but it's nice to feel wanted."

Owen looks over his shoulder, then risks a step closer. "Do I not make you feel wanted enough, Thea?"

No one has ever made me feel as wanted as Owen. "I like you like this. Happy and teasing."

He shrugs with a self-deprecating smile. "It's not my normal style. But it's easier with you."

I get what he means. I don't stress about what I'm saying with him. I just am. "Yeah, I know the feeling."

I love having this with Owen, but the second that thought crosses my mind, it feels like a bomb detonating inside me. The word "love" in relation to another person besides Addy and Vaughn has never crossed my mind. It's big and too unpredictable. I don't love him—I hardly know him—but I think I could, and that's terrifying.

There's so much at risk, and not just my own heart. It's only been ten minutes since we decided to give this thing a try, and we've already been discovered. How are we supposed to keep it together for another week? I'm mad at Addy, but that doesn't mean I'm willing to play around with her future.

I open my mouth, but Owen cuts me off. "Nope. We're not doing that."

"Not—we're not—what are you talking about?" I sputter out.

"I can see it on your face," he says with a little half smile. "You're spiraling over Gabriel catching us and coming up with all the worst-case scenarios. Were you about to tell me we couldn't be together?"

My mouth opens and closes like a fish desperate for water. I don't have an answer for him, because I *was* about to say that.

Owen glances up and down the hallway, then plants a quick kiss on my forehead. "If you decide I'm not it for you, I'll respect that. But don't let fear and our families steal it from us, okay?"

I look up at him, the determined set of his jaw and the earnestness in his breathtaking eyes, and nod. How could I make any other decision when he's in front of me?

"Okay then," he says, a boyish smile taking over his face. "I guess I'll see you tomorrow."

He sends another furtive glance up and down the hallway before lifting my hand and placing a kiss in the center of my palm. Then he walks off, leaving me boneless in his wake.

* * *

I blessedly make it back to my room without running into anyone and take a quick shower, already regretting the loss of Owen's scent on my skin. I need to steal something of his, a shirt or hoodie that I can throw under the bed if someone comes to my room.

My phone buzzes and Vaughn's name flashes across it. I answer on the first ring. "Hey, friend!"

His bark of laughter rings through the line. "Oh my god, you got laid."

I drop onto the bed. "I have no idea what you're talking about."

Vaughn hums. "Of course not. You always answer the phone all chipper like that. I guess my call to check in on how things are going was unnecessary."

My head jumps to *how things are going* with an image of Owen on his knees before me, the tight grip of his fingers on my thigh grounding me, the sweep of his tongue over me.

"You still with me, Thee?"

"Yup." I snap out of the vision and am suddenly flooded with everything else that's happened today, my stomach roiling over the argument I've been ignoring in favor of the memories of Owen. "Addy and I got into a fight."

"Not what I thought you were going to say," Vaughn says, his voice louder like I was on speakerphone, but my comment was enough to make him sit and pick up the phone. "What happened?"

A wildly complicated question. As hurtful as Addy's comments were, there are parts of her side that I get. Does the fact that our mother birthed her automatically earn her a position of respect?

Addy's all anger toward Mom. She doesn't remember the good parts—or really any parts—but those good parts did exist. Dance parties when she got a new job and long walks in state parks describing the dream home she'd never get. She got clean while pregnant with and nursing Addy because she loved us. Almost two years of perfection. But when neither of us was reliant on her body to survive, her illness let her justify starting back up.

It's easy to focus on the bad when she can't remember the good, but Addy *can* remember the good with me. At least, I think there was good. I tried to be there for her, to make sure she knew through all the instability that *I* was there. That she was loved. That I'd do anything—sacrifice anything—to keep her happy. Her lumping me in with her worst childhood experiences feels like a dismissal of all that.

I don't know how to describe this to Vaughn. He's always been quick to judge Addy, and I don't want to get into it with him.

"Not a big deal. She made a comment that hit a tender spot, and I lost it. But I let off some steam, so it's fine."

Vaughn's sigh is long and pained. "You plan to ignore it."

It's a comment, not a question. More than anything, it feels like a judgment on my relationship with Addy, and the surge of defensiveness I knew was coming rears up.

"Look, so far, all I've done since I arrived is screw up. I was late to the welcome party; sat in the damn cake; caused drama because everyone thinks I dated Owen; showed up to her shower late, dressed like a gremlin and with no gift; and started fucking her soon-to-be brother-in-law behind her back. So yeah, I think it's fair for me to let go of this one interaction."

"An interaction that hurt you," he says. "I can hear it in your voice."

Yeah, it hurt. It hurts to know I'm not good enough for her when all I want is to have a place in her family and her future, but I won't find that place by causing even more drama. The idea of pushing for a conversation and alienating her further makes me feel sick. What if she asks me to leave and I miss the chance to see her walk down the aisle?

"You deserve to speak your truth, Thea," Vaughn says. "Give her a chance to prove you wrong."

"I find it very inconvenient that you've gotten into therapy. Can't you just let me sit in my unhealthy behaviors?"

He laughs, and the familiar sound brings my stress levels down some. "I know you don't like conflict—"

"What are you talking about?" I interrupt. "I'm constantly arguing with people."

"People you don't care about. But you avoid it with us, me and Addy. There are plenty of times I've pissed you off and you don't say anything."

"Not tr—"

"Yes, it is. You can be mad at us and yell at us if we deserve it. We aren't going anywhere."

There's a lump in my throat preventing me from answering him. Shit, he's right. It's what I just did with Addy. Instead of staying and explaining why what she said hurt me, I ran, too scared that if I showed my anger, it'd push her away like everyone else in my past.

"You okay?" Vaughn asks.

"Ish?" I squeak out.

"If you promise you'll think about what I said, I'll distract you with a batshit story."

I accept, and that's how I end up spending the next thirty

minutes listening to a story about how an old hookup of Vaughn's got the keys to his apartment, let herself in, and presented herself—naked—on his bed for when he came home. Unfortunately, he'd also brought home the new guy he was seeing, and when she saw them both, she said she was willing to share. Vaughn paused just a beat too long before saying no and scared his date off.

I'm laughing so hard I'm sure it can be heard all the way down the hall, and I feel lighter than I have since I arrived in North Carolina. And with Owen's assurances of Addy's love for me and Vaughn's encouragement to be honest about my feelings, I feel strong enough to pull on my big-girl pants and go talk to my sister.

Chapter 21

THEA

Just over two hours have passed since this door slammed behind me, and a little part of me—okay, a large part—wants to run. The rap of my fist sets off a round of nausea inside me. I wait. And wait. And wait.

I'm put out of my misery when the door cracks open and Addy's face appears. She's still in her gown, but her eyes are bloodshot and swollen. I'm not sure what's stronger: the petty relief that she's upset, too, or the surge of guilt that I've upset her during her special week.

She inches the door open, leaving just enough room for me to squeeze inside, and the nausea kicks back up in full force. I don't know how this conversation's going to go. If she's going to apologize or demand an apology of me or just straight up call me an asshole and uninvite me to the wedding. But Vaughn's right, I can't keep running away from the hurt.

I planned it out in my head before coming to her room. Calmly explain why what she said bothered me, peeling the layers back so she can see why it hit so many of my soft spots. Instead, I blurt, "Do you hate me, too?"

That's the crux of it. I've always known Addy wanted more than me—more family and love and support—but I thought she wanted more *on top* of me, not instead. In my head, we've always been a team, a pair of sailors managing our tiny boat, equally vital to keep it from sinking. Now, I wonder if she looks at me as a liability, someone poking holes in the bottom while she's frantically trying to reach shore.

Addy's body jolts. "Hate you?"

"L-like her?" I stutter out. "Do you hate me like you hate Mom?"

"What?" she asks, her eyes flashing. "Why would you even ask that?"

I'm lightheaded, everything in me screaming to get out. *Leave before you drive her away like everyone else.* I never should have brought this up. It would have been so easy to apologize. We could have gone through the rest of this week like nothing happened, and we'd have been fine.

You deserve to speak your truth, Thea, Vaughn whispers in my ear. *Give her a chance to prove you wrong.*

Owen's soft voice echoes. *How could she know you as well as she does and* not *love you?*

I push past the sinking sensation in my gut. "You don't want the necklace because you're focusing on your new family instead of the one you could never rely on. That's what you said. *I'm* your family. *I'm* the one you want to leave in the past."

There. I said it, and there's no taking it back. I've opened Pandora's damn box. And shockingly, I don't regret it. It's a weight off to know it's out there, even if I'm still stewing in what it will mean for our relationship.

Addy's face drains of color. "No. Oh my god, no. I'm so sorry, Tia. That wasn't what I meant. You're my sister. My best friend. I didn't mean *you.*"

Her words and the accompanying relief knock the wind out of me. I know Addy better than I know myself. The way her jaw tightens when she's apologizing just to end the argument and how her eyes bounce around the room when she's lying. Right now, she's meeting my gaze head-on, her posture open and her eyes devastated, and I believe her.

Addy takes a step toward me but stops herself. "Please. Please forgive me. I'm sorry."

I close the distance, pulling her into a hug. "*I'm* sorry. I shouldn't have gotten so angry or run out."

We stand there, clutching each other and crying, the type of cathartic cry that washes you clean by the end. Her arms around me make me feel cherished. I need to be better about trusting our relationship. We may not be perfect like everything else about Addy, but we're real. Our foundation is strong enough to handle the shockwaves of our fights without collapsing.

"Tia?" Addy hiccups when our tears slow.

I squeeze her even tighter. "Yeah?"

"Can you please get me out of this dress?"

Both of us laugh, our bodies supporting each other as we collapse forward. I spin her around, undoing the buttons as quickly as I can. Once free, Addy throws herself onto the bed, starfished out in nothing but her shapewear.

"It's so nice to lie down. I've been standing for two hours because I was worried I'd get it all wrinkled."

"It's lace. Does it even wrinkle?"

Addy lifts her hands and lets them drop on the bed. "I don't know. Probably not. But I'm just so worried that I'll mess it up. That I'll mess all of this up."

I walk back over to the bed. "You know Harrison loves you for you, right? He's marrying you because you're amazing, not because you're perfect. It's okay if everything doesn't run exactly as planned."

She pinches her lips to the side, the love for him brimming from her eyes. "I know *he* does. He's just . . . he's wonderful, Tia. But his family's more than just him. I don't just want his love. I want to fit here, you know? I've never fit anywhere before."

She has the Fischers, but she's always felt separate from them. They've adopted three of their foster kids, but the other two were adopted as toddlers, growing up with Maria and Gary and—unintentionally—making Addy feel like a last-minute add-on. If they'd adopted her the first time we were placed with them, she wouldn't have this issue. I created this feeling of otherness for her.

Addy props herself up on her elbows, her tanned olive skin on display. "Anyway, how did you spend the past two hours?"

I'm hit with a wave of guilt. "Oh, you know, rage hiking around the property and talking to Vaughn." *And fucking your future brother-in-law.*

"I really am sorry," Addy says, her face pinching, and I feel even guiltier for keeping this secret from her.

"I know."

"I just kind of freaked out. Please don't be mad, but—Tia, I can't wear that necklace."

I can understand where she's coming from, and it shouldn't matter. What is it but a scrap of metal and a semiprecious stone? But it still hurts. Addy must see the way the words twist in my gut, because she jumps in.

"I love you, and you're one of the most important people in my life. But this is my wedding, and everything with our birth mother is wrapped up with a lot of pain and anger and complicated emotions, and I don't want to be thinking about that on such a big day."

I drop onto the bed next to her, wrapping my fingers around hers as we both stare up at the ceiling. "You're right. I'm sorry I pushed."

She faces me. "You aren't our mother. I'm sorry I made it seem like I was looping you two together when you've always put me first. I trust you. You're *nothing* like her. You'd never make selfish decisions like she did."

I don't point out that Mom wasn't selfish, she was sick. Even though I want to. Addy's relationship with our mother is her own, and I can't force her to feel the way I do.

And I refuse to give in to the guilt from her comment, in to the fear that the choice I made with Owen is selfish. It *would* be selfish if we came clean now, causing drama and issues with Diana just so I could touch him whenever I wanted, but we're waiting. And Owen is right, I deserve happiness, too.

"Join us for dinner tonight?" Addy asks, breaking me out of my reflection.

I smile, genuinely, because those fears of her not wanting me to be a part of the family were clearly unfounded. "Yeah, sounds great."

* * *

When Addy and I make it downstairs, Diana, Harrison, and Owen are already at the table. Harrison jogs over the second he spots Addy, his smile stretched across his face as he loops his arms around her waist and spins her. Addy's delighted squeal fills the space around us, and I can't stop my answering smile.

Camila's standing at the hostess station, her dark brown curls piled into a high bun with a poofy headband, and I stop for a quick hello.

"I thought you worked at the front desk?" I ask.

"I do. And the restaurant. And the tasting room. And sometimes housekeeping. At least bellhop is off the table," she says, gesturing to her bump. "Pretty sure my parents expected more of their five kids to join the family business, but it's just me. I need to hire some new employees before my maternity leave, but who has the time."

I lift an eyebrow. "Seems like something you make time for."

"Did you come here to have dinner or to attack me?" she asks, narrowing her eyes. "Because I believe someone is waiting for you."

She jerks her head toward the Hayeses' table. Owen's watching me, the weight of his gaze like a thousand electric pulses throughout my body. When we make eye contact, his lips quirk up. He rolls them together to hide the smile, and when that doesn't work, he rubs one hand over his mouth. But it doesn't matter that the curve of his mouth is hidden, because it's all there in his expressive eyes. His delight and desire, painted in shades of blue and green.

Everyone is seated when I make my way over. There are two free spots—one next to Addy and one next to Owen—and my body screams at me to take the seat I want. To feel the warmth of Owen's body in the small space between the chairs. But that would raise eyebrows, so I stop next to Addy.

Before I can pull the chair out, Diana rushes to her feet. "I'd like to sit there. Why don't you take the seat across from me?"

The free seat next to Owen.

"Mom, you've already sat down," Owen says quietly.

"I didn't think about it when I chose my seat, but I'd rather sit there," she says through gritted teeth, widening her eyes at Owen in a way that isn't as inconspicuous as she thinks.

"I'd like to sit by Addy, if you don't mind," I say, shooting for casual.

Diana makes a *psh* sound, walking over to maneuver me around the table. "Nonsense. You see Addy all the time. This is my chance to get to know *you* again."

She laughs, light and airy, but Addy flinches across the table.

"Mom," Harrison barks out, but I step closer to her before he can continue.

"Don't you dare make Addy feel unimportant again," I say in a vicious whisper for Diana's ears only, praying it doesn't reach Addy.

Diana meets my eyes, seeing the hardness there. Yes, this is my sort-of boyfriend's mother, but my job here is to protect my sister. Her eyes widen, like I'm watching her process that I won't sit back and let her treat Addy poorly, and she starts backpedaling.

"The perfect thing about this seat," she says, glancing frantically between the four of us, "is I get to sit close to both of the girls, which is all I want."

None of us mention she was fine not sitting close to Addy before I walked up. I'm hoping that Addy's so securely wrapped in her Harrison love bubble that she doesn't notice, but the forced nature of her smile says otherwise.

Diana scurries around the table to her new seat, fussing over Addy—how stunning her sundress is and how smooth and bouncy her curls are—shooting me glances that say, *See, I'm being friendly*, and I let out a sigh of relief. If Owen and I are going to make this thing between us work, the more Diana likes me, the better, but I won't sacrifice Addy on the altar of gaining Diana's approval.

The table's tight, like they squeezed six chairs at a table made for four, and every time either of us shifts, our arms brush. Owen casually slips his hand over, giving my knee a quick, reassuring squeeze before taking it back. I mourn the loss of contact immediately, even though I know he can't keep touching me here.

The beginning of the meal passes without anything of note. Diana peppers us both with questions. The tension in Addy's shoulders from her earlier comment doesn't disappear completely, but releases a bit more with every smile and thoughtful hum from Diana's lips.

I'm two bites into my filet mignon when Owen's hand slips back onto my knee, and every cell in my body goes on high alert. He doesn't look my way, talking about something with the group that I can't compute while he's touching me. His hand doesn't move, just rests on my leg. I sit in anticipation until his middle finger shifts, the smallest of circles that has other parts of my anatomy clenching. All my existence has narrowed to that one millimeter of space.

But two can play this game. I take a bite of my mashed potatoes and let out a borderline pornographic moan. His fingers tighten on my thigh in response, a five-point star of pure sensation.

"This is so good," I say, fighting to keep the words clear and strong when I feel breathless. Out of the corner of my eye, I see Owen's lips tilt.

"I've always loved this restaurant," Diana says. "The cook's phenomenal."

"I'm so impressed," Addy says, unaware that her brother-in-law's fingers are making a slow trek up my leg.

I didn't realize until now that Owen's left-handed, but I'm grateful for it. He keeps spooning his mushroom risotto into his mouth like nothing's happening, while his right hand teases, moving up until it meets the frayed edge of my shorts and slips underneath. I widen my legs, praying those long, rough fingers can reach where I need them. He pushes against the resistance of the denim, running the tip of his middle finger over my center before circling my clit.

While Addy, Harrison, and Diana are distracted, discussing the quality of the locally sourced vegetables, Owen leans over to whisper, "Next time, I want you in a dress."

My ridiculous whimper brings everyone's attention back to me. I cough. "It's . . . just really, really good."

Addy's brow furrows, and she glances between me and Owen like we're a riddle she's determined to solve. I fight against the flush in my cheeks.

"I like the changes they've made," Harrison says, leaning forward to catch my eye. "How does this compare to the restaurants you've worked in?"

Owen turns to me, a smirk on his face. "Yeah, Thea. What do you think?"

That smirk paired with his warm fingers should be illegal. He slips his hand from between my legs, stroking the sensitive skin of my inner thighs instead, and I don't know if I'm grateful for the space or desperate for him to finish what he started.

"It's, um . . ." I clear my throat, trying to focus enough to form a coherent response.

I glance around the restaurant. It's stunning when you stop thirsting over your sorta-but-not-quite boyfriend to look at the space. It must be a newer renovation, with light wood floors paired with crisp white tile along the main wall. Touches of greenery and light blues add to the soft, contemporary space. It looks like it popped right off a Pinterest inspiration board. But it's nearly empty, making what should be an airy, open space feel desolate.

"It's beautiful," I say diplomatically, "but . . . a bit . . . quiet?"

Now that I see it, I can't unsee it. I want to go back to Owen's fingers overwhelming all my other senses, but Camila's disappeared from behind the desk, and I see the expressions of horror on the patrons closer to the front of the restaurant from here, and I can't stop myself from checking in.

"I'm sorry, I'll be right back," I say, pushing back from the table and mourning the way Owen's hand slides off my thigh.

Camila slips out of the back as I walk up. "They scare you off already?"

"Just needed to stretch my legs," I say. "A quiet night?"

She winces. "Unfortunately, not. The restaurant used to be popular with the town *and* the guests, but we got hit with a kitchen fire a couple years ago and took the opportunity to renovate. Another nice restaurant opened downtown while we were getting up and running, and it's been hard to get people up the mountain ever since."

Before I can speak, Camila's face suddenly pinches like she's smelled something horrible.

"Excuse me," she says primly, walking a few feet to the door with WOMEN printed in bold across the frosted window.

A second passes before she starts retching. The same guests from before look dubiously at their food and then back at the door Camila disappeared through. I awkwardly wave, and they lift their hand in return.

Camila comes out with a bright smile. "Has Aunt Diana tried to turn this into a double wedding yet?

My brows pull together. "Are you okay?"

Her smile falters a bit. "Of course! Why would you ask?"

I look over at the patrons, who are all watching us closely, then position myself with my back to them. I point at the door, then mimic throwing up. And her eyes go wide.

"Y'all could hear that?" When I scrunch up my nose and nod, she mutters to herself in Spanish.

"Do you need to go home?" I ask.

She sighs, her hand landing on her bump. "Contrary to what Nana says, the condition is not, in fact, catching."

I point at the cantaloupe on her stomach. "Aren't you a little far along for that?"

"Yes, but this little parasite"—her smile is so indulgent that you just know her daughter is going to be spoiled beyond all reason—"is an overachiever. The doctor said it'll continue all the way through, and with the wedding events, I forgot to grab the refill of my anti-nausea meds before work."

"Can I get you anything? Ginger ale or crackers or something?"

"Oh, I tried all of that, trust me. The only thing that works is the medication and a flat surface until it can take effect." Her face goes pinched again. "Excuse me one minute."

She turns on her heel again, posture straight and a calm look on her face, but the chorus of gagging immediately picks back up. A minute or so later, she's back like nothing ever happened.

"So your plan is to just keep throwing up every ten minutes all night?"

Her smile is brittle. "This has been my life for the past four months. If there's a toilet in this building, I've puked in it. I can't leave the restaurant."

"What if I managed it?" I ask before I can think it through. I've never managed a restaurant, but I've been in them my entire working life. How hard could it be for a couple of hours? There are only three tables filled, for god's sake, including the Hayes table.

Her eyes go wide. "Seriously?"

"Of course. I've worked in restaurants for over ten years. I'm sure I can do it."

Camila rushes around the podium and wraps her arms around me, the little bump between us pushing against my stomach. "I could kiss you!"

"Not until you brush your teeth. And have written permission from Mira. I bet she could kill me with two fingers."

A devilish smile crosses Camila's face, and she bounces her eyebrows. "Oh, she could, and you'd thank her the whole time."

I'm still laughing when Addy pops up next to me.

"What's going on, Tia?" Addy asks, a tightness to her smile as she glances back to the table where Diana is watching us. She's frustrated at me for leaving the dinner, but I didn't plan on being away for so long. I planned for my check on Camila to be quick, but she needs me. The restaurant needs me.

While I talk her through the situation, Camila excuses herself right on cue, like the universe decided to provide evidence.

"What can I help with?" Addy asks when Camila comes back out.

Camila looks at me and shrugs. "Nothing, I think we're good. Thea's the one who worked in a restaurant, right?"

"Are you sure you don't need anything? I'd love to help."

"Just some Zofran and a flat surface." She smacks a kiss on my cheek. "I fucking love you, Thea Pappas."

Addy's lips thin, looking between the two of us, and I think that's envy running through her eyes.

"Why don't you help me?" I ask Addy.

She slides a hand over the smooth fabric of her sundress. "It's fine. I'll go back to the table."

Shit, she feels left out, and now I feel terrible. All Addy wants is to be a part of this family, and I can tell Camila choosing my help over hers—even though I'm the one with the experience—makes her feel like she doesn't have a place here.

"No, stay. I could use the help," I say, giving Camila a *help me out here* look that she doesn't register as her face turns green again.

"I said it's fine, Thea," Addy snaps, then sighs. "While you were gone, Diana invited us for a spa trip tomorrow afternoon."

"Owen and I are supposed to start on the cake tomorrow," I say, grateful to have the excuse not to spend the day with Diana doing god knows what people do on spa days.

"That's what he said, so Diana said we could go late." Addy must see my hesitation, because she steps closer. "Please. I need you."

"Wouldn't you rather get some one-on-one time with her?"

"She's only interested in me if you're there," she says, keeping her tone light and teasing, but there's an undercurrent of bitterness there. "Same for the rest of the family."

"Addy—"

"I'm joking," she says, rolling her eyes as she backs toward the table. "But please, come. Help me win her over. You're better at this than I am."

It wasn't a joke, but I can't say that when we're standing in the middle of a restaurant, the Hayeses still watching us and Camila coming out of the bathroom any second. The best I can do for her is show up and make sure Diana sees just how special Addy is, so I nod and promise I'll be there.

Once Camila finishes her fourth trip to the bathroom, she walks me through the space and runs off to get her meds. I settle behind the hostess desk, but it's quiet enough that I can walk around a bit, chatting with the couple of guests and asking about their stay. It's comforting, being back in a setting like this.

The rest of my table says a quick goodbye when they finish dinner, but Owen dawdles, coming up to me a few minutes after everyone else has left.

"You look like you're having a good time," he says, leaning his elbows on the opposite side of the hostess station.

I let out a contented sigh, looking over the restaurant that has filled up more in the last half hour. "I am. The bustle of a restaurant has always been my happy place. I just hope I can find it again at home."

"You will," he says, and his utter confidence rubs off on me. I *will* figure it out.

"Just so you know," I say quietly, "in my head, I'm kissing you goodnight right now."

His head drops forward, shielding his smile for a second before he looks back up at me. "Six days."

The heat and promise in those two words send a shiver down my spine. "Six days," I say back, and my eyes follow him as he leaves, giving me one last smile over his shoulder.

It's only three hours before Camila returns, rested and pumped with enough drugs to keep her from vomiting for the rest of the night. She demands she repay me with a drink, and the two of us sit on stools behind the hostess stand, whiskey in my hand and water in hers. We chat about her plans for the restaurant and ways to build community, things I've seen be successful at Cibare and other ideas that we all thought would work that fell flat.

The rest of the night flies by. And when I lie in bed that night, I can't help thinking about how much I loved the work at Cibare, even if Gordon was the worst, and how—maybe—if I can grovel in just the right way, I can get my home back.

Chapter 22

OWEN

Another night of dreams filled with Thea. Her touch and laugh and smile. I don't know how I'm going to make it through five more days of this torture.

I have a flight booked for Sunday night after Harrison and Addy's goodbye brunch, but I'm hoping Thea will let me join her drive home instead. Normally I'd avoid that drive at all costs, but time with Thea sounds incredible. Hours of talking, learning more about her. Us taking turns behind the wheel, never letting go of each other's hands.

A hand clamps over my shoulder, jolting me from my daydream.

"A bit distracted there, big brother?" Harrison asks, his dimpled smile stretching across his face. "I called your name three times."

"Sorry," I say, scratching at the back of my neck.

"Thinking about a certain future sister-in-law of mine?" His brows bounce, and I shake my head at him. "Oh, come on. You still have feelings for her."

"We're just friends now."

Only five more days of lying.

"Yeah, you saying my bride-to-be is afraid you'll want to kiss her sister again screams 'just friends.'"

I shove him but can't hold in my laugh. "You're the worst."

I turn to leave, but he grabs my arm. "Do you have a minute?

I wanted to talk to you about the stuff I mentioned a couple days ago."

Right. The business stuff. My head aches at the thought of the work this is going to create, but I can't keep putting it off.

"Sure," I say, "but we need to be quick. I'm supposed to meet Thea in the kitchen soon."

I've mapped out what we'll need to do to give Harrison and Addy the wedding cake they deserve. We'll bake the cakes and make the buttercream today. Tomorrow, we'll level, torte, and crumb-coat the cakes. I smile at the thought of Thea, her curls piled on her head and her tongue peeking out between her lips as she saws the cake leveler back and forth. Friday, while Thea's doing stuff with Addy, I'll add another coat of buttercream, getting that perfect texture. Then Saturday morning, I'll sneak Thea out of the bridal suite to help me stack and decorate the cakes. Maybe I'll even have time to sneak in a few kisses.

I follow Harrison into Camila's office, my muscles tensed. I wonder which department he'll want to move to now. Eventually, he's going to run out. And when he does, will he leave Hayes completely? The thought makes me sick.

Harrison releases a breath as he sits behind Camila's desk, then lifts his eyes to me. "I want to take on more of a leadership role at Hayes."

My mouth falls open. Not where I thought he was going with this. "What?"

At my surprise, Harrison straightens his posture, the muscles in his neck tightening. "Addy and I are building a life together, and I want to provide her with the stability she's always wanted. I've been at the company for three years now, and you became president after only one year. I'm not saying I want to be co-president or anything—I'm not trying to step on your toes—but I think I deserve a bigger role."

I open and close my mouth a few times before I can find my

words. "Yeah, I took the president role after a year, but I also worked there after school every day from fifteen on."

His jaw ticks. "I'm learning, and I don't think it's fair to punish me because you and Mom never cared enough about my future with the company to let me work there in high school."

To *let* him work? My hackles rise, but then a memory sneaks up on me. Harrison, sixteen with braces and a face full of acne, asking if he could work at Hayes. Twenty-four-year-old me, newly made president and so overwhelmed I could barely breathe, telling him to enjoy his time in high school, that there would be plenty of time for work. I was trying to save him from living my life. But in trying to keep him from having Hayes pushed on him, I took the choice away from him altogether.

"I'm sorry," I say, and his brows pull together. "I didn't realize. I didn't mean to make you feel left out of the company, and I'm sure Mom didn't either. Have you talked to her?"

He scoffs. "Mom and I don't talk." My brows pull together, and he scoffs again. "Don't pretend you haven't noticed. I'm the spare. She doesn't care what I do. Fuck, she's more invested in your ex than in my fiancée."

There's a knot in the back of my throat, making it impossible to swallow or speak. Was I so resentful of Mom that I didn't even see how it was affecting Harrison? He's always been so happy-go-lucky, the most confident person in the room, so I assumed there was nothing to worry about. I should have paid more attention.

"Stop," Harrison says, his voice strong. "You're beating yourself up. I'm not mad. Really, I've done a lot of work on this, and I've realized I'm not responsible for Mom's behavior. All I can control is what I choose. The same applies to you. I just want to think about what's next. We're co-owners of the company, and it's about time we started acting like it."

I'm not sure what to say. He has a point, and I wish I could go back in time and give him the choice instead of assuming he wouldn't want it either. As much as I'd like to pass along some of the responsibility, this decision won't just affect me. Hundreds of people depend on Hayes for their livelihoods, and I'm not sold on the idea that he'll stick around. I think he's more interested in the idea of our family company than the work itself, and we need consistent leadership. Not someone who may decide on a whim that Hayes isn't for him.

I roll my lips together. "I'm not saying no, but there's a lot we'd need to talk about. Why don't you focus on enjoying your honeymoon? We can talk more about it once you're back."

That's the best I can do. I don't want to call out his unreliable behavior during his wedding week. These are supposed to be the best days of his life. When he gets back, I'll explain my hesitancy and we can work out what needs to be done to earn my trust.

Harrison's shoulders droop. "Yeah. Sure. We'll talk another time."

A stone sinks in my gut at his devastated face, but he's out of the room before I can say anything else.

* * *

Thea's already in the kitchen when I arrive, fiddling around with some bowls I'd set out earlier. Her face breaks into a wide smile when she spots me, and some of the tension from my conversation with Harrison seeps out.

"Here I was thinking you were standing me up," she says.

I reach her in a couple of steps, dipping my head to place a soft kiss on the sensitive skin beneath her ear. "Never."

Her breath stutters, and I kiss her again just to feel her shiver against me.

"You gonna put me to work or am I just here to look pretty?" she asks, leaning against the counter while I pull ingredients out of the refrigerator.

I slide a bowl of lemons in front of her and smack her ass. "Get to work zesting, smartass."

"Yes, chef," she says in her husky voice, and I have to reach down to adjust myself. That's not what we need right now.

Addy gave me free reign on this. We settled on a lemon blueberry cake, relatively easy since Thea doesn't have much experience, but still delicious.

Thea and I get to work, and she nails each task. Yes, I give her the easiest jobs while I focus on the more complicated ones, but I love watching the way she lights up at every success—zested and juiced lemons, perfectly measured ingredients, everything combined as the mixer runs at a slow, steady speed. I want to teach her more. Teach her everything. To watch each time that disbelieving smile takes over her face. To praise her so often and so thoroughly that the disbelief fades completely.

With the cakes baking in the oven, I move on to the blueberry reduction. It's soothing, combining the blueberries, lemon juice, sugar, and water in a saucepan, letting all my other worries fade as the creation takes over my focus. Thea stands with her chin on my shoulder, watching every step in fascination.

"You lied to me," she says, but her tone is good-natured.

I glance at her, then back at the pan. "You slander me. I'd never. Haven't you heard? I'm the good cousin."

"Do you think they'd all still consider you the good cousin if they knew you had sex in their closet?" she asks, moving so she's leaning on the counter behind me.

A smile quirks my lips, but I don't want to give in, addicted to the push and pull of our conversations. I love when she throws out comments like that, unashamed of what we did. "No one would believe you."

"Oh, I have proof. You didn't see the camera?"

"Damn," I say, glancing over my shoulder, and her smile grows. "Did you at least get my good side?"

"They're all good sides," she says with a wink.

I've never had this before, this ease of conversation. With

anyone, but especially with someone I was romantically interested in.

Everything with Thea is different. I don't know if it's because we got to know each other a bit that weekend when romance was off the table, or if it's because she makes it so clear she enjoys my company, or if it's just something about *her* that can't be fully named. But I love it.

"Back to the lying," she says, and when I scoff, I get rewarded with that low, warm laugh that's becoming vital to my existence. "When we were talking in the vineyard, you told me you didn't have a passion."

My eyebrows draw together as I pull the reduction off the stove. "Because I don't."

She's looking at me like I'm dense. When I shrug my shoulders, she gestures with both hands around her. "This. This is what I'm talking about."

An incredulous laugh bursts out of me. "This is a hobby. Everyone should have hobbies."

"Are you telling me if you had the option to spend every day in the kitchen, baking and developing new ideas, you wouldn't take it?"

Something deep inside me warms at the image she paints, a little bakery where I can experiment with recipes. A small town full of friends who stop by first thing in the morning so they can grab whatever new muffin or scone I cooked up before they sell out. Thea giving me a quick kiss and swiping the to-go coffee mug I filled for her before she runs off to work.

But that's not real life, so I force a laugh. "Like anyone would pay for my cakes."

Thea slides over to the stovetop where the reduction is cooling, dipping a spoon into the mixture and bringing it to her mouth. The moan that rips from her throat nearly puts me back on my knees for her.

"Did you see everyone's reaction to your practice cake? I'd

murder people for something you baked. My morals may be questionable—you know, with the fucking in a closet and all that—but I'm sure all those good, virtuous folks would at least pay money."

I choose to ignore the dig she made at herself. The last time I challenged her on that, she clammed up, and we're having too good of a day to let it be ruined. "I'll just record the sounds you make. That's all the advertisement I'd need. People will come flooding in just in the hopes of catching you."

"What? These sounds?"

The noise that comes out of Thea's mouth has me howling in laughter. It's technically a moan, but it's so over-the-top. I rush over to cover her mouth, and she spins away from me. She tries to bolt, but I grab her hips a split second before she'd have been out of reach, yanking her back against me. I wrap one arm around her middle and the other over her mouth.

"You're going to get us arrested for public indecency. Or worse, bring my family in here," I say, laughing so hard both our bodies are shaking with the force of it.

She tilts her head to look up at me, licking my hand to get me to pull it away from her mouth, then grins triumphantly. "You'd look good with a couple prison tattoos."

"How about I stay out of prison, but I'll get a cupcake tattooed on my ass for you?"

Spending time with Thea has made me feel freer, like I'm someone with no responsibility to anything except my enjoyment. And when she laughs at my latest joke, staring up at me like I'm the real treat, I have a startling revelation. Even though she'd say I couldn't know after a couple of days, I'm certain beyond any doubt that I'm falling in love with her.

"If you two are having sex in my kitchen, I swear by all that is holy I'll sic Mira on you."

I cough and slide away from Thea as Camila lets the door swing closed behind her.

"Nothing's happening," I say, shooting a smile at Thea. "She's just a chaos demon."

Thea raises a brow at Camila. "I thought you couldn't be around the baking smells. Isn't that the reason you 'couldn't help Owen'?"

Camila rolls her eyes, slipping something small out of her pocket. "First, don't pretend you aren't ecstatic that I gave you an excuse to spend time with Owen. Second . . ."

She slips the little bit of plastic—a swimmer's nose clip—over her nostrils, and hops up onto the counter, holding her hands wide like she's displaying her brilliance.

"There, all smells stay out, and I can still bug you two," she says, sounding like Rudolph wearing his fake nose. "What are you up to?"

Thea smirks back. "I'm trying to convince Owen he's good enough to sell his own stuff."

Camila just shakes her head, a sad little smile on her face. "That's a pipe dream if I've ever heard one."

My chest feels like it's going to cave in. Not that I'd ever do anything with it, but that little dream Thea painted was tempting, and knowing my oldest friend—the one who patiently tried every failed concoction and begged for seconds of every success—thinks I can't pull it off hurts.

Thea face hardens. "If you don't think he can do this, I don't trust your judgment for shit."

Cami's eyes widen in glee. "Feisty."

Thea lifts her chin. I love watching her defend the people she cares about, her willingness to throw herself into a battle that isn't hers out of nothing but love. I mean, obviously she doesn't love *me*, but I like to think I matter, and the way she's subconsciously positioning herself between me and Cami, like she can protect me from the hurt of her words, says I do.

"What I *meant*," Cami continues, "was that he'd never make the choice to leave his family's company, even if he should."

She looks directly at me for the last part, like it's a given rather than something that's rearranging the world underneath my feet. I know Nana thinks I should leave. She's been bugging me about it for years, but it's always felt like she wanted me to come up to North Carolina more than she thought I should do something else with my life. I figured it was just her dreaming of a world where almost all her grandkids were in the same town as her.

Camila looks back at Thea. "While he spirals, can I talk to you?"

Thea reaches over to squeeze my hand once, then says, "What's up?"

"Alone," Camila says, shooting a glance at me.

"She doesn't want to be your mistress, Cami," I say, turning my attention back to the reduction.

Camila rolls her eyes, but Thea barks out a laugh, and I think I could be content with only making Thea laugh for the rest of my life.

"Sorry, but he's right. Should have made your move a few days ago," she says.

A low growl rumbles in my throat, and I tug her to my side.

Cami groans. "I hate being the only one who knows about this. Y'all are disgusting and Mira doesn't like gossip."

"Do you need to talk now?" Thea asks. "I offered to run into town to grab the wedding bands from the jeweler."

Camila hops off the counter. "No worries. Just find me when you get back."

After Camila leaves, Thea grabs her purse from the counter. Before she can reach the door, I snake my arm around her waist.

"You're leaving already?" I ask. "We haven't made the buttercream yet."

She lifts her brow at me. "You already told me that's a one-person job."

I drop my mouth to the place where her shoulder and neck meet. "What about my moral support?"

She laughs but tilts her head to give me better access. "Poor baby, having to make a batch of buttercream without someone to build up your ego."

I twirl her to face me, loving the way her hands land on my chest like they belong there. "Stay."

She nibbles on her lip. "I wish I could, but I promised I'd get the rings before the spa trip with your mom. We're supposed to meet her at four."

It's only 12:30 PM. It'll take about thirty minutes to make the Swiss meringue buttercream, plus a twenty-minute trip into town. Plenty of time to get the rings, even lunch, and still be back before she needs to meet Addy and my mom.

"We can make it work. Keep me company, and then we can go into town together and be back well before four."

"I don't know," she says as her fingertips absentmindedly drift over the fabric of my shirt. "I should probably just get them and get back."

I bend my knees to catch her gaze. "Imagine it. A couple hours of us hanging out with no worries about who may see us."

"That *does* sound nice."

"Then say you'll stay," I say.

She drops her head to my shoulder. I want to gather her even closer, to keep her there forever.

"Okay, but we need to be more careful. The wedding's so close. We can't get caught now. No more stolen moments in closets or staring at each other from across the room. And good lord, no more touching underneath the table."

I laugh, and she shushes me, placing both hands over my mouth as I tighten my arms around her waist.

"Fine, but I'd like to set the expectation up front that I'm going to kiss you as many times as possible today while we're away from my family," I say, the words muffled by her hands.

The sexiest smirk slides over her lips. "You better."

Chapter 23

THEA

We fucked up.

I can hardly see through the sheets of rain pounding the windshield. Thunder booms so loudly that it shakes my poor little car. My tires fight to hold on to the road as it weaves around the mountains.

"Thea, we have to pull over," Owen says, clutching the "oh shit" handle on the ceiling like Hell's trying to suck us through a portal and his grip's the only thing preventing our demise.

"We can't," I say. "I promised her I'd be there."

About twenty minutes ago, the beautiful, clear blue sky was suddenly taken over by dark, ominous clouds, and ten minutes ago—thirty minutes from us reaching the inn—the skies opened up.

If I had stuck to my original plan, I'd have made it back before the storm. Instead, Owen and I grabbed lunch at this adorable place a few blocks out of downtown that was covered from floor to ceiling with kitschy paintings of Scottish terriers and then wandered around downtown Elk Ridge.

I told myself that this thing with him isn't selfish. We're just exploring what we could be without making it a whole dramatic thing, right? But my decision today *was* selfish. I had a simple task—grab the rings and get back in time to back Addy up at the spa—and instead I spent the day laughing and flirting.

Owen lets out another hiss as we take a curve too close to

the edge for comfort. "Addy would rather have you at the wedding than you die trying to get back for a goddamn spa trip."

Logically I know this is true, but she's been so stressed over her relationship with this family. I don't think my friendship with Camila or Diana's obsession with me and Owen has helped. And even if I didn't feel guilty over my role in all this, she asked me to be there. That's enough. I screwed this up by choosing my wants over Addy's needs.

And it's not like we're *actually* going to die.

I plan to just keep driving and ignore Owen's concerns, until my tires hit a slick spot that sends our car coasting. Everything in me goes hot and tight all at once, and my eyes shoot to Owen to see the same look of panic on his face.

All the training from years of driving in Florida thunderstorms kicks in even as my heart thunders as wildly as the weather outside. I take my foot off the pedal, gently steering us until we get enough traction to pull off onto one of the runaway ramps, and I bring the car to a stop.

As soon as the parking brake's on, Owen's hands are on me, unclipping my seat belt and running up my arms and over my shoulders as he pulls me into his lap. "It's okay. We're okay."

I bury my head in his neck, muttering "fuck" on repeat as my heart rate comes down. His warmth isn't enough to stop the way my body shakes.

"We have to get off the road," he says, placing a kiss on my temple.

My eyes flood with tears. "We're only twenty minutes away. We can make it."

His hands come to my cheeks. "These roads are dangerous in the best of conditions. But right now, all it takes is one more puddle for us to go off the side of the mountain."

I'm not ready to give up. "Let's just call the inn. I'm sure there's someone with a big truck that can handle the roads like this."

"Doubt we have service," Owen says, but pulls his phone out to check, confirming what he knew he'd see.

"Let's just wait here for it to clear up."

"And wait for another car to hit that same spot and slam into us?" he asks. I glance out his window at the steep slope before he sets me back in the driver's seat. "These storms can go for hours, and I'm not letting you kill yourself because you feel guilty. Now put the car in drive and follow my directions somewhere safe."

I blink away the tears, but do what he says, driving slowly and carefully to a dirt road. Another couple hundred yards of mud later, he has me pull off by a wooden fence.

"Where are we?" I ask.

Owen leans forward, looking out the windshield at the torrent. "The far side of my Uncle Dennis's property. There's a barn about a hundred feet through that gate. Let's spend the storm there instead of stuck in this tiny car. Yeah?"

His question is soft, like if he presses too hard I'll break into a thousand shards, but when I give him a stiff nod, he throws his door open, bolting through the pouring rain. I head out right behind him, and within seconds, I'm drenched. It takes less than a minute to reach the barn, but I feel each step, each pelt of the raindrops on my skin, like the lash of a whip.

You broke Addy's trust.

She asked you for one thing.

You left her alone when she told you she needs you.

You're selfish, just like Mom, and Addy's going to hate you just like she hates her.

I bolt past Owen, yanking on the handle with enough force to send it flying. The barn door bounces aggressively off the metal stopper. It ricochets halfway back before Owen gets ahold of it, slipping in behind me and sliding it all the way closed. He huffs a laugh, shaking his head so water droplets fly everywhere.

My body is vibrating, and I pace the space between hay bales. "I can't believe I let this happen."

Owen walks over, rubbing his hands up and down my arms to warm me. "We'll head back once the storm stops. It should only be a few hours."

"In a few hours, I'll have missed the spa trip, assuming they even go when they can't find us. Fuck! They're going to cancel the trip and this was Addy's chance to win your mom over."

"It'll be okay," he says calmly, like the world isn't falling apart around me right now. "How could we have known a storm like this would come in?"

"We couldn't, which is why I should have just gone straight there and straight back."

"Sweetheart," he says, brushing one of my wet curls behind my ear. "We'll sort something out. It's just a spa trip."

"To you," I say, louder than I want. "To you, it's just a spa trip. But to Addy, that massage or facial or whatever the fuck we were supposed to do—this whole damn wedding—is a representation of her future with your family. And she asked for my help, trusted me when I've screwed up so many things for her. And I broke that trust. I was selfish and—"

"Stop," he says, his voice coming out sharp, and he paces a few steps away from me.

My heart screams, *Here it is, Thea. That last push that sends him running for the hills*. If there's anything my life has taught me, it's that everyone has their limit. Push hard enough, and they'll eventually break. And when they do, they'll leave you behind. Even knowing this, my traitorous heart held out hope that Owen would be different. It's crying out now, watching as he puts more and more distance between us.

When he turns back to me, there's fire in his eyes. "You are not selfish. From the second you stepped foot in North Carolina, you've done nothing but give to the people around you. Keeping up this ruse—which I'm to blame for—so that Addy and Harrison's day isn't ruined. Running all over these damn mountains to help Addy. Working for free so Camila can get her medication."

"Yes, I've helped, but I've also had to work really hard not to screw things up, too. Do you know how many times I almost bit your mom's head off in the past few days?"

"She's deserved to have her head bitten off!" Owen says.

I laugh through the tears, and he smiles, his smallest of smiles. The one he gives when he's almost embarrassed at having made me laugh.

He steps closer, taking my hand between his. "From what I've seen, you only get angry when someone's being treated badly, and it's beautiful to watch. You have the kindest heart, and you're protective of your people. That's a good thing, and I hate every person in your past who made you think you're anything less than perfect."

His words strike the middle of my chest, and I rub at the ache. "So everyone?" I whisper, unable to stop taking swings at myself.

"They're idiots," he says fiercely.

"Easy for you to say right now, but there's normally a reason for a pattern." I shrug, trying to brush off the way my insides feel like they're being eviscerated. "I'm not the type of person people keep."

Owen's eyes fill with tears. "What if *I* want to keep you?"

My limbs shake as heat spreads through me with the most overwhelming sensation of fear and exhilaration. I've never been wanted, not beyond a few hookups, and it makes no sense that this man—this kind, generous, gorgeous man—would be the first. It doesn't line up with my worldview at all.

But maybe he's right. Maybe my worldview is skewed and there's truth in what Cece told me on the mountain. That we believe what people say we are, and sometimes we need the right person at the right time to help us see ourselves clearly.

"Why?" I ask, stepping closer and bringing our bodies nearly flush. "Why do you want to keep me?"

Owen bites his bottom lip against his smile. "You're just digging for compliments now."

I shrug a little, running my hands up his chest. "Humor me."

He drops his head, running his nose along the curve of my jaw. "Too many reasons to count. How about how your laugh invigorates me more than my morning coffee?"

"I *do* have a great laugh," I say, and he smiles, the curve of it stamped onto my skin.

"How about the way everything inside me screams to touch you anytime you get within reach? To keep you close. That no matter how hard I tried, I couldn't make any of it feel fake."

He presses a kiss to the underside of my jaw, letting his tongue swipe against the pulse point there, and I moan. My hands come to his shoulders, clutching them to keep from sliding to the floor.

"And when I'm with you, I don't feel like the caretaker brother or reliable son or helpful cousin. I feel like I'm just me."

He pulls back to look at me. I run my hand up and into his hair, damp from the rain. "I'm glad I get *just you.* Because I think you may be my favorite person."

"I know you're mine."

Those words destroy our resolve to keep this new game going. I tug on his hair, smashing my lips against his. Our tongues vie for dominance as his hands move to my ass, squeezing tight, causing us both to moan and pant into each other's mouths. His grip shifts to the backs of my thighs, lifting until I wrap my legs around his waist, grinding down on him.

"Fuck," he moans, and I swallow the word. "I need you."

"Condom?" *Please, God, let him have one this time.*

He nods, but doesn't stop kissing me, taking my bottom lip between his teeth.

"Owen," I whine, still writhing in his arms. But I need more, so desperately I think I'll explode.

"Wallet. Back pocket," he says, then steals my lips again as he walks us farther into the barn.

I slide my hands down his body until I find it, letting myself get in one little grope of his ass. Owen sets me down, having blindly led us to the haystack in the corner. He grabs a blanket from the low wall a couple of steps away, laying it out over the makeshift bed before kissing me again. I fumble with his wallet, feeling for the telltale foil square. When I look at what I've pulled out, three condoms rest in my palm.

I look up at Owen with wide eyes. "Pretty optimistic, aren't we?"

He chuckles, pushing my half-dried, wild curls back from my face. "Went straight to the store to grab a box when we left the closet. I wasn't risking a repeat of last time."

I laugh, so loud it drowns out the storm, and Owen's smile grows, that elusive dimple popping in his cheek. I'm helpless against the urge to kiss it. When I pull back, our eyes meet, and his shine with such devotion that my breath catches. I'm sure he sees the same reflected from me.

He kisses me again, but it's different this time. Soft. Slow, like he's memorizing every millimeter of my lips and the way our mouths slide together.

As the kiss escalates, I wrestle with my jeans, but they've been suctioned onto my legs by the rain, and I groan in frustration. I need them gone. Need Owen's skin on mine. He chuckles at my pain as he sits me on the blanket, going to his knees to tug them off. The half smile I get when my legs are free has my heart shooting around my chest, slamming against the walls like it's trying to reach him. He plants a couple soft kisses to my calf, and I think he'll continue up my leg to the place I'm aching for him, but instead he stands, running his hands up the outside of my legs.

When I whine, he grins. "This isn't a hookup in a closet. No one's around for miles, the storm's raging, and I'm going to take my time."

I huff, pouting as I brace my hands behind me. He slowly unbuttons my flannel shirt, planting a kiss along my neck for every button he frees. Each kiss eats away at my resolve until I'm a squirming mess. He pushes it over my shoulders, revealing my plain white tank top. Nothing about it is special, but when Owen notices I'm once again not wearing a bra, he releases a groan that has my body clenching in anticipation. He reaches out one hand, slowly rubbing his thumb over my peaked nipple.

"Owen," I moan, arching into his too-light touch. "Put your mouth on me."

He runs his hand along the bottom of my tank, slipping just underneath so his warm hand stretches across my lower stomach, and I gasp.

"I want to see you, Thea. To savor my time with you. Can I do that?" he asks, sliding his hand another inch upward and bunching my shirt.

I've never been savored before. My past sexual interactions have been hard and fast. I told myself that was the type of sex I enjoyed, but I've never been more turned on than I am right now, with Owen's teasing fingers forcing me to wait for what we both so desperately want.

I want to say something clever. To be sexy, funny Thea, but there's no room in my mind for anything but desire, so I nod. That smile with the almost-dimple stretches across his face, but it's now laced with a reverence that I feel down to my bones. He slips his hand higher and higher, but still agonizingly slow, until the tank top is lifted away from me. I'm left in nothing but my cotton underwear, and Owen pushes my shoulder back to lay me out before him.

He stands over me, rubbing his hand over his mouth. "Fuck, Thea."

He slowly undresses himself, never taking his eyes off my body. I'd have thought being on display for someone would make me too self-conscious to be aroused, but the admiration in his eyes is intoxicating.

When he's finally undressed, he braces himself over me, running his lips down the column of my neck. I squirm, trying to hold back my reaction, but each place he touches lights on fire.

My arms tug him down, but Owen chuckles against my skin. "Not yet."

He explores every inch of me with his lips, a dedicated student of how to make me melt. A light brush over my collarbone earns him a shiver. His tongue laving my nipple gets him a full-body jolt. When he grazes his teeth over my hip bone, I cry out, lifting my hips toward him until he pins them with his forearm. But the most erotic part is the curve of his smile against my skin, the way he murmurs about how responsive I am. He never stops anywhere for long. Never gives me the relief I crave. By the time he settles between my legs, I'm shaking.

"You've been so good for me. So patient," he says, the heat of his words blowing over my underwear.

"Owen," I whine.

"Here?" he asks, running the flat of his tongue up between my legs and sucking my clit through the embarrassingly wet fabric. One swipe of his tongue, not even directly on me, and I'm seconds from coming.

Tears of relief slide down my cheeks. "Yes, right there."

He slips my underwear down, and the second the fabric is out of the way, his mouth is back on me. My hips jerk up toward his mouth, and he wraps my legs around his shoulders, burying his face between my legs like there's nowhere in the world he'd rather be.

He runs his tongue over me—one, twice, three times—and I'm already primed to explode.

"You're delicious," Owen says. "Your pussy is the only thing I want to taste for the rest of my life."

His words paired with the way his lips close around my clit, sucking hard, send me over the edge, screaming to the wood-beamed ceiling as my hands clutch at his soft bronze hair.

Owen drops his forehead to my lower stomach, panting against my skin. "You're just—god, you're perfect."

I blindly grope beside me for the condoms I'd dropped on the blanket earlier, throwing him the first one my hand closes around. "If you don't get up here and fuck me, I'm going to lose my mind."

"Pretty sure I lost my mind the second you walked back into my life." He grins at me as he tears the condom open.

Owen pushes himself to stand, eyes moving hungrily over me as he slips the condom on his incredible cock and gives it a rough tug.

"Owen, please," I beg.

In the thirteen years since I started having sex, I've never once begged. I've demanded and asked and taken, but I've never been so desperate that I'd beg to have someone inside me. But I need him, can feel where I'm empty and throbbing for him, and I'd crawl on my hands and knees to have him if that's what it took.

He lowers himself between my shaking legs. "You don't need to beg, Thea. Not for what's already yours."

I whimper when he nudges at my entrance. He goes slow, watching my face with rapt attention as he sinks in, inch by glorious inch. When he's fully seated, he lowers his mouth, brushing his lips over mine.

"You do know that, don't you?" he asks.

My brain is too scattered by the incredible stretch of him to even consider what he means. "What?"

"Do you know"—he grinds against me, filling me even more and putting the most perfect pressure on my clit—"that you already own me?"

He pulls back slowly, then fills me again with a hard thrust. I wrap my arms around him, running my nails down his back until I reach his ass, gripping it with both hands and reveling in the glory that is his body. He groans, dropping his head to the crook of my neck and nipping at my skin. I roll my hips to meet his, spurring him on.

More, more, more.

He growls, one hand coming to my thigh and squeezing so tightly it's almost painful, but the bite of it just pushes me closer to where I need to be.

"Tell me you know," he grinds out, his other hand twining in my hair and tugging to force me to meet his gaze.

No one's ever belonged to me. No one's ever *wanted* to belong to me, but there's no room for doubt when he looks at me like that. The intensity in his eyes shoots me off like a rocket, and I can't tear my gaze from his as I come around his cock, calling out, "I know."

He groans, hard and ragged and desperate, and his pace picks up. "Fuck, Thea—so good, so fucking good for me—fuck, fuck, fuck."

He slams into me one last time, his body shuddering as he follows me into ecstasy.

As he drops himself over me, peppering my neck with kisses, I believe him. He is mine, and I think I may be his, too.

Owen grabs his shirt, walking out into the rain, naked as Adam, to wet it again, then brings it back to run over my slick body, skimming his lips along my skin and murmuring praise. How good I was and how stunning I look and how special I am.

He pulls me into his arms after, his fingertips tracing circles on my skin as we both listen to the storm raging outside. Thunder echoing off the slopes. Droplets of rain hitting the roof. The way the world quiets for a couple of hours, freezing in time with nothing to do but wait and savor the moment. The calm *in* the storm instead of before it.

So I let myself embrace it, knowing there will be another storm to manage when we get back. But for now, I have warmth and joy and Owen.

And a three-condom promise that needs fulfilling.

Chapter 24

OWEN

I don't know if I've slept better in my life than with the comforting weight of Thea's head on my chest, which makes it even more startling when she bursts out of my arms like a wild animal escaping its cage. I jump up, pulling her behind me to protect her from the unknown threat, but as I look around the barn, there's nothing but us.

Thea whimpers, and I spin to look at her. "What is it? What's wrong?"

She's looking at the door, light drifting in through the slats. "That doesn't look like sunset, does it?"

Now that she's pointed it out, I can see what she means. The sun streaming into the barn is softer than it should be. The air is cooler, and even before I dig out my phone, I know we slept through the night.

"Shit," Thea mutters, moving around the barn to gather her things.

I follow Thea's lead. "It'll be okay. We'll get going now."

We make the short walk from the barn to the car, only for the morning to go from bad to worse. A tree limb lays across the hood, and I spot a crack in the windshield, splinters shooting out from the point of contact. I glance up at the oak trees over our heads, a dozen heavy branches stretching toward each other. With the storm as bad as it was, we're lucky the car was only hit by one.

I brace myself for Thea's reaction, facing her with my arms

outreached like I'm approaching a skittish animal. Her dark eyes are wider than I've ever seen them as she stares at the branch before slowly facing me. She holds my gaze for a handful of seconds, then a laugh bursts out of her mouth, so forceful it makes me jump. She bends at the waist, hands clasped over her knees as she continues laughing. I can't stop myself from joining—it's contagious, that sound on her lips—and I pull her to stand, wrapping her in my arms and kissing the top of her head. After a minute, she extracts herself and turns back to the car.

"Well," she says with shocking calm as she anchors her hands on her hips. "That tracks with how the past twenty-four hours have gone."

I slip my hands through her arms and rest them over her stomach. "I wouldn't say the past day's been all bad, would you?"

"There were a few highlights." She kisses the underside of my jaw.

I plant one last kiss on the side of her head, then walk over to the limb, giving it a tug. It's heavy, but not impossible for two people. I eye Thea's arms. "Got any muscles in those string beans?"

"I'll have you know I lifted ten whole pounds once."

I laugh, jerking my head toward the limb. She follows the unspoken instruction and takes a spot on the opposite side of the car. I count us down, and we lift. My side makes it a couple of inches off the hood, but hers barely budges. We try again. And again. And again, until she huffs and drops to the ground.

I walk around the car, expecting to find her crying or screaming in frustration, but instead she's lying flat on her back with her legs pointed up at the sky.

"What are you doing?" I ask, trying and failing to hold back my laughter.

She looks at me like it should be obvious. "My legs are stronger than my arms."

I laugh again, assuming she's just trying to lighten the mood, but she widens her eyes like an impatient schoolteacher waiting for her student to do what she said. She has me place her feet right under the limb, and I run back to my side. This time, after I count us down, we get the branch off the hood, making it half a foot down before it slips off Thea's feet, slamming back down onto the hood with a concerning thud.

Thea scrambles to her feet, eyeing the impressive new dent in the hood. "Fuck me."

I meet her on the other side of the car. "We should probably keep our focus on the car."

Thea laughs, then drops her head into my chest. "We're so screwed."

I run a hand over the dent. "This will need to be replaced anyway. Any objections to me just dragging the branch the rest of the way off?"

Thea shakes her head, and I wrap my hands around the limb. It slides off the hood, the knots leaving grooves no body shop owner could buff out.

I brush my hands together, looking over at Thea with a triumphant smile. "Let's see if this thing starts."

She rushes over to the driver's side, muttering what I think is a prayer under her breath. The key turns, but nothing happens. Thea groans and drops her head against the headrest.

"Can't a girl catch a break?" she yells at the ceiling.

I slip my phone out of my pocket—still no service—and run a hand down my face. "We'll have to hike to my uncle's house. It's only ten, maybe fifteen minutes from the barn."

She glances back at her car. "But what about—"

"I'll call my cousin Jourdan to come get it. She has an auto repair shop."

Thea looks over at the gate, and for a second I think she's going to refuse to leave her car, but then she groans, grabbing the ring box from the center console before climbing out. I'm a second behind her, and she gestures for me to lead the way. We reach for each other's hand at the same time, and I don't think I've ever wanted anything more than the casual intimacy of the move, the knowledge that she's seeking me out just like I am her.

We should rush, but by unspoken agreement we meander through the trees, savoring our last few minutes with nothing but the chirping robins to see our connection. My thumb makes slow, sweeping motions over the back of her hand as we share stories and dreams. She tells me what she loved about her old restaurant and the type of experience she wants out of her next job. I tell her my favorite things to bake and what staples I'd serve if I started something of my own.

When my uncle's house comes into view, Thea pulls me to a stop, placing a soft kiss on my lips, and my body melts at the sweetness of the gesture.

"I can't wait for Sunday," she whispers against my lips.

The day we can come clean and stop all this nonsense. "Me too."

We're on my uncle's doorstep when my phone recognizes the Wi-Fi and starts chirping with texts and voicemails. I share the password with Thea, and her phone lights up, too. One call to my mother, and they're on their way.

The bus pulls into Uncle Dennis's driveway ten minutes later, and dozens of my family members come pouring out. Lynne gets off last, looking down at the bus keys in her hand with a scowl, and I place a hand over my mouth to hide my smile.

My mom rushes over, tears rolling down her face. "We've been so worried."

I give her a tight squeeze to reassure her, then look over her head at Harrison. "We got caught in the storm and had to pull over."

Addy has her arms wrapped around Thea, her tears wetting Thea's shirt. "You're okay?"

"Yeah," Thea says, running a hand over her hair. "Yeah, I'm okay."

Addy's lip trembles, and Thea wraps an arm around her shoulder, whispering something into her ear that has her laughing even as she starts crying again. The sisters stay tangled up like that through the walk to the bus and the drive back to the inn.

"Can someone bring us breakfast in the kitchen?" I ask Harrison once we're back at the inn. "Thea and I have some work to do on the cake."

Thea steals another glance at Addy. "Is there someone else who can help? I just . . ."

I can see it now. Addy's shaking—subtly, but enough for Thea to feel it—and there's a blank expression in her eyes. When Thea pulls away to walk over to me, Addy's shoulders cave forward, like Thea's strength was the only thing keeping her upright.

The scent of cinnamon and fresh hay swirl around me when Thea comes close, triggering memories of the night before, the two of us wrapped around each other in our makeshift bed. "She needs me," she whispers.

I nod, running my hand down her arm. "I'll sort something out."

"Thank you," she says, smiling softly.

When I face my family, everyone's homed in on the small touch. I yank my hand away like I've been burned, and they all unfortunately clock that, too.

I turn to my mother, who's looking at Thea with a pinched expression, like she blames her for us getting caught in the storm.

"Can you help me with the cakes?" I ask.

Her face contorts into a pout. "I wish I could—you know I'd

do it in a heartbeat—but I'm going to town with Aunt Dawn today."

I cross my arms. "What for?"

She blinks at me, like she never expected me to call her out. And I guess there's legitimacy to her surprise. I've never done it before. It's been a defining part of our relationship that if she can't do something, I'll take care of it instead. But I can't do this on my own, and I'm tired of acting like it's fine.

"Well . . ." she starts, her eyes flashing around the group. "We were going to a new restaurant she wanted to try."

"I think she'd agree this is more important."

"You want me to just *cancel* on my sister? I taught you boys better manners than that."

There's a knee-jerk reaction to apologize and take full responsibility for the cakes, but I think about the conversations I've had with Thea over the past few days. Her questioning why I don't speak up for myself and challenging the perception that I have to take care of everything.

"Mom, I *need* you to do this."

She sputters, looking for any excuse and coming up short, then nods.

Addy gives Thea's arm a little tug, towing her away from me and into the inn. My mom follows them in, dragging her feet while I make a quick call to Jourdan about the car.

Working on this cake suddenly sounds a lot less fun.

We split the work of torting the cakes before filling each layer with the blueberry reduction–infused buttercream I made yesterday. It's soothing, even without Thea here to keep me entertained.

"You know," Mom says, breaking me out of my trance and making me almost fumble the cake I'm stacking, "your dad went through a baking stage, too."

I glance up at my mother, then back at the cake. "I don't remember him baking."

I remember his woodworking stage, his photography stage, his Italian stage, and, during one particularly strong remission period, his rock-climbing stage. He was constantly picking up new hobbies, like he knew his time was limited and had to squeeze in as many experiences as possible. I can't help but compare our lives, how much more *living* he did.

"It was while I was pregnant with you," Mom says. "I spent so much money on these cupcakes I was craving, so he decided to take it up. Within a few weeks, those cupcakes had nothing on his."

I love the idea of having a connection to Dad outside the business. "Why'd he stop?"

She laughs, loud and unencumbered, and it fades to an indulgent smile. "You know Dad. As soon as he mastered something, the hobby wasn't interesting to him anymore. I think his guitar phase was after that. He was always determined to do things well. You remind me of him."

There's a stinging behind my eyes I can't get rid of, no matter how many times I blink. "I've always thought Harrison's more like him than me. So carefree and enthusiastic."

She smiles down at the buttercream. "I guess you were both lucky to get parts of him."

Talking about Dad like this is nice. Her sharing stories without it being about my duty to his memory. I think this is what Dad would want, us celebrating who he was while he was alive instead of stressing about doing right by him in death. And the more I think about the way he lived, the more I think he'd encourage me to explore what I love. Something warm and vibrant expands inside me at the thought as I crumb-coat the cake tier.

"Baking again has been great."

She pats my cheek. "I'm sorry you haven't had time for your hobby. You've been working so hard, and it shows. Dad would be proud of what you've accomplished."

I focus on the cake to avoid looking at her. "I was thinking about starting a baking side business. Just something small out of my house for custom orders. Nothing that would take away from Hayes, but it'd be a fun way to make some extra money."

"I've seen the Hayes financial reports. You don't need to make extra money. Why don't you just spend your free time enjoying it."

My instinct is to back off, to take that little dismissal of my plans and dreams as a statement that I shouldn't pursue them at all. But Thea's thoughtful eyes flash through my mind. "This *would* be something I'd enjoy. I think it would be rewarding to hear people think it's good enough to pay for."

"And what about all your other responsibilities? You haven't had time to bake for fun. How are you supposed to find time to bake for others?"

"I don't know, but I'd like to explore it."

She huffs. "And how exactly would you do that?"

I've been thinking the same thing. If Harrison's serious, I could start training him. Make sure he knows the business inside out so I could have a true partner. Or, who knows, maybe let him take over Hayes completely one day.

"Harrison brought up wanting more—"

"Harrison's still a child," she cuts in.

Her words grate on my nerves, reminding me of what he said about Mom dismissing him. "Harrison's not a child. He's a grown man starting a family, and he's older than I was when I took over as president."

She waves the comment off. "You're considering rearranging your life for something you don't even know if you can do. We have a plan. Just follow it."

"Aunt Dawn thought I was good enough for the wedding."

"Aunt Dawn was desperate."

The words land like a blow to the stomach. Not her saying I couldn't do it—I've seen her react to enough things I've baked to know she thinks they're incredible—but her trying to manipulate me into giving up what I want in favor of her plan.

I grind my teeth together. "Camila and Thea think I could do it."

"I wouldn't give much credence to anything they say. This is just the latest in a long line of your grandmother's efforts to tempt you up here. She's so conniving. First with getting Thea to move here, and now this." The blood in my veins turns to ice. "It's a new low, even for her."

"What?" I say, but the word sounds far away with my blood churning in my ears. "What do you mean, Thea moving here?"

"She's going to work for Camila, managing the restaurant."

She's taking a job up here? There's no way my mom has that right. Thea wouldn't take a job six hundred miles away from me and not say anything. We haven't officially decided anything, but after our conversation yesterday—the way we both poured out our hearts—I can't believe she was planning on leaving me the entire time. It's just not possible.

Right?

Heat burns beneath my skin as I think back over our conversation. She opened up about her own fears, but she didn't promise me anything. Hasn't our relationship always been me seeking her out, desperate for her attention? We acknowledged we have feelings for each other, but that doesn't mean she's planning on a future with me. I filled in the blanks with what I wanted to see while she was busy building her own future—one that doesn't include me.

"When did this happen?" I ask. The words feel like sandpaper in my throat.

Mom hums. "I'm not sure, but you've seen how chummy Camila and Thea have become. When I came down to check on

Thea that night at the restaurant, the two of them were chatting, so I assume then. Camila needs the help, but it's selfish to take Thea when there are plenty of other managers out there."

I'm going to be sick, throw up all over this cake and ruin the wedding for real. How could I not have seen this coming? Didn't I expect this from the start? Every woman I've ever dated has gotten bored, has wanted something more exciting. How could the most thrilling woman in the world settle for someone like me?

I got so caught up in Thea's orbit, let myself trust in the way she looks at me and how open she's been this week. Let myself believe I could be someone worth sticking around for, when really she was just passing time while waiting around for a better offer.

Mom continues. "I'm sure that's what your nana's thinking. Convince the woman you love to move up here and fill your head with enough nonsense to get you to throw away your life on a whim."

I'm still spiraling about Thea, but I'm done letting Mom dismiss what I want.

"It's not nonsense," I say, harsher than I planned.

Mom jolts back. "Leaving your company, the company your father spent his last years fighting for, isn't nonsense? Abandoning the hundreds of people whose livelihoods depend on your work isn't nonsense? And what about your father's memory?"

She chokes on a sob, turning away from me. I step toward her, but she lifts her hand when she hears my movement.

"I'm not saying I'm leaving," I say, "just that I'd like to try something on the side."

"It's the first step," she says through tears.

"Mom, come on." It's a battle to fight down my frustration. It's an extreme reaction to me saying I want to do something outside the business. She's always been so concerned with me carrying on Dad's legacy, so controlling in leading me to the life he wanted for me, but I haven't said I'm leaving. I just want something for myself. Why does she feel entitled to my decisions, even the small ones?

"I can't believe you would do this," she says.

"I'm not trying—" I start, but Mom doesn't let me finish.

"And during your brother's wedding, no less."

Her words dig under my sternum, the guilt and pressure to protect Harrison clawing at my insides. But I've spent my life fulfilling this role, making choices for him and for them and for everyone but me.

I'm on the ledge, and I don't know what will happen if I jump. I may cave and hate myself for it, or I may lose it on her and make her skip the wedding, in which case I'll hate myself even more. My body is screaming, *Get out, get out, get out*. Words sit on the tip of my tongue, waiting for me to open my mouth and let them flow out like lava, destroying everything in its path.

I stack the cakes back in the refrigerator while Mom continues sniffling and going on about how she and Harrison wouldn't know what to do without me and how they and the Hayes community *need* me. I have to get out, to delay and distract until after the wedding, so I excuse myself, cutting the conversation off.

It's a battle to get a breath in by the time I reach the bathroom. I splash some water on my face, meeting my eyes in the mirror. They're wide and frantic. I force myself to hold my gaze, seeing the man I've become. A man pushed to the limit. I can't go back to how it was before, me sacrificing everything I want to keep the peace. Thea gave me that, even if she's leaving me shattered.

I don't know how I'm supposed to make it through the next three days with Thea, pretending like I'm fine when my heart has been ground to dust under the heel of her boot. And it's not just this weekend. Every year when I come up to what has always been my happy place, she's going to be here, reminding me of my stupidity for thinking I had a future with her, that she'd want me beyond a few hookups to pass the time.

At least I won't have to fake my heartbreak for my family anymore. How's that for a silver lining?

Chapter 25

THEA

Addy and I barely make it into my room before she breaks down in tears, and I pull her over to the bed. She drops her head into my lap, just like when we were girls and she was too overwhelmed by a new home and a new set of rules she didn't understand yet. I murmur soothing words, running my hand over her hair until her tears slow.

"It'll be okay, Addy," I whisper into the silence, and she hiccups in response.

Addy doesn't lift her head from my lap. "I was so scared something happened to you."

"But it didn't. I'm right here," I say, and Addy shivers.

"I can't lose you. Please don't leave me alone."

My heart squeezes. "I'm not going anywhere, but you aren't alone anymore. You have so much more than just me, so many people who love you."

She shakes her head against my leg, a new set of sobs shaking her body. We stay like that, me running my hand through Addy's hair, her tears soaking my jeans.

"Am I making a mistake?" Addy whispers, like she's scared if she speaks the words too loudly, they'll echo through the inn.

My hand stills in her hair. "A mistake in marrying Harrison?"

A little sob escapes her. "Yeah. I'm so certain of him, but what about the rest of them? No one else wants me in this family. His opinion should be the only one that matters, but I don't know how to stop caring about them liking me. I don't know if I can handle spending my life as an outsider in my own family."

"Why do you think you're an outsider?"

"They want nothing to do with me. I try, but I can't keep up. It's like a constant battle of wits and teasing, and by the time I get up the nerve to say something, they've already moved on to a different topic. I can tell they think I'm boring, and that only makes me more nervous. How do I ever break out of that cycle?"

Addy's not boring, but she is closed off to new people. If it was hard to break the perfect facade with our foster siblings who she knew were going to be out of our lives in a handful of months, it probably feels impossible to break it with Harrison's family—her dream materialized as flesh and blood. But those who are patient with her find the most precious jewel.

"Give it time," I say, twisting her on my lap so she can see me. "You love this man. Don't give him up because his family takes some time to warm up."

"I wish I was more like you," she says, eyes trained on the comforter.

I guffaw. "Oh yeah, who wouldn't want to be a mess who constantly screws up and embarrasses themselves in front of the family."

Addy's body tenses. "Of course you see it that way."

The words are quiet, almost incomprehensible. I open my mouth to ask what she means when a knock interrupts us. Camila is there when I open the door.

"Hey! We never got to talk yesterday. You free?" She looks over my shoulder, her posture stiffening. Addy's at the mirror, frantically wiping away the mascara streaked down her face. "I can come back later."

Addy sighs. "Might as well come in. Everyone's already seen me at my worst."

Camila slips inside, walking over to Addy and pulling her

into a hug. Addy's eyes are wide when they meet mine over her shoulder.

"Your sister was missing," Cami says. "I'd think worse of you if you *weren't* a mess."

The tension in Addy's body releases, and she relaxes into the hug. "Thank you."

Camila holds on for a few more seconds before letting her go.

"What's up, Cami?" I ask.

She shoots a furtive glance at Addy. "Can we talk, just the two of us?"

Addy scoffs, looking up to the ceiling and shaking her head. "Yup. I'll go."

"Addy," I call, following behind her as she walks for the door. "I can talk to Cami later. We should finish our conversation."

Her fist closes around the door handle. "It's fine. You talk. I need to shower anyway."

She's gone before I can say anything else.

"Is she okay?" Camila asks behind me, and I spin on her.

"No, she's not okay. Can't you make even the smallest bit of effort to get to know her?"

Cami's eyes widen at my tone. "Can *she* make an effort to get to know *me*? You think we haven't tried to talk to her? She's not like you. She just stands there and smiles. This is the first real emotion I've seen from her."

"Because she's anxious as fuck that you all won't accept her," I spit out. "And you telling her to leave so you can talk to me only makes it worse."

Camila's body deflates, and she drops onto the bed. "Shit, I didn't think about it like that."

No one in this family thinks about it. It's a sign of just how secure their relationships were growing up.

"Yeah, well, now you should," I say, the last of my anger seeping out.

Camila nudges me with her foot. "I'll work on it."

I drop into the chair, propping my feet on the bed next to her. "Now, can you please tell me why you've stalked me for the past two days?"

She laughs again, and I love the way we shift from arguing to being friends again.

"Come work for me," Camila says.

"What?" The word bursts out of me without consciously processing it.

"Come run the restaurant."

My mind is whirling, struggling to catch up with the lunacy of the offer. "But . . . but I have no experience."

She lifts an eyebrow. "You worked at another restaurant for twelve years."

"As a server," I say, too loud from the way it booms through the room. "Not as a manager. Fuck, they didn't even trust me enough to make me a shift supervisor, and you want to give me a whole damn restaurant?"

Camila shrugs. "I don't know what your old boss's problem was, but you did a great job a couple nights ago."

"I covered the restaurant for a few hours, and we served eight fucking tables, Cami."

"Look, I'll level with you," she leans forward, dropping her voice like she's sharing government secrets. "I'm desperate. I'm going on maternity leave in four months—and that's assuming this little girl cooks as long as she's supposed to—and I have nothing lined up. Mira's taking on a lot, but I can't leave it all on her, especially when she wants to spend time with the baby, too."

"I'm your last option?" I say with a laugh. This is more comfortable territory. She doesn't want *me*, per se, she just needs someone.

"You knew what you were talking about, and I like you. Working relationships have been built on far less."

I'd love to work with Camila, getting to spend my days in these mountains and my nights working at a restaurant where the owner respects me.

Camila continues. "I want to use your ideas on how to get the locals back into our restaurant. It's a trek up the mountain, but we did it before. And with you at the helm, I think we could do it again. Focus on special occasions. Build a community here."

God, it all sounds too good to be true. I genuinely like Camila and could see her being a friend, and there's something magical about these mountains, something that lets me feel like I can move past the persona I developed in Florida, just like Cece said.

"What about Owen?" I ask quietly.

Camila's mouth twists in a wicked smile. "Owen's a consideration?"

I nudge her with my foot. "Shut up. You know he is."

"I know no such thing because you won't tell me shit." She lifts her hands in front of her. "Look, I don't know how serious you and my cousin are. If it's real, I love that for the both of you. He's incredible, and he deserves happiness. But you don't belong to him. I'm offering you this job because I think you'd be great at it. I'm not going to cut you off from your choices just because you and Owen *may* be something."

Choices.

That word hasn't been a part of my vocabulary for as long as I can remember. A mythical thing, like unicorns and fairies.

"Just think about it, okay?" Camila asks, and I nod.

Obviously, I won't take it. Owen and I have plans. I think of his handsome face—the way he dips his head to hide a smile when he's embarrassed and the concentrated furrow of his brow while baking. If it's a choice between him and a new job—him and anything, really—there's no choice at all.

But that's not accurate. I know what it's like to truly have no choice. This isn't like me and Addy being forced to move homes because a broken system decided it was time. Or me taking a job at Cibare because it was the only place within walking distance when I was a kid, desperate for money. This is the first true, free choice of my life.

And I choose him.

Chapter 26

THEA

Camila's offer is still churning in my mind later that afternoon when the family gathers in the ballroom. I want to tell Owen about it before the family gossip train reaches him, but I need to find a way that doesn't make the infuriating, self-sacrificing man pull away because he thinks he's standing in my way.

We're supposed to get everything set up for the next couple of days—the rehearsal dinner in here tomorrow and the reception the following day—and the room is swarmed with Ellises. It's beautiful, watching the way this family comes together. The cousins are ridiculous and constantly mess with each other, but they show up in a way I didn't think was real outside the sitcoms one of my foster brothers obsessively watched on Nick at Nite.

As soon as I arrive, I subtly make my way over to where Owen is unloading chairs from the cart. His back shifts with each stack he lifts, and I want to run my hand down it, experience the roll of his muscles with my fingertips like reading a book in braille.

"Hey, hot stuff," I whisper when I get close.

Owen's throat bobs, but he doesn't look my way. "Hey, Thea."

Well . . . that's strange. Owen's always the one watching me, sending me secret smiles and covert winks. Now, he won't even look at me, and my stomach twists into knots.

"You okay?" I ask.

"Yeah, I'm good." He says, eyes still on the chairs. "Tommy, can you come unload these? I need to roll in some more tables."

"You got it," Tommy calls out, jogging over to the cart.

Owen claps him on the shoulder, then walks out of the ballroom.

And he still hasn't looked at me.

What the fuck?

This is what I asked for. I told him we needed to keep everything between us quiet, that we couldn't risk getting caught when we're so close to making it through. I'm sure that's all this is. How can I get upset at him for respecting my wishes?

Still, I can't get my nervous system to listen to my very logical reasoning. I'm jumpy, and I need to find something else to focus on, or I'll spend the entire afternoon fixating on nothing. Camila's across the room, set up with a clipboard and ordering people around, the only thing that will keep her pregnant ass stuck to the chair Mira pulled over for her. Addy's looking over the list with her.

"Where's Diana?" I ask as I pull another chair next to them.

Camila winces. "She's in bed with a *migraine*."

The way she says the word "migraine" makes it clear she doesn't believe it.

"She does this sometimes," Camila continues. "Adrian—that's my oldest brother who you probably haven't met yet—said he overheard Aunt Diana yelling at Owen about something in the kitchen this morning. Whenever she gets upset, she needs time to 'convalesce,' which is code, in my opinion, for guilting Owen into doing whatever she wants."

Owen's across the ballroom, and I clock the tightness of his shoulders and the straight line of his mouth. I hate that I can't go up to him, take his hand between mine, and ask what happened.

Gabriel pops up beside me, breaking my focus on Owen and bobbing his eyebrows. "We've got everything set up for that sound check and rehearsal."

I groan, dropping my head back even as a warmth blooms inside me. A part of me thought he'd forget, that it was part of his ploy to mess with Owen by flirting with me. It's shocking that there's a place on the stage for me even after he's pulled back on all that.

He quirks that adorable smile, his blue-green eyes twinkling. "It's always been my dream to sing with my wife."

Okay, so mostly pulled back on the flirting.

Addy looks between us, her brows knitted together. "I thought you decided not to sing with them?"

"I thought it was okay," I say in response, and Addy pastes on that fake smile. I hate the number of times I've been on the receiving end of it this week.

"Of course it's okay. Have fun."

She walks away to tick off one of the two thousand items on her to-do list without another word, and suddenly the ballroom is too cold. I have to make this better.

"Hey, Gabe," I say, pulling him to a stop on his way to the stage.

"Yes, darling."

I roll my eyes, but can't stop my smile. "I'll still sing with you, but I have a condition."

I fill him in on the idea while we walk over to the stage. The band and I chatted about their set list earlier, but this is our first time singing together. We dive into a few of the songs I know well. There are some hiccups, but once we get into the swing of it, I have the time of my life. The cousins stop setting up to watch us, even as Camila yells from her perch about the schedule. I have no illusions about the quality of our music. It's passable. We won't be signing any recording contracts, but it's fun. We're playing off each other, and I feel like I'm wanted and appreciated as Gabriel compliments me for the fortieth time.

My eyes track Owen in the crowd—the only cousin who keeps working. The temptation to jump off the stage and grab him, to force him to stop being so responsible all the time, is almost too much.

"How're we doing, Ellises?" I call into the mic, and they cheer. "We have a treat for you, but to make it happen, we need your help. I'm sure you've all been dreaming about my much more talented sister's voice since the bar. She's been busy with wedding stuff, but she deserves some fun, too. Can y'all help me get her up here?"

Everyone starts clapping, those closest to Addy nudging her toward the stage. A light blush takes over her cheeks, and she looks at me with so much gratitude.

When we start our song, Owen finally stops moving. My body is primed for his reaction, for the way he watched me at the bar, but he stares into the middle distance. He meets my gaze briefly, then shoots away. My stomach roils. It's one thing to keep his distance while we're working, but this feels different.

Just like that night at the bar, Owen makes me miss my cue, but this experience is so different. I'd felt like I was on fire then, slowly melting like a candle under Owen's flame. I'm freezing now. How dare he pull his warmth away after making me dependent on it?

My concentration on Owen is broken when the song ends and Addy wraps her arms around my shoulders, whispering, "Thank you, Tia."

Camila comes up on stage and unplugs my microphone. "That's enough, sirens. They've gotta get some work done."

Everyone grumbles except for Lynne, who jumps up on the stage with the wireless microphone they use for wedding MCs. "Or we can pass the time with a game? Cami can't unplug this one!"

The microphone is clasped between both her hands like she's a pop star. Camila whines that there's too much to do, and Lynne agrees not to start the game until everyone picks back up their jobs. I'm rolling out another round table with

Mira when I hear Lynne call out. "Ellises and guests, welcome to the Newlywed Game. Single elimination, so don't mess up. We'll start with Addy and Harrison versus the oldest couple in the room, Uncle Dennis and Aunt Patricia!"

Dennis and Patricia holler about how they aren't old while the rest of the family laughs.

Lynne dramatically shushes everyone, still clutching the microphone like a lifeline. "I have a list of a hundred questions. The couples will go head-to-head, and the first to get one wrong is kicked off until there's only one couple standing. I need to help Cami oversee the setup, so who wants to be our MC for the day?"

A dozen cousins rush for the stage, tripping and tackling each other until one of the twins—Tommy or Johnny, who can say—scrambles up in front of Lynne. She smiles angelically, pushing the microphone into his hands. He looks down with a furrowed brow a second before keys with a bright yellow key chain tumble from his hands, the metallic clang echoing through the room.

"Son of a bitch," he screams into the microphone, so loud I cover my ears. "You tricked me!"

"If you weren't so desperate to be the center of attention," Lynne says, pleased with herself, "you wouldn't have ended up on driving duty."

"But Cole texted me they got a new whiskey for tonight!"

Lynne cups her cheeks in mock horror. "Oh no! What will you do?"

The Ellises howl in laughter.

"The night's not here yet," he says, looking out over the crowd with an almost demonic grin as he slips the keys into the back pocket of his jeans.

He starts up the game while the rest of us keep working. Addy and Harrison take down Dennis and Patricia in one question, and as they exit the stage, the room can hear Patricia complaining that her husband of almost fifty years doesn't know her favorite ice cream flavor. Addy and Harrison make it through three more challengers before they're dethroned by a couple I haven't met yet. The couples on the stage keep rotating after that, viciously arguing and taunting each other. The Ellises don't play when it comes to competition.

I'm shaking out a tablecloth when Camila's scream echoes through the ballroom. Mira rushes to her side with terror etched on her face. Her feet stop in their tracks when she spots the telltale yellow key chain hanging from Camila's fingers, a bag of Poppy popcorn mix spilled out at her feet.

"You can't scream like that, Camila," Mira yells, running her hands up into her hair.

Camila's pointing at Gabriel, who has a shit-eating grin stretched across his face. "What the fuck, Gabriel?"

"Johnny paid me forty bucks to slip them into the bag and give it to you."

"How?" she screams. "He's been on the microphone the whole time!"

"Twin-tuition," Johnny and Tommy—who's on the stage with his boyfriend—say together. They high-five without looking.

"You can't use my Asheville Mix cravings against me," Camila whines. "That's cheating."

Gabriel turns to me. "Is there a rule against using pregnancy cravings?"

Camila begs with her eyes, but the rules must be maintained, so I shrug. "Sorry, Cami. It's every man for himself in the Ellises, right?"

I glance over at Owen, looking for a smile or a laugh or anything, but he just stares blankly at me and walks away.

Something's wrong, and I feel sick. There's too much attention on me right now, but I'm sneaking away the second I can to corner him. He can't spend the week making me obsessed with him, and then just take it all away without an explanation.

Mira holds out her hand. "I'll take the damn keys."

"No," Camila says with the fire of a vengeance demon. "This isn't over."

"Maybe not," Johnny says into the microphone, "but this round *is*, which means we're out of couples, and we have a winner. Everyone give it up for my twin and Jayce, who are only a year and a half into their relationship and still wiped the floor with all y'all."

"What about Owen and Thea?" Gabriel calls out, and I glare at him. "They haven't had a turn."

"We're not together, asshole," Owen says.

The room sucks in a breath. This isn't the Owen everyone knows, the one who is sweet and accommodating. That Owen would never curse in front of the family, would never call out Gabriel's behavior like that. He'd have walked onto the stage, no matter how uncomfortable it made him. I'd be proud of him, if the way he was looking around the room didn't feel like it was really aimed at me.

"But you were," Gabriel says, unfazed by Owen's callout. "And for almost as long as Tommy and Jayce. Don't let Tommy win. We'll never hear the end of it."

I don't get what's happening—the scowl on Owen's face and the way he won't look at me directly. I want his smile back, the dimple I have to work for and the soft look in his eyes.

Owen's jaw tenses. "Are we done?"

He doesn't wait for an answer, just slams his way out of the French doors.

"What was that about?" Addy asks while I blink at the door.

"I . . . I don't know."

It takes a few extra seconds, but then I charge after him. I run to catch up, calling out his name as he reaches the inn. He doesn't pause, pushing through the front door.

He's halfway up the first flight of stairs when I catch up to him. "What's going on?"

Owen's long legs don't stop, eating up the space between him and the third floor where we're both staying. "Nothing."

"Oh yes," I say, a teasing lilt to my voice that I hope will break through whatever's going on in his head. "This definitely feels like nothing."

My stomach drops further when he doesn't respond, reaching his room and tapping his key card against the lock. He walks through the door without a backward glance. My instinct is to walk away, to say fuck it—fuck him—if that's how he's going to behave.

But he let me yell and rage. He was supportive when I was at my worst, and he deserves a bit of that patience given back to him. If he thinks this conversation is ending here, he doesn't know me as well as I thought.

Chapter 27

OWEN

The door almost makes it closed before Thea slams it open.

"Talk to me. What's wrong?" she asks, letting the heavy wood swing closed behind her.

The click feels ominous in this space that's way too small for all the things I'm feeling. Hurt and anger, but also this intense longing to go back to yesterday when we were curled up together on a bed of hay, sharing our secrets and our bodies. I was filled with hope. Blindly optimistic about our future.

She's breathtaking today in a turquoise dress, the first dress I've seen her in since the welcome party. Way more casual, but no less devastating. Something about the fabric makes her glow—her golden skin and golden hair—like Midas's most prized possession. Of course I couldn't hold on to someone like that.

God, I've never felt so ridiculous in my life. She's perfect, gorgeous and funny and clever, and I let myself believe she'd want me.

"What did I do?" she asks, and it's the most vulnerable I've seen her. It makes me want to throw myself at her feet.

Instead, my legs give out and I drop onto the bed. I'm exhausted. Seeing her upset is killing me. Even now, I don't want to hurt her. It's not her fault that I built this up to be more than it was. She deserves the opportunity to do something she loves. I know how much she misses her work, and Camila would be a great boss. She'd be happy here. Fulfilled. How fucking selfish am I that I'm mad at her for building a good life for herself?

She stands in front of me, and without my conscious consent, my legs spread, and I pull her body closer. My head drops to her chest, and she runs her hand through my hair in a move that makes me feel like every cell has suddenly sprung to attention.

"Please talk to me," she whispers, and my grip tightens on her hips.

"I'm sorry," I say. "I'm not being fair to you."

"I don't understand."

Her voice is so much softer than I've heard it, but there's tension in her body. She's battling her knee-jerk reaction to fight, all for me, and it makes me melt into her a bit more.

It's moments like this that have fucked with my head. I can see what our future would be like, how we'd argue, but that each of us would try to put the other first. I'd be such a good partner to her, treat her like the equal she is while worshipping the ground she walks on. But she chose a life that doesn't fit me.

"I'm happy for you. Really, I am. You deserve it," I say, pulling back to look up into her beautiful face. "I'm just going to miss you when you move."

Her large brown eyes go even larger. "Are you talking about the job offer from Camila?"

"Is there another reason you'd move up here? Are you planning on eloping with Gabriel?"

She clicks her tongue. "Not yet. Gotta wait until he's old enough that I can't get arrested for it."

I drop my head back to her chest, laughing into her skin, but I sober just as quickly. "You don't owe me information about your choices. I just . . . I don't know. We shared so much yesterday and I thought we were on the same page, so learning that you're keeping this huge thing from me, it felt like a betrayal."

"Owen—"

Shit, she's going to think I'm such a dick, believing I'm entitled to her decisions.

I rush to add, "I know it wasn't one. We agreed we'd take the week to see if we wanted to pursue this, and I promised you could walk away if that's what you wanted."

She wraps her fingers in my hair, giving it a tug. "When would I have told you? You've refused to talk to me all afternoon."

"I don't know, maybe some time between us baking the cakes and you coming on my cock?"

She laughs, and I can't tell if her reaction pisses me off or soothes the ache inside me. "She offered me the job this morning."

I blink up at her. "This morning, as in . . . today."

"No, this morning as in a month ago," she deadpans. "Yes, this morning!"

I feel like a total asshole. I've given her the cold shoulder all afternoon, had decided what this meant for our relationship before she'd even been offered the damn position. But just because she hadn't known yet doesn't mean that she isn't going to take it. I can't let myself hope only to be crushed again.

"I'm such a jackass. My mom told me about it first thing this morning and said it was a done deal. I'm sorry." I force myself to swallow before asking, "And what do you think about it?"

There's a pressure in my chest as I wait for her answer, so strong I have to fight the urge to look down, sure I'll see an anvil pushing against it. Or maybe the hard barrel of a shotgun, ready to destroy my heart on her word.

Her mouth pulls to the side. "About the job? Of course I'm not taking it."

All the tension in my body is sucked out in an instant, but it's followed by crushing guilt. I think of her face—the smile that stretched across it and the light in her eyes while talking to the customers—and I hate the idea of her passing up something that would bring her joy.

She must see the concern in my eyes, because she goes on. "Did you really think I'd walk away from this? That I'd do it without talking to you?"

I look up at her, my gorgeous, heart-stopping girl. "I think you're the most incredible person I've ever met and so far out of my league it's laughable."

"Then I'm not doing my job." She traces the line of my jaw with her fingertips, and I lean into the feeling. "You should know you're perfect and that I think I'm the luckiest woman in the world that you're willing to even look at me."

I shake my head. "Part of me still thinks this is a very elaborate dream I'm going to wake up from at any moment."

She brushes my hair off my brow. "It's not."

I give her body a tug, and she falls into my lap, legs on either side of my hips. "You're real?"

She sighs and lets her lips drift over mine. "I could ask the same of you."

My grip on her hips tightens, grinding her down against where I'm rapidly hardening and showing her just how real I am. Her head drops back, and I run my lips down her neck, reveling in that spicy scent. I lap at the spot where her pulse is beating wildly, and she moans.

"Owen," she whimpers, and I love the sound of my name on her lips, the way she whines like she's coming apart at the seams. She's always so strong. Watching her turn soft in my arms is a drug I don't think I'll ever be able to kick.

I inch up her dress until I glimpse her light blue lace underwear, and a loud groan tears from my throat. She's so perfect. When she rolls her hips over mine, her heat is right over my aching cock, and I wrap my arms around her, anchoring our torsos together.

"I'm sorry," I whisper into her neck. "I should have just talked to you."

She stops the erotic way she's grinding against me, brushing a soft kiss on my temple. "It's hard, being vulnerable. Trust me, I'm absolute trash at it."

"It's not an excuse for me to be a dick to you."

She pulls back, trapping me in her dark gaze. "You're not one moment, and the good of you far outweighs the bad."

They're an echo of the words I said to her in the closet, and the way her eyes shine, she knows it. A whole Fourth of July fireworks show sets off inside me, and I'm hyperaware of every place we're connected as I drag her lips back to mine. She moans into the kiss, and I want that sound seared into my brain as a reminder of how much she wants me on the days my asshole brain tells me I'm not enough for her.

"I can't figure out how to stop wanting you so badly." My head drops to her shoulder as I pant onto her skin, and she shivers against me. "It's never been like this."

"Me neither," she whimpers, tilting her hips and gasping at the pressure she's putting on her clit.

I slide the straps of her dress over her shoulders, pushing down until she gets the idea and pulls her arms out. The fabric pools at her waist, leaving her in nothing but a lacy bra that matches her panties. She's stunning like this, but I want it all. I can't resist the temptation, yanking the dress back up and over her head so I can see the set together.

I stand, keeping her legs wrapped around my waist, and she makes the most adorable squeak that has me chuckling on her lips. It only takes two steps to reach the antique desk set up across from the king bed, and I drop her on top of it, running my hands down her legs as I take a half step back to look at her.

The lacy bra doesn't hide much, her nipples pushing against the material and begging for my attention. I delay the gratification, letting my eyes take their fill of her. Her heels are still anchored around my back, forcing her thighs wide and giving me the most enticing view of the dampness between her legs. There's a little tear in the lace of her underwear, and my hand goes straight to it, fingers playing with the bit of skin that I shouldn't have access to.

My eyes track back up her body, and there's a trace of vulnerability in her eyes. "Not my nicest lingerie."

I can't abide her thinking she's anything less than perfect. "You're the most glorious thing I've ever seen. Nothing has ever come close. Not the waves in the Atlantic Ocean or the Blue Ridge Mountains or any other thing people travel the world to experience. None of it can compete with you, just like this."

Her throat bobs, and my hand drifts up until it wraps around her neck. Thea's back arches. I could spend the day this way, letting my fingers map and explore her just to see the way she squirms.

Her self-control breaks, and her hands come to my jeans, opening and pushing them down with lightning speed. I groan when she closes her fingers around me over my boxer briefs.

"Why is it always you getting to look at me?" she asks innocently. "What if I want to look at you?"

"Next time," I pant.

My grip around her neck tightens, and I pull her mouth to mine. I want to taste every inch of her, to imprint the feeling of my lips on her skin so no one will ever compare. She's so fucking sweet, my favorite meal I'd happily gorge myself on just to keep the taste on my tongue.

My hand comes back down to her underwear as she pushes mine down my thighs, giving me the skin-to-skin contact I'm craving. My finger finds that little hole again, like it's a homing beacon calling out to me.

"Are you attached to these panties?" I ask against her lips, and she shakes her head. "Good, I'll buy you more."

I hook my finger through the hole, bringing my other hand down to yank the lace in half, leaving her fully exposed to me. She laughs, but the laugh turns into a melting moan when I cup her pussy possessively.

I groan. "Fuck, you're already so wet for me."

My mouth goes to one of her breasts, licking over the material and turning the lace even more translucent. I bite down on her nipple, and her back arches, pushing her more firmly in my face. She whines when I pull my hand away from her pussy, but she can wait. I push her breasts together so I can skim my mouth back and forth over her nipples. She retaliates by grabbing my hips, pulling my dick against her warmth. I thrust on instinct, my hard length pushing against her clit.

"Condom," she says. "Now."

"I haven't even tasted you yet." But I blindly grope on the desk behind her for the box of condoms I bought after our hookup in the closet, slipping one out and tearing it open.

She pulls my face to hers, kissing me deeply. "Next time."

Our tongues battle for dominance as I slide on the condom, but I pull back before more. I'm desperate to watch this moment, the way her eyes go wide and her head drops back when we're joined. I started slow last time, but now I know she can take me. That she takes me so fucking perfectly it's like she was made to hold me.

I maintain eye contact as I rub the head of my cock over her clit a few times until she gets the most adorable little furrow between her brows. "Fuck me, Owen."

The demand—the confidence and power in her voice—makes my cock pulse in my hand, desperate to comply. I line myself up, still holding her eyes, and slam all the way home in one thrust. She moans loudly, and I slide my hand over her mouth.

"We aren't in a barn in the middle of nowhere anymore, Thea. No screaming this time."

She narrows her eyes on me like it's a challenge and then brings her hand to my ass as she fucks herself on my cock. The desk rattles beneath her, even louder than her moan, and I scoop her up, keeping myself buried within her as I move us to the bed.

I lay us down, never breaking contact, and roll my hips against hers, earning me another glorious moan.

"We made it to a bed," she says with a breathless laugh.

"Proud of us," I say, rubbing my nose against hers.

It earns me a giggle, something I've never heard from Thea. I love her usual laugh, the raspy sound from somewhere deep inside, but I love this, too. The airy sound, like she's letting herself have a bit of lightness.

I pull back, almost to the point of leaving her body, then thrust back in, hard. She clenches around me, so tight I almost go over the edge, but I'm not ready for this to be over. My girl hasn't even come yet, and that's not acceptable, so I slow my thrusts, grinding against her instead. My hand comes to her clit, rubbing circles, and I'm rewarded when Thea's head tilts back, thrusting her breasts into my face. When I close my teeth around a nipple again, she shoots off, and I drag my mouth back up to hers just in time to swallow her scream.

Watching Thea come is my new favorite pastime, and I'm so fucking close that if I don't pause, I'll finish right here. With my cock seated inside her, I lick and kiss up her neck, whispering praise in her ear. I'm about to start moving again when she scrambles out from under me. My dick aches from the loss of contact, but she pushes my shoulder to lay me down.

"I want to ride you," she says.

In seconds, she's thrown her leg over my hip and taken me back inside her. She pins my body with both hands as she moves, and I'm in heaven. Her eyes are trained on my face, watching every shifting expression—the way I respond when she rolls her hips compared to when she bounces, nails down my chest versus a featherlight touch—and I've never felt so important. Like my pleasure is the most vital part of the experience for her.

"Take off your bra," I say, intending it as a command, but it comes out as a plea.

Her lips tilt up in the sexiest smirk as she lifts her hands from my body, sliding the scrap of lace up and over her head and letting me see her fully.

"Better?" she purrs.

"Was already good," I grunt out. "Always so fucking good for me, Thea."

She lowers her upper body so our torsos are lined up, bringing our mouths back together. I grip her hips, unable to stop myself from thrusting up into her. It doesn't take long with me so close to the edge, and my fingers tighten as my hips lift from the bed, pushing as deeply inside her as I can as I come so hard my vision goes white.

She drapes herself over me as we both breathe hard, trying to come down from the high of the last twenty minutes. Eventually, she slides off me, heading to the bathroom while I tie off and throw away the condom. I'm worried she'll go right for her clothes, but she surprises me by climbing back into bed.

My arms come around her, pulling her as close as she can get. I place a kiss on top of her head, leaving my mouth against those stunning curls even though they tickle my nose. I'll take the closeness I can get until I can keep her close forever.

Chapter 28

THEA

Owen's warm at my back. Steady and comforting in a way I've never known.

"We need to get dressed," I say, and his arms tighten a smidge more.

"Not yet." He nuzzles into my neck, and those damn butterflies are back.

I twist in his arms so that I'm facing him, running my finger along his jaw and up to his lips, and he nips at my finger. He grins so wide at my giggle that those three little terrifying words I've never said romantically spring up in my mind. The ecstasy and terror mix inside me like a Mentos dropped into a soda bottle.

I wiggle out of his arms, rushing around to get my clothes. Owen pushes up on his elbow, the comforter pooling around his waist. He's an erotic fantasy brought to life, all messy hair and firm body and a delicious line of hair just begging to be traced down below the blanket.

His lips kick up in a half smile. "If you keep looking at me like that, I'm going to drag you back into bed."

"Stay," I command, narrowing my eyes at him.

He pushes off the bed, crawling toward me with a challenging smirk. "I'm not a dog, Thea."

I pull my bralette and dress over my head, backing up toward the door. His smile grows, and I know I have seconds before he pounces. I love this side of him, the playfulness that he doesn't normally show. Another time, I'll indulge it all day long. But right now, I need to get back to Addy and her to-do list. I slip on my sandals, sacrificing my ruined underwear to the cause of escaping.

I get the door half an inch open before he spins me toward him, pushing me back against it. His hand wraps around my neck, and then he's devouring me again. I melt into the kiss, incapable of doing anything but accepting it. One more kiss, and I'll leave.

"You're terrible at following commands," I mumble.

He smiles against my lips. "Guess you'll have to stick around to train me."

I laugh, pushing against his stomach until he staggers back with a dopey grin on his face.

I stumble out of the door, my smile stretched so wide I resemble the Joker, but the smile falls when I spot Addy leaning against the opposite wall.

"All done?" she asks with faux calm.

"Were you listening to us?" I ask, and I feel a surge of protectiveness for what I just shared with Owen.

She makes a gagging sound. "Don't worry, I left when I heard just what you two were getting up to. You know this is a family establishment, right? I didn't need to know what you sound like during sex."

I cover my face with both hands to cover a laugh. When I pull my hands away, I realize the laugh I'd expected from Addy after a comment like that is missing. She looks hurt and scared and really fucking pissed.

I step closer to her. "I'm sorry, Addy. I didn't mean for this to happen."

"You promised," she says, so low I hardly hear her. "You told me you'd keep your distance and wouldn't cause problems. When you two break up again, you'll walk away, and I'll be left with the fallout."

"You don't know that we'll break up."

"Of course you'll break up, Thea." Her hands fly out to the side before slapping back against her legs. "If you didn't make it the first time, why would you make it now?"

I bite at my lip, trying to decide what to tell her. I think of the earnest look on Owen's face, his willingness to deal with his mom for the chance to be with me. It's going to get out eventually, so I might as well tell Addy now. We're only a day out from the wedding. She wouldn't have to keep the secret for long, and maybe if she knows we never broke up in the past, she'll see our potential, too.

I glance up and down the hallway to make sure we're alone. "We didn't have a first time."

Her eyes blink rapidly. "What do you mean you didn't have a first time?"

I suck in a breath. "We faked our relationship. Owen wanted to get his family off his back, so he paid me to come to the wedding and pretend to be his girlfriend. But it wasn't like . . . well, like it is now."

Her dark eyes nearly double in size, and she drops back against the wall, sliding down slowly. "This is a disaster."

"No, it's okay. We were just going to keep up the ruse, but then everything happened between us, and Owen has a plan now. It'll be fine, I promise." I can hear the desperation in my voice, but she stares blankly at the wall.

"What's Owen's plan?" Addy asks, finally looking up at me.

I start to squat down so we're level, then remember my pantiless existence and go to kneel in front of her instead. "He's going to tell Diana while you're on your honeymoon, so it'll all blow over before you're back."

She points down the hallway like Diana will magically manifest. "Have you met that woman? There's no way she's going to get over something like that in years, much less in two weeks."

I flinch.

Addy clutches my arm, and it's so reminiscent of the way she clung to me as we moved from home to home that my heart squeezes. "I get why you like him. He's great, and you have chemistry, but do you think that's enough to build a relationship on? It's all secretive and romantic now, but what about when you get home?"

She pushes to stand, and I scramble up after her. Is she right? Am I just caught up in the beauty of the mountains and the freedom of a new place? Will I destroy Addy's relationship with her new in-laws for something that will go bad before the milk I bought last week?

Addy rubs at the skin under her eyes, like preemptively swiping away tears. "I can't have Diana hating me."

"She won't hate you," I say, desperate for an excuse to cling to.

"She barely tolerates me now! I think the only reason she does is because of you, so what happens when she decides she hates you?" she asks. "She's emotionally reactive and unstable, and you're gambling with my future."

My body goes numb. "I . . . I'm not . . ."

She takes my hands between hers. "Please, Thea. I'm not above begging. Please don't take this from me. There are billions of men on this planet. Why does it have to be him? Please just leave me this family."

My heart bellows, furious that she'd equate Owen to anyone else. No one could compare.

Before I can conjure up the words, she continues. "I love Harrison so much, and I want to build a life with him. A family. One that includes a grandmother who doesn't hate the mother of her grandchildren. Something happy and stable, like we never had."

Tears escape her eyes, speeding a few inches down her cheeks before she swipes them away, and suddenly she's a child again. Three years old and sobbing for our mama. Six years old and crying because she's being forced to leave a home she's finally comfortable in. Ten years old and begging me to play nice with our foster parents so we aren't moved because a teacher believes in her for the first time. A few months later, on the walk to school, trying to hide her tears over having to say goodbye to her because I couldn't keep my promise.

"Addy, dear," a voice calls from down the hall, and I get another gut punch.

"Maria! Gary!" Addy calls, swiping away the tears as that perfect smile slides into place.

Maria and Gary Fischer are the type of foster parents the system always hopes for. Kind and loving, in it for all the right reasons. While they are nowhere near wealthy, they both have jobs and don't treat the kids they foster like a paycheck or unpaid labor around the house. In the six months we lived with them, they never raised a hand to me, even through our worst arguments. And even they—the archetypes for the perfect foster parents—couldn't bring themselves to put up with me.

Maria shifts on her feet. "You look well, Thea."

This is only the second time I've spoken to Maria since I left her home at eight years old. When Addy was reassigned to them a few weeks after I aged out, I came to the house to ask permission to spend time with Addy. I got a forty-five-minute lecture about how this was a chance for Addy and that I'd only be allowed to see her if I didn't lead her into trouble. After that, I'd wait outside for Addy to come to the car. I hit every schedule they set in the fear that one missed curfew would make them rip her away from me.

"Thank you, Maria," I say, turning my awkward smile on Gary. "I'll let Addy get you two settled, and I'll see you at the rehearsal tomorrow."

I turn to leave, nausea churning at the reminder of all the things I've stripped from Addy over the years. I'm almost to the end of the hallway when Addy calls to me.

"You'll think about what we talked about?"

There's no need to think about anything. I already know what I need to do.

My tears start falling before the door of my hotel room swings shut. I can hardly see the screen of my phone, but somehow navigate to the name I need. It rings a handful of times before he picks up.

"How's my girl?"

"Vaughn," I choke out through the sobs. "I fucked up."

Chapter 29

OWEN

I've been to a lot of weddings. With a family the size of a football team, there's always a next event on the horizon. Someone's wedding or a big anniversary party or first birthday party. I may live six hundred miles away, but the Ellises show up for each other.

But through dozens of weddings, this is the first time I'm excited for a rehearsal.

It hasn't even been twenty-four hours since Thea left my room, but I'm itching to see her, to maybe sneak her away for a kiss. She shot me a text last night saying she had some things to take care of and couldn't come out with the family, and I almost canceled and went to her room instead.

I was in the kitchen all morning getting the final coat of buttercream perfect. I wish Thea could have been with me, even though I knew this wasn't something she could help with. Even without her there, it was fun, and I breathed a sigh of relief when I looked over the work. The cake is going to be perfect. All we'll have to do tomorrow is assemble and decorate it.

Then I went to Mom. She was still in bed with the curtains drawn when I reached her, exactly as she'd been when I checked on her the night before. I apologized and pleaded and finally got her to agree to come to the rehearsal. It's temporary, a way to get us through the wedding until we can have an honest conversation, but it still feels wrong—a betrayal of myself—in a way it didn't before.

I can feel the moment Thea steps onto the lawn, and when my eyes find her, the air is sucked from my lungs. She's so beautiful it hurts, in a lavender dress that flows down around her knees, swishing with each step as she walks. Her curls are loose, the wind blowing them away from her face, and I want to gather them up in my hands, to twist one around my finger and tug, just to see it bounce back into place.

Her eyes skate to me, then jump away, back to Addy who is walking by her side, talking animatedly to a couple I don't recognize. That's when I clock the emotion on Thea's face. She's smiling, but the closer she gets, the more I can see the cracks in the facade. These must be Addy's adoptive parents—the ones who chose not to keep Thea—and I instantly hate them.

Introductions are made and we run through the rehearsal without any issues, except for the fact that Thea won't look at me, but I doubt Aunt Dawn would consider that a wedding-related emergency.

When the two of us walk back up the aisle behind Harrison and Addy, I whisper, "Everything okay?"

Thea nods, but it's stiff. "Just a big day."

Something's wrong, but I don't know what it could be. Yesterday, we were in bed together, talking about the future. I want to pull her away, but Addy stays plastered to her side.

The small group of us from the rehearsal make our way to the ballroom where the party is in full swing. It's ridiculous. We're practically having two receptions, but the Ellises never say no to a party.

Cousins and aunts flood Addy and Thea as they walk in, all reaching for a piece of them. I keep my eyes on Thea the whole time, looking for an opportunity to talk. But before I can, Gabriel's voice rings through the ballroom.

"There's our star. We've been subjecting you all to Roy's singing for long enough. Thea, get your ass up here."

Aunt Ximena calls out, "Watch your language, mijo," and

his bandmates tease him while Thea squeezes through the crowd.

I make my way through the buffet line to distract from the overwhelming frustration of not getting Thea alone, then sit at a table near the back, watching her laugh and sing on the stage as they cover song after song. She doesn't look at me, like I'm another stranger in the crowd, too unimportant to warrant a glance. My blood's boiling in my veins, and I'm fighting against the urge to rush up onto the stage myself and drag her away, to lock her up until I get an explanation.

"Okay, y'all, we're mixing it up. This one's for you Swifties," Gabriel says.

Thea gives him a nod, stepping up to the microphone as the opening bars of "Cruel Summer" ring through the speakers. They play it in a lower key, and the verse is perfect for Thea's voice, deep and sultry like the song she sang at the bar that's forever burned into my memory. She's up against the stand, clutching the microphone between both hands as she brings her head close. There's something so intimate about the way she sings this one, the straight line of her lips and seriousness in her eyes. The tune shifts, pushing the top of her range, but she follows the melody as it flows into the chorus. She owns this crowd. She owns me, but that's nothing new.

When the bridge hits, her eyes find me, so unflinchingly that I know she knew my location from the start. The lyrics of the song break through, ones I could have sung before this moment, but that feel new from Thea's lips. Her eyes are sad, and when she holds my gaze for the last line of the bridge, I feel like my heart has been ripped out. Because no, the idea of her loving me is nowhere near the worst thing I've ever heard, and I don't understand why she'd think it was.

By the end of the bridge, she's looked away, back to performing for the crowd instead of me, and there's ice in my veins.

The bridge hits even harder the second time. It's equal parts wistful and angry, and it's so perfectly Thea that I don't know if I'll ever be able to listen to the original again. A tear slips from the corner of Thea's eye, and she swipes it away like she's pissed it's there to begin with.

An eternity passes before the song ends, and Thea laughs into the microphone. "It's a bop, but damn if it's not emotional, right?"

She asks the question to the rest of the band, like directing attention to them will make everyone else ignore her obvious reaction.

"Hell yeah, it is," Gabriel says, smiling at her with a bit of concern in his eyes as his mother once again yells, "Language." Gabriel just laughs. "How about we give this gorgeous woman's vocal cords a break? It means y'all have to deal with Roy's pitchiness, but she deserves it after that killer song."

Thea steps away from the mic, and Roy immediately takes her place. Gabriel's happy-go-lucky mask slips as he meets her at the side of the stage, whispering something to her. Thea's face is somber as she nods, then she smiles slightly before slipping off the stage and disappearing through the back of the ballroom.

I'm on her trail in seconds, dodging family left and right until I'm in the hallway. She's just about to pass the closet where she rewrote every expectation I have for a sexual experience when I catch up, grabbing her arm and tugging her inside with me.

Her face is wet, and it sends a sharp pang through me. I place my hands on either side of her neck and wipe the tears away with my thumbs.

"Talk to me," I say, meaning it to come out soft, but there's a harsh desperation in my voice. I know what she's going to say even before she opens her mouth.

"This has been the most incredible week of my life," she says, a little hiccup interrupting her sentence and giving me the chance to break in.

"No," I say, shaking my head. "We're not doing that."

She laughs as more tears escape the corners of her dark eyes. "You said to talk to you."

"But not to say this. We're not done."

"We can't tell your mom—"

"Thea, no."

"—without making issues for Addy, and I can't do that," she finishes like I didn't speak at all.

"Please. Please don't do this."

"She cares so much about what people think about her, and it's my fault. I was the one who kept ripping her away from home after home and made her terrified of losing people's approval. It's the consequences of my own actions. She'll never be happy if your mom decides she doesn't approve of her."

"What about you?" I ask. "Don't you deserve to be happy?"

Her smile is so sad, and I want to gather her in my arms and make the hurt go away. "I'll never be happy if I've caused her unhappiness."

I shake my head, my fingers sliding up into her hair. "There has to be a way to make it work."

"You can't tell your mom the truth. I need you to promise me you won't tell her. Please, do this for me?"

This isn't *for her*. She's sacrificing her own desires out of a sense of obligation to Addy, and it's making me see red. But I won't betray her, so against every desire and instinct, I nod.

She smirks, and the artificiality of the expression feels like knives dragged down my back. "You'll be fine. It's easy to get caught up when you're related to every other woman at the wedding. There's a beautiful, smart, kind girl waiting for you back home who will take over your mind so completely that you won't even remember the hot girl you had a wild fling with in North Carolina."

I'm already losing her, watching as she slips back into that shell of self-deprecation, and it makes me sick. My hands tighten in her hair, tugging her another inch closer to me. "Don't fucking do that. Don't dismiss the way I feel about you. You may walk away from me, but I'll never stop wanting you. I'll spend the rest of my life begging Addy for scraps of your life, praying that you'll show up at the next family event at her side. You are not replaceable."

"Owen."

She says my name like a benediction, but I'm the one who wants to worship her. It takes only the slightest pressure on the back of her head to bring our lips together. It's messy and desperate, and the way she moans into my mouth has me making vows in my mind she doesn't want to hear. I don't care how long it takes. If it's months or years or decades. I'll make sure we find our way back to each other.

She pushes against my body, never taking her lips from mine as she backs me against the shelves. Her hands come to the buckle of my belt while I grab her leg, hitching it around my waist as I grind into her. She's perfect for me, and I slide my hand up her leg until I'm grasping her ass. She gasps into my mouth as she frees me from my pants, her hand closing around my aching cock.

"I need you," she whispers against my lips as she slips my wallet from my back pocket, and I'm so relieved I replaced the condom there.

I drop my mouth to her neck, resisting the urge to suck and bite. The idea of sending her back onto that stage with my mark on her neck is almost too tempting, but I won't back her into a corner, won't take another choice away from her.

Thea puts the condom package between her teeth, ready to rip it open, when the door behind her swings open. We both freeze, and Thea turns her head, condom still hanging from her mouth. My mother is in the doorway, watching us with a manic look in her eyes. And my dick is still out. Thank god for Thea's body placement.

"Shit," Thea says, the condom dropping and landing with a little *thwack*.

Mom's eyes home in on the unmistakable foil packet and she titters. "Oh, I didn't . . . That is . . . Excuse me."

I groan, mortified, as Mom spins and lets the door fall closed behind her. Thea's immediately off me, straightening her clothes.

"Stop her, Owen. Please." Thea's face is terrified as she stares at the closed door. *"Please."*

I put my clothes back in order and rush out after my mom, leaving Thea to follow a few steps behind. When we make it to the ballroom, Mom's already talking to my aunts.

"Mom, can I talk to you?" I ask.

"This is all your grandmother's manipulation." She turns to Aunt Dawn. "Did you hear Mom made Camila offer her a job so she'd move here and drag Owen with her?"

"It wasn't a trick from Nan—"

"And now she has him wrapped around her finger again and is going to steal my son away from me."

I'm about to scream, or at least drag her away kicking and screaming, when another voice rings through the room. "Thee, I missed you so much."

Vaughn—whose idea started this mess to begin with—strides across the room before he wraps his arms around her and presses a hard kiss to the top of her head.

My heart stops. I know they're just friends, but it looks bad, and the last thing we need is an added complication when the walls are falling in on us.

My mom steps forward, pinning Thea with a glare. "So not only are you playing with my son's heart, but you have a boyfriend?"

The room goes quiet for a few seconds, and then everyone starts talking at once.

Chapter 30

THEA

As much as I want to burrow into the warmth of my best friend's hug, I force myself to push away and deal with the shit show around me.

"Am I supposed to be your boyfriend?" Vaughn whispers.

"What?" I whisper back. "Of course not."

He smiles that movie star smile. "Just making sure I'm not supposed to be *My Best Friend's Wedding*–ing you."

"What the fuck does that mean?"

"You know, when her queer best friend shows up to pretend to be her boyfriend so people aren't suspicious of her?"

I can't stop the short laugh that bursts out of me.

"I'm glad you find this so amusing," Diana says, her hands anchored on her hips.

"It's not what it looks like," I say.

Diana turns her nose up at me. "It looks like you've decided one man isn't enough for you."

Addy steps forward. "She and Owen aren't together."

"She's right," Gabriel says from the stage, his voice amplified by the microphone so that everyone straining to hear from the edges of the room can be privy to his part of the conversation. "A couple backslides never hurt anyone."

He looks so proud of himself, so earnest in his helpfulness, that I almost feel guilty crushing his joy when I shoot daggers at him.

Diana raises a brow, an empress studying an ant. "Is that

what we're calling what I just caught you doing in the closet? A backslide? My generation called it going at it like jackrabbits."

"Not in my closet," Lynne moans dramatically.

"You guys must really like that closet," Gabriel says, and it rings through the room.

Addy gasps, her eyes going hard. "You promised, Thea."

"This is just a big misunderstanding," I say.

The room quiets down to hear whatever drama's going to spill from my mouth next. I almost expect Lynne to come running up with the wireless microphone, but she's probably still recovering from learning about our extracurricular activities in her closet.

"Vaughn's just a friend, right, Vaughn?"

I kick him, and he jumps to attention. "Yes, just friends."

"And yes, Owen and I may have had . . ." *Brain-altering sex. Unabashedly honest conversations. The most authentic connection I've shared with someone since my mother's death.* ". . . a few moments. But we just got caught up in the magic and romance. We agree we don't work. Right, Owen?"

I can see what the lie costs him—the pained expression in his eyes and the way his mouth draws into a tight line—but he still nods. Still sacrifices what he wants for what I need.

"So this was all just a fun game for you?" Diana asks. "Playing with this family's emotions for your own entertainment."

"She's not playing with anyone's emotions, Mom," Owen says, and I can tell he's holding back an eye roll.

"Of course you're going to side with the trollop."

"Don't talk about her like that," Owen says, more fiercely than I've ever heard him speak.

"What century is this?" Gabriel mutters, but he's still close enough for the mic to project it around the room.

"Can you turn off the fucking mic, Gabe?" I snap, and Diana gasps dramatically.

"Such foul language, too. I can't believe I thought you were good enough for my son. I'm ashamed of the role I played in trying to get you two back together."

Patricia—Diana's archnemesis who sees an opportunity to get back in her good graces—steps to her side. "My twins told me that she's been making a scene all week."

One of the twins—I'm too overwhelmed to figure out which—says, "We never said that," but neither woman is paying attention to him.

"I'm not surprised," Diana says. "She's desperate for attention. With the way she keeps jumping on any stage that will have her and toying with my son's feelings. She makes him fall in love with her, drops him like last week's newspaper, then strings him along like this? It's disgusting."

Cece stomps to the middle of the group, her embroidered dress catching the light like she's a living disco ball. "Diana Ellis Hayes, get control of yourself."

"I don't think there's room for you to talk, Mother. You've been trying to manipulate Owen for years."

All the Ellises are murmuring, the noise getting louder and louder as each new family member shares their opinion. The buzzing is too loud, too muddled to know what's being said, but I imagine the worst. My body preps for fight or flight. I've never been inclined to run, but if I follow my instinct, I'll just make the situation worse.

"Oh my god, stop attacking Thea. She didn't do anything wrong," Camila hollers from her seat at one of the tables. "It was all fake!"

The entire room goes silent, their eyes swinging between me and Owen. And holy shit, I'm going to need the Ellis-Gutiérrez siblings to stop trying to help me.

Diana looks at Owen, a stricken expression on her face. "What does she mean?"

I look at Addy, whose face is as devastated as Diana, but with an edge of guilt. This isn't what I wanted for her. I tried so hard to keep this from coming out, but it still happened in the end.

Owen sighs and rubs his forehead. "Thea and I pretended to be in a relationship back at Camila's wedding. I wanted to avoid everyone trying to set me up all weekend."

Diana spins to me. "I'm guessing this was your idea."

"No," Owen says emphatically. "It was mine."

"Of course you'd say that," she says. "You're trying to protect your *new* girlfriend."

"We both made mistakes," I say. "And we're so sorry for any stress and pain we caused."

Diana turns her vicious glare on Addy. "Did you know about this?"

"I . . . well . . . it's just . . ." Addy stammers.

Harrison steps up next to her, sliding a protective arm over her shoulders. "Yes, we knew."

Owen's brows pull together. "You knew?"

"Yeah," Harrison says, the usual warmth when he looks at his brother noticeably missing. "Addy told me yesterday. Always fun to learn your brother's secrets from someone else."

Owen's shoulders cave, and I fight against every instinct to step closer, to comfort him.

"I'm sorry, Harrison," he says, and Harrison scoffs in response.

"Oh," Diana says, spinning in a circle and projecting her voice louder. "So they *all* knew. How lovely."

"Diana, please—" I start, but she doesn't let me get another word out.

"You two are poison," she says, the words spitting from her mouth.

Maria pushes through the crowd, slipping her hand into Addy's. "Don't speak to my daughter that way."

Diana clasps her hands together. "You seem lovely, but you adopted her at fourteen. The damage was already done."

"Mom," Harrison says. "You need to calm down. If you keep speaking to Addy that way, you can consider your invitation to the wedding rescinded."

Diana scoffs. "Like I'm coming to the wedding. You boys *never* lied to me, and the moment the Pappas sisters come into the picture, you both start. I should have known they would ruin you the second I heard about their messed-up family."

My hands start shaking as a rush of pure rage flows through my body. She has the right to be angry about the lie, but she doesn't have the right to attack my sister, to make her feel ashamed for something she had no choice in. I'm about to light into her when Addy turns on her heel, running out of the ballroom. For a moment, I consider letting her leave while I bring down the force of my fury on Diana, but she's my priority.

Harrison starts after her, but I grab his shoulder. "Please, let me do this?"

He grinds his teeth together, looking toward the door where Addy disappeared before nodding once, a harsh, sharp movement. "Make this right."

I follow Addy a couple of steps behind. Instead of heading to the inn, Addy runs out into the vines.

She must be fueled by something special, because even with my longer legs, I can't keep up. "Addy, please wait."

She twirls on me, and there's a look I've never seen on her face. Pure, unadulterated rage. "Don't you think you've done enough?"

I flinch. "I'm sorry. I was telling Owen it was over and it just happened."

"How many times did you hook up this week?"

I wince, counting back. If we include the kisses . . . "Five times."

"Knowing I wanted you to keep your distance from him?"

"I tried," I plead with her, and she straightens her shoulders.

"You *tried*? Do you really believe that? You could have stayed away from him. You could have told Dawn and Diana you couldn't help with the cake because it would be too hard to spend time together. Or you could have not let him come with you to pick up the rings. Or, I don't know, maybe you could have just not fucked him."

I flinch, because she's right. She told me she was worried, asked me not to go there. I could have made any number of decisions this week that would have let her walk down the aisle tomorrow without this hanging over her head.

She rubs her hand over her mouth like she's trying to stop the flow of words, but there's no dam in the world strong enough to hold back the flow of her feelings now. "This whole week has been about you. Ellises left and right asking if I know what happened between you and Owen. Cousins brainstorming ways to push you together. Everyone trying to show you that you're admired and how much they want you in the family. Meanwhile, I—the person who *wants* to join the family—am ignored and pushed to the side, until I get looped in with you for the shit you've pulled. You didn't try to avoid something with him. You chose him, over and over."

"I didn't think it would—"

"Would what? Turn into this?" She gestures around herself. "But you knew it could. You knew how Diana would react if she found out, and you still chose your own pleasure over me. God, you're just like our mother, making the selfish choice because you care more about feeling good for a moment than my long-term happiness."

Her words land like the blows of a boxer who got the upper hand in a match, pummeling the opponent with one fist after another until they're left bleeding out on the floor of the ring.

"Why does no one I love choose me?" Her voice breaks on the words. "What did I do in a past life to earn me a family who doesn't think I'm worth protecting?"

"I'm sorry," I say, my voice weak.

She swipes at her tears. "Just go."

"Addy, plea—"

"I said fucking go," she yells, and I flinch away from her.

I nod as I blink back my tears, turning away before she can see them. I've caused enough damage, and she doesn't need to be subjected to my messy emotions, too.

I'm numb by the time I reach my room. Vaughn's leaning against the wall with his suitcase in hand. "The pregnant one wouldn't give me a key. Said she wasn't letting some creepy-ass man into her friend's room. Nice that you made a friend."

"I don't have the energy, Vaughn." I swipe the key without looking at him.

He follows me inside. "You sounded like you needed me. I'm sorry if I made it worse."

I grab my bag and start throwing things in without paying attention to what's going where.

"What are you doing?" he asks. "You're not running away."

"No, Addy asked me to leave."

"You can't leave," Vaughn says, flipping the suitcase closed. "Thee, come on. Emotions are high. Let's just give it the night."

I would, except she's finally let out all those feelings she's kept hidden. Waiting would only give her time to feel guilty.

"Please don't make this into an argument," I say. "I have to go."

He rolls his lips together, then sighs, flipping my suitcase open again. Without asking, he packs up my bag, refolding the things I haphazardly threw in and gathering everything else around the room, and I feel a pang of gratitude for him. While I wait, I realize there's one more thing I need to do before I leave. I sit at the beautiful desk, pull over the little notepad and pen, and start writing.

I make it through three pages before I feel content, folding them over on top of each other. "I'll be back in a couple minutes."

Vaughn opens his mouth to speak, then thinks better of it. I leave without giving him a chance to change his mind, heading a floor down until I find the room I'm looking for. I knock. And wait. I knock again, and again, and again, until the door swings open to reveal a scowling Diana.

"What do you want?"

I hold out the folded sheets of paper to her. "To give you an explanation."

"I don't need anything from you."

"Just read the fucking letter, Diana," I snap, and her skin turns a deep shade of red. "I get it. You hate me, and honestly, the feeling's pretty mutual. You've been horrible to the most important people in my life, but for some reason, they still want a relationship with you. So read the letter. Addy doesn't deserve to suffer for my mistakes, and Harrison deserves a future with the woman he loves."

She eyes the papers like a snake she expects to strike at any moment. After a full minute, Diana reaches out to take them. Her eyes are steely, but she tucks the pages into the pocket of her fluffy robe.

I nod and leave. That fifteen-second interaction drained the last bit of fight from me. The warm hallways of the inn that felt so homey the past few days now feel heavy, like the walls are going to cave in and crush me at any second. My door is in sight when Owen's voice calls out from behind me. I consider slipping into my room and pretending I didn't hear him, but he doesn't deserve that from me.

He wraps his arms around me, and I let him. The damage is already done. What's one last hug?

Owen pulls back, placing his hands on either side of my neck just like he did a few hours earlier, but it's not the same. There's no thrill at the contact, no tingling of my skin or racing of my heart. I've gone numb.

"I'll fix this," he says, strong but frantic in his conviction. "I promise you, I'll make this right."

I nod, because what else can I do. Whatever happens, I won't be around to see it.

"Thea, please say you believe me."

"Of course." My voice is scratchy, like I've gone days without speaking.

"I'm going to let my mom sleep on it. She'll be easier to manage in the morning, but I'll head there first thing. It'll work out."

"Okay." My voice is as dead as my relationship with Addy.

"Can I stay with you? I don't want you to be alone."

"Vaughn's here," I say, my voice and body stiff as an oak tree.

Owen nods. "Can I kiss you goodnight?"

I close the gap instead, gifting myself one last kiss. It's a bizarre experience, touching someone you care about so deeply, knowing it's the last time. I let myself savor it all. The softness of his lips. The way his breath hitches at the slide of my tongue. The fresh taste of him and that deep sugary smell that will follow me until my last breath.

Owen breaks the kiss first, tilting his head so our foreheads rest together. "Go get some sleep. Everyone will be in a better headspace tomorrow."

He smiles and kisses my forehead before heading down the hallway. It isn't until he's out of sight that I can force myself to leave, too. When I enter the room, my things are neatly packed away.

"I'm coming with you," Vaughn says.

I smile, but it dissolves into tears that have Vaughn rushing over to hold me. My world is falling apart. I have no job, no sister, no significant other. But I have Vaughn, and that's worth more than I can say.

"I'm asking a lot," I say, wiping my face with a tissue before grabbing my purse and suitcase. "But I need you to stay. Please. To bring my car home when it's fixed and to smooth everything over."

"How the hell am I supposed to do that?"

"You have more charm than Jonathan Bailey. You'll figure it out. If I stay, it'll just cause more issues. Please make sure the wedding happens tomorrow."

He looks like he wants to argue, but nods. I believe him. He'll do it.

But I won't be here to see it.

Chapter 31

OWEN

I didn't sleep. All night I paced my room, wondering if I should go check on Thea. She looked so broken last night, and I hate the idea of her working through this alone.

The moment the sun breaks over the horizon, I head to my mom's room. I need to calm her down, to appease her for the wedding. The thought of her getting away with how she acted last night grates, but I know it's what Thea wants. And there's nothing I wouldn't do to see Thea's brilliant smile again. I can hash everything out with Mom after.

Mom's door swings open mere seconds after I knock, like she's been up and waiting for me to come by.

"I assume you're here to apologize?" she asks.

I swallow my pride. "Yes. I'm sorry for lying to you, then and now. I shouldn't have done it."

Shockingly, she reaches out and pats my cheek. I was primed for hours of groveling. "It's not your fault. I'm just glad that toxic relationship is out of your life."

I smile in relief—everything's going to be fine—until my brain fully processes her words. "Wait, what do you mean?"

I follow her into her room as she walks to the desk, waving around a few pieces of paper. "Thea dropped this off."

I snatch the papers out of her hand so quickly she's lucky she doesn't get a paper cut. The letter is long, and my mind struggles to focus on the words with the blood pulsing in my veins, but I catch the most important ones.

Please forgive Owen and Addy. This was all my idea. . . .

. . . Addy is incredible and shouldn't be punished for being born into my family . . .

. . . manipulated Owen into the lie so I could make some extra money . . .

. . . You can accept Addy into your family knowing you'll never have to see me again. . . .

"When did she give you this?" I ask, my voice so harsh that Mom jumps.

"Last night."

"What time?" I yell, and she flinches.

"I don't know. Around nine?"

When I saw her in the hallway. She already knew she was leaving, and she didn't tell me. But of course she wouldn't. She knows I'd never let her walk away, not like this. Not when she's throwing herself under the bus so Addy and I don't have to deal with the consequences.

She's gone. She's gone, and I can't breathe. I don't know where she is or how to get to her. My fierce warrior—who fights for everyone but has been told she's not worth fighting for—is heartbroken and alone. I brace my hands on my knees, trying to get air into my lungs.

I never should have left last night, should have known she'd do something like this. If I'd been thinking clearly, I'd have spent the night running my fingers through her curls, telling her every little thing that I love about her. All the big and little ways she makes the lives of everyone around her better. That if she weren't here, these mountains would lose their luster, everything dimming to black and white. I should have fought for her like she fought for me and Addy.

That's what I'm going to do now. I don't care if it disrupts the wedding, if it forever alters the way my family looks at me. I'm going to get her back, and then I'm going to spend the rest of my goddamn life making sure she knows there's at least one person who will fight for her, who would burn the fucking world down to make sure she's safe and happy.

I run for the door, ignoring Mom calling after me. My feet skid on the carpeted hallway when I come to a stop at Addy's door. My fist comes down so hard on the wood that the whole thing shudders. I only make it five seconds before knocking again.

"Addy, open the goddamn door," I call out.

Harrison pops his head out of the room next door. "What the fuck, Owen?"

I bang on the door again, barely sparing him a glance.

When I lift my fist again, Harrison grabs my shirt, pushing me against the wall. "You lie to us, fuck up my wedding, and crush my future wife, and then think you can come up here like this?"

My blood is roaring in my veins. "I'm sorry for the lie, and I'm sorry for what happened last night." I don't sound sorry, and Harrison raises a brow. "I'll give you the apology you deserve later, but I can't do this right now."

"I don't care if you *can't*. You're going to."

"Thea needs me. What would you do if Addy needed you?"

I'm desperate, begging him to understand. I've seen how much he loves Addy, the things he would do for her. If anyone can get how I'm feeling right now, it's him. Harrison's jaw tightens, but he nods as Addy's door swings open. She's in her robe, fresh-faced and still wiping the sleep out of her eyes.

My mom rushes down the hallway to us, huffing out a breath. "Owen, what is the meaning of this?"

I hold the papers out to Addy. "Read."

Her eyes skim the paper, going wider with each second while I dig my phone out of my pocket to try Thea. It goes straight to voicemail, and I scream in frustration.

"Where did you get this?" Addy asks, her voice wobbling.

"She dropped it off with my mom last night." I dial Vaughn next, and he picks up on the first ring. "Where is she?"

"She's gone," he says. "Addy told her to leave."

His words land like a match to gasoline. I'm a living flame, and I'm going to burn everyone down with me. I jab at the phone to put him on speakerphone. "Say that again."

"Owen, come o—"

"Fucking say it, Vaughn."

He pauses for a minute, then repeats, "Addy told her to leave."

Addy's face goes white. "She's gone?"

"Yes, she's gone," I scream, and Addy flinches. Harrison steps between us, but I have no intention of hurting her with anything but my words. "You told your sister, who has spent her whole life prioritizing you, that you don't want her here. What the fuck did you think would happen?"

"I didn't think she'd leave," Addy whispers, almost like she's talking to herself.

Harrison slides his arm around her shoulder, murmuring in her ear.

"I said the most horrible things to her, Harrison." A tear slips from her eyes, and she swats it away with a jerky movement so reminiscent of Thea that I want to cry myself. "I was angry and scared I'd lose you."

He kisses her forehead. "We'll sort it out."

"Driving or flying, Vaughn?" I ask.

He hums, an infuriatingly passive-aggressive sound that has me thankful he's on the phone and not close enough for me to punch. "Not sure."

"Bullshit. Her car's still in the shop, so if she drove, she'd have to take your car. Did you fly or drive here?"

"She doesn't want anyone to follow her, Owen," Vaughn says, almost sympathetically. I've always liked him and regretted losing touch when he left Hayes, but I'm at the end of my rope.

"You know what? It doesn't matter. Either I'll catch her at

the airport or I'll get on the next flight back to Orlando to go after her." I stab the end call button as a replacement for the fist I want to put through the wall.

"What about the wedding?" Mom asks.

"Like I'm going to the wedding," I say sarcastically. "Isn't that what you said yesterday when you were humiliating Thea?"

She gasps like I've attacked her. "Well, I don't—"

I don't care enough to hear what she has to say, instead turning to Harrison. "You know how much I love you, right?"

His normally jovial face is written in harsh lines right now. For a minute, I think he's going to lay into me about the lying, but then he walks to me in a couple of long strides and pulls me in, a clinging full-hearted hug. "Go. We're fine."

Mom grabs my arm. "Owen, this isn't like you. I get why you're so charmed by her—we all were—but she's not worth throwing away your family for."

I turn back to her, reading the terror underneath her angry facade. I think, for the first time in thirty-two years, I may understand her. She's been dealt a shitty hand, watching the love of her life waste away. Seeing Thea eaten away by disease would break something inside me, too. It's easy to assume her issues are about wanting control, but maybe it's something more. Maybe it's her fear of what happens if she *does* let go.

Part of me—a very, very large part after last night—wants to write my mother off. She has manipulated me my entire life. I now realize she's hurt Harrison with her indifference. And worst of all, she drove Thea away. I'm not sure that's something I can forgive.

But the truth is none of us have been honest with her. We haven't given her the chance to change, at best ignoring her behaviors and at worst enabling them. Maybe she won't hear us—maybe she's too buried in her own issues to dig herself out—but I have to at least try.

My heart's pounding, beating out a rhythm that says, *Get to*

Thea, get to Thea, get to Thea, but I force myself to slow down. I want a future with her. A real future, where we can build our lives together. And to do that, it needs to start from a place of honesty. I don't know how my mother will respond, and I've realized I can't control that.

"Mom, I need to tell you something, and I need you to hear me. I don't have time to say this more than once, and I'm not going to fight with you. First, and most important, everything Thea said about me in that letter is a lie. She was telling the truth about Addy's involvement—she found out the day before you did—but it wasn't Thea's idea. I didn't even know her until after I'd come up with the plan, and our mutual friend introduced us so I could ask her to pretend to be my girlfriend. She didn't influence or manipulate me. It was all me."

My mom's eyes fill with tears. "I don't understand why you'd do something like that."

"I know you don't, because I've never been brave enough to tell you. I know things were hard before Dad died and only got worse once he was gone, but I've always felt responsible for keeping this family together. Every time I've tried to do something off the path of what you've decided for me, you shut down."

"That's not true," she cuts in.

"Mom," I say, leveling her with a stare. "I mentioned I want to start a side business for something I love, and you went to bed for a day. You almost missed Harrison's rehearsal."

"Would have been better if she had," Harrison mutters, and I shoot him a glare. She doesn't need us ganging up on her.

I continue. "I don't want the life I'm living. I've never enjoyed the work, but I've done it because I felt obligated to do what was best for this family, to maintain Dad's legacy. I wasn't willing to sacrifice my relationship with you. But I can't keep living like this—giving up what I want because I'm walking on eggshells. And I won't lose Thea because I'm too scared of the fallout with you."

She sniffles. "You think I'm that bad of a mother?"

I rub my hands down my face. "If this is how you're going to respond, then I'm going to go. I'm not missing the chance to catch Thea because you refuse to hear what I'm saying."

I head down the hallway, disappointed with her reaction but not terribly surprised. I feel lighter. It's a relief to have it all out there.

I only make it a few feet before a small hand closes around my bicep. Addy stares up at me, her chin thrust high.

"I'm going to get her," she says.

I scoff. "Like hell you are."

"I'm the one who did this," she says, her voice breaking on the words. "She's done everything for me, and I drove her away. *I* need to fix this, not you."

My fists clench. She's not wrong, but the thought of leaving this to anyone else grates at my soul. Thea's mine, and I want to be the one to protect her, to help her when she's hurting.

"I'm not staying here," I say.

Addy's posture goes even straighter. "Together, then."

I nod, and she sprints back to her room to get dressed.

Harrison walks to me, slipping his hands in his pockets. "You never told me you don't like our work."

I shrug. "Didn't see the point."

"Of course there's a point. We're co-owners. You've always been in charge, but you don't have to take it all on. If you don't want it, *I* do."

"Come on," I say, crossing my arms over my chest. "You don't want Hayes."

"Yes, I do," he says. "I know you don't take me seriously, but I've been working my ass off to get to know the company."

After the last twenty-four hours, I don't have the emotional energy to hold back my thoughts anymore. "Harrison, you bounce around from department to department. That's not the behavior of someone who enjoys their job."

His lips pinch. "Is that what you think? I've been trying to get to know what each department does. I can't lead the company with you if I don't understand it."

My mouth drops open. "What?"

"How else am I supposed to learn? No one cared enough to teach the spare, so I had to figure it out myself. But I love my work. I love Hayes, not because it was Dad's, but because it's mine."

For a moment, I'm stunned into speechlessness. There are better ways to learn, but how could he know that when I never took the time to teach him? I created my own idea of who Harrison is and pushed him into that box, never stopping to ask why he wanted to move around the company so much. I'm not too different from Mom, telling Harrison who he is instead of letting him tell me.

And selfishly, I can't help but think about what this means for me if he's serious. No, not if. I'm done questioning him. If he says he's serious, I believe him.

I clap him on the shoulder as Addy comes back out. "Okay. Let's talk."

The three of us take the stairs at a run, stumbling into the lobby. It's packed full with dozens of family members. Camila and Mira, still in their pajamas. The twins and their partners. Lynne and Jourdan arguing about god knows what. And right in the middle of them all is Vaughn, grinning like the Cheshire cat.

"Figured you could use some backup," he says.

I walk over, pulling him into a back-slapping hug. "Thanks, man. It's great to see you."

"You can fawn over me *after* you get Thea back."

Gabriel flies through the front door, swinging the bright yellow key chain around his finger. "Bus is out front."

"I brought breakfast for everyone," Camila calls out, lifting two giant bags of pastries that Mira rips from her hands.

"And I've got crafting supplies," Lynne yells, lifting poster boards and a bag of markers.

"Why the hell do we need crafting supplies?" Johnny asks.

"To win her back, obviously," Lynne says with an epic eye roll.

I smile at my wild, overwhelming, supportive, *perfect* family. "If you're coming, get on the damn bus and let's go."

I'm the last one on, taking the seat Harrison saved for me up front.

I rub a hand over Gabriel's hair. "Drive like a maniac, kid."

For once, he doesn't make a comment about not being a kid. He just grins a slightly terrifying smile and turns the key.

And I settle in to figure out what I'm going to say when we reach the airport. Assuming she isn't already gone.

Chapter 32

THEA

One fun fact I never thought I'd have to learn? When you're in your late twenties, sleeping on an airport seat is not an acceptable choice. My back is aching so bad I don't know if I'll ever stand properly again. A crick in my neck is forcing me to keep it tilted just slightly to the left, making the world around me lopsided.

By the time I dropped off Vaughn's rental car at the Asheville airport, TSA was closed for the night. Getting a hotel room was out of the question after draining my account for this plane ticket, so I found a seat by the baggage claim carousels and fell into a sleep that included mutilated versions of all the best moments from the week. Baking with Owen, until Diana kicks in the door and drags me out by my hair, or us together in the barn, only to have it collapse, burying Owen and making it impossible to get to him.

When the sun rises, I drag myself to the TSA checkpoint, turning my phone back on to access my ticket. Messages flood in. Owen's name over and over again until it swims in my vision. I ignore it, scanning my ticket quickly and turning it back off.

I go through security, getting questioning looks from the agent who clocks my puffy eyes and splotchy face. It earns me a special pat-down, but I'd take anything to distract from the way my heart is back at the inn, leaving me with nothing to pump the blood through my veins.

I find another hard seat, wondering if I should grab a crappy airport sandwich from the little kiosk, but the idea of eating makes my stomach roil. My eyes close, hoping for the smallest bit of rest after such a shitty night. I'm drifting off, in that space between waking and dreaming where everything feels a little magical, when I hear my name. It's soft and kind, relieved, like the speaker has been searching for me all their life. It feels like home. My lips lift, thanking my brain for making this dream pleasant—no angry mothers or murderous barns—when a hand closes over my shoulder.

My brain takes a few minutes to catch up, to recognize that I'm not, in fact, dreaming. Addy's standing over my seat.

"You haven't left yet," she says.

"There were no flights until this afternoon," I say, my brain struggling to catch up. "I'm sorry, I tried to leave sooner."

She drops into the seat next to me. "I'm so sorry, Tia."

I blink at her, my mind not at full operating capacity after a shitty night's sleep. "You're . . . I'm sorry, what?"

She takes my hand. "I never should have said what I said last ni—"

"But it's true," I cut in as my eyes flood with tears again. I'd have guessed I'd be too dehydrated at this point to produce more. "I *am* selfish."

"No—"

I don't let her finish, words pouring out as my breaths come too quickly. "I'm not like Mom. I'm worse. She was sick. Owen isn't an addictive substance. He didn't strip me of my free will. It was all me, every moment where I could have walked away and chose not to. Every second was all my selfishness."

"No," Addy says, clutching my hands so hard it hurts. "*I'm* the selfish one. I asked you to give up your long-term happiness so I could avoid a bit of discomfort. I saw that this thing between you and Owen wasn't temporary, and I ignored it because it was easier for me. I hate myself for trying to take him away from you. It had nothing to do with you and everything to do with my paranoia that I'd lose Harrison because that's what happens when I have something good. It never lasts, and I've been waiting for months for the other shoe to drop."

I hate that she's been fighting that fear, and I hate that I'm the reason she has it to begin with.

I suck in a shuddering breath. "I'm the other shoe."

Addy releases a surprised laugh. "What?"

I want to laugh with her, but I can't when I feel destroyed. I can't even look at her, staring instead at my ratty suitcase. "I'm the reason we were moved so much. The reason you had so many of those good things stripped away. The reason you weren't adopted by the Fischers as a toddler. Your life would have been so much better without me."

Addy kicks my suitcase out of the way before kneeling in front of me. Her jaw is as tight as the grip on my hands. "None of that is true. We lost every home because the system is broken, not because you are. You protected me. You're the reason I'm still here. I don't think I'd have made it through our childhood alone. You saved me."

I choke on a sob. As much as I want to believe her, I know the truth. "I know you feel guilty about last night and think you need to fix it, but you—"

Addy starts crying, too. "I *do* feel guilty, because you've been there my entire life, and I'm just realizing that I've never thanked you. I never made it clear that you've been the light of my life. I don't know why the Fischers didn't adopt us together, but they made a huge mistake missing out on a life with you. And whatever their reasons were, I don't care. I wouldn't trade you for anything, much less those extra years with them."

"But it's not just them. It's your future with Harrison, too."

"I wouldn't trade you for that either, but luckily I'll never have to pick. He'd never ask that of me because he knows how much I love you. Things with Diana may not be what I was hoping for, but that's *her* fault, not yours. She's the one who chose not to have a relationship with us. And I think she's going to regret it, because you're the best person I know."

I nudge her with my knee, unable to stop the little smile curving my mouth. "Stop."

"No, seriously!" She moves back to the seat next to me, tucking my curls behind my ear. "I hate that I've made you think there's something wrong with you when you're incredible. You're hilarious and kind and loyal and perfect."

"I'm really not. You're the perfect one."

"I try to be." Her smile doesn't reach her eyes. "But I'm broken. God, I'm just so fucking broken."

Her voice cracks on the words, and my instinct is to jump in, to fix it. I want to tell her that one difficult week during an extremely stressful time doesn't make her broken. But the pain on her face tells me this isn't new, that maybe there are feelings Addy's hidden even from me, and brushing off those emotions—even in an attempt to help—will just make her feel worse.

"Addy." I take her hand back between mine as she blinks up at the ceiling.

"I'm sorry," she says. "This isn't about me. It's about you."

"It's about *us*," I say, squeezing her hand. "You're a pretty important part of us. How are you broken?"

The inhale is shaky, and for a second I don't think she'll answer. "I don't let people in because I'm terrified that when they see how messy I am, they'll run away screaming, and then I get angry that no one cares about knowing me. I ask for your help trying to connect with the family, then resent you for becoming close with them. I worship you, then get jealous of the things I idolize."

I jolt at that statement. We've always been close, but I thought it was because I was the only consistent thing in her life. The idea that Addy—smart, capable, level-headed Addy—wants to be like me is incomprehensible.

Addy swipes away a tear. "I wish I was comfortable in my skin the way you are. You say what you think, and people love you for it. Meanwhile, I'm frozen, so nervous about saying something wrong that I don't end up saying anything at all. I've always wanted to be like you. I watched you with the Ellises all week, and seeing how those traits I've always tried—and failed—to imitate got this family to accept you . . . I think I started resenting you without realizing it. It wasn't fair."

Her tears are falling in earnest now, a half dozen emotions warring on her face. Guilt and exhaustion and embarrassment and hurt. Regret. Loneliness.

"I'm not the easiest person to get to know," Addy continues through her tears. "I convinced myself that you being so open and wonderful was the reason they weren't getting to know me, but it wasn't you. It was me. And I hurt the most important person in my life because I was too scared to admit I'm the problem. I'm so sorry, Tia."

Warmth blossoms in my chest at her apology even as a knot forms in my throat. I hate that she's been fighting this without me, that I haven't been able to help her through it. Our fight hurt me in so many ways, but I can see her words for what they were—pain and fear, just like all those times I lashed out when I was younger.

There's more for us to work through, but there's one vital thing I need Addy to know before anything else. "For what it's worth, I think you're really easy to love."

She lets out another sob. "Stop being nice when I was such a bitch to you."

"I love you. And Harrison loves you, more than I knew was possible. And the rest of them will come around if you open yourself up a bit. Just pretend they're me. Lord knows you've never had a hard time telling me how you feel."

I laugh as Addy groans and drops her head to my shoulder. "I'd never forgive me."

"Well, lucky for both of us, I'm not you."

Addy pulls back to meet my gaze. "Please come back. I can't get married without you. You're my family, my true family."

I force a tight smile. "I'm fine. I want you to have the beautiful wedding you've imagined with no mother-in-law drama. You go, take a million pictures, and show them to me at brunch or something when you get back from your honeymoon."

Addy's eyes rove over my face. "Yeah, that's not happening."

She taps at her phone before holding it up, showing a ticket for the same flight I'm scheduled to be on.

My eyes go wide. "Addy, you can't be serious."

"Dead serious. Either we go back to Elk Ridge together, or we go back to Florida together."

A short laugh bursts out of me. "This is blackmail. Wait, extortion?"

Her nose scrunches up. "Coercion, maybe?"

A flurry of nerves erupts in my stomach. I want to go back, more than I could possibly say. I want to watch Addy walk down the aisle and hold her bouquet while she pledges her life to Harrison.

"I don't want to ruin your wedding day."

"Then stop being stubborn and come back with me. The only way you can ruin my day is by making me get on that plane. I really want to get married today, Tia."

Adrenaline shoots through my veins at the prospect of facing the Ellis family again. I think about the disdain from Diana as I dropped off my letter. About all the whispers moving through the crowd at the rehearsal dinner, the way everyone's faces got more and more wary with each revelation. I think of Owen, who must feel so betrayed by me leaving without telling him. The idea of seeing that hurt on his face makes me sick to my stomach.

But—God willing—Addy will only get married once. And if she wants me there, nothing can keep me away.

"Okay," I say, and Addy jumps up like she needs to get us moving before I change my mind.

"Thank god." She tugs on my hand, using her full body weight to force me to stand. "I didn't want to cancel this wedding."

She wraps her arm around my waist, and I throw mine over her shoulder, closing my eyes against the moisture pricking them. I let her blindly lead me from the gates to the airport exit, and when we step through the sliding doors, a round of cheers goes up.

My eyes pop open. There's a giant group of Ellises right outside security. The crowd is littered with posters with handwritten phrases in blocky letters, surrounded by glittery swirls and stars and hearts. I spot Camila holding one with a stone-faced Mira that reads, COME HOME, THEA. The twins are in there with their own signs—DON'T LEAVE US and WE MISS YOU ALREADY. Vaughn's next to them with a sign that reads REMEMBER I LOVED YOU FIRST. Others jump from the back, trying to lift their own posters over their taller cousins' heads like fans outside the *Today* show.

And right there at the front, his hands stuffed into his pockets like he's physically holding himself back, is Owen. He doesn't look betrayed or angry like I expected. All I see is stark relief shining out of those stunning eyes. There's no stopping the tears this time.

"What are you all doing here?"

Owen steps forward, his hands still restrained but now within reaching distance of me if he let himself. "We couldn't let you leave."

"I drove," Gabriel yells from behind him.

Camila smacks him upside the head, muttering a curse in Spanish. "Can you let them have their moment, please?"

"Just saying," he grumbles, and a watery laugh flows from my lips.

Owen lets one of his hands free to run it down his face,

mumbling something I can't hear before bringing his gaze back to me.

"This week's been intense, and there's a good chance you'll walk away because who in their right mind would want to keep this family, but there are things I need you to know before you do."

He steps closer, bringing our bodies almost flush and sliding that freed hand along the side of my neck. An embarrassing whimper escapes me at the contact, and his eyes flare.

"I won't say 'I love you,'" he starts, and my stomach bottoms out. "I know you don't believe in love after such a short time."

"You can't know someone well enough to love them in a week," I say, regurgitating the same concept I've always believed, but something deep inside me revolts. What could this feeling be if not love?

His mouth twitches. "Yes, I've heard the spiel. And when I say those words to you, there will be no doubt in your mind that I mean them."

When. Not *if*.

Shit, my heart's going to give out.

"But what I can tell you," Owen continues, like he hasn't done enough damage to my cardiovascular system, "is that I've loved every part of you I've gotten to see. I love your sense of humor and your questions. I love how passionate you get when you're upset and that you let me see the emotions underneath it all when you're ready. I love how protective you are of the people you care about, that you're willing to fight for them if necessary. I love the way your brain works and that one touch from you wakes me up, like I've spent my life asleep until your hand brushed my skin."

"Didn't need to know that one," Gabriel calls out, and the crowd laughs.

Owen doesn't take his eyes off me, even as his smile grows at the goading.

"I've spent my whole life trying to make others happy. You're the first thing I've wanted enough to go off the path. I know the past twenty-four hours have been miserable, but if you give me the chance, I'll spend the rest of our lives overwriting them with happy memories."

Owen's a blur before me, and it's by instinct alone that my lips find his. He sighs, his other hand weaving through my hair. The kiss is a clash of contradictions. The sweetness from whatever pastry he had this morning mixing with the salt of my tears. His lips are soft on mine while the hand in my hair grips tight like he owns me. I'm not sure if I want to collapse into him and cry, or if I want him to drag me into the closest bathroom and fuck me until I'm certain I'll always be his.

"So happy for you two, but could you do this *after* Addy and I get married?" Harrison says from the crowd, and Owen and I pull away, laughing.

"Let's get you back where you belong," Owen whispers, his forehead dropping to mine.

We head back to the bus that Jourdan's been circling around the drop-off lane for the past thirty minutes. My eyes scan the group, and I see so many people I've gotten close to this week. Everyone but Diana and Cece.

Addy's arms are wrapped around Harrison as she beams up at him. Owen seems content as he weaves our fingers together, pressing his lips to the back of my hand. They're all happy. Untroubled. But I can't help but wonder how long the happiness will last with what's waiting for us at the inn.

Chapter 33

OWEN

Relief doesn't cover it. Elation. Euphoria. Ecstasy.

My family's waiting on the pickup platform for Jourdan to bring the bus around, and we have just enough time for a moment away from their prying eyes. I catch Harrison's gaze and jerk my head to the side. He rolls his eyes, but nods and taps his watch. I give him a little salute, then use the hand twined through Thea's to tug her to the side before the sliding glass doors, backing her against the stretch of wall.

Thea smiles up at me, a bit teasingly but still so soft. "Mr. Hayes, someone could see us."

"Let them watch," I murmur, bringing my mouth down to hers.

She's delectable, far surpassing every recipe I've obsessed over until I considered it perfect. I want to drag her away, lock her in a tower only I can access, like a princess in a fairy tale. The second we get on that bus, everyone's going to pull her away from me. I'm not ready to share her when I just got her back.

I pull away, planting a soft kiss on her nose. "You never said yes."

"You never asked a question," she says. "Are you asking me to be your girlfriend?"

She bats her lashes. It's over the top and ridiculous and so perfect I could cry. "Boyfriend and girlfriend" feels so flippant, so small compared to the size of my feelings for her. But even I can recognize that saying I want to call her my future wife after only seven days is absurd, so I smile.

"Will you be my girlfriend, Thea Simone Pappas?"

She kisses me again, smiling against my lips, but I refuse to be distracted.

"Answer the question," I practically growl.

She hesitates, and I'm instantly flooded with adrenaline.

"I want to," she whispers.

"Then say yes."

"But what does this look like? What happens with your mom? Is each interaction with her going to be a fight, or are you planning on cutting her out? And if you do that, how long before you come to resent me?"

I place a finger over her lips to stop the flow of questions. "I get why you're worried. Mom and I had a blowup before we came to get you, and I don't know what it's going to look like. But I told her everything, including how miserable I've been at my job. Even if she doesn't accept it, it's all out there now."

"And you won't regret that?"

"Regret living for myself?" I scoff. "Absolutely not. I've never felt so free. I did it for us, but I did it for myself, too."

She blinks away tears and nods, leaning up to kiss me. "Then yes."

I pull away before her lips can distract me again. "There's something else. I'm leaving the company."

She blinks up at me with her wide brown eyes, surprised at having her kiss thwarted, but her face breaks into a smile. "Owen! That's amazing!"

I rub the back of my neck, feeling sheepish about it now. "Yeah, on the bus ride here, Harrison brought up buying me out. He loves the work, and he said if we could set up a payment plan, he'd give me the out. It'll take a while for me to get him ready, but we've set a schedule. Six months of intensive training, and then he'll take over, with me on speed dial if any issues come up."

She runs a hand up my chest. "How do you feel about that? You've always felt trapped there. Are you worried you're doing the same thing to Harrison?"

"There are those questions I love." I press a quick peck to her lips, a small thrill shooting through me every time I say the word "love" to her. "No, I don't feel that way. He's explored other options, interned with different companies while he was in school, and he's going in with clear eyes. I love it for him, and knowing that someone else will carry on my dad's passion takes some of the pressure off."

My stomach flips as I prepare to say the next thing, and I'm not sure if it's nerves or excitement.

"But there's one more thing. If I'm not tied to Hayes, I'm free to do whatever I want. And *wherever* I want."

Her eyes go wider. "Are you saying . . ."

"I have a lot to figure out, but yeah. I want to start a bakery up here. Which means you can take that job with Camila." My body flushes. "Not that where I am would be the determining factor of whether or not you'd take the job, because you should do what you want, and we don't even have to stay—"

She cuts me off with a kiss. "I want to be where you are. But I'd be especially happy if it was up here."

"Thank god." I'd follow her back to Florida, but I'm so excited about the chance to stay up here, in a place I've always loved.

She chuckles, laying her head on my chest. I keep us anchored together as I lean back, glancing out the glass door to see almost everyone's on the bus now. "We need to catch up."

She groans. "Fine, but I'm staying in your room tonight."

I kiss the top of her head, a rogue curl from her night sleeping in the airport tickling my nose. "You better."

I weave our fingers back together, loving the freedom to do it without worrying who'll see. The entire bus erupts in cheers when we climb the steps. Just like I expected, everyone wants to talk to Thea, trying to pull her into seats beside them and peppering her with questions.

"Y'all wanted us stuck together in the back of the bus on Monday, so that's where we'll be," I say, towing her behind me. "If you need us, don't."

Thea's laugh is booming and free, and I've never been happier in my life. The cousins boo, but no one tries to stop us. I pull her down next to me in the back row and do exactly what I wanted to do on Monday. I kiss her the whole way home.

* * *

We all pile out of the bus when we reach the inn, everyone ribbing us for how we spent the drive, but my face is stretched wide in a grin. Thea keeps popping up to kiss the dimple that's on permanent display now.

When I wrap my arms around Thea's waist from behind, I catch sight of Addy a few feet away. She's watching Thea, a soft smile teasing at the corners of her lips. It's the most genuine expression I've seen on her face, and I think there's a chance I'll be able to forgive her for the hurt she caused Thea. Eventually.

"Can I borrow my assistant for an hour?" I ask Addy, my arms tightening a fraction.

"I'm supposed to get ready with Addy," Thea says, kissing my jaw.

"I'll be fine for an hour," Addy says, turning toward the rest of the family as she twists her hands together. "Would, um . . . would any of you ladies . . . would you like to come get ready with us? Keep me company until Thea's done?"

Camila and Lynne blink at each other in surprise, but then Lynne speaks up. "I have to do some things for the wedding in a bit, but I could hang for a glass of champagne."

"Or a bottle," Jourdan says, sliding up next to them.

"You two talk like you'll stop at one bottle," Mira says in her typical exasperated tone. "It's like when these two get together, they think the first person to puke wins Miss fucking America."

A laugh bursts out of Addy, but it quickly turns into a snort, and her eyes go wide in embarrassment.

Camila throws an arm over Addy's shoulder. "Oh yeah, we're going to have fun with that."

The five women head off into the inn, and Thea releases a sigh, her body melting even more into mine. "She's going to find a place with your family, right?"

I nod, placing a soft kiss to her shoulder. "Of course. Now let's go finish a cake."

Thea's the one who reaches for my hand this time. I wonder how long it will take for these casual touches to stop destroying me, scattering my brain cells until nothing exists but where our bodies meet. I hope it takes forever.

I'm so wrapped up in her that it takes me a few seconds to realize we aren't alone in the kitchen. My mother and grandmother are standing together, lifting the second tier over the bottom tier of the wedding cake.

I step forward, dropping Thea's hand to reach mine out. "Stop! What are you doing? Have you even put in the support structure?"

My mother throws her hands in the air, Nana precariously balancing the cake for a few seconds before I slide into place, helping lower it to the counter next to the bottom tier. Mom's already massaging the space between her brows.

"I was trying to help." She straightens her shoulders and meets my eyes.

This is her version of an apology. It's what I've accepted for years, where she does something nice to make up for whatever she did wrong without having to say the words "I'm sorry." And it's nowhere near enough.

I step back beside Thea, slipping my arm around her waist. "That's what you want to say to us right now?"

Mom lets out a little whimper. "I'm sorry my help isn't good enough for you."

Nana runs a hand down her face. "Diana, what did we talk about?"

She twirls on Nana, lifting a hand at me. "I'm supporting the wedding. I'm *helping*, and he doesn't even say thank you."

Nana opens her mouth to argue, but I cut her off. "Mom, if you want a relationship with me—and with Harrison, too, if I had to guess—you owe Thea and Addy an apology."

I think she's going to resist, but Nana steps forward, slipping her hand into hers and squeezing. Mom looks at her, a trace of pain and vulnerability sliding over her face.

Mom turns back to Thea. "I shouldn't have spoken that way last night."

"Diana," Nana whispers, drawing the word out.

Mom drops her eyes to the kitchen floor. "I'm sorry."

Thea looks at me like I'll guide the conversation, but I'm as surprised as she is.

"Thank you," Thea says, but it sounds more like a question.

Mom purses her lips. "I don't hate you. And I hope—if you're going to be in my son's life long-term—that eventually you'll stop hating me."

I look at Thea with a raised brow, and she winces, whispering, "I may have gone off on your mother before I left last night."

Fuck, I love this woman.

Thea bites her lip, her body tense like she expects me to be upset. Instead, I lean down and kiss her.

I whisper against her lips, "Remember how much I love your protectiveness?"

Thea's body relaxes against me, and she mouths *thank you* before I turn back to my mother.

Mom faces me. "The things you said to me this morning were . . . very upsetting."

"I'm not trying to upset you," I say. "But I'm not going to make my decisions for you anymore. I need to live for myself, and there's a lot you aren't going to like. You'll have to decide whether or not you can handle that."

Tears flood her eyes. "I just want what's best for you."

She loves me. I know she loves me, but that's not enough. And I can't keep following this instinct to comfort her when it only makes things worse.

"You need to see someone, Mom." She flinches away, like she just realized I'm an electric fence and she's scared of getting shocked. "I get why you reacted this way after everything with Dad. Why you've felt this overwhelming need for control. But Harrison and I aren't toys you can move around your dollhouse. You need to get help."

"I don't think it's as bad as all that," she says, shifting on her feet.

"It is," I say, refusing to let the discomfort scare me off. "You've come so close to losing me. Your relationship with Harrison isn't much better—but that's something you need to work through with him. These problems aren't going to magically disappear, and I'm telling you right now, I won't tolerate you taking out issues you refuse to deal with on Thea. I want a relationship with you, but I can't force you to do the work."

She keeps her eyes trained on something over my shoulder, and I brace for her ire. Instead, she swallows thickly and nods.

"Maybe . . ." She clears her throat. "Maybe I can help you with the rest of the cake? You can tell me more about your thoughts for that baking side business you mentioned."

I shoot a quick glance at Thea, and she nods. "It's not going to be a side business. Harrison's going to buy me out so I can focus on it full-time."

She closes her eyes, and I can practically hear the wail she's holding back. This is hard for her, and I think putting it all out there is the best choice. One severe injury that needs to heal instead of small cuts at random.

"And I'm going to start it up here. I've loved these mountains my entire life, and I want to live here."

She lets out a little whimper, and I let go of Thea's waist to pull Mom into my arms. "I'm your son. I'll *always* be your son."

I want to ask for her to be happy for me, but I don't know if she's strong enough for that, and I don't know if *I'm* strong enough to know the answer. Hopefully, this will help Mom realize she needs to process her trauma. But until she finds a way to heal, I'll live my life and recognize that I can't control her reactions.

As I step back from my mom, I glance at Thea, a question in my gaze. My mom's been difficult all my life, but she's been cruel to Thea, and I won't force her to spend time with her if she's not comfortable.

Thea steps to my side, placing a possessive hand on my back that has my pulse kicking up. "We'd love your help, Diana."

I'm so in love with this woman—this beautiful, kind, forgiving woman—and I can't wait for the day when I get to tell her.

Chapter 34

THEA

"Is this real life?" Addy asks, staring at her reflection.

She's outfitted in that perfect gown, her hair and makeup beautifully done. I'm in my crystal-green bridesmaid's dress, the same color as the rings around Harrison's and Owen's pupils.

"It is, and your life is going to be as stunning as you look right now."

Addy meets my gaze in the mirror. "Can you grab the jewelry box from the desk?"

My body tenses—I don't want to think about the necklace she refuses to wear when we just got back to a good place—but I do as she asks.

Addy takes the box from my hand, popping it open and pulling a necklace out by the long chain. "I didn't handle the situation with our birth mother's necklace well, but when I said I already had jewelry planned, I meant it."

She holds up the gem so I can see the forget-me-not blossom that's been preserved in resin next to a little blue bead, the type children use to make jewelry.

"What's this?"

"Do you remember the bracelet you made me the first day you went to school after we went into the system?"

I do. Our mom died in late May, which meant we had almost three months in the system where I was with Addy constantly. It was considerate of Mom to die then, if you think about it.

We had just moved to our second home when it was time for me to start up school again, and four-year-old Addy had begged me not to leave her alone. During crafting time in art class, I made her a little bracelet with all the colors of the rainbow.

"You kept it?" I ask, looking up at her.

She nods, rolling her painted lips together. "Took it with me to every home. Away to school. Everywhere. I had to cut it up to get one of the blue beads off for the necklace, and I sobbed, even though it hasn't fit me in over a decade."

The tears that flood my eyes take me by surprise, flowing down my face before I even realize they're happening. "Shit, Adelaide, I'm going to have to redo my makeup."

She sniffs, struggling with her words. "You wanted our mom to go down the aisle with me, but when I think of who raised me, who gave me the love and support to become who I am, you're it. I'm sorry I made you doubt your importance in my life."

I wrap her in my arms, both of us crying until we're interrupted by a knock on the door. Maria and Gary Fischer come in, both immediately tearing up when they see Addy.

"You look gorgeous, darling," Maria says, clutching Addy's hand.

"Thank you, Mom."

There's a bit of hesitation before the word, and from the little sob Maria hiccups out, I know it's the first time she's ever used it. When Addy smiles at her, it's *my* smile, genuine and joyful, with a touch of mischief. Her real smile. And instead of the feeling of fear I always expected to feel, I'm at peace. Because I want that for her. Real, open relationships that aren't contingent on her behaving perfectly. I feel confident in my place in her life. A truth that solidifies when Addy breathes deeply through her nose and steels her shoulders.

"Mom. Dad. I hope that this doesn't make you upset because you—you've been so, so good to me." She stumbles over the words a bit, because even though she's working on being open, she's still herself. "But Thea's going to walk me down the aisle."

I don't hear Maria or Gary's response. All I can focus on is the love shining from my sister's eyes, and the realization that maybe I'm the foundation of the family I've always been determined to find for her.

* * *

The wedding is as beautiful as expected, the mountains stretching out as far as the eye can see behind the bride and groom, but I spend most of the ceremony lost in the eyes of the best man. There's intention in that gaze, a promise that we'll be back here one day with our roles flipped. When Harrison says "I do," Owen's lips quirk, like he wants to say the words, too, and a reckless part of me wants to say them right along with him.

As we walk back down the aisle after the ceremony ends, I whisper, "What do you think about elopement?"

He chuckles. "Not against it, but Camila would kill us if she wasn't invited, and if we tell her, she'll tell everyone, and then the family will show up. Doesn't it seem easier to do it here than to manage Gabriel in Vegas?"

I laugh, feeling light enough to let the sound boom out of me and fill the wide-open space around us. Our relationship—everything related to Owen—feels so safe. It's something I've never experienced before, and I'm more grateful than ever for this man beside me. The one who saw behind the anger and hurt and fought for the right to be my person.

The night flies by in a blur. Camila pulls me and Owen in for a round of pictures at the photobooth, including one where she writes "I knew all along" on a small blackboard. Gabriel makes me sing a dozen songs before he releases me to Owen on the dance floor. Cece corners me and Owen at the bar to pepper us with questions about our move. We tell her I'm moving up immediately, and Owen's going to follow me after he finishes training Harrison. Six months of long distance is a small price to pay so that Owen can start his new life free of any guilt over leaving Hayes.

I find Addy at the edge of the dance floor by herself, watching everyone with a longing look on her face. She takes the water I offer her, chugging it down in a few gulps. I drain mine, too, taking both our glasses and setting them on the closest table.

"Thanks, Tia. I don't know if I've ever danced this much."

I jerk my chin to the dance floor. "You looked like you were having a great time out there."

Her eyes trail to where Harrison is chatting with Cece, his arms flying as he tells some story. He catches Addy's eye and winks, and a lovestruck smile takes over her face.

One of the twins—Johnny, from the woman on his arm—walks over to greet us. His wife, Misha, gives Addy a giant hug, then pinches her chin between her thumb and her pointer finger. "Look at this woman, Johnny. Isn't she glowing?"

I nudge Addy with my elbow. "Being head over heels in love will do that to you."

Addy laughs, carefree and open, and heat radiates through my chest.

Misha turns her attention to me. "You're one to talk. You're glowing, too."

"Closet sex will do that to you," Addy says, so quickly I know she didn't think it through.

Our group goes quiet as Johnny and Misha's eyes widen, and Addy freezes next to me. I can feel her anxious thoughts swirling in the middle of the group, like a hurricane pulling up water, becoming more powerful by the second.

But then laughter bursts out of both of them, Misha clutching her stomach while Johnny doubles over. He stands up and scans the crowd until he spots his brother.

"Tommy!" he calls, cupping his hands around his mouth. "Tommy! You have to hear what Addy just said." His brother's too wrapped up in his boyfriend on the dance floor to notice, and Johnny groans. "Guess we're going to him."

He grabs Addy's hand, tugging her along with them. Addy glances at me over her shoulder, widening her eyes. I nod and wave her off, like a mom on the first day of kindergarten. It feels like fireworks have gone off inside me when I see them all chatting, laughing at Tommy's response to Addy's joke.

A sweet, earthy scent envelops me seconds before two strong arms wrap around my waist. Owen places the softest kiss to my shoulder, and I lean back into him.

"Have I mentioned that you look breathtaking tonight?" he whispers in my ear.

"If I say no, will you say it again?"

His chuckle reverberates through my back. "I'll say it as many times as you let me."

I twirl in his arms, giving him a light kiss he chases when I pull away. Instead, I drag him back out for one last slow dance. He takes my hand, spinning me in a circle. His eyes catalog every inch of me, and it sets me on fire on an atomic level. He pulls me close, sliding one hand over my hip.

I bite my bottom lip as a smile stretches across my face. "Do you remember dancing at Camila's wedding?"

He groans. "You in that red dress? Absolutely."

His reaction emboldens me. "Do you remember when I asked what you'd do if this was real?"

His pupils dilate until the green disappears. The light blue follows, until all I see is a sliver of navy around the black. "Yes. In fact, that conversation has starred in more than a few dreams."

It still blows my mind that he dreamed of me all those years, of what he'd do to me or what I'd do to him if we had the chance.

"And those dreams ended differently than that night?"

His smirk grows. "Very different."

I brush my lips against his. "Show me."

My laugh echoes through the room as he tugs me off the dance floor and into our new life. A life with love and respect. A life with family.

Epilogue

THEA

FIVE YEARS LATER

Owen's warm breath gusts over my neck. "Do you know how much I need you, sweetheart? How desperate I am for you?"

I settle back into his arms. "I love it when you beg."

He chuckles, running his lips down my neck. "You know I'd make it good for you."

A screeching wail makes us jump apart, and we spot Camila at the entrance to the restaurant with her eyes narrowed on Owen. "Get your sneaky, poaching ass out of my restaurant. You can't have her."

Camila and Mira's four-year-old, Riya, comes flying toward me, throwing herself into my arms with complete abandon, knowing beyond the shadow of a doubt that I'll catch her. I'll never get over how freely this little girl's trust is given.

She presses her forehead to mine. "Mama said a bad word."

"I heard," I whisper back.

Riya beams up at me. "Hi, tía Tia," she says, and the two of us dissolve into giggles.

My heart almost exploded the first time Riya called me Tia, the only other person besides Addy who calls me that. And when she got older and realized my nickname is Spanish for "aunt," she started calling me tía Tia, laughing so hard each time she said it that her little body collapsed under the weight of her joy.

Owen lifts his hands, walking around the podium for his standoff with Camila, who's still glaring at him like he's public enemy number one. "So you no longer believe Thea should know all her options?"

She points an aggressive finger in my direction. "She's *my* employee."

He crosses his arms over his chest. "She's *my* wife."

It's been four years, but him saying those words still sets off a round of butterflies inside me.

"You can't take her," Camila growls.

"You can't stop me," he says, leaning against the hostess stand, all casual confidence.

When Owen started his bakery up here, it was a grab-and-go place. Mostly cupcakes and pastries. He did a lot of custom orders—wedding cakes and special events sent his way by Dawn—but there was no need for anything beyond a couple picnic tables out front.

News spread about his breakfast pastries, especially his incredible cinnamon muffins that half the town would gut each other over, and people started begging for a place to eat and enjoy a cup of coffee. A few weeks ago, he closed on a new location that includes a café space, and Camila became convinced he's going to steal me away to run it.

I'd never leave our restaurant, and Owen knows that. I've built something special here. Camila and I started a monthly town dinner to bring people back up the mountain, where we set up massive communal tables so everyone can get together and gossip about Elk Ridge life. I've partnered with the vineyard on wine-pairing dinners that guests and townsfolk alike love. The restaurant is flourishing, and I'd never leave my baby.

But Owen can never pass up an opportunity to fuck with Cami.

I lift Riya up on my shoulders, stepping between the two of them. "Camila, please don't murder my husband. And Owen, please stop riling up my boss. You know I won't leave."

"Oh, I will kill him, becau—" Camila cuts off as she processes my words. "Wait, you aren't considering going with him?"

I set Riya down, and she immediately jumps into Owen's arms instead.

I face Camila, planting my hands on my hips. "Oh, ye of little faith."

"But last night, Owen said . . ." she trails off, narrowing her eyes on him. "You're such a liar."

She chases him out of the restaurant, and I hear his laugh echoing through the inn. I love how carefree he's become since moving here. By the time I make it to the lobby, Owen's standing near the front desk, holding a giggling Riya between him and Camila like a shield.

Camila snatches her daughter out of his arms and places her back on the ground. "I still don't trust you. You're lucky I don't kick you out."

"He's here to meet Harrison and Addy," I say, and Camila twirls to face me.

"The babies? I thought they weren't coming until tomorrow!" Camila screams and, as if on cue, a matching scream floats in through the open front door.

Addy and Harrison's oldest, Jackson, sprints in, tackling Riya in a giant hug. With only seven months between them, they've always been close. One of them demands a video call every other day, which is mostly just them pointing the camera directly up their noses and not speaking.

Addy comes in, corralling their sweet three-year-old and toddling two-year-old. Camila does her best Jackson impression and half tackles Addy in a hug, whose booming laugh turns into that perfect, ridiculous snort.

My heart swells, seeing the genuine love between them—how

comfortable Addy's become with all the Ellises in the past half decade—but I'm only so patient. I yank Camila off her. "Give me my sister, you hog."

I wrap my arms around her and she squeezes back, so tight I don't think either of us can breathe properly. "I've missed you, Tia."

"Me too."

We break the hug when Harrison stumbles through the front door, one eight-month-old twin strapped to his chest while the other is strapped to his back, and he and Addy give each other tired smiles.

"Remind us never to drive up with this many kids again," Addy says, popping a quick kiss to my cheek before walking over to wrangle one of the twins out of the carrier.

Harrison sighs. "I'm not coming to the next wedding."

Addy nudges him. "Liar."

He smiles down at her, somehow still as in love as he was before having five kids in as many years.

"Where's Mom?" Owen asks, looking over Harrison's shoulder at the door.

Our relationship with Diana is still complicated. She started seeing a therapist after she got back to Florida, and things have gotten consistently better, but Owen still struggles with opening up to her. He started seeing someone himself a couple of years ago to unpack his resentment, but there's a long way to go to total forgiveness. The distance has helped. She doesn't see enough of our life here to interfere.

Whatever else I can say about Diana, she's an extremely engaged grandmother, and the babies have healed something between her and Addy, too. We get pictures of them every few weeks—covered in sand at the beach or beaming through the sweat and exhaustion at Disney with five little kids. Every time Diana's and Addy's faces are pushed together, the smile that was just mine for decades is always on Addy's face. Now, she gives it to the whole world.

Harrison and Addy share a conspiratorial glance. "She decided to fly, so she won't be here until tomorrow," she says. "Apparently, ten-plus hours in the car with them is the official limit of the love for her grandchildren."

Dammit, Owen and I were counting on her being grandchildren-ed out by the time she got up here. When the time came to decide what future we wanted, we both agreed we wanted to stay kid-free. After a life looking after our siblings, we wanted the chance to be a bit selfish, which is exactly what Diana called us when we told her. It was the one major backslide we've experienced in the past five years.

Owen was pissed. So pissed he considered cutting her off. He said this was the most intense thing she could meddle on. A job you could quit, but kids were for life. I could see where he was coming from, but she'd been doing so much better. I didn't think we should cut her off because of one conversation.

When I reminded him none of us are just one moment, all the tension in his body evaporated. His smile was so soft when he kissed me. "None of us deserve you, Thea Hayes."

Here's hoping that we don't have a repeat of that fight.

The door of the inn swings open again, and Gabriel bounds in with his never-ending energy.

"The party is here, people!" he calls out. "Lynne and her fiancé are already at the pickleball courts, so we need to get over there to warm up. I don't care if she's the bride, none of us want to deal with an insufferable Lynne if she wins. Better move those car seats over!"

Harrison and Addy distribute their twelve thousand kids between us so they can take care of it. More and more cousins show up, filling the lobby with as much love as noise. I still can't believe this is my family, that not only Owen but the rest of them have welcomed me and Addy into their lives so wholeheartedly.

Owen makes his rounds, catching up on the latest in everyone's lives before making his way back to me. He takes the twins that I have anchored on either hip, giving me a soft kiss on my forehead.

"I left you a surprise in your purse," he says. "Go find the brown paper bag."

I moan. "Owen Hayes, did you save me a cinnamon muffin?"

He winks. "I don't know. Why don't you go check?"

I run to the restaurant to grab my things, digging in my giant purse while heading back to the lobby. But instead of a fluffy, delicious muffin, my hand closes over something cold and hard.

Owen's watching with delight when I pull the bright yellow key chain out of my bag.

"What the fuck, Owen? We're supposed to be a team!"

Riya's eyes go wide. "That's a *bad* bad word, tía Tia!"

"You're right, RiRi. I'm sorry," I say, then turn my ire on my dear, loving husband.

He scrambles toward the door. "Gotta get these kids back to their parents."

"Yeah, you better run!" I yell after him while all the cousins laugh and holler at my expense.

"Oh hey, Thea?" he calls from the front door, and I twirl back to him, eyes narrowed.

"What do you want?"

His giant smile softens, and even though I have plans for payback, everything inside me goes a little bit gooey. "I love you."

And just like every time he's said it for the past five years, I believe him.

Acknowledgments

Not to pull a Jane Austen, but she was right when she said there are some universal truths. One of those truths, at least in the world of traditional publishing, is that book two will be a fight for your life. Another truth? If I'm told something will be extremely difficult, I'll assume they're exaggerating.

Dear Reader, they are not. Writing is still the most fun job of my life, but your relationship with the work changes when you know it will be read and, for better or worse, compared to book one. Is the banter bantering as hard? Are the characters as developed? Is the conflict believable? Will the second desk sex scene be good enough to satisfy (she says suggestively)?

But through all the challenges and fear, I'm more proud of this book than I could have anticipated. I love Owen and Thea, and I hope you loved them, too. If you're struggling to continue writing, don't stop. Even when it's messy and scary, it can lead to something beautiful, and the hard days are worth it for the good ones.

Now the part where I acknowledge the people who kept me from throwing my laptop into the lake (because it was a close call many, many times).

First, my brilliant agent, Jem Chambers-Black. I'm so lucky to have you in my corner. If you're an aspiring author looking over people's acknowledgments to find good agents—like I was a few years ago—please know Jem will be your cheerleader, your protector, and your creative partner all rolled into one. Thank you for believing in me, even (and especially) when I didn't believe in myself.

To Christina Lopez, my wonderful editor, thank you for helping me make this book what it is today. It's been such a joy exploring these worlds with you, and I'm so lucky to have your eyes on my characters.

To Kejana, Alyssa, Vivian, and the rest of the St. Martin's Griffin team, thank you for believing in my stories and putting your own talents behind them. I'm so grateful for your support. To my cover artist, Kelly Wagner, thank you for bringing Thea and Owen to life, and creating another beautiful cover to grace our shelves! I'm so honored that our art could come together this way.

Anyone who follows my social media knows that community is, in my opinion, the most important thing for a writer to have. That was true when I was first writing and querying, and it still is today, with two books out in the world.

To my critique partners—Amanda Hopkins, Heather McBreen, and Kjersten Piper—who have been with me since the beginning. I wouldn't have finished this book without your hilarious thirsty notes, your thoughtful challenges, your resounding no whenever I asked the question, "Is this *too* spicy?" I'm forever and always grateful for you.

To Laura Marie Meyers, thank you for being my rock and never judging when I send four 5-minute voice notes back-to-back. By the time you're reading this, your brilliant debut will be out in the world, and I hope you feel as loved and celebrated as you make me feel.

To Michelle Mitchell, my other voice-note victim, I love the way our friendship has deepened over the past year. I'm so honored to be a part of your journey and to have you invested in mine.

To the other writers who have encouraged me over the years. Yes, I know this list is obnoxious, but so am I, and these people have dealt with it for years! The least they deserve is their name in this section! Gina Banks, Erin Connor, Betty Corrello, Peyton Corinne, Chelsea Curto, Sarah T. Dubb, Ivy Fairbanks, Katy Jakes, Jessica Joyce, Naina Kumar, Mallory Marlowe, Taj McCoy, Annie McQuaid, Noreen Nanja, Danica Nava, Megan Oliver, Ellie Palmer, Shameez Patel, Ila Sikorski, Scarlette Tame, and Alexandra Vasti. I don't deserve you all!

To everyone who blurbed *The Best I Never Had*, thank you for using your very limited free time to help me. I'm not listing everyone here because the list isn't final and the thought of accidentally leaving someone out makes my anxiety spiral, but I love you all.

To my orl girlies—fozi, ila, and nela—finding you all has been one of the greatest blessings. You're the ultimate ride-or-dies, and I'm so happy RYC brought us together.

To Valentina, who is also an orl girlie but would yell at me if she didn't get her own callout. You're my number-one hype girl and one of the best friends I've ever had. Thank you for managing my many, many crash outs with a gentle hand and a funny comment.

To Tiffani, my other hype girl, you are joy incarnate. Thank you for filling our little bookish family with enthusiasm and humor, and for never letting me forget that I'm making a difference.

To Jane and the whole team at The New Romantics, words cannot express my love for you. You've brought light and community to Orlando in a way I didn't even realize was missing. I'm forever grateful for your enthusiasm and love. And to all the other indie bookstores supporting me and so many other authors, you're the lifeblood of this community.

To my non-bookish best friends—Aly, Ayesha, Erinn, Lauren, Robyn, and Sara—thank you for keeping me grounded outside of this all-encompassing work. If I haven't scared you off at this point, I've gotta assume you're in this for the long haul. I love you.

To my family, thank you for cheering me on through this process! You've always been there for me, and I've appreciated every encouraging text, event attendance, and friend you've forced to buy the book out of love.

To my irl creations, Bria, Emmy, and Lucas, I'm not sure how your dad and I made three such perfect things. You're all gifted, hilarious, and most importantly, kind. And no, you're still not allowed to read my books. I love you more than all the stars in the sky.

To Brandon, I know this was a tough one, but you stood by me through it all. You're my soulmate, and I'm so lucky to do this wild, hilarious, sometimes overwhelming life with you.

And lastly, to the readers, thank you for giving me your time and your headspace. The world is a scary place right now, and I hope this book gave you a bit of hope and light like so many other books have given me.

Thank you for reading!

About the Author

Erinn Brown Photography

Amy Buchanan has had a lifelong love affair with romance. After decades of devouring love stories written by others, she decided to share the ones pinging around in her own brain. She writes spicy contemporary romances with relatable heroines, swoon-worthy heroes, and loving found families.

She lives in Central Florida with her three littles, two pups, and one husband. On top of writing, she uses her master's in higher education administration to run a scholarship foundation for first-generation college students. When not working, she trolls travel sites for luxury rentals outside of her budget and—poorly—trains for half-marathons.